THE BIG SCAM

A Novel of the FBI

PAUL LINDSAY

SIMON & SCHUSTER
New York   London   Toronto   Sydney

SIMON & SCHUSTER
Rockefeller Center
1230 Avenue of the Americas
New York, NY 10020

SIMON & SCHUSTER and colophon are
registered trademarks of Simon & Schuster, Inc.

For information about special discounts for bulk purchases,
please contact Simon & Schuster Special Sales:
1-800-456-6798
or business@simonandschuster.com.

Manufactured in the United States of America

10 9 8 7 6 5 4 3 2 1

Library of Congress Cataloging-in-Publication Data

Lindsay, Paul.
  The big scam : a novel of the FBI / Paul Lindsay.
    p. cm.
    1. United States. 2. Federal Bureau of Investigation—Fiction. 3. Government
investigators—Fiction. 4. Organized crime—Fiction. 5. Mafia—Fiction. I. Title.

PS3562.I511915B54 2005
813'.54—dc22   2005045172

ISBN 978-1-4516-2393-2

Acknowledgments

I'd like to thank the usual suspects: David Rosenthal, my editor and publisher of thirteen years, for his patience, instruction and friendship; Esther Newberg, the Grand Archimage of literary agents, for her prescient advice and inexplicable loyalty; my daughter, Larisa, for her grace and intelligence during first-reading chores; Ruth Fecych, my editor, for her remarkable endurance; and Barbara Yergeau for her relentless eye for imperfection.

Additionally, Mark Codd, the good ASAC and loyal son of New York City for his invaluable assistance; and Gus Sander and Angel Pilato, both generous patrons of the arts.

And, as always, my wife, Patti, for everything else.

FOR PHIL STELNICKI AND JOE PECORARO,
WHO, EACH IN HIS OWN WAY, TAUGHT A BUNCH
OF NEIGHBORHOOD KIDS THAT SUCCESS HAS LITTLE
CHOICE BUT TO SURRENDER TO PERSEVERANCE

THE BIG SCAM

1

YEA, THOUGH I RIDE, IN RELATIVE LUXURY, THROUGH the valley of the shadow of death . . .

Despite being imprisoned in the carpeted darkness of the full-size Mercedes' trunk, Paul Dimino had a rough idea where he was, and worse, where he was headed. Starting at the point of abduction, through each turn, and with the speed at which the vehicle was now traveling, he guessed they were on the Cross Bronx Expressway. For men of his profession, that borough had only one purpose: making a body disappear. He tugged at the plastic cuffs that bound him. The ends had been expertly looped through the back of his belt, allowing his hands little movement. Another was wound tightly around his ankles, and a precut length of duct tape sealed his mouth from earlobe to earlobe, the taste of adhesive bitter.

Inexplicably, calm seized him. Although the remainder of his life might be measured in minutes, he seemed to accept his fate with a previously unrealized strain of dignity. Not that finding himself in such a situation was unexpected. Like a single malignant cell, the possibility that something like this could happen, whether provoked or not, had been in the back of his mind since the day he was sworn into the life. A product of Catholic schools, he had been shaped by the notion that consequences, although sometimes brutal, were intrinsically redemptive. *Penance—the workingman's therapy.* Apparently there was more altar boy in him than he knew, because the relief he was experiencing, with all its intricate opiates, seemed to have dissolved the need for fear.

He had murdered three men—*in the line of duty*, he reminded whoever might be monitoring his last-minute codicil—and each of them had nothing but panic in their eyes as their final moments slipped away. But now placed in the identical situation, he was interested only in timing the patterns of surging rain on the trunk lid, each a tiny, mathematical fugue. A slow, tranquil breath warmed him.

For some reason, he was being offered a last few unencumbered moments to weigh his life. A wife and son, he guessed, were its measurable total. A wife and son, but not a family. He had made no such investment. Instead, he had given free rein to base instincts, leaving everything else to pale with insignificance. Never having tasted the bittersweet affirmation of hard work or sacrifice or selflessness, everything now seemed useless and ephemeral. Even the difference between living and dying.

The Mercedes hit a deep pothole, slamming his head against the floor. He tested the cuffs again. When the two men had forced him into the trunk at gunpoint, he noticed that they had even thought to disconnect the interior safety release. Briefly, he had considered trying to buy them off, but they had treated him with complete indifference—an indication that this was not the first time they had murdered someone.

His first time had been difficult. It was not a question of whether he could kill somebody, but whether he wanted to. He knew the decision was irrevocable. Had he been offered a bribe at that instant, he now wondered if he would have chosen differently. Probably not. He didn't particularly like murder, but it was a tool, the most complicated one men of his tradition used, something that was both exciting and repulsive, a necessary passage if a man was to be taken seriously.

He had never seen either of these men before, and the one who did the talking sheared off the ends of longer words to their last hard consonant, leaving the slightly fractured, staccato accent that was peculiar to the Chicago area. He assumed that they had been brought in from out of town, which was unusual. The endless government assault had robbed the five New York families of their swagger, along with their most prized possession, the illusion of invulnerability. Uncertainty had caused them to become extremely provincial, trusting only their own. That these two were imported meant someone comfortable with the old ways, someone with patience, had issued the contract for his death. That suggested only one person—Bastiano "Buster" Delvecchio, the head of the Corsalini crime family.

Delvecchio must have finally discovered that Dimino had been stealing from him. To a reasonable person, some degree of mitigation for being a thief could be offered. After all, hadn't he done everything his boss had asked of him, including the three murders? And though he knew things that could hurt the old man, he never breathed a word, not even when serving a year and a half on a weapons charge. For his loyalty, he was thrown only crumbs. As much out of anger as greed, he began skimming from the family's vending machine interests. Suddenly, deceiving his boss became as addictive as the stolen money. Paradoxically, as dictated by the counterclockwise rules of organized crime, stealing had returned power to him. It proved that he was more cunning than the old man. Dimino barked a muted laugh through the duct tape. *So smart that I'm now the one in the trunk.*

In the bumpy darkness, he smiled. *I would do it all again.* It was all about respect, and part of that was dying without complaint or apology. But there was enough Sicilian outrage left in him to argue that while a man could accept violent death, he must also plot against those who caused it.

Given the circumstance, he could think of only one way to avenge his own death. He stretched his left hand to his right and, with some difficulty, slid the flawless star sapphire ring off his little finger. His initials were engraved inside. He wriggled around until he found a seam in the carpeting, probably leading to the tire well, and pushed the ring down into it. If it were found, his last moments alive could be traced to the Mercedes and, with a little luck, back to Delvecchio.

But the ring was valuable, and if found by the wrong person would simply disappear. He had to leave other evidence, the kind the law has special equipment to find—DNA. Lying on his side, he raised his head until it was touching the trunk lid. Finally he found an edge on the metal, but it wasn't sharp enough to cut him by simple contact. *Fucking Germans.* With a quick jerk, he raked his ear against it. When he didn't feel the dampness of his own blood, he did it again, harder. Still he felt nothing. The car veered to the right and slowed down, an indication they had gotten off the expressway. There wasn't much time left. He smashed his head as hard as he could while raking it against the lid. Almost immediately, he felt blood. He started rolling around the trunk, leaving stains in detectable amounts. *Take that, old man.*

Suddenly the Mercedes jerked forward as the driver stomped the accelerator and started taking corners at dangerous speeds. Then Dimino heard a siren. After a few more turns, it seemed to be closing.

A gunshot boomed from the Mercedes. As quickly as he could, Dimino turned himself so his feet were pointing toward the back of the car and curled up in a ball, hoping that if the cops returned fire, he would be hit only in his feet or legs. But no shot came from the pursuing car. Again the Mercedes fired. Still no return fire. Did they know he was in the trunk and didn't want to risk hitting him? He hoped so. *Goddamnit—whoever you are—don't lose us.*

After a couple more sliding turns and accelerations, the Mercedes fishtailed to a stop. Dimino was thrown forward, hitting the front wall of the trunk. Then he heard the car's doors open, followed by quickly shifting footsteps. "Hold it! FBI!" came from the distance.

Now there were multiple gunshots. He heard the rear window above his head explode. He tried to shrink into a smaller ball. More gunfire erupted, and then along with the sounds of everyone running, it trailed away. Complete silence followed as the rain drummed on the trunk lid, matching the rate of Dimino's pounding heart. Waiting until there no longer seemed to be any danger, he started kicking the sides of the trunk and mumbled urgently through his gag. Outside, a man's voice said calmly, "Hold on, we'll get you out of there." Dimino could hear him walk around to the driver's door—almost in slow motion—and felt the car lean slightly as the person got in and took the keys from the ignition. An instant later, the trunk lid opened. Two men dressed in windbreakers stood over him. The older one, pulling the tape from his mouth, asked, "Who are you?" in the damaged, irresistible baritone of a longtime whiskey and cigarette abuser.

"I assume you're the FBI."

Each agent grabbed an arm and pulled him out of the trunk. "I'm T. H. Crowe. This is Dick Zalenski. Yeah, we're agents." Crowe's face was heavily creased with age. Zalenski, who looked thirty years younger than Crowe, just nodded. Even under the dark, unpredictable sky, his face glowed with an unassailable innocence as if someone had granted him absolution of all future sins. Dimino thought they could have been some kind of before-and-after advertisement. *Just Say No*—to becoming an FBI agent.

"I'm Paul Dimino."

Crowe said, "Dimino? Aren't you connected to the Corsalini family?"

Dimino knew he was about to make a decision that would change the rest of his life. Either he had to play dumb and get away from these men—which would mean disappearing permanently, because Bastiano Delvecchio was a patient man—or he could seek federal sanctuary, which meant turning against the head of his family. "How did you guys know I was in the trunk?"

"Someone tipped our Chicago office that these two guys were coming out here to zip someone. Their surveillance crew put them on the plane at O'Hare, and we picked them up when they got off at JFK. Looks like your lucky day." They were standing in the parking lot of an old factory. Crowe pointed up at the wall next to where the Mercedes had dead-ended. In faded letters, Dimino could just make out the name of the business:

LANTRELL'S CHICAGO-STYLE SAUSAGE

"Not to seem unappreciative, but if you were following them since the airport, why didn't you grab them as soon as they put me in the trunk?"

With what Dimino supposed passed for a smile, Crowe said, "Actually, my vote was to wait until your toes were in the grinder—"

"We had to wait for backup," Zalenski interrupted. "We get

calls like this all the time. We cover them, but until tonight they've always been BS. When we saw this was for real, we called for help."

"Did they get away?"

"Other units in the area are looking for them. If we don't find them, it'll just be temporary."

"Well, I guess I don't have to say thanks."

Crowe inhaled a slow, bracing breath before he spoke. Everything about him seemed lethargic. Speaking appeared to drain him even further. *"Are* you affiliated with the Corsalini family?"

Dimino looked up at the sign on the wall and then at the younger agent before turning back to Crowe. Even though he was about to disappear forever into a black hole of anonymity, he smiled. "Not since I joined the Witness Protection Program."

After cutting away the flex-cuffs, the agents led him to their car. Before getting in, he ran back to the Mercedes and dug out his ring. Slipping it on, he turned his face up to the steady rain and opened his mouth, catching its sweetness on his tongue. Maybe it was true what the Bible says, he thought, that the wages of sin is death, but apparently it depended on what kind of week you put in.

As soon as the Bureau car containing the government's newest informant pulled out of the lot, the two men who had abducted Dimino came from a prearranged hiding place behind the plant. The taller one, Jack Straker, took out an unfiltered cigarette and rolled it against the tip of his tongue, wetting the end. He lit it and slowly pulled the first drag deep into his lungs. Howard Snow watched the tiny ritual, and, without a cigarette, he inhaled a breath of equal size, rhythm, and reward.

In his flat Chicago accent, Straker said, "That was a pretty convincing chase. I almost lost it coming around that last turn into the lot. Thought I was going to take out the fence. You were looking a little white-knuckled yourself there, Howie." He was smiling. Jack Straker was not particularly good-looking, until he smiled. Although perfectly balanced, his features had a strangely anonymous quality. At rest, his face had a look of chronic boredom that threatened to drain the energy from those within its range. But when he smiled, planes shifted and its remarkable equipoise was revealed. His cheeks drew up under high cheek-bones and his eyes were pulled into flawless teardrops, suddenly shining. The lower lip flattened, allowing the cleft in his chin to become shadowed, bisecting his face and exposing its symmetry. When the transition occurred, the smile's target, most often female, felt the small, jolting euphoria that came with discovering something so well hidden. Occasionally, whether out of actual boredom or maybe to determine if there was a limit to this endowment, almost in parody of himself, he would bare his teeth farcically. It didn't seem to matter. Anything from the most reticent smirk to a full, howling jack-o'-lantern—it all worked.

Howard Snow, on the other hand, was short and slight of build. His hands were small and childlike, constantly seeking any object to fidget with. Even dressed in an expensive warmup suit with three thick gold chains around his neck, he looked more like a librarian than a mobster. His face had the perennial expression of being slightly puzzled by everything within range of his myopic eyes. He reached into his pocket and took out a pair of glasses. Even with his vision adjusted, he looked around as if the correction was still somewhat suspect. His left hand went to one of the gold chains and started fingering its sharp links methodically.

Snow smiled appreciatively. "I could use a change of underwear."

Straker laughed. "Christ, Howard, that's actually pretty funny. For you, it's damn near hysterical."

Snow looked down, slightly embarrassed by the compliment, and then to ease his discomfort walked around the back of the car and examined the shattered window. "Dreagen's going to be pissed about that."

"Dreagen? What does the administrative ASAC have to do with this? Or anything that real agents do?"

"He told Nick that he wanted this for his personal Bucar after we were done tonight. I guess it won't be too bad to get fixed."

Straker laughed in the peculiar way he always did when he was about to say something sardonic. "That's perfect. Assistant Special Agent in Charge Bernard E. Dreagen. A sniveling asshole, who has never worked a case in his life, wants to drive a Mercedes that some poor hump agent worked his tail off to seize as part of a drug forfeiture, a car he could probably use undercover to make more cases." Straker got a black leather bag out of the backseat and pulled a handheld radio from it. He tossed it to Snow, who caught it clumsily. "Call for any of the units that are still in the area who can give us a ride."

"Aren't we taking this?" He watched the rain slant in the jagged opening where the rear window had been. "It isn't that bad." Straker got behind the wheel without answering. "What are you going to do?" Snow asked, his voice slightly elevated, more pleading than questioning.

Straker took a drag on his cigarette. "Evidently you've forgotten how delighted Dreagen was to dump you on this squad."

"Come on, Jack."

Straker took a final, long drag and flipped his cigarette in a lazy, tumbling arc. "Call for the car . . . and you better give me a little room."

Snow shook his head and backed up.

The Mercedes' oversized engine caught with a roar. Straker's eyebrows snapped up and down as he raced the engine. He fastened his seat belt without bothering to close the door. He dropped the shift into reverse and gunned it. The car accelerated a hundred feet before striking a concrete light pillar, caving in the rear end of the vehicle. The fifteen-foot metal light stanchion collapsed and fell on top of the car, shattering the sunroof. Straker then put it in neutral and revved the engine to near capacity. With a formal salute to Snow, he closed the door and shifted into gear, holding the accelerator against the floor. The tires spun briefly on the wet pavement, then the vehicle catapulted forward. It reached almost fifty miles an hour before slamming into the wall, taking out a couple dozen courses of brick. The engine sputtered, choked, and died as steam escaped up into the cool rain.

Snow ran to the car as Straker stumbled out, his forehead bleeding. "Jesus Christ, Jack, are you all right?"

"Fucking air bag failed," Straker said through clenched teeth, testing the cut with his fingertips. "I think I screwed up."

"Whoa, John William Straker second-guessing an impulse?"

"Jesus, Howie, first a joke, and now you're taking a shot at me?"

"I've been running with a bad crowd."

"And yet another shot. Maybe there *is* hope for you." Snow smiled self-consciously. "But I think you're missing the point. If I had been more patient, and with a little bit of luck, the ASAC could have been killed driving this thing."

2

MIKE PARISI SAT AT THE FIVE-DOLLAR BLACKJACK
table, trying to slow-play what remained of the hundred-dollar
stack of chips in front of him. It seemed foolish to worry about
such a small amount when ten thousand dollars of his own
money had just been bet on another one of his crew's "can't-lose"
schemes, but for some reason, watching this hundred dollars
trickle into the lava flow of cash and credit card numbers headed
toward the Mohegan Sun counting room was making him even
more anxious. Part of it was that even though he had been their
boss for two years, he knew they still didn't accept him. And sitting and waiting for this latest scam to play out, he wasn't sure
whether it was more prank than con. He even began to wonder if
he wasn't the mark.

"Your bet, sir," the dealer said, this time with a little less diplomacy. Parisi looked at him slowly and then again at the two cards
that lay face up in front of him.

When he became engaged to Danielle, going to work for her
uncle had seemed like a reasonable idea, at least financially. The
downside was that his new employer, Anthony Carrera, was head
of the Galante crime family. Not that breaking the law had ever
kept Parisi awake at night. As a kid he had earned himself six
months in a New York State juvenile facility for stealing cars. Of
all the lessons incarceration could teach, the two he came away
with were: never break the law out of boredom, and if the punishment for the crime outweighs the reward, you've fucked up. In

recent years, before he met Danielle, he had been involved in some pyramid sales schemes, getting out just ahead of the regulators. And when nothing else was available, he worked a few boiler-room operations, defrauding people whose greed made them foolish enough to trust a voice on the telephone.

Carrera had offered Parisi the bulk of his loansharking and gambling interests to oversee. With that responsibility came a crew, or as Carrera had called it with a formality more suited to his generation, a regime. Parisi would be its *capo*. The previous captain, he was assured, had died of natural causes. Parisi was to be paid 10 percent of whatever his crew brought in, which, based on the don's estimate, would bring him roughly a hundred and seventy-five thousand dollars a year. Additionally, he would be given 10 percent of any additional revenue his crew could create.

But memories of juvenile confinement warned Parisi of the consequences of easy money. He told Danni that before he could accept her uncle's offer, he had to be sure they had a way out— and in no more than three or four years—before it all became too comfortable and brought with it the inevitable prison sentence, or worse. A boyhood friend of Parisi's, Colin O'Brien, who had done well in northeastern New Jersey real estate, offered a possible solution. His father had a friend who owned a Cadillac dealership in southern Florida and was looking to retire. The asking price was ten million dollars, which by current standards was more than fair. O'Brien told Parisi that they could get a loan from the banks, but the downstroke would be 30 percent, making Parisi's end a million five, a number Parisi knew would be impossible to accumulate legitimately. Since the laws that he would be breaking for the don were not a priority for law enforcement, Parisi drew in a cautious breath and accepted.

In the last two years, he had managed to save close to three hundred thousand dollars, funneling it into an account used for his "consulting" business. His wife pitched in by working as a hostess at a local restaurant to bring in additional income. Their only disagreement over money was her insistence on buying the works of local artists, many of which were exhibited in the restaurant. While he thought most of them were amateurish, he never objected too strenuously. He supposed it was because of the way she went about it, buying them without apology, never asking for an opinion, confident in her choice. It was a strength he admired. He wished he were equally sure of himself with his crew. If he had been, he wouldn't be sitting in a casino in Connecticut in the middle of the night.

"I'll take a hit," he said, and when the dealer turned over his third card, it was a queen, giving him twenty-three. He tossed in another five-dollar chip and looked at his watch.

Less than three hours earlier Jimmy Tatorrio had called him at home with his latest "surefire" moneymaker, a bet that would return eleven thousand dollars to Parisi on a loan of ten. What Tatorrio didn't say was that if he lost the bet, the chances of Parisi ever seeing his money again were extremely small. A judicious person would have said no, but Parisi was the outsider. The rest of his crew had come up together, ripping and running through the streets of Brooklyn. They had trusted one another their entire lives. His position as their boss had been gained solely through the sacrament of marriage. He felt he had little choice but to say yes.

"Ten thousand? No problem," he said, trying to strike the pose of casual recklessness the members of his crew seemed to thrive on. Since taking over, he had tried different things to cast himself in the role of mobster, but with little success. Barely five foot seven and thin, he was not physically imposing. He was in his early thirties but looked younger, possessing one of those boyish faces that would probably change little over the next twenty years. He was wearing the kind of warmup suit some of the older men wore, but its bagginess made him look even more misplaced. A gold crucifix, slightly too large, hung across his chest. Tucking it inside his jacket, he pulled up the zipper a couple of inches and took a watery sip of his scotch, another thing he didn't like. He took a larger swallow to punish himself for his pretense.

He glanced at Gus Dellaporta sitting next to him. There was a mobster. At 270 pounds, he was their chief enforcer, but his hovering presence usually precluded any need for actual violence. If his crew had any respect among the other families, it was thanks to Dellaporta. No matter how badly one of their little enterprises fell apart, he never panicked, but methodically found a way to get out, managing to salvage some dignity for the crew.

Jimmy Tatorrio was another story. He lived purely by his wits. If his request for a loan had come during the day, Parisi would have guessed that the money was needed for another "lock" at the track. "What do you need it for this late?" Parisi had asked, hoping for a loophole.

"Did I ever tell you the story about the time I helped the FBI put the bug in the old club?"

Tatorrio had a flair for throwing out the one line that begged for the rest of the story. "No," Parisi said, forcing as much disinterest into his tone as possible.

Tatorrio fought the urge to entertain him with the long version. "Remind me to tell you about it sometime. But a guy from the Parrinos had to lend me ten grand that night. Then the SOB gouged me for nine months. Every week when I'd pay him the juice, he'd make sure somebody else from his crew was there so he could enjoy rubbing it in. I've been working on a deal to get even for a year now, waiting for just the right time. He walked in the club tonight and started busting my balls. You know my temper, so I started this in motion without thinking. But honest, Mike, this can't miss."

"I'm going to need more than 'it can't miss.'"

"It would take too long to explain. We're leaving to drive up to Mohegan Sun in less than an hour, and I've got to get over to my parents' and pick up their dog and then get back here."

"Why the dog?"

"He's the bet," Tatorrio said. "Mike, you're the only chance I got."

It sounded like a disaster in need only of financing. He started to search for other reasons why he couldn't get involved and finally said, "I'll be there in a half hour."

At the club, Tatorrio's car was parked behind a black Lincoln that Parisi didn't recognize. Dellaporta and Tatorrio were sitting in the back room drinking with two other men. A golden retriever lay obediently next to the table. Tatorrio stood up and shook Parisi's hand.

Six foot two, Jimmy Tatorrio was narrow at the hips and shoulders. His entire body, including a long neck and head, could be best described as a narrow cylinder, the most salient feature of which was a gnarled Adam's apple that appeared to be as prominent as his shortened chin. When he spoke, all the surrounding features seemed to stand fast while the dominating knot of cartilage bobbed excitedly. His eyes protruded like those of a creature that had survived because of a few extra degrees of peripheral vision. That Tatorrio had escaped a lifetime of obvious nicknames was a testament to his ability to never take himself seriously, a point of silent but inestimable admiration among Parisi's crew.

"You're a lifesaver, man," Tatorrio said. "This is Joe Chianese. Joe, Mike Parisi." In his late forties, with an oily, out-of-date hairstyle, Chianese had the impatience, the racing emptiness of a degenerate gambler. "How are you?"

Chianese shot a thumb over his shoulder. "This is Billy." Parisi nodded.

No one said anything further, and Parisi realized all eyes were on him. "You're waiting for the money."

"That's why we're all here." Dellaporta said.

"Can I at least know what the bet is?"

Tatorrio said, "That I will be able to get Rusty here into the Mohegan Sun." He leaned down and stroked the dog's head. "And he will not only be allowed to sit at the blackjack table in a player's chair, but to actually play."

"For one hour," Chianese interjected.

"Yes, Joe, for one hour."

Chianese said, "If this is some kind of trick with words or some other bullshit, all bets are off."

"The dog will be allowed to play blackjack with me at the Mohegan Sun for one hour," Tatorrio said. "Period."

Parisi looked at Dellaporta for some sign of reassurance. "Don't ask me, Mike. I know they don't let animals in a casino under no circumstance. And as far as playing . . ."

Parisi stared at Tatorrio hoping to get some indication of how he was going to do it. Asking the wrong question might expose whatever sleight of hand Tatorrio had devised and cancel the bet. Tatorrio stared back evenly. Parisi handed him the small gym bag he was carrying. Tatorrio placed the bills on the table. "There's mine, Joe."

Chianese riffled through one of the bundles and tossed it back on the table. He handed his car keys to Billy, who headed out the door. "It's okay with me if Gus holds the money."

"I appreciate this, Mike," Tatorrio said. "I'll see you tomorrow when we get back."

Parisi looked over at Gus, who was examining the bundled bills. "I think I should go along."

"Really? Sure, Mike, I just thought, you know, you'd have better things to do."

"If I was a little smarter, I probably would. But I should at least get some entertainment for my money, don't you think?"

Billy came back and handed Chianese a bulging manila envelope. He gave it to Tatorrio, who turned it over to Dellaporta and said, "Okay, let's ride."

Parisi said he'd go with Tatorrio and with the newest member of the Galante crime family, Rusty. The other three went in Chianese's Lincoln. As soon as Tatorrio pulled away, Parisi said, "Okay, Jimmy, I know this is another one of your scams."

"Like I said in there, there is no scam."

"Then how're you going to do it?"

"Don't you trust me?"

"I'm driving up to Connecticut in the middle of the fucking night. Does that sound like I trust you?"

Tatorrio smiled disarmingly. "Like I told you, I've been working on it for a while. I *really* need to get this guy. You said you wanted to be entertained. When we get there just go inside and get a good seat. It'll be much more enjoyable if you don't know what's going to happen. If I told you now, you might get all nervous, and Rusty can sense that kind of stuff."

"You mean my money is in the hands of a fucking dog?"

"Paws, Mike. Paws."

Parisi could feel the anger rising, not at Tatorrio, but at himself for not pressing him further. He just gave this man ten thousand dollars, and the guy didn't even feel the need to explain himself. He slouched back in silence.

When they finally pulled up to the main entrance of the casino, Tatorrio dialed Dellaporta's cell phone. "Gus, you guys inside?"

"Yeah, we got a table that's empty. The five-dollar table. Just come straight back through the lobby and you'll see us."

"That's what you think."

"What's that mean?"

"Patience, Gus."

Parisi now understood that his ten thousand dollars was about to bankroll a James Tatorrio performance, one that he hoped would result in a tale of such epic proportions that it would distinguish itself amidst an already impressive oeuvre. "I'll see you inside, Jimmy."

Parisi looked down at his cards again—twenty. The dealer had blackjack. He pushed in another chip. The four men played distractedly for the next fifteen minutes, watching in the general direction of the front door.

Then in the distance, they saw casino patrons walking around something coming toward them. A few seconds later, the obstacle materialized. Tatorrio, wearing dark glasses, was being led by a uniformed security guard and was holding on to a double-strapped leather harness with Rusty at the other end, placidly following the casino employee. Parisi burst into laughter. Tatorrio's face was slightly askew. Even Joe Chianese, who sensed he was about to lose ten thousand dollars, started chuckling.

When they got close, Tatorrio said, "Officer, is there a five-dollar table?"

"Yes, sir." He led Tatorrio over and put his hand on the back of an empty chair next to Dellaporta. "Right here, sir." The dealer held up his palms questioningly to the guard, who shrugged. "Upstairs said it was all right. Whatever he wants. When he's done, call us so we can get him a cab."

"How's he . . ." The dealer decided that to question how a blind person could read the cards was not only insensitive, but unnecessary. Instructions would have to be issued shortly.

"Chips, sir?"

Tatorrio pulled out five one-hundred-dollar bills, each folded in the same peculiar way. He fingered the edge of two of them. "Two hundred dollars, please."

The dealer straightened the bills before pushing the chips across the table until they touched Tatorrio's left hand.

"I'm sorry, dealer, what's your name?"

"Randy."

"Randy, I'm John Waylon, and in order for me to play, I need Rusty to sit in the chair next to me."

As soon as Parisi heard the phony name, he knew that Tatorrio wasn't completely confident about the success of his plan. Parisi started visualizing the con going bad and the four men and dog legging it to the nearest exit.

"Rusty?"

"My dog."

"I'm sorry, there are strict rules about the chairs. They're only for playing customers."

Tatorrio smiled in the general direction of the dealer. "Randy, not to be a pain in the butt, but it sounds like you're making up rules to fit the situation. I've been blind since birth, and I've heard every excuse there is for denying me access to the things that are apparently reserved for the sighted. I've spent my life trying to prove to myself that being blind is not that big a handicap. Something as simple as counting to twenty-one certainly shouldn't be."

A small crowd had started to gather. The shift supervisor, noticing the swelling knot of people, walked over. "Everything all right, Randy?"

"This gentleman says he needs a chair for his dog so he can play."

"The dog's going to play?"

"No, the man. Says he can't play without the dog sitting next to him."

"I'm sorry, sir," the supervisor said. "Why do you need him next to you? Wouldn't he be more comfortable on the floor?"

"This dog is my eyes."

"You mean when you walk."

"Right now I mean when I play. You might find this hard to believe, but I don't watch a lot of TV. So, at night, Rusty and I work on tricks. I have a Braille deck, and I have taught him to play blackjack. Now unless you have a Braille deck, I need him to sit next to me to read my cards. We actually play the hand together."

"I'm afraid I find that a little hard—"

"Let him play, I want to see this," someone called from the

crowd, which had tripled since the supervisor had come over. The potential for embarrassing the casino seemed only one or two bad decisions away. "How about we get an employee to sit with you and tell you what your cards are?"

"You're not getting it. Do you think I came here to gamble? I came here to prove to myself that there's something else in the world that my blindness can't prevent. It's only a lousy chair. What's the problem? Is this casino that crowded?" A couple of voices in the crowd started booing. "I'm sorry, I know I'm putting you in a bad position, but it's just for an hour or so."

"It's just that—"

"Did your dealer take my two hundred dollars?"

The dealer nodded to the supervisor. "Yes, sir, he did."

"And since he gave me chips, I assume my money's good."

"Of course it is, sir."

"Let's say, I'm . . . let's say I'm crazy, and this dog doesn't know a jack from a jackass. The only thing that will happen is that I'll lose two hundred dollars very quickly."

"Can you hold on, sir, while I call upstairs?"

"Sure. And maybe I could get a drink."

A cocktail waitress said, "What can I get you, Mr. Waylon?"

"Vodka rocks, and I'd like to buy a drink for everyone at the table, for the inconvenience."

"There'll be no charge, sir," she said.

As the supervisor hurried to the nearest phone, the crowd started chanting, "Let them play! Let them play!" *Them?* he thought. *Now they're cheering for the fucking dog.*

His boss had apparently already seen the commotion on the surveillance cameras. "What's going on down there?"

The supervisor explained Tatorrio's demand. "And it's starting to get ugly down here."

Parisi took another sip of his scotch. Tatorrio was still in character, head cocked, humbly accepting slaps on the back from the crowd. Parisi had to hand it to him, Tatorrio was able to judge his own lack of beauty so objectively that he had found a use for it. Now he was in the process of turning it into legend.

The supervisor's boss came back on the line. "Andrews said this could be a publicity bonanza. You're to do whatever you have to, just keep him at the table. It'll work better than free liquor to get the crowd pumped up to gamble. Comp him whatever you have to. I'm going to get the photographer down there. Andrews wants pictures of this for the website."

As soon as the crowd saw the supervisor coming they started to boo again. He held up his hands and smiled. "Mr. Waylon, I'm sorry for the delay. It's always a little confusing when someone is about to make history." The crowd started high-fiving one another. "We'd be honored to have you and Rusty at our table for as long as you like. I have been authorized to extend you every courtesy of the house."

A corner of Tatorrio's mouth curled up. "Maybe I could play longer, if I had a room for the night."

Having accomplished his prime directive, the shift supervisor said with rising elation, "With the compliments of Mohegan Sun, sir."

"I'm sorry, do you have anything with two bedrooms? Sometimes Rusty snores."

"That shouldn't be a problem."

"Thank you."

Dellaporta, who was sitting next to him, got up. "Here, John, Rusty can have my seat." He lifted the animal effortlessly into the chair. The dog, sensing that it was finally time to perform, instantly became alert. Parisi was now sitting on the other side of Rusty. The waitress arrived with the drinks and put Tatorrio's in his hand.

Clumsily, Tatorrio found his stack of chips and, taking two from the top, handed them to the waitress. He pushed another one out crookedly in front of him. Parisi, Chianese, and Dellaporta anted up.

Tatorrio said, "Randy, you need to put my cards right in front of Rusty. Think of it as him playing and I'm just his voice." The dealer dealt everyone two cards face up, carefully arranging Tatorrio's directly in front of the dog. Tatorrio leaned over and patted the dog. With his head cocked, he listened carefully as the others played their hand. When it was his turn, he leaned closer to the dog and said, "You ready to play, boy?" The dog shifted on its hindquarters eagerly. Tatorrio's cards were a seven and a five.

With his left hand, he tapped the table in front of the dog. Rusty extended his nose toward the two cards. "Do we need a hit, boy?" Almost immediately, the dog raised its right paw and placed it across Tatorrio's left forearm. "We'll take a hit, Randy." A murmur of cautious approval shot through the crowd. The dealer turned over a six, totaling eighteen. "Do we need a hit, Rusty?" Tatorrio asked, tapping the table again. The dog sat frozen. "We'll stand."

The dealer, with a ten showing, turned over his hole card, a seven, for a total of seventeen, disqualifying him from taking a hit. "You win, Mr. Waylon." The huge ring of spectators exploded with cheers.

The shift supervisor watched Tatorrio carefully during the next four hands, only one of which he won. He called to his bosses upstairs. "Can you see how he's doing it?"

"No, but what difference does it make? He's losing. I wish he was winning, it'd make a better story. Just keep him happy, that photographer should be there by now." Three more hands were played before the photographer arrived. During that time, Tatorrio did not change his body alignment, presumably so his arm would be within range of Rusty's paw. But to Parisi, something about his positioning seemed unnatural. For one thing, he had never seen Jimmy sit with his hand in his pocket.

The photographer arrived. "I'd like to get some pictures of you and your dog, Mr. Waylon, for the casino website, if you don't mind."

"Is my hair on straight?" Tatorrio asked, using both hands to smooth the sides.

The photographer laughed. "You look fine, and so does the dog. I just need you to sign this release."

Tatorrio smiled in his direction. "I'm sorry, I didn't bring my reading glasses." The crowd laughed. "I'm sure it's perfectly harmless, but I don't know what I'm signing."

Parisi surprised himself when he said, "John, I'm an attorney. I'll give it a quick once-over if you like."

Tatorrio turned toward him, and Parisi could see through the dark lenses that he was surprised, too. "That's awfully nice of you . . . I'm sorry, what is your name?"

"Mike . . . Reynolds."

"Mike Reynolds. Good name—you know, for a lawyer. Has that ring of integrity. Thank you."

Parisi took the document from the photographer and pretended to read it. "It's a standard release."

"Then hand me a pen." As Tatorrio signed it an inch above the signature line, he said, "And could somebody please get my attorney a drink?"

The game slowed for the next half hour while the photographer asked Tatorrio to pose in different situations, everything from Rusty pawing for a hit to the dealer pushing a fictitious winning stack of chips in front of the courageous John Waylon. When he finished, Tatorrio said he'd like some copies and gave the mailing address for the Sons of Catania Social Club. A few more hands followed, and then Tatorrio pushed a button on the side of his wristwatch, flipping the crystal up. With his head still looking forward, he fingered the dial. "Ten minutes to one, can that be right? Have I been here an hour already?" Through his sunglasses, he stared at Joe Chianese, who smiled and nodded his defeat. "Randy, could I talk to your supervisor, please." When the dealer waved him over, Tatorrio said, "I'm a little tired. If you don't mind, I'd like to go up to that room and take a load off for a few minutes."

"No problem, Mr. Waylon. I'll be glad to take you up."

Tatorrio turned in the general direction of the other players. "Gentlemen, I wouldn't have been able to do this without your patience. I'd be honored if you'd come up to the room for a drink."

"Sure," they answered in unison. Dellaporta lowered Rusty to the floor and handed Tatorrio the harness grip.

As soon as the supervisor closed the door to the suite behind him, Tatorrio held a finger up to his lips. After a few seconds, he peered through the peephole. He took a long stage bow, which evoked laughter and applause from his four-man audience.

Chianese was shaking his head. "How the fuck did you get the dog to do that?"

"In a minute. I've got to make one quick call. Get yourselves a drink from the bar." He went into one of the bedrooms to use the phone. When he came back, he told the dog to sit. Holding his left forearm near the dog, he put his right hand in his trouser pocket and said, "Rusty, do you want a hit?" The dog immediately raised its paw and draped it over the offered arm. Tatorrio took his right hand out of his pocket. In it was what looked like a push-button door-lock device for a car, the kind found on a key ring. He held it up and pushed the button. Rusty raised his paw, reaching for Tatorrio. Then laying the dog on its side, he took off the harness. Something hard the size of half a pencil had been sewn inside the belly strap. He placed it in Chianese's hand and pushed the button again.

"It's vibrating."

"The guy who sweeps the club for bugs built it for me. It's part of a beeper. Pretty simple really. The only thing I had to do was teach old Rusty to paw me every time he felt the vibration."

Chianese said, "I've got to hand it to you, Jimmy, it was fair, and it was square. And your act, man, you had every one of them. Hell, for a while there I actually thought the goddamn dog could read cards."

For the next hour, they drank and retold the story, each from his own perspective. Then there was a knock at the door. Tatorrio checked the peephole and said, "In appreciation of everyone's assistance, I've ordered room service." He opened the door to reveal five young women. "My treat."

3

IT WAS A LITTLE AFTER SEVEN A.M. WHEN NICK Vanko's phone rang. "Global Fish," he offered, using the undercover name of the squad's off-site location.

"Nicky, how are you?"

When Special Agent in Charge Ralph Hansen was in a buoyant mood, he added a *y* to everyone's name. Intended to give the appearance of familiarity, the gesture's real value was to discourage serious discussion, and therefore leave unsaid any delicate detail that Hansen might later have to deny under oath. Being an FBI boss had taught him that whatever success was being celebrated had more often than not been gained by violating Bureau rules or even committing the occasional high misdemeanor, either possibility capable of ending a career.

And Vanko understood that the SAC, no matter how strongly he urged candor, did not want specifics. "It sounds like the Dimino debriefing went well."

"Nobody called you?"

"Not yet, but my guys didn't hand him off to Leary's squad until after eleven-thirty last night, so I'm sure everyone's running late."

"Well, as of fifteen minutes ago, he was still talking. Gave up Delvecchio on some murders and a ton of other stuff. We should be able to take out the whole top shelf of the family."

"I'm glad it worked out," Vanko said.

"He said something about someone trying to kill him."

That Dimino had so completely believed the production surrounding his conversion made Vanko smile. "These people have to invent reasons to justify becoming an informant. I can guarantee you his life was never in danger."

"That's good enough for me. And I guess you were right about every wise guy hiding things from their bosses. Dimino was skimming from Delvecchio's vending machine operation and was under the impression that a contract had been put out on him because of it."

"Wise guy" had been pronounced with slightly more enunciation, in the way of a person trying to sound familiar with a world in which he had no experience or insight. Before Hansen had worked his way through the management ranks to SAC, the majority of his time as a field agent had been spent in foreign counterintelligence, a specialty that kept its agents at a calculated distance from violent crime. Evidently his only exposure to organized crime had been at the movies. But Vanko preferred having him in charge because he was practical enough not to get in the way. "As much as hard work is necessary in these cases, it'll never be as productive as a few well-placed moments of paranoia."

"You are unbelievable. You get a call that it would be nice to turn Dimino, and the next thing I know he's in, and we have to slap him to shut him up."

"The world is overflowing with best-laid plans. Executing them is the hard part, and last night the troops did that with only a few minor problems. They're the ones you should be telling this to."

"Okay, *your people* did a hell of a job last night."

"If you mean that, I'd like to do something for Howard Snow. He was largely responsible for this thing going so well."

"Nick, I seriously doubt that he had that much to do with it. His history is that of a screwup. If it was anybody else, I'd do it simply because you asked, but I can't. I appreciate you trying to help him, but he's got major baggage with OPR. Sticking an attaboy in his file isn't going to help. This is one of the few times I can remember an agent actually being investigated for incompetence. I think we both know he's terminal."

Hansen was right about the Office of Professional Responsibility investigation threatening Snow's future as an agent, but still Vanko felt he had to try. "Out here, he's been indispensable."

"Christ, Nick, he got a search warrant for the church of a high-profile black minister based on the information of an unproven informant. Then he executed it during a Sunday prayer meeting. He damn near started a riot. I suppose he's a decent enough person, but as an agent, he just doesn't get it. There's a common-sense gene or something missing."

"But they found the stolen equipment inside the church, exactly where the informant said it was."

Hansen took in a deep breath and let it stream out. "Let me give you the three *un*official reasons Snow is in trouble, each infinitely more important than any official reason, each indisputable. *High-profile. Black. Minister.* What's legally right or wrong doesn't matter. This is the twenty-first century. Politics trump the law."

Vanko knew what the SAC said was more true than not. "Could you put a memo in his file anyway? Who knows, it might help."

"I—"

"Please."

"Okay, okay. It's a mystery to me how you get anything accomplished with that collection of freaks."

Freaks. The word made Vanko touch the right side of his face where the skin sagged against two long, thin horizontal scars, one along the hairline and the other immediately under the eye, giving it the appearance of melting wax. The word was invariably stated with disdain, the strongest nonprofane expression against the lower forms of the species. In a culture where most intolerance was spoken in hushed tones, it was pronounced with grinding conviction, a universally acceptable pillorying of those perceived to be clinging to the edges of society—the identification and distancing of caste.

Vanko picked up the framed photo on his desk. It was taken at the twenty-fifth anniversary of his parents' restaurant in New Jersey. Everyone was crowded into the room his father liked to advertise as "suitable for banquets." Years earlier, after a free, anesthetizing meal, the fire marshal had generously allowed its occupancy to be listed at twenty. Vanko smiled at the photo's asymmetry. At his father's insistence, everyone was squeezed into one end so there would be room in the shot for the serving dishes brimming with all the menu items. His father in an ill-fitting tuxedo and his mother in a glistening beaded top were flanked on one side by Vanko's brother and sister and on the other by Vanko and his girlfriend, Caly Panos. Actually she was more than a girl-friend. Anyone who dated a male member of the family for more than a month, especially if she was a "good Greek girl," was as-sumed to be a fiancée in waiting. His father was beaming, his arm locked around Caly's waist, pulling her toward him.

Vanko tried not to look at his own image. His face wasn't scarred then, but, even so, wasn't handsome enough for someone as attractive as Caly. She had the kind of creamy olive skin the camera loved. Vanko thought about the last time that he'd seen her. It was just before he had gotten out of the hospital. Fearing the inevitable, he had taken off the bandages to show her the damage the doctors said was irreparable. Her eyes flashed. Tradi-tion or not, he knew they were through.

"There're a thousand agents in the division, Boss," Vanko said. "That's a lot of people to expect to be in lockstep. Not all of them are meant to wear wingtips. I know that their motivations don't always line up with the Bureau's, but whatever it is that drives them off course is what makes them invaluable when we need to do something that's not exactly in the Bureau handbook."

"Not exactly in the Bureau handbook" was not a phrase the special agent in charge of New York liked to hear, especially when it came to covert operations. His voice became more hurried, slightly more foreboding. "Well, it came out right last night, and contrary to your protests, I'm going to assume that's as much your doing as theirs. Now, is there anything you need?"

"There was one small problem that came up. The UC car they used was wrecked. I understand that Bernie Dreagen wanted it for his own personal car. These guys don't need any more ene-mies downtown than they already have."

"I'll have the administrative ASAC in for a little chat." The SAC's audible code softened abruptly. "Anything else?" He was about to request something he wasn't comfortable with.

"Not unless you had something."

"You know the inspectors are coming in Monday."

Vanko had forgotten the inspection staff was due so soon.

Every couple of years middle managers charged into each of the field offices convinced that they were about to save the Bureau's reputation. Their cover story was always the same: they were there to ensure "compliance," a euphemism that to everyone but them explained why they had chosen management as a career path. The inquisition had been instituted under the long, totalitarian reign of J. Edgar Hoover; its mission was professed to be quality control. That the practice had survived while the agency did everything possible to free itself of the first director's image proved the appeal of reminding the Field just who was in charge. Without exception, the process began with what street agents regarded as the most outrageous—and the most laughable—statement ever floated by management: *We're here to help you.* It was just another in a long list of pious fictions that agents pointed at to demonstrate the dark comedy of the ever-widening distance between themselves and their future leaders who, experience had taught, would someday obstruct them. The inspection battle cry, "The Betterment of the FBI," invariably turned into an indiscriminate scalp count as the inspectors feverishly worked to discover what degenerative viruses the inventive street agents had released into the system since their last visit.

But for Nick Vanko, inspections meant something different. "So I'm about to welcome some new members to the squad."

"Nick, I feel bad about this, but with the inspectors inbound, everybody's looking to hide their problems, or, to be honest about it, get rid of them. With your squad being off-site, it's kind of ideal for that."

"How many?"

"For now, just one, but I'm sure a few others will trickle down in the next couple of days. I'll call you as I get the requests."

"Who's the one?"

"Bradley Kenyon. Have you heard anything about him?"

Vanko laughed. "So he's bad enough that even I might have heard about him."

"It's not that he's bad, he's, ah, different. He's fairly new. He's been working some art theft cases and actually has made some nice recoveries."

Vanko waited a moment before saying, "But?"

"Well, he's single and he's been hanging around with some . . . some . . . I don't know how to say this diplomatically. He's been spotted hanging around some gay bars."

"Maybe it's work-related?"

"It could be, but how are we supposed to find out? This isn't something we have experience with. At least, I hope we don't. All this stuff is so goddamn touchy these days. The bottom line is everyone wants him at arm's length."

"Just so I'm clear, why are you sending him out here?"

"You have an ability to read people. Maybe you could find out?"

"If he's gay?"

"It's not like we can ask him. I might as well dial up the ACLU and tell them we hate queers and what are they going to do about it."

"When is he getting here?"

"I think today. Sorry, Nick, with the inspectors coming, I just want to minimize potential problems."

"I know."

The next question Hansen was reluctant to ask. Previously, he had mentioned to Vanko that the office was getting a lot of heat concerning the disappearance of a local judge, and because it was thought to be organized crime–related, had hoped that Vanko, like he had with Paul Dimino, could use his unorthodox bunch to somehow resolve it. "Have you got anything going on Judge Ferris?"

"Nothing concrete yet, but we're working on some ideas," Vanko lied. The SAC had mentioned it casually right after the incident appeared in the papers, but Vanko found that the SAC liked to throw out "intuitive" ideas to his managers without any real thought or direction. Too many supervisors put into motion elaborate plans no matter how counterproductive for their agents. Their subsequent reporting of "progress" to the SAC further convinced him of his leadership acumen, which, in turn, caused the release of even larger and more unstable trial balloons. Vanko never did anything until Hansen mentioned a problem at least twice.

Vanko's answer was as specific as the SAC wanted to get. "Good enough," he said. "I don't suppose I could get you to come out of hiding and let me buy you a drink."

"I appreciate the offer, but things are a little busy right now."

Inexplicably, Hansen, even though assigned to New York for almost two years, had never seen Vanko in person. The supervisor always offered some undefined urgency to keep from meeting with the SAC or, for that matter, anyone outside of his squad. Although Hansen was tempted to order him in and end the odd but minor breach of protocol, Vanko's selfless shunning of credit in matters like the Dimino case made Hansen examine his own motives more closely. He decided that such a demand would simply reveal a need to pull rank. He was sure Vanko had a reason for his reclusiveness. His file stated that he had been involved in a bad automobile accident as a young agent. Someone had been killed, and he had suffered permanent facial damage.

The agents in the office referred to his squad as the Opera House. When Hansen first arrived, he asked why it was called that. One articulate supervisor, who had a deeper understanding of the art form than most agents would care to admit, said, "Everyone who is sent out there has this long, sad, emotional song. It's a place where subplots of anguish and recrimination go to exhaust themselves. You know, just like an opera."

But the SAC was well aware of the gallows humor of agents and suspected this wasn't the real reason for the squad's nickname. When he discovered that Vanko's face had been disfigured, he understood. That he had never heard the word *phantom* connected to the phrase was an unusual tribute to Vanko's reputation. "I understand, Nick. And again, thanks for the work last night. You'll let your people know?"

"They already do."

4

MANNY "THE LAG" BALDOVINO SAT IN HIS CAR trying not to think, especially about bridges. Ever since developing gephydrophobia a year earlier, his thoughts always raced back to his fear of the overwhelming structures that delicately laced the five boroughs of New York City together. The phobia was bad enough—only being able to use tunnels and the ferry to get around—but it invariably dead-ended at the same inescapable taunt: a fear of bridges had cost him the only chance he would ever have to become a made member. He was just thankful that his father, who had died five years before, did not have to endure the disgrace of a son's weakness.

Joseph "Joey Stones" Baldovino, so named for his courage during the gang wars of the seventies, had been a captain in the Galante crime family and held the unusual distinction of being both feared and respected. During his eulogy, his best friend had said that he died of a heart attack because his heart was too big. Contrarily, with the malicious wit of children, Manny had been designated "the Lag" because he was never able to keep up on any level. As a child he had looked forward to the day he would outgrow the name, but it had clung to him. Not only did it remind him of the disappointments of his youth, but now it slandered his father's memory. Most of all he hated the nickname because he suspected it was accurate.

Joseph Baldovino had been handsome, tall, squarely built, and powerful. His hair was thick and imperial, its forward edge extending low onto his forehead, giving him a black-and-white movie star quality, while Manny's, even though he was only in his thirties, was disappearing both in density and expanse. Like his mother, he was short, and as a child he had possessed her slender frame, but with the advent of middle age and an impulsive diet, he had become round-bodied. He had a reputation for being nonconfrontational no matter how harshly provoked, hardly an asset among men whose primary industry was intimidation. These impairments led him to suspect that the bridge phobia— or at least its pre-existing conditions—had seeped into his psychological undercarriage through the maternal half of his DNA. All of Manny Baldovino's shortcomings as a gangster found their way to the surface the night he was sent to kill Rocco Gaggi.

An associate of the Galante family, Gaggi had been spotted coming out of the Federal Building in Manhattan. Normally such a sighting would have aroused mild curiosity, but coupled with his arrest forty-five days earlier for receiving and concealing, the risk of his being flipped rose considerably. The family underboss, Danny DeMiglia, had only one rule of thumb when it came to security: settle all close calls with murder. Manny was given the job with Tommy Capps as backup.

One night, they followed Gaggi around Brooklyn, waiting for an opportunity to end his life. As Gaggi started to cross the Williamsburg Bridge into Manhattan, the two would-be killers quickly decided that once he reached the other side, they would drive up alongside and shotgun him. But without warning, Baldovino started feeling faint. His heart raced and his breathing became labored. Sweat coursed down the middle of his back. At first, he assumed it was just the anxiety of his first murder. As they approached the bridge, fear of his own imminent death closed in around Baldovino. He was seized by an urgent need to flee, to turn around, to do anything to avoid the bridge. When he pulled over, Capps stared at him in confusion. "Didn't you see them!" Baldovino demanded with as much false anger as he could muster. "The undercover car. Might have been Feds. We can catch up with Rocco tomorrow."

"Manny, you don't look so good. You okay?"

"Don't know. Maybe it was that risotto I had for dinner. Fucking clams." But he knew it wasn't. A wildfire was sweeping through his central nervous system, and he looked over his shoulder to make certain that he could no longer see the bridge.

"Want I should take you to the hospital?"

"Naw, I probably just need a Alka-Seltzer or something. How about I drop you off at the club? My nephew's got a thing at school tonight."

He lay awake all night, his mind unable to erase the overscaled steel and concrete geometry of the Williamsburg Bridge. Eventually he drifted into a light sleep and found himself driving through the concrete portals of the Brooklyn Bridge, which, despite thousands of crossings, he had never noticed before. The tented stone arches and thick steel cables suddenly seemed tenuous, unsafe, death-defying. Without further warning or explanation, he felt himself free-falling from its height. As his feet started kicking the accelerating air, he awoke.

The next day he went to his doctor. The receptionist, a heavily built woman in her sixties who was normally a heartless enforcer of the waiting list, saw the urgency in his eyes and sent him right in.

"Doc, you're like a fucking lawyer, right? Anything I tell you has to stay right here."

"Just like a fucking lawyer," the doctor answered with just enough sarcasm not to be detected. Without revealing the previous night's mission, Baldovino told him about his symptoms and their apparent cause.

"Sounds like either an anxiety attack or some type of phobia."

"Phobia? You mean like scared of something?"

"I'm not a psychiatrist, but yes."

"How in the fuck can you be scared of a bridge?"

"People are afraid of a lot of things: grapefruit, cotton balls, wind chimes. It can be anything." The doctor pulled a book from the shelf behind him and flipped through some pages. "Since last night have you had any more thoughts about bridges?"

"That's all I've been thinking about. I'm really dreading the next time I have to go across one of them. In fact, I've been planning these alternate routes. Or maybe just staying in Brooklyn."

"Well, Manny, this really isn't my field of knowledge. You need to see a specialist."

"You mean like a shrink? I ain't going to no fucking shrink."

"There are some behavior modification treatments now that can help you overcome these kinds of problems."

"Ain't you got some kind of pill I can take when I feel this start?"

"I can give you something, but wouldn't you rather eliminate the problem?"

"Doc, I think you know what I'm about. If I was built for self-improvement, I'd be hustling time-shares in Arizona or something. Please just give me the pills."

Later that day he found himself alone with Tiny Russo, his *capo*, trying to explain what had gone wrong the night before. Baldovino gave him the same excuse: that he had spotted cops, or maybe the FBI.

Russo didn't answer right away. "Tommy said you got sick or something."

"I think I had some bad clams at Little Rocky's."

"You okay now?" Russo put his hand on Manny's shoulder, but it felt insincere.

"Yeah, I went to the doc. He gave me some pills; I should be fine."

"How about that guy?"

"The guy from last night?"

"Yeah, what other fucking guy would I be talking about?"

"I'll grab Tommy and we'll go try to find him right now."

"You sure you're okay?"

"Fine, I'm fine."

But as soon as Baldovino and Capps got in the car, Manny's heart started to race. He had Capps drive him home and promise not to say anything to anyone. A week later, while Manny was home "sick," Capps caught Gaggi coming out of his girlfriend's house one morning and cut him in two with a shotgun. Three months later, Tommy Capps was made.

Contract killings had as their primary purpose the elimination of impending financial and legal problems, but they were also considered a relatively reliable evaluation tool. During the Cosa Nostra induction ceremony only one question was asked: Would you kill for the family? Apparently Manny wouldn't. When allowing himself to think about it, he could only conclude that some things were just not meant to be.

Sitting in his car, he reconsidered, for the hundredth time, his being chosen for the Gaggi contract in the first place. Recently promoted to underboss, DeMiglia had openly opposed the old ways. Tradition had failed, he argued. While their family had far fewer problems than the others, too many of their members were either dead or in prison. That was their *real* tradition. Things had to change if their organization was to survive and prosper. They had to quit sitting around trying to relive the good old days.

While not naming Baldovino specifically, DeMiglia stated that certain individuals needed to be thinned from their ranks, not only because of their inability to conduct the everyday business of organized crime, but also because of their links to the past. Enough of a tactician not to offend the old mustaches, DeMiglia gave the Gaggi hit to Manny, probably figuring that he would fail and eliminate himself from the family's rolls. It was an expedient DeMiglia had used in the past. And Manny had to hand it to him—it worked.

But being kept on Cosa Nostra's lower rungs was not all bad. Shortly after the failed murder attempt, Manny was sent over to another crew and now answered to Mike Parisi, who had been made a captain when he married the niece of the family boss, Anthony Carrera. Because the don had been close to Baldovino's father, he had asked Parisi to take Manny in as a personal favor even though DeMiglia had wanted Manny severed from all family interests.

Since leaving Russo's crew, life had become much easier for Baldovino. Almost defying the underboss's edicts, Parisi did not pressure his men to make money. He ran the family's gambling and loansharking operations with unusual efficiency. At the present time, Parisi had almost two million dollars on the street in shylock loans, which brought in close to twenty thousand a week in interest. That was a million a year. Gambling, stronger during football, usually averaged twelve to fifteen thousand a week. So, without looking for new opportunities, the crew brought the family about $1.75 million a year, not spectacular numbers by organized crime standards, but steady and dependable enough to allow the don to take risks in new areas without running into cash-flow problems. Some of the other *capos* felt that Parisi's crew was the spoiled stepchild of the family and, when given an opportunity, would voice their displeasure to the boss. He responded by telling them if they all ran their regimes as successfully as his nephew did, everybody would be a little richer with a lot less looking over the shoulder, an argument that usually put only a temporary halt to the grousing.

All in all, everything had worked out for the best for Manny. He even had to admit that it was only right that if somebody was afraid of bridges, they couldn't expect to be a big-time gangster.

Still, he had to take care of himself, and that meant hustling a buck. He wasn't married and not a gambler—at least not a degenerate gambler—so his needs were modest. He picked small enterprises and loyally tithed the proscribed tribute to his *capo* without bothering him with details. To that end, he had come upon a new opportunity three weeks earlier when he struck up a conversation in a bar with a guy named Jake Tanager who had done time with someone Manny knew. While in prison, Tanager learned how to operate a stamping press. After being paroled, he went to work at a plant in New Jersey. Not really caring, but enjoying the conversation, Baldovino asked, "What do you make there?"

Tanager had an unequivocally warm smile, but the question put a tinge of embarrassment in his quick eyes. "You know, stuff."

"What kind of stuff?"

"You're not going to laugh?"

Baldovino smiled. "I'm sorry, even that question makes me laugh."

Tanager laughed and the embarrassment disappeared. "Believe it or not, license plates. Made them on the inside, now I'm making them on the outside." After a few more drinks, Tanager explained that he was in charge of the production line that punched out New York plates. And some of their runs were handicap plates.

"Man, you don't know how many times I wish I had one of those. Fuckin' New York. There's eight million people and one parking space in the whole city."

"You want one, Manny? It's as good as done. How about your family, they need any?"

Baldovino thought about the rest of his crew. He could be a hero for a while, but it probably would be seen as another one of his harebrained schemes. He could hear Mike Parisi now. "Manny, think about it. As often as the FBI comes through here running plates, what are they going to think when there's nothing but handicaps registered to everyone?" This was good, Manny decided; for once he was thinking ahead. But this was too big an opportunity to pass up. "Jake, maybe we could make some money on this. How many of those plates could you get?"

"Hey, Manny, I was trying to offer you a courtesy because we have a mutual friend. I don't need any more trouble than I already got. My parole officer is a real prick."

"There's millions of license plates issued every year in this state. Is someone going to notice a few extra handicaps? And if they do, I'm the one selling them. It'll come back on me. You can check with our friend, I don't give people up."

"That all sounds good, but the joint is full of guys who thought something sounded good."

"I'll tell you what, I'll give you two hundred a set." Manny could see that Tanager immediately began multiplying in his head. There was nothing easier to sell than easy money.

"I could definitely use the cash. How many sets are you talking about?"

"Get me twenty sets, and we'll see how it goes." Manny figured he would make maybe seven or eight hundred on each of them in return, maybe even a grand in Manhattan where parking was impossible. "I guarantee this won't come back on you."

Tanager drummed his fingers on the bar for a few seconds, then reached over and offered Manny his hand. "I'll see you here, in the parking lot, a week from today at noon."

Where is this guy? For the tenth time since parking, Manny flipped on the air-conditioning, hoping that some mechanical miracle had repaired the system that hadn't worked in three years. Damp, rubbery-smelling air churned out of the vents. He turned it off again. To divert himself, he took a napkin from the glove compartment and started figuring the optimum return on his investment. Twenty thousand minus four—sixteen grand. He would give Mike five. Eleven thousand, not a bad little gig. Parisi would ask where it came from, but Manny didn't think he should tell him. Parisi had taken Baldovino in when everyone else would have rather pretended he didn't exist. All in all, the crew thought Mike was a good captain. His only problem was that because he had not come from the same background as the rest of them, he occasionally tried a little too hard to be a gangster, to be a little tougher than he obviously was. Although he had done some time as a kid, he hadn't been involved in the hardcore felonies that were the normal precursors for acceptance into an organized crime regime—unless your father was Joey Stones.

Ultimately Parisi was an honorable guy, and in their business, that trumped all minor violations, and quite a few of the majors. For instance, Manny had the distinct feeling that Parisi had figured out his fear of bridges, because every time he started to send him on an errand across one of them, he would stop himself and find an excuse to send someone else, never confronting Manny with any suspicions. And because he was a standup guy, of the five grand turned over to him from the plates, Parisi would kick two or three up to the don, making sure that Baldovino got credit for the tribute. It wasn't big money, but it showed respect.

Tanager pulled into the lot. He was only a few minutes late. He parked his ancient Toyota next to Baldovino's equally seasoned Lincoln and scanned the parking lot as he got out. He was carrying a large pink cake box. Tanager got in and handed Manny the box, its weight too heavy for bakery goods. "As promised, twenty sets."

"Any problems?"

"Smooth as silk. I had an overtime job last night and stayed late. I just ran them before I did my other work. Kind of funny, getting paid overtime to make them."

"You're going to have to trust me for the four thousand."

"Goddamn it, Manny, that wasn't the deal."

"Hey, it's not like I'm going to stiff you. I'll be back for more. I can't do that and expect you to deliver. As soon as I sell four grand worth, it's yours."

"Do you have *any* money? I was counting on this. I owe, and it ain't to the fucking Chase Manhattan."

Baldovino took out his wallet and stretched it open to prove his insolvency. "I'm busted. But like I said, as soon as I see anything, it'll get to you."

"When are you going to start selling them?"

"You just saw my wallet—today, right now."

"I'm curious; where would you go to unload something like this?"

"Brooklyn, the old neighborhood. You know, kind of test the waters to see what they'll bring."

"Okay, here's the deal. If I don't have my four grand by Saturday, don't call me again."

"I'm on my way to Brooklyn right now."

"Please don't fuck me, Manny."

"I'm on my way, I swear."

Tanager shook his hand with less enthusiasm than when he'd gotten into the car. "Saturday."

5

DICK ZALENSKI KNOCKED ON THE DOOR FRAME
and stuck his childlike face in Vanko's office. "Nick, this is Brad
Kenyon. Found him in the reception area. I don't know where
Abby is."

"She's running some errands." As Vanko stood up, Kenyon
thanked Zalenski with an elegant nod of the head. He wore a black
turtleneck under an expensive black and white houndstooth jacket
that seemed to strobe in the dusty fluorescent light. His brown hair
was swept back from his delicate face in glistening cords. Vanko
shook hands and motioned him into a chair. There seemed to be an
air of restraint about Kenyon, as if he had been miscast as a government employee and was as amused as anyone by the occupation he
now found himself in. Vanko suspected there might be money in
his family, an unusual occurrence within their ranks, and could see
why others might consider him a potential problem. Distrust had
always proven itself a reliable ally of agents, both outside their
ranks and within. Whether accurate or not, judgments tended to be
made quickly. It was better to be wrong than to be taken in. Agents
felt most comfortable with newcomers who were in character: bargain suits, just-out-of-the-military haircuts, and a trace of angst
swimming just beneath the surface. Not only was Kenyon void of
these conformities, but he had successfully recovered stolen art.
Being out of character and still accomplishing things was more
than likely his real crime.

"So, you were working art thefts on your last squad."

"Was."

"And you're still in your first year."

"I'm still on probation if that's what you're asking."

"I don't know what you've heard, but just because you've been sent out here, don't think I'm looking for a way to get rid of you."

Without any noticeable apprehension, Kenyon studied Vanko's damaged face. His new supervisor did not try to use lighting, distance, or positioning to mute its effect, but instead held it out to scrutiny with an enviable dignity. "Fair enough."

"I understand you made some nice recoveries."

"Yes, I guess I did. Art is kind of a niche of mine." The word was pronounced as a European might—"neesh." "That's why it's a little bit of a mystery why I was transferred here. This squad works organized crime, doesn't it?"

"More or less."

The walls in the office, like those throughout most of the squad's space, were covered with cheap wooden paneling that had been painted a color that was either pale green or an oxidized gold. Hanging opposite Vanko's desk were several black-and-white photos of men, obviously under surveillance; some were going to gray, the heavier ones wore designer warmup suits. The photos were neatly skewered with pushpins and spaced at perfect intervals. "The enemy, I assume."

"Something like that," Vanko said, his tone neither superior nor contentious.

On another section of the wall, almost lost in the shadows, were more than a dozen photos. Kenyon got up to take a closer look. The people in these were obviously not members of organized crime. The first one was a picture of an Asian man. His body strained against the weight of a heavy metal container, which he was pushing through the garment district. His expression was an amalgam of the bewilderment of an outsider and the hopeful confidence of impending acceptance. If he worked hard enough, long enough, and made good choices, one day he would be inside looking out. And if not him, undeniably his children. Next to it was a photo of a black woman, her dreadlocks disobediently emerging from underneath a knit hat.

"These are exceptional. Yours?" Vanko nodded with neither pride nor self-consciousness. "How did you get them all with the same expression?"

"Patience."

"How many photos did you have to take to get these?"

"Hundreds, I don't know, thousands. We have a makeshift darkroom here. We're kind of the jacks-of-all-trades for the office, always getting called to photograph someone or someplace for arrest and search warrants. Most of us have had to become photographers to survive. It's just more practical."

"These are all immigrants."

"Yes, they're kind of an interest of mine. I came here with my parents from Greece when I was six."

Kenyon turned back to the supervisor, his voice no longer contained. "I'm sorry, but I'm really wondering what I'm doing here. There's something I've got to ask you."

"Go ahead."

"I've heard some rumors, so I'm just going to ask you. Was I sent here because they think I'm gay?"

Vanko hesitated. He didn't want Kenyon to think it was a foregone conclusion. "They think it's a possibility."

"Why didn't someone just ask me?"

"I think you know why."

"Lawsuits."

"That and precedents."

"This seems like a very roundabout way to deal with it."

"When you're here a little longer, you'll find that only in the most blatant cases does the Bureau get rid of someone because of their actual sins, at least not their sexual sins. Usually they just find some uncontestable *t* that hasn't been crossed and let it do their dirty work for them."

"Which in my case is not that difficult because I'm still on first-year probation."

"I've already told you, I'm a supervisor, not an executioner."

"Aren't you going to ask?"

"No."

"Well, just for the record, I'm not. This isn't the first time people have thought that about me. I know I don't come off exactly as a barroom brawler, but I do like women." He grinned. "I've got some telephone numbers if you'd like testimonials."

"Like I said, I've got enough to do. If you want, as soon as inspection's over, I'll call the SAC and get you sent back to the squad you were on."

"I think I'd find it hard to work for that supervisor after this."

Vanko opened a drawer and took out an office directory. He found what he was looking for and dropped the list back into the drawer. "When I had about as much time in as you do, I was working on a squad that handled bank robberies and kidnappings. I really liked it. Then I got into it pretty good with the supervisor over something that really wasn't that important. But I had my pride, so I requested a transfer off the squad. Six months later, the supervisor was transferred to FBIHQ, and I was never able to get back to that squad. According to the directory your supervisor is here just getting his ticket punched. If you really like working art theft, don't give it up because you're trying to get even with him. In the meantime feel free to hide out here until he leaves."

Kenyon found himself involuntarily nodding at Vanko's logic. "I'll keep it in mind." As he turned to go, a photograph he hadn't noticed before caught his eye. Apparently homeless, a black man was leaning into a trash basket. By the gauzy light, it appeared to be early morning along some Manhattan curb, and he was digging through the twenty-four hours of flotsam contained inside. Next to him on the sidewalk was a gigantic clear plastic bag filled to near capacity with aluminum cans, hundreds of them. Kenyon could almost feel the summer heat shimmering off the damp pavement at the man's feet. He had on a threadbare sport coat that had the top button fastened formally across his midsection. He also wore high black rubber boots that inexplicably seemed useful for what he was doing. They gave him the look of a fisherman efficiently excavating clams at low tide. At the last moment before the photo was snapped, he had instinctively stared up at the camera with a look of disrespect that gave him an implicit dignity.

"This one is different."

"Yes, I thought so, too. He has a kind of grace." Vanko smiled warmly. "Makes me think there's hope for all of us."

"So he's the poster boy for this squad."

Vanko laughed. "I just like the photograph, but you may be right."

Kenyon knew that his supervisor understood these photographs far better than anyone. After all, his empathy had created them. He looked back at Vanko's face and, in the stinted light, froze it in a single-frame image. It explained Vanko's understanding and fraternity with the men and women on the wall. He too was an outsider, once by birth and now by the residue of tragedy, more enduring than most. So was Kenyon, sentenced to this unfamiliar world as every member of the squad had been—immigrants, castaways all.

6

TRUE TO HIS WORD, MANNY HEADED STRAIGHT FOR
Brooklyn. He had the perfect guy to sell the first set of plates to—
an Arab who owned a convenience store. He was a known fence
in the neighborhood. Baldovino had once sold him fifteen thousand dollars' worth of stolen food stamps. But the Arab was a
tight bastard, giving only ten cents on the dollar.

As always, he was behind the counter where he could observe
every square foot of his store. Manny walked in, put the box on
the counter, and shook hands. The smell of brewing coffee hung
thickly in the air and mingled with the scents of Middle Eastern
spices that filled large scoop bins. The store owner's grip was
strong, but his eyes gave no indication of friendship. They shifted
to the box suspiciously.

Baldovino said, "Have I got something for you."

The Arab smiled slyly. "Not cake?"

Manny opened the box. "Not cake."

The Arab's eyes widened as he turned the plates in his hand,
running his fingers along the edges, then inspecting the backs for
any detectable flaws. "These counterfeit?"

Just then a man in his thirties walked in and went directly to
the snack aisle. He was wearing a windbreaker and sunglasses.

Manny lowered his voice. "These are the real deal. They're as
good as the plates on your car. They're made by the state. Fool-
proof."

"One hundred dollars," the Arab offered.

Manny smiled with some satisfaction at having the upper hand and put them back in the box carefully to suggest their worth. When he started tying the string, the Arab countered, "Two hundred."

"A thousand."

"Take them and get out."

Manny rationalized that the Arab would be a more difficult sale than the rich white people he would sell the rest of them to, but right now he needed some walking-around money. "Okay, eight hundred."

The storekeeper ignored him and raised his voice to the customer. "Can I help you find something, sir?"

The man was inspecting the nutritional information on a bag of pretzels. Looking up, he said, "Ah, I'm looking for something that's not loaded with fat. Do you have a health food section?"

"Sorry, you're looking at everything we have right there."

"Five hundred," Manny countered.

"Two fifty, end of discussion."

"Okay, okay." Manny took out the plates and handed them back to the store owner, who was smiling the same malicious smile he had used when he'd bought the stolen food stamps. The Arab handed two hundred-dollar bills and a fifty across the counter.

The customer said something in a low voice. Unable to make it out, the Arab assumed he was reading another label to himself. He set the plates on a shelf under the cash register.

While only getting a quarter of what he hoped the plates might sell for elsewhere, Manny walked out feeling like he had fought the cheap Arab to a draw. For him, not a bad piece of negotiation.

As soon as he got in his car, a gun was pointed at his face. "FBI!" Another agent was standing at the passenger's side with a gun drawn. Two more men ran into the store. Manny was pulled out of the car and handcuffed.

After they searched him, one of the agents took the box from the front seat and opened it. "They're in here." He took the plates out and started counting them. "Nineteen sets."

The first agent led him to a Bureau car. "You have the right to remain silent—"

"That's it."

"That's what?" the agent asked.

"I'll take that one—to remain silent."

"Fair enough, but I have to read them all to you."

While the agent offered the option of afforded or appointed counsel, Baldovino realized that even though being arrested for the first time was something he had always dreaded, it now carried a certain liberation. He suspected, if nothing else, it would earn him some respect.

The Arab was brought out in handcuffs, led by the man who had posed as a customer. It occurred to Manny that he had not been reading the package but talking into a hidden radio. He must have been followed. But how had they known?

Manny suddenly questioned his latest enterprise. Where were New York plates made? Why would it be in New Jersey? And how did the FBI get onto this so fast? He was set up. He had to smile at the expression. *Set up*—a defense so overused that it had actually become subtle evidence of guilt to all but the most stubborn of jurors. Tanager had to be either an FBI informant or worse, an undercover agent. He had been very smooth: in hindsight, too smooth, and he lacked the uncleansed cast of someone who had survived years in correctional warehouses. Baldovino laughed out loud. The agent in the front seat looked at him. "Are you all right?"

"Am I all right?" He laughed harder. "I'm fucked." As much as it hurt to admit, Baldovino had again earned his nickname. The Lag had been too slow on his feet. The FBI had hooked strings to him and pulled them in the most uncomplicated sequence possible. And he had performed flawlessly. He closed his eyes tightly, and the fatigue he sometimes forgot he carried burned the underside of the lids. He was so glad his father wasn't alive.

"Maybe we could let you work this off."

Before he could reply, something occurred to Baldovino. The government had gone to a great deal of trouble to target him. He was small-time, and the case certainly wasn't the kind that normally warranted the attention of the rubric-seeking FBI, but with the agent's offer to exchange freedom for information, everything suddenly made sense. They were after Mike Parisi. Then something far more immediate struck him. "Where are you taking me?"

"To the magistrate. For arraignment."

"Yeah, I know that, but where?"

"In Manhattan."

Baldovino felt his breath coming faster. "Can we take the tunnel?"

"We'll take the bridge, it's faster. You do want to try to make bail tonight, I assume."

"Fuck bail. I want the tunnel."

Not understanding what was going on, but sensing an advantage, the agent suggested, "Like I said, maybe we could work something out."

For the first time Baldovino took a close look at him. He appeared too young to be arresting people. It was a game to these college boys. A year from now, Baldovino would be in prison, and they would be working elsewhere, going to their kids' games and school plays, their only remembrance of him an exaggerated sense of accomplishment. Maybe he wasn't as smart as everyone else, but loyalty didn't take any talent, just the ability to endure self-punishment. It was something he had inherited from his mother that he could finally use. His mouth twisted into an uncomfortable knot of resolution. "Fuck it, kid, let's take the bridge. Any bridge. The bigger the better."

7

ALTHOUGH THEY HAD BEEN HEADQUARTERS supervisors together in Washington, Bernard Dreagen had not seen or spoken to Charles Lansing in almost three years. Their career paths diverged when Dreagen was promoted to the coveted position of administrative ASAC of the New York office, while Lansing, his junior in years, continued his duties in Washington, awaiting any similar opportunity. With the sudden, dramatic arc in his career, Dreagen placed the memory of those left behind into his mental shredder, making room only for those who could bring future advantage. But today was the first day of the month-long inspection, a time when authority's pecking order was annoyingly jumbled.

As Lansing entered the office, Dreagen rose dutifully and offered a practiced smile along with his hand. "Chuck, how are you?" From the crooked grin on Lansing's mouth, Dreagen sensed that he, like all inspectors, expected to be treated with deference.

Lansing was wearing the unofficial uniform of FBIHQ: a blue blazer, medium gray trousers, white shirt, and a regimental-stripe tie with just enough red not to call attention to itself. His hair, sandy and thinning, was frozen in place by some kind of fixative that left his shining scalp substantially more noticeable. Dreagen ran his hand gratefully through his own thick, dark hair.

"I'm good, Bernie. How about yourself?"

Dreagen held his arms out to encompass his unlimited good

fortune. "The center of the universe, my friend. Center of the universe. How long have you been on the inspection staff?"

"This is my third time out."

"And you're finding it . . . ?"

"Uneven. One minute everything's running like a solid gold Rolex, the next, you're feeding some guy's career into a wood chipper."

That Lansing had used the word "career" implied a threat. It meant the "guy" was management. Street agents, those rank-and-file men and women whose only responsibility was to investigate and solve cases, weren't thought of by managers as having careers. Lansing's reference indicated that he had come here to commit the misdemeanor of inspection extortion. He was looking for an informant who could relieve him of the inconvenience of tediously going through files to determine which agents could be taken out.

Dreagen wondered if he had become a target. The grin he'd screwed onto his face weakened and slipped away. Hopefully Lansing had other priorities, because Dreagen wasn't ready for another confrontation. He had just come from SAC Hansen's office, where it had been explained to him, in relatively unpleasant terms, that he had no right to convert to his own use a Mercedes or any other seized vehicle in the FBI's possession. The ASAC then made the mistake of arguing that the "Bureau dregs" under Nick Vanko's supervision were irresponsible and had probably wrecked the car on a whim and then deceived the SAC as to how it happened. "You're the admin ASAC, you have no idea what that squad does. Just handle administrative matters. Leave the heavy lifting to the real agents." The SAC, a veteran of clashes with ambitious men, knew that Dreagen would not hesitate to seek revenge for the minor whipping on those he perceived as responsible. "And stay away from them. If you have any problems with Vanko's squad, come to me, and I'll handle it. Do you understand?"

Dreagen put the smile back on his face. "So what brings you here, Chuck? Am I in trouble already?"

"I really haven't started yet, so it would be premature to try and answer that."

With a little bit of playful suspicion, Dreagen said, "Small FBI. We used to work together, and you draw me for the inspection."

"If you're asking me if I *arranged* this assignment—guilty. I thought since we were in the same unit once, we might be able to give each other a hand."

"And what am I giving you a hand with?"

"Any areas that you might think need my attention."

"And I would do that—why?"

"I imagine that unless you drop one in the end zone, you'll be going out as a SAC before much longer."

As veiled threats went, this one wasn't very artful. Apparently, in too big a hurry to get himself promoted, Lansing was making the deadly mistake of not observing the speed limits of ambition. Too many shortcuts, especially in the FBI, inevitably led to biting oneself in the ass. Dreagen knew how to use this against someone, but he had also learned that a hook was best let out slowly. "In other words, you want me to do your work for you."

"I would think that someone in your position would want to ensure that any impending air strikes were as surgical as possible."

Normally Dreagen loved the masculine metaphors of management argot. It was as cool as a guy wearing a fifteen-dollar tie could get. It was their secret handshake, not understood by the unwashed masses, that seven-eighths of the agent population—the portion of the FBI iceberg that floated beneath the waterline of importance. But Lansing, having the advantage of being stationed at Bureau headquarters, the seat of the insider dialect, was too current, too practiced in its use. Dreagen decided it was banal and elitist. "So I'm looking at a pass . . . for my entire part of the office's operation."

"It'll add at least a month to your life."

Lansing was right; the inspection had a way of suspending time for everyone while those four adversarial weeks ground nerve endings into a fine powder. Besides, ASAC Dreagen needed to settle a score he had been ordered not to. Here was someone offering to do it for him, and it would take absolutely no investment on his part. "Okay, I've got something, but when you go for them, you and I never had this conversation."

"*Them?*"

"That's right, *them*. An entire squad. And, if you're thorough enough, you may be able to get just about every person on it. But first you've got to convince me this won't come back to me."

"How would it? Why would it?"

"I'm sorry, hypothetical questions aren't what I need—I need collateral."

Lansing hesitated, eyeing the ASAC closely. "This is that good*?*"

"It'll make you employee of the month. Have you ever heard, in the history of inspection, of an entire squad being gutted? And not just censored; I'm talking about actually getting some of them fired."

"Seems a little too good to be true."

"What you have to remember, Chuck, is that one-tenth of the agents in the FBI are in this division. Hell, there are almost a hundred different squads. That's going to produce some serious personnel problems. And in New York, the most serious are all buried on one squad."

"What kind of problems are we talking about?"

"You name it, everything from total incompetence to having a screw loose to criminal behavior."

"Criminal behavior?"

"One guy is about to be sent out there while OPR's looking at him for insider trading."

"Insider trading? How would an agent have access to that kind of information?"

"He was working as a UC at a brokerage house." Lansing's eyebrows raised. "I'm telling you, you'll have a field day. Fish in a barrel."

"Who's the supervisor?"

The ASAC was aware that the requested "collateral" had not been provided, but he wanted Lansing to believe that he had outmaneuvered him. "Nick Vanko."

"What's he like?"

"A ghost. I've never seen the guy. In fact, I've never even talked to him. The squad works out of an off-site."

"Why off-site?"

"They're tasked with special projects. And before you ask, I don't know what that is. I think it's mostly surveillance, photographic assignments, odds and ends like that. But I'm not positive."

"And they need a separate office for that?"

"I've wondered the same thing, and whenever I ask, I've been given the distinct impression that I didn't want to know."

Lansing's lips tightened with determination. These were exactly the kinds of potentially embarrassing things an inspector worth his salt uncovered. "Well, it sounds like something I'm going to want to find out."

"Let me warn you, Chuck, you're going to get the runaround. I get it when I ask, and I'm on the home team. Maybe they've got something on the SAC because anytime somebody tries to hold them responsible for anything, he jumps up in their defense." Dreagen thought throwing the SAC in as a possible trophy couldn't hurt.

"I'll stay out there the entire month if I have to."

Perfect, Dreagen thought. All today's problems were about to take each other out.

8

THE MORNING'S TABLOID HEADLINE READ:

MOB GOES FROM MAKING LICENSE
PLATES TO . . . MAKING LICENSE PLATES

In an almost bullying departure from the delicately ham-
mered rhetoric of FBI spokespersons everywhere, James Wade of
the Manhattan office was quoted in the article as saying, "Because
we feel the FBI is largely at fault for the lack of entrepreneurial
opportunity that organized crime faces these days, we're going to
urge the United States Attorney's office to show Mr. Baldovino
some leniency. Possibly allow him to plead to a lesser offense,
something like interstate transportation of counterfeit instruments in a pink cake box."

Released that morning on bail, Manny Baldovino stared out
the narrow front window at the Sons of Catania Social Club.
Some of the others from Mike Parisi's crew sat around a table behind him, arguing and laughing over a pinochle game. Never before had Manny understood the luxury of their idleness, and he
now admonished himself for not enjoying it more when it had
been his. He stood close enough to hear them, but kept his back
turned in self-exile as punishment for embarrassing himself and
his friends.

Outside, evenly scattered clouds, their undersides flat and gun-
metal gray, covered the neighborhood with alternating patches of

dry, blanched sunlight and pewtered opacity. Back in the kitchen, sauce was cooking. The oily singe of garlic, the sweet pungency of tomatoes—it reminded him of Sundays at his mother's house, the ultimate safe harbor of his life. Squinting out at the recurring cycle of light and dark, he imagined each a silent frame, each a day and then a night, flickering by, distancing him from his problems.

"Hey, Manny, quit watching out the window," Gus Dellaporta said. "You expecting the FBI? Oh no, that's right, you wouldn't know them if you saw them. For future reference, they're the ones with the cake boxes." A spattering of laughter erupted as Baldovino turned around and waited while his eyes adjusted to the dimmer light. Dellaporta sat with his thick hands folded gently in front of him like a boxer lowering his arms to taunt an opponent with superior skills. But Baldovino could see that it was not done maliciously, but rather to show him he was among friends, and the mistakes they all made were inherent in trying to exist outside the law. Dellaporta was calling for return fire.

"If all it took was cake boxes to figure out who the FBI was, Gus, you'd be the most valuable guy in the outfit."

Even Dellaporta had to laugh. "Come on and sit down. Use those hands for something besides slapping yourself around. Play some cards. This'll go away, you just have to get off it."

Dellaporta stood up and stretched. As always, he was wearing a sport coat over his 270 pounds, this one powder blue. It was all he ever wore, even during a snowstorm. He squatted down and bounced to loosen his heavily muscled thighs. For his size, he was remarkably light on his feet. At parties or weddings, those who knew him looked forward to the moment when he had had enough to drink to step out onto the dance floor. Once he did, no matter how many times they had witnessed it, his friends could only shake their heads at the apparent suspension of the physical laws of the universe as he floated above the hardwood surface with an endless string of eager women.

While Baldovino didn't consider himself especially insightful when it came to people, his bridge phobia had made him aware of the mind's ability, in times of stress, to hide larger problems behind smaller ones. Subsequently, he had discovered an anomaly of omission within the Gus Dellaporta mystique: as big as he was, no one ever saw him eat. At restaurants or any occasion at which food was a focal point, he would just sit and drink whiskey, and not as much as an olive would pass his lips. For Manny, the conclusion was obvious—Dellaporta had to be a closet eater. And whatever drove him to overeat was also driving his need to hide the act itself. If no one saw him, then it wasn't really happening. There was no visible cause, so the effect really couldn't be considered a weakness. Somehow Gus Dellaporta was just a big man.

While Manny was not a person who found pleasure in another man's misery, he found it reassuring that even the most respected of his associates had problems. He liked Dellaporta. There was a gentleness about him that in rare, unguarded moments escaped almost unnoticed. Baldovino gave him a slightly sad but appreciative smile and turned back to the window.

"Manny, if you think this is embarrassing, have Jimmy tell you about his career in—the fuck you call it, Jimmy?"

"Countersurveillance."

"Yeah, countersurveillance. Tell *that* story."

Jimmy Tatorrio straightened with a storyteller's pride. "This is what started that whole thing that ended the other night at the Mohegan Sun. It happened when we were still at the old place. In fact, I think my fuckup is why we moved out." Some of those who knew the story started to laugh, indicating that Tatorrio was improvising on an old theme, adding a characteristic twist of self-deprecation. "Nino had the crew then. He was a great captain, but if things didn't go right, he could be one mean SOB. God rest him. So, at the old joint, we had this jukebox, and it never worked right. I think we robbed it. One day Nino finally tells someone to call and get the 'damn thing' fixed. It wasn't me he told, so, you know me, I'm paying absolutely no attention. That weekend, I think it was Labor Day weekend—whatever it was, Monday was a holiday, and this is a Friday when he orders it fixed. Saturday night I'm out all night. But I left my car at the club, so I get dropped off. It's just starting to get light, which means it is now Sunday morning. What comes next, a guy with one brain cell would have figured out, but naturally I didn't. I come around the corner and there are these two guys knocking on the club door. One old and one young. I walk up and ask, 'You the guys to fix the jukebox?' The older one—in hindsight—looks like I just put the barrel of a nine-millimeter in his mouth. 'Ah, yeah, that's it, we're here for the jukebox.' So being a good soldier, even though it wasn't my job, I take out my key and let them in."

Manny turned around and smiled at the tempo of Tatorrio's storytelling, now knowing where it was headed.

"So I'm following them around, asking if they need anything. The next thing I know, I'm standing there at the jukebox holding the flashlight for the young one, and he's fucking around behind it. You know me, I'm talking a mile a minute, never wondering where the other one is. Twenty minutes later the old one walks up and says to the young one, 'You're done, aren't you?' in this voice that's really saying, Let's get the fuck out of here. So me being the gentleman that I am, I offer them a drink. The old one gets this goofy look on his face and says, 'Sure, why not?' So we go to the bar and I pour shots all around. Not that I needed any more. Then I ask them how come they're there so early on a Sunday morning. The young one thinks for a second and says, 'Our boss, he found out who the club belongs to and didn't want any problems.' So I'm thinking here we go again, getting something because of who we are, but at the same time, you don't want to make enemies over a fucking jukebox, so I pour them another drink. An hour later I'm even more fried, and these two pricks are so bad they can't find the front door. Anyway, they leave and I pass out on the couch."

Dellaporta said, "If you think this is funny with Jimmy telling it, what do you think the FBI version sounds like?" More laughter erupted around the table.

"So now it's Tuesday, the day after the holiday. I come in late in the afternoon and everybody's there. I'm saying hello to everybody, and Nino asks whoever about the jukebox, and whoever says, 'Yeah, the guy came Friday and fixed it while I was here.'"

Everyone was laughing now, even those who had heard the story before. "Being the moron I am, I'm wondering why this guy is lying about him getting the jukebox fixed. I've actually got my hand in the air, about to say, But I took care of that on Sunday. Suddenly the light goes on. To make matters worse, Nino's standing—actually leaning—on the jukebox, and he's talking about some late payments on bets. So I bolt over to the machine and play a song. Nino looks at me like I'm the rudest prick in the world. He goes in the back room. I say something clever like, 'This isn't loud enough' and go behind it like I'm looking for the volume knob. I'm trying to remember where the young guy was working and I can't see anything that looks like a bug, not that I knew what one looked like. Then it hits me, the young guy was the decoy; the older one was planting the bug. So now I don't have a clue where it might be. I thought he might have been in the back, and naturally now Nino is *in the back* talking business to a couple of other guys. What was I supposed to do? Tell Nino? He would have killed me, and I don't mean the nice kind either. So I decide I've got to get everyone out of the club. I think, I'll call in a bomb threat. I know it sounds stupid, but, in case you haven't been listening, this story isn't about me being smart. But we had just robbed a couple dozen cases of booze, so the guys are in there drinking it up. A bomb could go off and they wouldn't leave. The only thing I know that'll beat free booze is free food with free booze. I tell everyone I had hit the trifecta over the weekend and was taking them all to dinner wherever they want. They can't get to the cars fast enough. I explain to them I'll meet them there because I'm expecting a call. As soon as they're out the door, I called my lawyer and had him bring over his electronics guy to sweep the place. It cost me two grand because of the short notice, but he finds the bug back in the office. Now, by the time I get to the restaurant—and naturally it's one of the most expensive in Manhattan—the bill for drinks and appetizers is already thirty-five hundred. These pricks are buying for the house. They said it was punishment for me not being a proper host. Of course they're just busting my balls, trying to make sure my good fortune is completely bled dry. But I figure, what the fuck, I can't get too mad, that's who we are. And, of course I've only got about twelve dollars on me. So I'm fucked. I've got to come up with the cash or explain why I pulled everybody out of the club. Okay, Manny, at that point, who had the bigger problem, you or me?"

Baldovino chuckled and swept a hand elaborately toward Tatorrio.

"I needed a shylock. But because of what it's for, it couldn't be from anyone in our family, so I called this guy with the Parrinos, Joe Chianese. He came over and I had to sneak outside and get ten K off of him. The whole night cost me seventy-five hundred. So I take the twenty-five hundred that's left over—which a smart person would have put back on the nut—but not me, no, I had it all figured out. I'll take it and run it up to ten grand at . . ." Tatorrio's rising tone invited everyone to respond.

"The track," they pronounced in unison.

"Three races. That's all it took. And about a year to pay it back. And every time I made a payment, Chianese busted balls. I did finally even the score the other night, but that year was a nightmare. Manny, the next time you screw up, I'll tell what I had to do to get *that* money together." Everyone's laughter turned into applause. "Manny, please. Come back when you're ready to play in the majors."

Baldovino nodded his appreciation and had decided to give up his post at the window when a familiar silver Cadillac made a careless U-turn and pulled up in front of the club. A bridge-sized surge of adrenaline knotted his stomach as he saw Danny DeMiglia, the family's underboss, get out. Manny could only hope that the rare visit to the club was not about him, but with the morning's headlines, he knew that was extremely unlikely. Since the don's stroke two months earlier, DeMiglia had been assuming more and more authority, much of it a questionable departure from the traditions everyone was comfortable with.

Now forty-four, younger than most who rose to that position, he had worked his way up from the streets, enforcing his decisions with unhinged violence. Within the organization, his brutality was so unpredictable that recollections of it were related only in the most guarded tones. But violence often created the very problem it promised to cure. This was the case when the honorable William G. Ferris had disappeared.

Judge Ferris had exhibited more political ambition than self-preservation when he publicly named two members of the Galante crime family who had tried to extort a portion of a cement-hauling contract that had been impartially awarded to one of the voters from Ferris's district. He played a recording for the media of one of the Galante men making a threatening call to the contractor. The newspapers ran front-page stories for a week. DeMiglia hated specifics about the family's operation being aired in the press. Four days later, Ferris's wife reported him missing.

For a month, the media attempted to link the Galante family to the judge's disappearance. Manny didn't know for sure whether DeMiglia was responsible or not, and he would have liked to say he didn't care except that, like the judge, he too had been a source of bad publicity for the family.

Hurrying to the back room, he found Mike Parisi on the phone. "DeMiglia's out front."

"I'm on the phone here," Parisi said, waving him away absentmindedly. But Baldovino stood in front of him, his expression insistent. He wasn't sure Parisi understood the gravity of the underboss's visit. For that matter, he wondered if he understood DeMiglia at all. When the don was healthy and his authority unquestioned, DeMiglia had treated Parisi with some regard, but the two men had not met since Carrera became ill. Baldovino feared that the crew's existence, as they knew it, was about to take a turn for the worse; if that happened, his ill-planned efforts to be an entrepreneur would be pinpointed as the catalyst.

When the don had made Parisi a *capo*, resentment floated openly throughout the organization, most of it traceable, with little effort, back to DeMiglia. He referred to the appointment as nothing more than a wedding dowry, a custom, which—not unlike the don's leadership—was out of date and out of place.

Parisi could no longer ignore Baldovino's increasingly panicked expression. "I'm going to have to call you back. But get started on that roof by Monday, or we're going to have a problem." He hung up and said to no one in particular, "Fucking contractors." But his words lacked conviction, which caused Manny to smile. Everyone on the crew understood that Parisi was trying to prove that he belonged, trying to convince them that even if he hadn't married the boss's niece, he still had the stuff from which real mafiosi were made. None of them thought so, but then most of them didn't think they had much of the real stuff either.

"DeMiglia's here," he repeated a little more urgently.

"Christ, Manny, you look like you're going to piss your pants. I heard you the first time."

"He's probably here about me."

Parisi lit a cigarette and held the filter half-crushed between his molars. "So what. You're on my crew. If he has a problem with any of my people he has to come to me."

"Mike, you didn't come up in the neighborhood. I know you were involved in some shit in Queens when you were a kid, but these guys around here are different. We've seen Danny operate since he was a kid. He isn't a—a whaddaya call it—chain of command kind of guy."

"Then I'll go see the old man."

"Have you seen DeMiglia since your uncle got sick?"

"No, why?"

Baldovino didn't answer, but Parisi finally recognized the fear in his eyes and decided some caution wouldn't hurt. "Okay, go on down to the basement and stay out of the way until I get rid of him."

While Parisi waited out of sight of the front room, he listened to the conversation around the card table.

"Don't *even*, ya fuck," Gus Dellaporta warned.

"Me fuck? You fuck." Jimmy Tatorrio slammed down a queen, taking the final trick. "Ba-*boom.*"

When they were by themselves, Parisi had noticed that the crew's language became more abbreviated than usual, a kind of shorthand they prided themselves on. It demonstrated friendship and, as an ancillary benefit, provided a certain amount of increased security. Usually the first thing to go was their use of interrogative pronouns. The who, what, and wheres were replaced with an all-inclusive "the fuck." *The fuck's that guy's name? The fuck is going on here? The fuck is my drink?* Sometimes when Parisi walked in on one of those conversations, he would start laughing, not because of the content, but because the whole thing had the tantalizing confusion of a too-hip beer commercial. Reacting that way made him doubt he could ever be one of them.

Danny DeMiglia walked in followed by his driver, Angelo. He peeled off his sunglasses and smiled at Parisi. Almost imperceptibly, a couple of the crew at the table stiffened. "Mikey, how are you?"

Danny DeMiglia was no more than five foot six, even in his

heeled boots. He wore a custom shirt of pale lavender, whose collar could not disguise his thick neck. He stood with his arms angled away from his torso like a bodybuilder at the end of a posing competition. His hands, as wide as they were long, extended from the sharply starched cuffs, one bearing the initials DMD in purple thread. The knuckles on his right hand were scarred and irreparably misaligned. His suit iridesced in the subdued light, accenting his stiff movements. The men around the table stole glances at his clothes and considered how only Danny DeMiglia could wear a monogrammed lavender shirt with impunity.

His bodyguard seemed twice his size, but if bets were placed on the two of them squaring off, most suspected that the underboss would prevail on pure viciousness. Parisi hadn't thought of DeMiglia that way—he had never had to. But after Baldovino's warning, he couldn't help but feel some apprehension. "I'm good, Danny, how about yourself?"

DeMiglia made sure each of the men saw his anger. "If you're asking me that, I guess that means you didn't see the papers this morning. Where is the dumb fuck?"

"Let's go in the back." DeMiglia gave a slight nod for his driver to remain with the others.

In the back room, one of Parisi's men, Tommy Ida, sat reading a book. Seeing the mood of the two men, he got up to leave. DeMiglia shook his hand. "Tommy, how have you been?"

"Good, Danny, real good." Ida seemed nervous, and Parisi realized that if the most composed member of the crew sensed danger, there had to be more to it than Manny's nervousness. Ida closed the door behind him.

"Every time I see that guy, he's reading something. Gives me the fucking creeps."

"He just likes to read, Danny. He doesn't mean anything by it."

"Still, it gives me the creeps. It's like that fucking guy that stabbed Julius Caesar in the back. What's his name?"

"Cassius."

"Yeah, with the hungry look. He thinks too much. You got to watch that, Mike. That's about the only thing I remember from high school. Worst two weeks of my life." The pronouncement of his failed education was spoken boastfully, implying that his hard-won "blue collar" success was the antithesis of Parisi's rise within the organization.

Parisi smiled carefully. "I'll keep an eye on him."

Suspecting Parisi's reply contained some nuance of condescension that he was incapable of deciphering, DeMiglia looked Parisi up and down, letting his eyes intentionally drag across the warmup suit and gold necklace, his leering smile an obvious insult. "See, that's the difference between you and me. You remembering that name, and me not giving a shit. I don't know, sometimes it's like you think you're entitled to this life, and at the same time I get the feeling you think it's beneath you."

Apparently Baldovino had been right about Parisi not knowing the real DeMiglia. Proceeding with care, Parisi mustered as conciliatory a tone as he could manage. "What is it you would like to hear?"

"See, there's the problem. You want to offer me words. Words are not action."

"Okay, what do you want me to *do*?"

"I want you to start running this crew like a business, not a summer camp for losers. This whole thing with the Lag is a symptom. It reflects no leadership on your part. If your guys were out making real money, busting real balls, they wouldn't be embarrassing the family, giving this FBI asshole the opportunity to rub our faces in it."

"We bring in our share of money."

DeMiglia, still not getting all the signals he was used to, leaned in and let his voice harden. "You bring in what was handed to you as a wedding present, nothing more. I've been around this most of my life, and that's taught me one thing—the old days don't cut it anymore. The FBI's got all those laws on their side, all that RICO shit. Every phone is tapped. We have to improvise or we're through. Especially gambling. That's all done on the phone. When's the last time any of your places got hit?"

"Not in the two years I've been here."

"You know what that tells me—you're way overdue. If they're hungry enough to put a sting on a slug like Manny, they got to be all over your gambling operation."

"The don doesn't seem worried about it. As far as I can tell, he's happy with the way things are going." The anger in Parisi's voice had risen another notch, and it seemed to please DeMiglia.

"You of all people shouldn't be bringing up your uncle. Your crew's lack of production is disrespecting him. Besides, he is not in good health. He's not going to be the head of the family forever. In the meantime, I'm giving the orders. I want you to start earning your way around here."

"We've got something we've been working on."

"Which is?"

"There's this guy over in Queens, he's a loan officer at a small bank. He approves all the home equity loans and lines of credit. Turns out he made himself a couple of loans to play a few can't-miss stock deals. When they missed, and he needed to put it back before the auditors found out, he came to us."

"How much?"

"With this week's vig, almost fifty K."

"Fifty, that's it? This better start getting real fucking interesting real fucking fast."

"He's missed payments the last three weeks, so I sent Manny to talk to him. Now he's scared—"

"The Lag scared him? He must be easy."

"Well, evidently he is, because now he has this idea for these scam lines of credit. He tells us that if we come up with people who own their own home and have at least a hundred thousand in equity, he'll dummy up the application and get seventy-five thousand for each of them. You know how these old-timers are, they got the first dollar they ever made. Most of their houses are paid off and have doubled and tripled in value since they bought them. We just have to give him the names and addresses that have that much equity. He's even got a guy who'll dummy up appraisal reports for a hundred apiece if we need him. Then, as soon as he approves them, we get a checkbook and can write checks on each of them for seventy-five thousand."

"How many we talking about?"

"Tommy's found a way to get all the information on any home we want from the county tax assessor through the Internet. So far he's searched hundreds of houses, so there's no limit to it. As soon as this banker gives us the word, we'll hit it hard until it breaks down."

"What's that work out to be?"

"Every thirteen—you know, times seventy-five thousand—is almost a million dollars."

"What part of the city we talking about?"

"Right here, Bensonhurst."

"You're doing this in our own backyard?"

"We thought it was best to stay local, you know, in case something went wrong on the homeowner end. It would be easier to reason with people who know who we are."

"How come you didn't tell me about this?"

"Well, it's not completely in place yet, and you're the one always talking about too many ears."

"And when it collapses, what then?"

"Then he'll have to do three or four years in one of the federal hotels. He's about a hundred pounds overweight. So he'll get himself in shape, get his teeth cleaned, get his cholesterol and blood pressure down. He'll probably live twenty years longer. We'll be saving his life."

"Who can he give up?"

"Just Manny. He gave him the original loan and will handle all the contacts with him."

"Might be worth risking it just to get Baldovino to take the fall. I'd pay for the call to the auditors myself."

"I told you, I'll take care of Manny."

DeMiglia's eyes answered with a bright flash of anger. Finally, he drew in a big breath and spoke with a nonchalance that was practiced and chilling, an unmistakable warning that further insubordination would have irreversible consequences. "No, I don't like it. You know who handles it when the banks are ripped off—the FBI. This thing sounds shaky to me. Everything going out of the bank and nothing coming in. They're set up to spot bad money trends like that. They're probably already looking at your guy for cooking the books from when he was loaning himself. It's probably one of those stings, like Manny's deal. Either that or they already got him and are setting you up. Either way I'm not giving you another chance to let those assholes humiliate us. You stay away from this, understand?"

"We've put a lot of time in on this. Tommy's got the info on all those houses already. This could be a big payday for everyone."

"We don't do business in our own backyard. The reason these people protect us is because they know we'd never screw them. You got a lot of balls doing this here. You're from Queens. You don't have any idea about these people and obviously could give a good fuck less about them."

DeMiglia's argument might have been convincing if Parisi thought the underboss cared about anyone but himself. With his injunction now registered, it suddenly became clear to Parisi that this wasn't about getting caught. Other than Manny's exposure, the bank scam offered little risk. The real purpose of the underboss's visit had still not been revealed. "Well, that's the best we've got right now. Unless you've got a suggestion."

A little surprised that Parisi didn't argue his case further, DeMiglia lit a cigarette, taking the moment to stall, to make sure he wasn't missing something. "Yeah, I do. It's a once in a lifetime score. Whether your crew has the finesse to pull it off is another question."

DeMiglia's tactic was so obvious Parisi couldn't help but misdirect him. "Well, if you don't think we do, maybe I should look around for something else."

DeMiglia stood up. "Come on, we've been talking too long in one place. Let's go for a walk." Parisi couldn't tell whether he was on to him or not.

When they were within earshot of the others in the front room, DeMiglia asked, "When's the last time you had this place swept for bugs?"

"I don't know."

"Weren't you told a minimum once a month? I have my joint and car done once a week. That's the way they always get us. But they'll never get me. Why the fuck can't you people understand that?"

Outside, the underboss scanned the neighborhood for anything out of the ordinary. The clouds had cleared and the heat had again become oppressive. They walked for a block before DeMiglia spoke again. "So, I assume you talked to Baldovino."

"I had a long talk with him."

"Where is that stupid fuck?"

"I've got him doing something for me."

"Selling handicapped license plates, what kind of a thing is that for a grown man to do? First the thing with the bridges and now this." Parisi looked at him. "What, you didn't think I knew about him being afraid of bridges? Everybody knows."

This time Parisi was careful to keep emotion out of his voice. "I'm taking care of it." With forced nonchalance, he lit a cigarette to further demonstrate that there was no need for concern.

"See, that's exactly what I mean. You say you're taking care of it, and then nothing happens. Meanwhile your crew isn't making a cent. On top of that you're making us look ridiculous in front of the whole world. You know I've got people to answer to. Both inside the family and on the commission. They ain't going to like this thing with the license plates. Not only is the whole world laughing at us, so are the other families. You know the one thing that makes our thing work—it's fear. After that article, who's going to be afraid of us? Motherfucking FBI!"

"Manny's a guy who acts without thinking."

"That doesn't make me enthusiastic about his future."

"His heart's in the right place." Parisi regretted the statement as soon as he said it.

"His heart's in the right place? What do you think this is, some fucking soap opera? What we do isn't about good intentions, it's about money. I didn't come here to start trouble, but I was given this position to make sure business is good and that nobody goes to prison. And so far, everybody else is doing all right. I know the don's your uncle, but while he's sick, I've got to do what I've got to do."

"Okay, what is it that you think you have to do?"

"To get you to start contributing, and the sooner the better."

"And what if I can't?"

"There is no *can't.*"

"It's just that—"

"Do you want to keep this crew?"

Even though at the moment he wasn't sure, Parisi knew the best answer. "Yes."

"I'm going out of my way to give you a perfect score and you're whining. You know why? Because you didn't earn this. You're the only captain in the whole family who hasn't filled a contract. You have paid *no* dues. Here's your chance. Are you ready to uphold your commitment, your oath to this family?"

Parisi had to see his uncle. He lit another cigarette off the first and inhaled deeply. "Yes."

"That's more like it. This score can't miss. I've been sitting on it for a while. Ten million minimum."

"Ten million, and it can't miss? I thought the bigger the score the bigger the risks."

"Why is it that people think if they're fucking pessimists, they'll be taken as some sort of expert. Who's done more scores, you or me?"

"You have."

"Mikey, these are the kind of numbers you need to respect your uncle. To bring yourself into the fold so to speak." Parisi gave him a reluctant, appeasing nod. "Good. This is a hit on one of those vaults down in the diamond district."

"The diamond district? I always heard there were more off-duty cops on that stretch of Forty-seventh Street than are on duty in the rest of Manhattan."

"I've got a guy who will take you inside. You know Jackie Two Shoes across the river?"

"The bookie."

"Yeah, he's got this yid that's into him for a little over two hundred K on sports bets. He's one of them Orthodox Jews, you know with the hats and the curls—"

"You mean Hasidic," Parisi said.

DeMiglia just shook his head. "He works in one of those big buildings down there. Jackie says if I buy his paper and send someone big enough to explain our payment plan, he'll do whatever we want. According to Jackie, at this time of the year, there's at least ten million in uncut stones."

"Are you talking about during the day?"

"Those vaults are all on time locks, so, yeah, during the day."

"So there will be witnesses."

"Hey, it's ten million. Do you know how many times in your life you're going to see that number? Probably never. So if there's a problem that needs to be taken care of, you take care of it."

The idea of murdering innocent people sent a wave of disgust down Parisi's spine. That DeMiglia was suggesting it so offhand-edly indicated that his real purpose was something more compli-cated than boosting the family revenue. The don would know. But until Parisi could see him, he had to stall. "How many wit-nesses do you figure?"

"Including the guy taking you in, three or four tops. Who the fuck cares? They're Jews, they're used to dying."

"Multiple murders don't go unsolved in this city."

"You're a smart guy, you'll be the first. This is a courtesy I'm extending you, an accommodation out of respect for the don. If you don't take it, I will feel insulted and certain adjustments will have to be made."

If "adjustments" was meant to be vague, it wasn't. "But what does ten million come to fenced?"

Anger crackled across DeMiglia's face. "It comes to a fuck of a lot more than you're making right now."

Both men walked in silence for a while before DeMiglia spoke again. "Your uncle—although I have the deepest respect for him—isn't the man he once was. Everyone thinks of him as semi-retired, at best. I've been pretty much handling the day-to-day operation since his stroke." He took out a handkerchief and wiped the sweat from his forehead and upper lip. "My first prior-ity is to improve the economy. I'll call you in a few days when I get this thing worked out. Don't tell anybody until I do, you un-derstand?"

When Parisi didn't answer, DeMiglia grabbed his elbow. "Mike, don't get on my enemies list, it comes with a lifetime guarantee . . . which usually isn't all that long."

9

DESPITE THE THICK WALL OF PLEXIGLAS BETWEEN the receptionist and Charles Lansing, he couldn't help but feel a little intimidated. She had hard New York eyes, black female hard. But he had no choice but to deal with her.

The name on the door said Global Fish, and while he could see no visible evidence that the small building housed an FBI operation, he knew it was the right place. He could smell banana oil, an odor familiar from as far back as new agent training at Quantico. It was the most pungent ingredient in the solvent used to remove exploded cordite from their weapons. Behind the vaguely mercantile façade of Global Fish, someone was cleaning a gun.

From everything he had been led to expect of this squad—its personnel problems and the lack of motivation—that someone was conscientiously maintaining a firearm, to ready himself for the almost impossible chance of close combat, seemed the severest of contradictions.

The receptionist asked coolly, "May I help you?" He could tell from the flat, impatient delivery of her words that she knew exactly who he was—the enemy.

Trying to muster some of the condescension used with subordinates at FBI headquarters, he said, "Charles Lansing . . . with the *inspection* staff."

"May I see your credentials, sir?" "Sir" had a slightly insulting edge to it. Both of them knew her request, which could be defended as procedural, was really being used as a brief reversal of

power to say, *This is the real FBI. You are, at best, an inconvenience.*
She didn't let him see it, but a bit of pleasure pulled at the outer
corners of her eyes as Lansing fumbled through his briefcase. He
held up his credentials to the glass.

After checking the photo, she made one final appraisal of his
face and then reached under her desk. A loud metallic clank
sounded off to the inspector's right. He looked for its source and
saw that a section of the wall was hinged and had opened slightly.
A few seconds later, the woman pushed out the door. "Sorry for
the Dungeon and Dragons. This neighborhood specializes in
walk-in weirdos."

For the briefest moment, he considered an attempt at charm,
to ask good-naturedly if he was that indistinguishable from the
local rabble, but her answer might be another veiled, unpunish-
able insult.

Leading him through a narrow maze of right-angle turns, past
cinder-block walls and cheap paneling, the receptionist came to a
small windowless office. "Nick, that inspector's here."

"Thanks, Abby." Vanko rose and offered his hand with unexpected warmth. "Nick Vanko."

Lansing noticed the drooping right side of his face, but forced
himself to lock onto Vanko's eyes. "Charles Lansing."

"You found us okay? It can be a little tricky."

"Yes, in fact, I didn't have any trouble until I ran into your receptionist. Is she that testy with everybody?"

"Sorry about that. Actually she's the squad secretary. She can
be a little territorial, probably because she pretty much runs the
place. Once you get past her growl, she's hard to live without."

"I'm only going to be here a month, which probably wouldn't
be enough time."

The left side of Vanko's face smiled disarmingly, diplomatically, making Lansing feel a little petty. "So what are you going to
need from us?"

Lansing took out a thick stack of forms. "I've gone through all
the interrogatories. They're pretty straightforward. You have nine
agents on the squad?"

"With me, ten."

The point was not lost on Lansing. Vanko considered himself

an agent, which all managers were but most would not claim. Lansing suspected that ground rules were being put in place. "I'm going to need to interview each of them."

"Some of them aren't available. One is serving a forty-five-day suspension. One is at a two-week in-service at Quantico. Two are more or less working a permanent wire for the strike force. One is assigned to a security observation post in Manhattan. He'll be gone for three months."

"Sounds like when it comes to getting crappy jobs, your squad is taken advantage of."

"As long as their checks show up every two weeks, I don't think you'll hear any complaints from them."

"And your squad, as a primary mission, is assigned one of the regimes of the Galante crime family?"

"That's right, the Michael Parisi crew," Vanko said.

"And how's that going?"

"Has anyone told you about the Galante family? Most of their made members are from the same town in Sicily, so they are extremely close-knit. They have a great deal of allegiance to one another, making them extremely difficult to compromise. That's why the family has been broken down and squads assigned specific regimes."

"You're telling me this to explain your squad's lack of statistical accomplishments."

"Isn't that what inspections are all about? You find problems, and I make up excuses to explain them away?"

Strangely, Lansing didn't think Vanko's answer was meant to be amusing, or even masked sarcasm. Nor did he seem intent on gaining absolution. Rather, it had a self-contained, almost naïve honesty that made Lansing uncomfortable because it meant that this supervisor wasn't afraid of him. That was not the atmosphere in which Lansing wanted to conduct his inquiry. Too much civility could mute the bright lights by which flaws were exposed. "Let's face it, every agent on your squad, at one time or another, should have been fired."

Vanko waited a moment, then said, "Is that a question?"

"Let's make it one."

"Most of these agents were sent here due to, let's say, incompatibilities on other squads. But not one of them has had a problem since arriving."

"Are any of these 'incompatibilities' currently being investigated by OPR?"

"Two members of this squad have open cases with the Office of Professional Responsibility. Yes."

Vanko's use of the full name rather than the more colloquial "OPR" made the unit sound excessively pedantic, as though those under investigation were victims of some extreme enforcement of all-but-expired rules. "Let's try this a different way. Have any of the agents assigned to your squad ever been fired?"

"Yes."

"For?"

"A variety of things."

"You're not going to make this easy for me, are you?"

"Just tell me what you're looking for me to make easy."

While the response contained a latent resistance to the line of questioning, he couldn't help but warm to Vanko's manner. Maybe it was his voice, low and unrushed, its persuasion contagious.

"My job."

"Isn't it your job to evaluate how this squad is performing? Past problems have either been punished or are being investigated by OPR. Whenever an agent has been reassigned to this squad, the first thing I tell him is that he has to answer only for what he does, or doesn't do, while he's here."

Vanko was right; investigations of misconduct were not within the scope of Lansing's responsibilities unless they happened to be uncovered during inspection. He decided that coming on too strong might prove counterproductive. "I was just curious. You know, trying to get a feel for your personnel. It must be difficult trying to get things done never knowing how long an agent is going to be with you."

Jack Straker walked in and tossed some paperwork into Vanko's in box. When he noticed Lansing sitting off to the side, he said, "Oh, sorry, Nick, I didn't know anyone was in here."

"This is Charles Lansing, he'll be inspecting the squad."

He extended his hand. "Jack Straker."

Although the thought of taking on an entire squad of problem agents was somewhat overwhelming, it had been Lansing's experience that the actual size of an enemy was never as large as its reputation. Each of the agents had been sent there because of an inability to comply with rules. And Lansing knew the rules as well as anyone. He stood up and shook hands.

Straker was big and good-looking. He looked directly at the person he was talking to, giving the impression that, until proven otherwise, that person was worth getting to know better. A bandage above his right eye appeared to be covering stitches. Lansing found this a promising inconsistency. Attractive people were usually more careful. It told Lansing that he had found a possible starting point. "Nice to meet you, Jack. What happened to your head?"

Straker smiled artfully. "An automobile accident."

"Bureau car?"

"Actually, no." He backed out of the office. "I'll get out of your way. Nice to meet you."

Lansing made a mental note of Straker's evasion. "I've been told that your squad also does special projects. Like what?"

"Mostly surveillance. Special photography or videotaping. Basically anything that others don't have the time or desire to do."

"And that doesn't bother you?"

Vanko laughed. "Not as long as we're asked nicely."

"Let's get back to your lack of stats."

"Well, we did arrest one of Parisi's crew recently."

"The guy selling the handicapped plates."

"I know it's not exactly a contract murder, but it is an arrest. We did have the satisfaction of getting a UCA next to one of them. And who knows, maybe he'll have a change of heart and roll over."

"This undercover agent, he was Bureau approved?"

"That's the rule."

"And your squad always follows the rules."

"I doubt that you'll find anything to indicate otherwise."

It was clear that, if pushed hard enough, Vanko would be defiant. Up to that point, his diplomacy and powers of persuasion had been impressive, but Lansing felt he had found a vulnerable spot. "I've got to go back to the office, but starting tomorrow, I intend to spend most of my time here. I assume you have no problem with that."

Vanko stood up. "We'll be here."

"I hope I'm not going to have to be strip-searched again to get in."

Vanko took a key out of his desk drawer and handed it to Lansing. "You can come in through the back. The door next to the garage. That's the way we get in. Just park around back. There's a spot marked Visitor."

He had to hand it to Vanko, to wrangle this bunch of misfits successfully took creative leadership. But there were inherent advantages in supervising agents who were in trouble. Each one arrived with his livelihood dangling precariously, leaving him little choice but to be dutiful.

He looked again at the supervisor's face, trying to decide if it had been handsome before being injured. Its recesses had the smoky Mediterranean darkness that appealed to some women, but Lansing suspected that without its distracting damage, Vanko's face would probably look oversculpted, too susceptible to emotion, too European. But apparently Vanko had learned to draw strength from the disfigurement. It gave him purpose.

10

MIKE PARISI TURNED ONTO BENSONHURST'S Eighteenth Avenue and pulled up in front of a grocery store whose windows were covered with bright yellow and pink signs advertising sale items. At least half of them were in Italian, most of which he couldn't decipher. His wife had explained that if he was going to see her uncle, it was Sicilian courtesy not to show up empty-handed. Even if he only brought a loaf of bread, it showed respect.

He stepped inside the store. Despite the air-conditioning, the fragrances were so thick they felt like they could be swallowed—sweet, smoky meats, the slightly sour tang of cheese at room temperature, ginger, garlic, sage, and from a different direction the dusky bitterness of chocolate. Loops of fat sausages hung overhead alongside pink and white hams and salamis wrinkled with age. Carved wheels of white and yellow cheeses sat on top of counters, and small, perfect pyramids of glossy green and red apples, all impossibly the same size, filled the bins along the back wall. Shelves that ran to the ceiling were stacked with cans of varying sizes and shapes, their labels red and green, like the apples, like the flag of Italy.

His wife had refused to tell him exactly what to bring. *The tradition is meaningless unless it comes from the heart.*

He had come to this store because should his offering somehow prove inappropriate, its package being printed in the mother tongue might lessen the degree of sin. When he saw that the price of a whole Prosciutto di Parma ham was over two hundred dollars, he asked for one to be wrapped up. When the owner held it out to him and began explaining in a voice made more passionate by his heavy accent that it came from the mountain region in Parma, Parisi's thoughts wandered back to the previous day's conversation with Danny DeMiglia about how he would never be part of the community.

As he left, he noticed two old men sitting outside the pastry shop next door drinking espresso. One was reading *La Gazzetta* and seemed impervious to the other, whose lighted cigarette danced excitedly through the air as he spoke. The smoker stopped and eyed Parisi with some suspicion. Parisi nodded at him.

Still a few minutes early, Parisi drove slowly through the neighborhood. At the houses that had yards, clothes dried on lines, rosebushes grew next to tomato vines and pots of basil. Occasionally, he spotted a small Saint Anthony shrine displayed with some prominence. In a small park, two men, wearing dark clothing in spite of the heat, sat staring at the pieces on a crumbling concrete chess table. The homes on the blocks immediately surrounding Anthony Carrera's house were duplexes, some frame, mostly brick, tightly wedged up against one another, all painstakingly maintained.

Don Carrera's brick house was three stories. Its architecture and craftsmanship had been brought to the area by Italian immigrants almost a hundred years earlier. Around its perimeter was a waist-high brick wall with irregular diamond-shaped openings. Two gateless entryways led to a double set of stairs with wrought-iron railings that came up to a landing and then turned into a single staircase leading to the second-floor entrance. Along the second story, delicately shaped metal railings supported awnings across the entire front of the home. Although he had been there before, he had never really paid much attention. There were no elaborate gardens, no fountains or statues. Considering its size and who lived there, the house had an inviting simplicity. The owner did not think himself any more privileged than the men who played chess or sipped coffee.

He drove back to the pastry shop. The smells were different from those in the grocery, but just as distracting—lemon, vanilla, cinnamon, and almond. The more perishable items, many of them covered with pastel icings, were displayed in spotless glass cases. Behind the counters, wire bins held loaves of bread, brown and crusty, some long and thin, gathered upright in their containers like tied sheaths of wheat. He chose one of the thick loaves that were stacked in the bin, reasoning that because there were so many of them, they had to be the most popular. He paid the clerk and told him to give the two men outside another round of espressos. Ignoring the smoker's icy stare as he walked past, Parisi bid them both, *"Buongiorno."*

"How's my niece?"

"She's terrific, sir. We just found out Friday, she's pregnant."

"Salute. I hope it's a girl, they're a lot less trouble."

"From someone with four boys, I'll take your word for it, but I think it might be a little late to change my order."

Anthony Carrera laughed carefully, conserving strength. He sat up a little straighter and leaned back against the headboard of his bed. The small movement exposed the paralysis in his left shoulder and arm, which lay disobediently at his side.

"How are you feeling?" Parisi asked.

"Every day I am a little stronger, except for this." Carrera waved disgustedly at the arm. "But getting older is about making adjustments. I'll be fine."

For fear of taxing the don's strength, Parisi, like most of the other relatives, had not visited him since his stroke. Instead he had faithfully called once a week to pay his respects and give Carrera a brief, coded report of their business interests.

Parisi was surprised by how good his uncle looked. He had lost some weight, the stroke burning off the bloat of too rich an existence, almost as if, as an ancillary benefit to his illness, he had been granted a small step back toward his youth. His jawline appeared harder, a knot of determined muscle pulsing at each of its hinges. "You really look good."

"Good genes are better than all the doctors in the world. I'm sure your concern for my health is sincere, but since you've come here during my illness, I have to assume it has something to do with business."

Parisi hesitated, still not sure of the propriety of bringing trouble at such a time. He smiled, shaking his head in admiration of the don's ability to read people.

"It's all right, Mike, you're my nephew. You can tell me whatever you need to."

Parisi explained the demands DeMiglia was making. As he was finishing, the don's eyelids fell shut. Parisi thought he had fallen asleep, but as he rose from the chair, Carrera said, "You know this has nothing to do with you. It's about him becoming boss." He opened his eyes. "He thinks I am through. That leaves only you. He sees you as a final obstacle because we are related by marriage. So he orders you to do something he knows, in all likelihood, you won't. In turn, that act of disobedience could be offered to the commission as proof of your disloyalty. You would be discredited, and because I made you a *capo*, I would be dishonored, making any future vote in favor of DeMiglia's interests much more acceptable. It's a very clever ploy. Everything is taken care of at the same time. I'm out, and he's in, and you're gone."

"The commission has to be able to see through that."

"He is very smart and has made friends on the commission. You remember when Frankie Falcone in Buffalo was murdered?"

"Yes."

"Do you know why?"

"I've never really paid much attention to those kind of things."

"I'm aware of that. I hope, if nothing else, this problem has taught you to see that ignorance in this business can never bring bliss. Your survival is at stake. And to be honest, so is mine. What you need to know about Frankie's murder is *why*. He ran his regime well for this family. He was a good earner and was always loyal, so it was both a personal and business loss for me. If I didn't authorize it, then where did it come from? One of the reasons he was a good earner was because he would never back off when the other families wanted a piece of his action. Frankie was fearless. He was a pain in the ass to the other families, especially the Parrinos. Although they wanted him out of the way, they didn't want to risk a war with us, so they went to someone in our family to get permission. It was still illegal, but at least they didn't have to worry about a war."

"And you think DeMiglia gave them permission."

"By doing that he gains the Parrino vote when it comes time to appoint a new boss of this family. I suspect he has made similar deals with some of the other families. Once you are out of the way, he will be my successor."

"Why does he want to eliminate me? I have no ambition to become boss."

"He doesn't know that for sure. When the opportunity presents itself, not many men in this business can resist. And there's another benefit to getting rid of you. The loans and gambling you take care of are very low profile, not likely to bring in the government. And it's almost two million dollars a year. He may have scoffed at it as small potatoes, but, unless I miss my guess, he wants it very badly. He'd be crazy not to."

"What can I do?"

"First, you have to understand, panic is an enemy."

"Tony, I take care of your businesses. It's like DeMiglia said, I'm more a bookkeeper than a gangster. I don't know anything about the rest of it."

"Do you think I gave you that crew simply because you married my niece?"

"I don't know . . . yes."

"Before you came, everyone I put in charge of those interests stole from me. Not enough to do anything drastic about, but enough to be disrespectful. When I met you, I could see you had character."

"You've always treated me as if we were related by blood. That means a great deal to me. Everything I have I owe to you. But being loyal to you and taking on someone like DeMiglia are two very different things. I barely get over on my own crew," he laughed, "and they're easy."

Carrera smiled softly. "It is the wise man who can see the genius in someone he fears. From him, he must try to steal some of that genius."

"How?"

Carrera motioned toward the large table next to the bed. "Hand me that bowl with the nuts." Carrera chose a walnut and handed it to him. "Break it open for me."

"Where are the nutcrackers?"

"There are no nutcrackers. You're on your own."

Parisi placed the nut between the heels of his hands, laced his fingers together, and applied as much pressure as he could. "I can't do it."

"That's right, you can't. Not like that." Carrera took back the walnut and picked out a second one. He manipulated them in his fist and then flexed his large, veined hand with surprising quickness. One of the shells shattered. He popped a piece of the walnut meat in his mouth.

Parisi nodded that he understood the point of the demonstration. "But who could I use?"

"Someone outside the family would be best."

"I got to tell you, Tony, this is scaring the hell out of me."

"Just remember, the more dangerous a man is willing to be, the more vulnerable he becomes. Violence is a weakness; it causes other weaknesses. You have to find them."

Parisi stood up to go. Carrera handed him two walnuts. "You are lucky, Mike, most men never get a chance to find out what they're made of."

Parisi smiled. "If they live."

The don turned on his side and closed his eyes. "If you live."

After closing the door quietly behind him, Parisi stood in the hallway. Using one hand, he tried to break the nuts against each other. He repositioned them several times and squeezed as hard as he could, but nothing happened. Then he used both hands. One of the walnuts exploded into small pieces. *I guess I'm someone who has to cheat a little.*

Outside Vanko's office, a dozen or so desks for the squad members were jammed into the limited space. For the duration of the inspection Lansing had been given the one closest to the "vault," a narrow room with cinder-block walls and a heavy-gauge steel door. Because of break-ins in the sixties, every FBI space, even one as detached from the daily treadmill as Global Fish, had been mandated to have an "extra secure" area where sensitive documents could be locked away. Inside the room was a six-hundred-pound safe with four drawers, one of which had been cleared out for Lansing's files. He had been given a key to the door and the safe's combination and was assured that the only other people who had access to it were Vanko and the squad secretary.

Among the files Lansing had brought from downtown were the squad's personnel folders. They were usually not allowed out of the office, but Lansing had asked Dreagen to make an exception. Part of the process was to interview each agent and analyze his or her performance—or lack thereof—since the last inspection. With the files in hand, finding inconsistencies would be markedly easier. For good measure, he was also given the expense and budget documents for the off-site, another exception Dreagen approved.

The previous day, Lansing's presence at the off-site had brought him an unexpected benefit. While he was retrieving a folder from the safe, Howard Snow had entered Vanko's office, the back wall of which abutted the vault. Lansing realized he could make out a surprising amount of their conversation. The source appeared to be an electrical wall outlet. Using a penknife, he unscrewed the cover plate. The rest of their exchange, although slightly metallic, was clear enough to understand. As best he could tell, Vanko was providing Snow with a strategy to defeat the ongoing OPR investigation against him. He also had Snow initial a letter of commendation the SAC had sent for what Vanko referred to as the "Dimino scam." Lansing made a note of the name and crouched down to put the plate back on the outlet. While trying to thread the single screw back into place, he imagined how he would look if someone walked in. The screw slipped between his fingers and rolled behind the safe. Unable to reach it, he just hung the plate on the outlet. It would make it easier to remove next time.

Nick Vanko's phone rang; it was Abby at the reception desk. She spoke in the low, unenunciated monotone. "That one you said was coming is here."

"Okay, bring him back."

Garrett Egan had been arrested, in a very public manner, by the Securities and Exchange Commission a week earlier for insider trading at a small Wall Street brokerage house. What the world had yet to learn was that he was an FBI agent working un-

dercover in an elaborate sting operation designed to draw organized crime members into illegal transactions.

Because of the government's increasing success in prosecut-
ing traditional Mafia crimes, mobsters had to find new sources of
revenue. With increasing frequency, they were involving themselves in stock market fraud. Their most common ploy was a
white-collar twist on one of their longtime staples—loansharking. They made loans to stockbrokers, most commonly for personal debt or business expansion. Then they would buy from
them, under coercion, low-priced shares in a company before its
stock went public. Through transactions that the brokers were
forced to make among themselves, or in some cases faked transactions, the shares were rapidly inflated. The brokers were also
made to recommend the stocks to customers, further driving up
their price. The mobsters then sold everything, causing the over-
valued stocks to nose-dive.

Those in charge of the Bureau's New York office ordered the
few who knew about Egan's arrest not to discuss it with anyone
for fear it might be leaked to the press, but as usual, the "undis-
closable" facts of the case swept through the office at the speed of
light. Garrett Egan's insider trading, executed using his undercover name, Sam Shelby, was not part of the FBI project. The arrest affidavit for Shelby stated that he had used information
obtained from sources, still undetermined, to conduct personal
trades in the market. During the last quarter, these transactions
had netted him $268,000.

Lansing watched from his desk as Abby led the new agent in
the expensive suit into Vanko's office. The inspector thought he
knew who Egan was because his name had come up two days
earlier during a conversation with the ASAC. Lansing had gone
to see him seeking the exception to Bureau procedure concerning the removal of personnel files from the main office. "Bernie, to
do this right, I'm going to need the files at the off-site."

"Not exactly kosher, but I think I can arrange it."

"I'll be careful."

"Your timing is good. That agent with the insider trading
problem? He'll be out there in the next couple of days. You'll
want his file, too. If nothing else, it'll show a pattern that

Vanko's squad is a safe haven even for those who commit felonies."

"I appreciate the heads-up."

"Just remember, this conversation never took place."

Lansing flipped open Garrett Egan's file to the photo attached to the inside cover. His face seemed older than the photo, which had been taken the day he was hired eight years earlier.

Lansing was about to get up and, with as much casualness as he could summon, make his way into the vault. But he noticed T. H. Crowe staring at him. According to the files, Crowe was the oldest agent on the squad and apparently had been through enough inspections that they no longer intimidated him. Or had he seen Lansing in the vault, removing the cover plate and listening? He looked away and within a few seconds looked back. Crowe maintained his emotionless stare. Egan's was a conversation he wasn't going to hear.

Vanko offered the newest arrival a seat. "Do you know anything about this squad?"

"No." Although just a single syllable, the answer was charged with resentment.

"We work organized crime, the Galante family. Specifically, the Michael Parisi regime."

"Great, cops and robbers. That's what I need to get my mind off my problems. This is going to cost me a hundred thousand dollars in lawyer's fees with no guarantee I won't go to prison, so excuse me if I can't get too excited about locking up some Italian who's extorting money from some other guy who's probably a bigger asshole than he is. Besides, I've spent a night in jail. I wouldn't wish that on anyone."

This was not the first time Vanko had endured the diatribes of a reporting agent, and he knew that the source of Egan's anger was more than his onrushing legal problems. Arrival at the squad was final proof of exile, of being jettisoned from respectability just as an agent was frantically searching for self-respect. The Bureau was in the process of turning its back on him, stripping him of the safety of its community, attempting to leave him with the perception that his only remaining duty was to go off quietly to whatever fate he had brought upon himself.

Nine years earlier, after his accident, Vanko had been similarly excommunicated, exiled to the complaint desk, a cramped room that most agents couldn't find if they wanted to. Call-in complaints were maddening. A high percentage of them were from the psychologically unstable, and the "legitimate" ones were usually too convoluted to be investigated or were completely without merit. And, of course, the more unqualified the complaint, the more outraged the callers were about being denied their "right to justice."

Vanko had understood the purpose of the reassignment and in a strange way agreed with it. When someone makes an error in judgment as large as his, he needs to be tested for resolve, to determine if he is in the midst of a disastrous pattern. In his case, a woman had died. The subsequent inquiry concluded that he was not at fault, but premature death, even when adjudicated, invariably left an aftertaste of suspicion.

His scarred face hadn't helped, either. It served as an indelible reminder of potential bad judgment. The complaint room was the perfect answer. Neither the public nor the other agents had to be exposed to his disfigurement or reminded of its origin. The bleak cubicle had been known to break the resolve of even the most unyielding probationers. But Vanko accepted the transfer, hoping that, if nothing else, its piercing loneliness would prove cathartic.

Almost a year passed, and he began to wonder whether he would ever be returned to the mainstream. Why should they let him? He was doing an awful task well, his hard work preventing the very thing it was meant to recapture: his freedom. Then one night, as he was about to leave, a female caller said she had information about a kidnapping being planned. When Vanko pressed for details, the woman became evasive, saying she feared the conversation was being recorded. The kidnappers would not hesitate to kill her if they found out she had called. It took almost an hour for Vanko to persuade her to meet him.

After being initially startled by his appearance, she soon became convinced by its dark honesty. Once assurances of anonymity took hold, she started supplying specifics. The target was identified as the daughter of a wealthy investment banker, and a long night of work by dozens of agents began. The SAC reported to the com-

mand post to oversee the investigation, and he found himself rely-
ing heavily on Vanko's previous kidnapping-squad experience. By
first light, the crime had been prevented and four men were in custody. As an unexpected bonus, they all turned out to be members
of organized crime. The case made national headlines, and the SAC
provided flawless sound bites for television newscasts. A few days
later, Vanko was called to the SAC's office and offered the chance
to start a new clandestine surveillance squad, one that would pri-
marily work organized crime cases. The SAC ordered ten supervisors to provide one man apiece, and each of them gladly gave up
their most unmanageable agent. With its heritage established before the fact, Global Fish came limping into existence.

As he did with each new arrival, Vanko wanted to know if—
beneath the almost obligatory indignation—Egan was actually
looking for a new beginning.

"Just about everybody on this squad arrived with baggage."

"Baggage! They're here because they got caught going to grad-
uate school during working hours, or because they pissed on the
ADIC's wife's shoes at the Christmas party. None of them were
facing prison."

"What I'm saying is that these things always seem monumen-
tal at first."

"So you think I'm blowing this out of proportion? How do
you think it was for my son when one of his friends at school said
he saw me on TV being arrested? Thank God my kid didn't see it,
and I could tell him it was a mistake. The papers ran the story
with my UC name but no photo. And let's be honest, the only
reason the Bureau hasn't given me up to the media is because
they want that undercover project to continue. If they had to
come out and say I was a UC, they'd have to shut it down, and it
cost them over a million dollars to set up. So if it seems like I'm
making a big deal out of this, it's only because I know it's going to
get much bigger."

"Maybe you should take some leave."

"I've checked. Even if I get fired, which I'm sure I will be, I get
paid for any unused leave on the books. I'm going to need every
dime."

"I was talking about unofficial leave; just take off for a while."

"Let's get something straight: I'm not looking for friends. And quit pretending that this is some new beginning for me and the slate is wiped clean. You know as well as I do that this is not going to have a happy ending."

A cold resignation came into Vanko's voice. "Go see Abby, she'll find you a desk. I'll have something for you to do by this afternoon."

Egan got up to leave. "While I was waiting I thought I heard the secretary say there's an inspector here?"

"There is."

"The goofy-looking guy who doesn't think he's losing his hair?"

"The one wearing a tie, yes."

"Great, he looked at me like I was his lunch. It just keeps getting better."

11

MANNY BALDOVINO SAT WITH HIS FACE OVER HIS coffee, trying to cut an opening through the morning fog inside his head. He had slept fitfully again, but not because of any anxiety over bridges. Ever since Danny DeMiglia had visited the club, Mike Parisi had seemed preoccupied. Manny had tried to feel him out about how it went with Danny, but Parisi's only answer was a pensive, "Fine." His captain had been threatened in some way, and Manny knew it was his fault. Maybe he should just have his lawyer get him a deal and go off to prison, screw the delaying tactics, be stand-up. And when he got out he could move to another state. He always wanted to see California. Get a regular job, if there was such a thing. Maybe sales, he was pretty good on the short con. He took a moment to picture himself with a wife and kids, going off to work each morning, coming home and . . . He shook his head. "Jesus Christ," he said out loud, "I can't do that." What he had now, the leisure, the freedom—he had never known anything else. Without really tasting it, he took a sip of coffee. Sitting around the club all day, playing cards, out all night eating and drinking with his pals—it was hard to imagine having to catch a train or bus. And answering to someone whom he didn't respect, that would never work. Sure, the life he had chosen came with the occasional inconvenience or worry, but those who take for a living were used to those small, emotional downdrafts. In fact, they provided the only stirring in an otherwise unchallenging existence. Routine required endurance, and men became criminals because they lacked that exact resource.

He reached across the counter and picked up the mail that had accumulated for over a week. Bills and advertising, nothing personal, nothing to say that Manny Baldovino was an individual worth corresponding with. He started to push the pile away when the hand printing on one of the envelopes caught his eye. It was addressed to the attention of "Joseph Baldovino or Emmanuel Baldovino." God, he hated that name, from some uncle a thousand years ago. He couldn't imagine who would know it other than his parents.

The return address was the Seaside State Bank in Little Egg Harbor, New Jersey. The name of the town sent Manny drifting back to his preadolescent summers. He, with his mother and father, would go to the Jersey shore for a month. Other than being called in to explain his latest errant behavior, it was the only time he could remember spending alone with his dad. They would fish from the shore, and supper was always at a restaurant surrounded by tan, relaxed people, most of whom weren't Italian.

He held the envelope under his nose, hoping for a hint of the beach, for memories so distant their only images were tiny flashes of sepia-burned photos. His nose twitched at the smell of dusty paper.

Sensing that some window to the past was about to be opened, Manny carefully slit the flap with a kitchen knife and pulled out the enclosed notice. It stated that the rental agreement for the safe deposit box in the name of Joseph Baldovino had expired, and if not claimed or renewed within thirty days, it would be opened and its contents disposed of. The original date of rental was twenty years earlier, and the last five-year renewal had been paid shortly before his father's death. Also enclosed were photocopies of signature cards for the two people with access to the box. One was Joseph Baldovino, and the alternate designee was Emmanuel Baldovino. Manny didn't remember signing it, but that was definitely his childhood signature, its loops larger, more patient, the *i*'s dotted with small circles. He looked at his father's writing with its Old World flourishes and could still picture the quick, conductor-like movements of his hands.

The significance of the notice dawned on him slowly—safe deposit boxes were for valuables, in the case of his father, the infamous *capo*, possibly secret valuables. Then he took a deep breath and reminded himself that he was Manny Baldovino. If there was an Italian version of Murphy's Law, it was Manny's Law. Things didn't fall into his lap; if anything, they fell through. But at the very least there had to be some family items: birth certificates, photos, other documents. Whatever it contained was at least twenty years old, and that in itself excited him.

He cautiously placed the documents back in the envelope and pushed it off to the side where nothing could be spilled on it. As he lifted the mug to his mouth and imagined the possibilities that awaited him in Little Egg Harbor, he realized the coffee was no longer hot. He poured it down the sink and hurried to the shower.

Manny pulled his fourteen-year-old Lincoln into the gas station across the street from the club. He told the old guy who worked there to fill it up, wash the windows, and check the oil. It was burning almost a quart a week, and he figured that was the equivalent of a drive to the Jersey shore.

He found Mike Parisi in the back room talking to Tommy Ida. "Mike, can I see you for a minute?" Ida wandered into the front. "Can I borrow three hundred?"

Parisi pulled out a modest fold of bills and counted out six fifties. He handed them to Manny. "Seems like you're in a hurry. You going somewhere?"

Discovering a safe deposit box in only his and his father's name suddenly seemed like a secret they had shared for twenty years. And after everything that had happened in the last year, to have his father's trust was worth more than if the box were full of diamonds. It needed to be kept secret, even from Parisi. "I've got to get out of town for a couple of days. Thought I'd go to Atlantic City. You know, maybe change my luck."

Parisi grinned. "You're coming back, right? I mean aside from this, you owe me ten grand for the bondsman."

"Come on, Mike. You know I'd never stiff you."

"I'm just busting balls a little, Manny. If there's one guy in the world I would trust with everything I have, it's you."

Baldovino looked down as he smiled, wondering why someone like Parisi would treat him with such friendship. "If I win anything I'll split it with you."

"In that case maybe I should go with you to make sure your count is right."

"Maybe you should."

Parisi stripped off another two hundred and handed it to Baldovino. "Since you're going to win all this money, I'll need to make a little more of an investment."

Parisi seemed different somehow. His clothes were different, a golf shirt and khaki pants, no jewelry. But more than that, there was an air about him, as though he were finally comfortable being in charge. Manny felt certain that the mess he had kicked up with DeMiglia was responsible for the change. His first impulse was to feel guilty about Parisi's problems, but it looked like maybe his mistakes had finally done some good. Maybe the curse of the Lag had gone full circle, now able to change bad into good. Maybe his childhood daydreams were finally coming true, maybe his lack of speed was now a good thing. The time had come. Tipping into Manny's favor, and everyone was looking to him for their cues. Manny "the Cue" Baldovino. And just maybe the final proof of his long withheld ascendancy was waiting for him in that New Jersey safe deposit box.

A small storage room, accessible only from the garage, had been cleared out at Lansing's request. Vanko had offered his office for the squad interviews, but Lansing didn't want someone wandering into the vault and realizing how easy it was to overhear conversations inside the supervisor's office.

Lansing finished arranging his papers while Howard Snow unbuckled his wristwatch and stood it up as if hoping to place a time limit on the interview. "Sorry about the cramped space. Howard, I've got to be honest with you, I've been through your personnel file and have read some of the preliminary complaints against you in this latest OPR inquiry. And that I have to use the word 'latest' shows that you are indeed on the verge of serious consequences. Two OPR investigations in just four years of service—kind of a flag, wouldn't you say?"

"I suppose it is."

"Of course I don't have all the information that OPR does, but I'd say there's little question that your job is in jeopardy."

With a just-noticeable hint of defiance, Snow looked up in silence as though everything Lansing had said was as predictable as a script for an old B movie. When the inspector matched his stare, Snow said, "I suppose it is."

"You know, it's okay to say something other than 'I suppose it is.'"

"Do you suppose it is?"

Lansing gave a short, appreciative laugh. "Let's try this from a different angle. About a week ago you were involved in a case, and during surveillance, or whatever you were doing out there, an expensive automobile was totaled. Do you remember that?"

"About a week ago?"

"A Mercedes was wrecked, do you remember *that?*"

"A Mercedes, I think I heard something about it."

"You were out there, what do you mean you 'heard something' about it? Do you people wreck that many cars?"

"Not that I know of."

"Do you know the number-one charge lodged against agents after they're interviewed about misconduct? It's lack of candor. And frankly, Howard, there's not a lot of room left on the list of charges against you. So let's give it one final try. What was the name of the subject your squad was working the night you think you may have heard that a Mercedes was possibly wrecked?"

Snow picked up his watch and let his thumb slowly trace its different geometric shapes. "I think it was Dimino."

Finally, corroboration of what Lansing had overheard: "the Dimino scam." "And what happened?"

"You mean to the Mercedes?"

Lansing said, "At this point, I'll take anything—the car, Dimino, what color pants you were wearing, anything."

Snow looked up. "Sorry I'm so vague, but I was alone in my car and never really did get close enough to take the eye. At the end, someone came up on the radio and said we could break it off and head home. You know agents, you don't have to say that twice."

"So you don't know anything."

"I know that Dimino rolled over and gave up his boss."

"Rolled over to whom? Who had contact with him that night? And why did he roll?"

"You know who'd know? Nick."

"I'm sure he would, but I'm asking you."

"That's about all I know. We didn't even hold on to him that night. He was turned over to the squad working the Corsalinis."

"Why were you working another squad's subject?"

"Nick told us to. You'd have to ask him."

Lansing turned the file in front of him 180 degrees so Snow could see his name on it. "I've read your *entire* personnel file. I've got to hand it to you, you busted your ass to get this job. When you were turned down the first time, you went and got your master's, even took flying lessons. Why was that?"

Lansing was pleased with the results of his question. He had found that chink he had been looking for. Something had gone soft in Snow. "When I was turned down after my first interview, I looked at all the different programs the Bureau hired under and saw that they sometimes recruited pilots, so I took lessons."

"Well, Howard, I've got to tell you, if I had to go through all that, I don't know if it would have been worth the trouble to me. It'd be a shame to lose someone like you. Did OPR give any indication what was going to happen to you?"

"With all respect, they told me not to discuss particulars with anyone."

"That is standard procedure." Lansing started paging through the file. "The preliminary statement says that although you are an extremely hard worker, you appear unable to interpret the most basic social clues."

"That's probably true. My people skills are not what they could be. But I've been working on them, and they are getting better."

"I'm glad to hear that, but I worked in OPR before I came to the inspection staff and I've got to tell you, your future isn't what you deserve."

"Meaning?"

"Meaning, you're probably going to lose your job over that search warrant disaster."

"You can't be sure of that."

"The OPR investigation, and if I tell them about your lack of candor regarding this Dimino case, I think I can predict exactly that."

"I've told you I don't know anything that happened with Dimino."

"Then why are you the only member on this squad with a let-ter of commendation for it? You're lying to me."

Snow's eyes dropped, and his voice strained to override his hollow bravado. "Then I guess I'll lose my job."

"Hardworking *and* loyal. This would be a shame."

Snow's eyes locked on Lansing's. "Would be?"

"You need someone who's in a position to help you, and I think we both know that isn't Nick Vanko."

Snow shook his head vigorously. "No!" He threw his watch at the tabletop. It bounced and fell to the floor.

His response was an overreaction, one of self-admonishment rather than protest. No matter how deeply Snow thought he be-lieved in loyalty, he was considering the alternative and was sud-denly angry with himself because of it. The importance of remaining an FBI agent threatened the rules he had set up for himself.

"You've already given me enough here to finish off your ca-reer. You have to decide whether you want me as an enemy or an ally. Do you want me to help you save your job?"

"What guarantee is there that you could, or would?"

"The only guarantee I can give you is that I'm going to report your part in this coverup to OPR."

Snow was still shaking his head. But the motion had slowed, its arc longer, changing its message from one of halfhearted defiance to one of impending surrender. Lansing knew it as a sign of self-preservation, the most dominant of human instincts. With time, there was a better-than-even chance that Snow would come around. "I'll give you one week. Then this will be turned over to OPR."

12

THE BANK MANAGER OF THE SEASIDE STATE BANK
seemed as musty and yellowed as the old account cards that he
had taken out of the safe deposit box folder. He had introduced
himself as Mr. Jordan. Manny watched him compare his twenty-
year-old signature with the one he just provided. Jordan's neck,
long and thin, craned forward to scrutinize the handwriting. With
his head bowed, a bald spot on his crown became visible. His hair
was the same mottled gray and brown as his shapeless suit. His
narrow black tie, its knot chalky with use, dangled from a shirt
collar large enough to accommodate two of his necks. Manny
tried to calculate who was president when the tie was last dry-
cleaned.

Finally the banker straightened up. "This all seems to be in
order, Mr. Baldovino. I assume you'd like to retrieve the contents
of your box?"

"Yes sir."

"Do you have your key?"

Manny gave his friendliest smile. "Hey, Mr. Jordan, it's been
twenty years. Who knows where it is? Hell, I'm not sure where I
parked my car."

Jordan went on as if Manny hadn't spoken. "We'll have to drill
out the lock. There's a hundred-dollar fee involved."

Baldovino handed over two of the fifties Parisi had given him.
"Perfectly understandable."

A half hour later Jordan shut the door to the small private

room in the safe deposit vault. Manny put the long box on the table and waited a few seconds before opening it. He mumbled out loud, "Don't get your hopes up. If it was that valuable, Pop would not have left it here. He would have spent it. Or told me or Ma where it was." On the other hand, his father was a saver and had died without warning. Maybe it was an inheritance, the kind that couldn't be taxed. By having Manny's name on the signature cards, it was tantamount to a will without all the legal intervention. Even if nothing of value was inside, the contents were something his father thought worth preserving, and that alone would be worth the trip.

He swung the lid open. On top sat several banded bundles of currency under which were maybe twenty pieces of jewelry. While he wasn't an expert, most of it looked to be of fairly good quality. He lifted out the cash. It was all ten-dollar bills, and as he fanned through them, he could see they were Silver Certificates. The face value totaled twenty thousand dollars, but because they were old bills, they might be worth more. He began to fill the plastic grocery bag he'd brought with the cash and jewels. Then he slid his hand under the half of the top that wasn't part of the hinged lid to check for anything he might have missed. He felt a flat, thin book with a cloth cover and pulled it out. A smile overwhelmed him. In a voice intended to be just loud enough for his father to hear, he said, "You're going to change my luck, aren't you, Pop?" He sat down.

The first ten pages or so were columns of figures, precise accountings of outstanding loans, payments, and other gambling income and the date, each neatly entered in his father's handwriting. Manny recognized them as old numbers accounts along with some loansharking balances next to names he had never heard of.

The mob hadn't bothered with the illegal lottery in decades, so the book had to be at least twenty years old. That meant the ledger might have been the original reason for renting the box. If so, it had to have some value other than long-expired accounts.

He thumbed through it. The rest of the pages except for a couple at the end were blank. Tucked inside the back cover was a piece of paper folded into quarters, its creases worn through in places. He unfolded it carefully.

The left-hand edge looked like it had been torn away. What remained was about the size of a half sheet of typing paper and appeared to be a hand-drawn map. Age had faded the ink to a cocoa brown. An undulating line had the number "28" written just above it. Another, that ran parallel to the first, was marked "Esopus Creek." Next to it were some crudely drawn objects that Manny thought might represent trees. Below the line marked "28" was another, long and curved, which was marked with short perpendicular lines, the traditional symbol for a railroad track. He looked closer and saw that an X marked a blank area above the three linear designations, north if the map was oriented properly. It didn't seem to have any specific relation to any of the landmarks.

Written in a different ink, not quite as aged, along an edge was "Lulu's map." It appeared to be his father's handwriting. "What *is* this?" he asked aloud.

He picked up the notebook and turned to the last few pages. His father had written:

October 23—Me and Auggie got the map from Tony Luitu as collateral on overdue loan. His mother was Marty Krompier's sister. He gave it to her the night he was shot. Luitu found it in her papers after she died. Says he never told anyone.

October 25—Me and Auggie head to Phoenicia to look. Map confusing. Can't find a thing. Need someone who knows the area and can be trusted.

November 17—Feds busted Auggie. Had Gleason go see him in jail and ask where his half was. Said it was in his numbers ledger. The Feds took it as evidence.

June 8—Auggie sentenced to five years. Had Gleason petition to get Auggie's book back. Denied because his conviction was under appeal and had to retain all evidence. Have to wait until Auggie comes out.

It had to be a treasure map. Suddenly the boundless fantasy of buried treasure returned him to his childhood. He could feel his heart accelerate, almost audibly. New opportunities sprang from that box, and, more important, different endings.

Then Manny stood up. He was suspicious of unrestrained elation.

Whenever those small chain reactions of anticipation started pounding in his chest, he reminded himself to apply the brakes. Whatever this was, his father had thought it valuable. Normally that would have been good enough for Manny, but it had been forgotten in the bank vault for twenty years. Maybe it was no longer worth anything. Maybe what had been hidden had already been found. Then possible scenarios started multiplying faster than he could keep track of them. He'd have to take it to Mike Parisi—he'd figure it out.

Baldovino got to the Sons of Catania late the next morning. He had overslept, the first good night's sleep in a long time. As soon as he walked in carrying the plastic bag from the bank, Gus Dellaporta, from his usual seat at the card table, said, "Manny, the fuck you going?"

"Nowhere, why?"

"You've got your Puerto Rican two-suiter."

Everyone laughed. In response, Manny good-naturedly shot out an arm, slapping the elbow with the traditional up-to-here salute. "I guess we know how you did in Atlantic City," Dellaporta replied.

In the back room Tommy Ida was sitting at a side table reading as usual. Parisi was pouring a cup of coffee. "Manny, you're back already? I thought you were going for a couple of days."

"Something came up."

Parisi could see the excitement on his face. "Something good?"

"Maybe."

"You want some coffee?"

"Yeah, sure. Thanks."

Parisi watched over his shoulder as Manny put the bag carefully on the table. He finished pouring the second cup and brought it over to him. "You didn't hit the jackpot in Atlantic City, did you?"

"I don't know." He heard Ida put down his magazine and get up. Manny took out the stacks of silver certificates. "My old man had a safe deposit box with these in it." He laid out the jewelry on the table next to the money. There were a dozen rings, mostly with good-sized diamonds, an emerald brooch, and the rest were expensive-looking gold watches.

Ida picked up one of the bundles and riffled through the bills. "Uncirculated, sequential silver certificates. In mint condition."

"That's good, huh, Tommy?"

"How much is there?"

"Twenty Gs." The men from the other room started filing in.

Ida said, "I'm no expert, but with crisp, uncirculated silver certificates, I think you'll be able to sell them for—these are legit, right?"

"As far as I know."

"I mean they're not from some old kidnapping where the FBI is just waiting for the serial numbers to show up. That's why they always used sequential numbers, they were easier to record. Your old man was never involved in anything like that, right?"

Manny took half a step back from the table. Maybe his luck wasn't changing after all. Ida laughed. "Manny, I'm just jerking you around. Your old man was a hell of a lot smarter than to get caught with dirty money. Besides, these are old enough that the statute of limitations ran out a long time ago."

Baldovino chuckled. "You had me going, Tommy. So what do you think they're worth?"

"Maybe two or three times face value. Maybe more."

The others started picking up the bundles and some of the jewelry. Jimmy Tatorrio slipped a woman's diamond ring on his little finger and held it under the light. "This stone is very clean." He picked up the emerald brooch. "This stuff is good quality."

"The fuck you get it?" Dellaporta asked.

"My father had this safe deposit box for twenty years. In New Jersey. The rent finally ran out on it, and the bank asked me to come and clean it out." With everyone now giving him their full attention, Manny couldn't help but orchestrate a little drama as he removed the final item from the bag with two fingertips.

"The fuck is that?" someone asked.

Manny unfolded the piece of paper and laid it on the table with the reverence due a religious artifact. "*That* is a map. I think to something valuable. I think, I don't know. It's pretty old. Maybe it's worth nothing."

"Mind if I look at it?" Parisi asked.

"That's why I brought it, Mike."

Carefully, Parisi picked it up. "Lulu's map. This was some broad's map? You know who Lulu is?"

Manny shook his head. "Not a clue."

"Maybe your old man had a little something on the side," Dellaporta offered.

Manny felt a small burst of anger. "I never saw anything to indicate that."

"Hey, he was your father, I think he had more style than to shove it in your face."

Baldovino's eyes narrowed, but before he could say anything, Parisi intervened. "Manny, what's in the book?"

"There's some stuff in it about the map." He handed it to Parisi.

Parisi looked at the handwriting. "This is your father's writing?"

"Yes."

"So he's the one who wrote 'Lulu's map.' Same handwriting, same color ink."

"Yeah, I think so." Parisi read the dated entries out loud and everyone tried to decipher their terse description and language.

"Wasn't Auggie G. your father's partner?" Tatorrio asked.

"Yeah, Auggie Grimaldi. He was a lot older than my dad. He died in the joint, serving time for making book. And my old man's lawyer for a lot of years back then was that Patrick Gleason guy."

"Phoenicia, anybody know where that's at?" Parisi asked.

"I think it's up in the Catskills," Dellaporta said.

"But we still don't know what it's a map to." All at once everyone noticed Tommy Ida. He was leaning back against the chair with a smug expression across his face.

"What?" Parisi demanded.

"Lulu isn't a woman. It's Lulu Rosenkranz. He was Dutch Schultz's right-hand man. This is a map for Schultz's treasure."

"Dutch Schultz's treasure," Dellaporta said. "Yeah, I remember hearing about that. He buried a chest somewhere."

"In Phoenicia," Ida said. "Treasure hunters have been looking for it since him and Lulu were murdered in the thirties."

"What's he supposed to have buried?" Parisi asked.

"Cash, gold, diamonds, whatever. He had a big trial coming up and was afraid of going to prison and didn't want it stolen. They say he was a cheap bastard, never spent a dime, so I guess it made sense to everyone that he wouldn't leave it laying around."

Dellaporta and Tatorrio moved closer to get a fresh perspective on the map, which had suddenly become more valuable. "The fuck's it supposed to be worth, Tommy?" asked Dellaporta.

"Supposedly, it was worth millions back then, so it could be worth maybe ten times as much now."

Tatorrio whistled. "That's a lot of ching."

"Hold on a minute," Parisi said. "This sounds like bullshit. All those people looking all those years, somebody would have found it."

Ida said, "Maybe they couldn't find it because they didn't have a map. At least not this one."

"According to the ledger, half a map," Parisi corrected. "If it's even legit. This guy Tony Luitu might have been running a scam on Manny's father—no disrespect, Manny—an overdue loan, they might have been getting ready to bust him up, and he was just trying to buy some breathing room."

"Let me see if I can't check some of this out," Ida said. "If we can find out who Luitu is and this Marty Krompier, maybe something'll match up."

"How're you going to do that?" Parisi asked.

"I'll run over to the library."

Dellaporta gave a short, hard laugh. "You think they got books on this stuff?"

"Maybe. If not, they've got free Internet service. That's where I was running all the addresses we were going to use for those home equity scams. If there's any information available on this, that's where it'll be."

"How long you going to be?" Manny tried to disguise his excitement.

"If there's a computer available, an hour, more or less."

"Hey Tommy, they got any magazines there?" Dellaporta asked.

"Not that you'd like."

"The fuck you know what I'd like?"

"All theirs have words."

13

JACK STRAKER AND HOWARD SNOW SAT DOWN across from Vanko who asked, "Is the inspector out there?"

"His Majesty, Charles the Sniveler?" Straker said. "I saw him leave about fifteen minutes ago."

"Jack, we're trying to lull this guy to sleep. Please don't go twisting his nipples."

"Nick, he isn't about to go to sleep with his career making all that noise."

Vanko looked at Snow. "Any chance you can help keep your partner in check?"

"Shouldn't be a problem, I'll just use the same approach I did when I got him to baby that Mercedes."

Vanko shook his head. "After I'm fired, I'm going to look for a job working with adults."

"That's the attitude, Nick," Straker said. "Screw him."

"Actually, I've got you in here because of another problem. Something to keep idle hands busy. The SAC wants to see what we can do about the Judge Ferris disappearance."

"Let me save you some time," Straker said. "It was Danny DeMiglia, in the library, with the candlestick."

"I know it's been a while since you've been in a courtroom, but juries have this quirk about not voting guilty based on hunches, even if they are yours, Jack."

"I thought the state police were taking the lead on it," Snow said. "At least they're the only ones I see on the news talking about it."

"This would be more of an unofficial inquiry."

"In case you're wondering, Howie," Straker said, "that means, Let's have the expendables do something stupid and see if it works. If it doesn't, it's not like they're losing real agents."

"Like you'd want it any other way," Snow said.

Vanko handed a sheet of paper to Straker. "I reviewed the intelligence file on DeMiglia. That's a list of his known associates. I'm sure you could charm one of them into helping us. And for the time being, this is just between the three of us."

"Because of the new guy? What's his name—Egan?" Straker said.

"Let's just say not all loyalties have been established yet."

As the two agents were leaving, Abby appeared in the doorway. "You didn't tell me we were getting another agent."

"Why, is someone here? No one called me."

"Yes."

"Okay, bring him back." Vanko settled behind his desk. "What's his name?"

Over her shoulder, Abby laughed and said, "Sheila."

Vanko bolted to his feet. He had never had a female agent on the squad; he had never even considered it. As a rule, women in the Bureau didn't get into trouble, which was the usual route to the Opera House. Dropping a woman into the midst of his little penal colony could cause problems. It was difficult enough keeping the troops focused on the task at hand without a pair of breasts distracting them. He walked out through the hinged door to the reception area. "Hi, I'm Nick Vanko."

The woman emerged from a shadowed corner, and Vanko was struck by how plain her face was. While none of its features were particularly unattractive, its composite was one of overwhelming ordinariness that would be difficult to memorize. Her age was hard to judge. Her skin was coarse and stippled and had a worn maturity to it that he suspected had haunted her even in childhood. At the same time, it did not have the looseness of middle age. Surprisingly, she wore no makeup, as if she had surrendered all social expectations and had convinced herself that appearance and its eventual purpose, companionship, were no longer a possibility, or even a desire. She was noticeably underweight, and from her baggy black pants suit, he guessed that she had lost a good deal of the weight recently. Her slender figure didn't seem to have a curve to it, but it was impossible to tell under the shapeless clothing.

Although he had deflected a thousand reactions to his own face, he could not pull his eyes from hers. Then he noticed her hair. He could see that given a little care, it would have been striking. It was rich and thick, but it appeared to have been pushed into its present disorder with the towel that had dried it. Was she afraid that exhibiting its fullness would further diminish her face? Her eyebrows and lashes were dark and lustrous and made her skin seem even paler, irreparably coarser. Her pupils, bezeled by pure cognac irises, were widely dilated and gave her a look of hollow distraction, of chronic exhaustion. The survivor of a catastrophe, or possibly still in its grasp.

An agent's appearance was a difficult thing to stereotype, but Vanko started to wonder if she even was an agent. She seemed to possess none of the requisite hauteur of authority that was issued with a badge and gun and, with rare exception, jealously maintained.

She extended her hand and looked at him like no one had since the accident, totally free of discomfort. "Sheila Burkhart." Her voice was worn out, husky, yet sensual.

Her handshake was surprisingly firm. "What squad are you coming from?" It was a question subtly designed to test whether she was an agent, but he immediately regretted it.

She opened her credentials. "I assume this is what you're really asking." She smiled and suddenly he saw her confidence. Although vulnerable to the pressures of the moment, it was part of a thick vein that ran deep, ingrained by the kind of successes that came from hard work.

He glanced at her photo and saw a different person. The issuing date was three years earlier and she looked noticeably more robust, but still unquestionably plain. "Oh no, that's all right."

"Don't be embarrassed, I've had to show them more than once lately."

"Sorry," he said. "Come on in."

Instead of sitting behind his desk, he took a chair next to her. "What squad *are* you being transferred from?"

"You really didn't know I was coming."

"It's been kind of crazy with the inspection and all."

"You don't have to make excuses to spare my feelings. You'll find I'm pretty impervious to criticism."

He smiled. "That would explain how you got here."

"I like that. Most supervisors wouldn't admit that their squad was the office dumping ground."

"Most agents wouldn't admit they had been dumped."

"If that's your way of asking what I did to be sent here, it's pretty clever."

"I'd rather hear it from you than the front office. I have a feeling your version will contain a lot less topspin."

"Fair enough. In a word, they think I'm crazy."

"Are you?"

"Probably. A little, anyway."

"Then I'm afraid you're underqualified to be around here."

She laughed. "I smell coffee. Can I get a cup before I burden you with your newest problem's autobiography? I've only had thirteen or fourteen so far today."

Vanko stood up. "Sure. How do you like it?"

Sheila stood up. "No, I'll get it." Vanko directed her to the coffee machine. "Can I get you some?" she asked.

"No thanks. Ten's pretty much my limit."

Holding the paper cup between both hands, she sat back down and took small scalding sips between sentences. "I was working on a violent crimes task force. Mostly NYPD, a little bit of ATF, a couple of DEA, state police, blah, blah, blah. But the work was first-rate. Mostly serial offenders, rapists, a bank stickup crew, a couple of home-invasion gangs. Then a year ago, some *fucking* animal up in Harlem raped and strangled a twelve-year-old girl." Vanko was stunned, not by her expletive, but by the hatred with which she spit it out, as scorching as any man he had ever heard. "It is my opinion that he has killed other girls since then." The last sentence was slower and more formal, as if it had been delivered too many times before as a defense.

"I don't think I've read anything about it."

"Clever *and* tactful. I've only been here five minutes and you've figured out why I was sent packing from the task force."

She waited for him to say something, then continued. "I was the only woman on the task force, and because Suzie Castillo—that's the twelve-year-old victim—was a female, they made me lead investigator. Which makes sense. So I start working it, knowing nothing about homicide investigations. But I do know a little about serial offenders because of the cases we were working. No matter what the profilers tell you, each one is different. You have to learn as you go, not only about how to, but you've got to learn about the individual you're looking for. So I start working it like a maniac, and before I know it, this thing's got ahold of me. I'm working sixteen hours a day, sometimes straight around the clock. I don't notice it, but everyone is starting to pull back from me. I guess they could see that it was taking me over. But I couldn't." She sipped her coffee.

"And that's why you're here?"

"More or less."

"'More or less' usually means more."

"Hey, I'm sure you want me to leave a little mystery, something for you and the people downtown to gossip about. Or are you trying to tell me that you're not going to call the office to find out if what the wacko has told you is really true."

"The minute you leave."

She took another sip and looked at him. "What happened to your face?"

Vanko felt himself flush, but he sensed that she was asking the question more to find out about him than about his face, and his reaction would reveal a lot. "People don't usually ask that," he said without the slightest trace of anger.

"Look at this face. The only thing it's ever earned me is the right to ask that question."

He did look. There were small indications of her dissatisfaction with its effects on the world. In unguarded moments, fatigue turned down the corners of her mouth and her eyebrows knitted themselves together sadly.

"There's nothing wrong with your—"

She held up her hand. "*Bup, bup, bup,* I've only known you fifteen minutes, but you seem like an unusually honest guy. Don't ruin it."

"Fair enough. Nine years ago, I was working surveillance and we had a multi-kilo deal on some Colombians. The guy I'm on gets hinky and takes off. I'm a relatively new agent, but fortunately off probation. I take off after him. He gets it up over a hundred on the expressway, and I'm on him. But, as I was about to find out, I was out of my league. Intentionally, he cuts into this woman and forces her into me. And . . ." He pointed at his own face. Momentarily, the life disappeared from his eyes.

"And her?"

In a strained voice, he said, "She died."

"Jesus!"

They both lapsed into silence.

Finally she said, "Maybe you're right, maybe I'm not crazy enough to fit into this squad." When he failed to smile, she asked, "So tell me about the worst day I'm going to have around here."

Vanko pinched the end of his nose with his thumb and index finger. "If the inspector we've drawn has his way, they'll all be the worst."

"I'd offer to sleep with him, but that usually makes things worse." Vanko finally laughed. "In case he asks, what am I supposed to be doing around here?"

"Well, we do a lot of photography. Have you had any experience?"

She stood up and moved over to the row of his immigrant photos. "Actually, I'm pretty good." She examined each of the photographs. "Some people try to become accomplished photographers so they'll always be asked to take the photos." She turned back to him. "That way they never have to be in them."

Just before Tommy Ida returned from the library, Baldovino maneuvered Parisi into the back room. Manny took out half of the silver certificates and handed them to his boss.

"What's this?"

"I told you we'd split whatever I made in Atlantic City."

"You didn't go to Atlantic City. Besides, this is a gift from your father." Parisi tried to hand them back.

"My father was an honorable man. This gives me the chance to be what he taught me. Please."

Parisi could see that Manny needed to do this, to offset the problems he had brought to the crew by the only means at his disposal. To Parisi, the gesture represented more than money. For the first time he understood that loyalty had a downward arc. Not only was he responsible for protecting the don, but, just as important, for protecting the men who had sworn their allegiance to him. "You know, Manny, sometimes you knock me out."

Ida walked in, carrying a thin roll of papers. The others filed in without a word.

He laid the pages on the table. "There's quite a bit of stuff on the Internet about the Dutchman's treasure. There's chat rooms, maps of Phoenicia, there was even a television documentary done on it. They all say the same thing: a map does exist. Schultz, whose real name was Arthur Flegenheimer, was about to go on trial and thought he had a better-than-even chance of doing some time. So he and Lulu Rosenkranz drove up to Phoenicia one night with this iron box. Like I said, the Dutchman was a real miser, so it was loaded with most of what he had accumulated—gold, jewels, and cash. It was supposed to total seven million."

"What's that in today's money?" Dellaporta asked impatiently.

"There are some variables, like how much of it was gold or diamonds, which have increased at different rates, but the general figures that are thrown out are"—Ida hesitated for effect—"thirty to fifty million." Everyone groaned. "So after they bury it, Rosenkranz, who's not the smartest guy in the world, decides he'd better draw a map so he can find it again. But he's got a big mouth, and eventually Dutch hears that he's been talking about it. He tells Lulu to give the map to his next in command. And who's third in command? Marty Krompier." Remembering the name from Joseph Baldovino's ledger, the room began buzzing again. "Now on"—Ida checked one of the pages—"October tenth, nineteen thirty-five, the Dutchman, Lulu, a guy they call Abba Dabba Berman, and Abe Landau are sitting in the back room of the Palace Chop House in Newark tallying up the weekly receipts. In walk two guys, one named Bug Workman, and they wind up shooting all four of them. At the same time Marty Krompier, who was Schultz's chief enforcer for the Harlem numbers, and some of his people, are ambushed in a barbershop in Manhattan."

"Just like in *The Godfather*," Tatorrio said. "Taking care of all the family's enemies at once."

"Just like in *The Godfather*, but thirty years before the book was written," Ida said.

"There's a book?" Dellaporta asked.

"Now Krompier is hit bad, and his brothers Jules and Milton had to give him blood transfusions. But he still doesn't know if he's going to make it, so he tells Milton about the map and that he should hold on to it for Dutch. See, at the time he didn't know Schultz had been shot."

"What happened to it then?" Parisi asked.

"That's where the story ends. There was one rumor that some unnamed gangsters got it after killing some of the Dutchman's men. That's the last anyone ever heard of the map."

"So the last thing we know for sure is that Milton Krompier had it."

Ida smiled as if about to pull one last rabbit out of the hat. "Did you know that you can trace your family tree on the Internet, for generations and generations?" Everyone just looked at him with a blank stare. "Yeah, the librarian showed me how to do it. Something the Mormons started."

"Probably so they could keep track of all their wives," Tatorrio offered.

"So I plugged in the name Anthony Luitu. And guess who his parents were—Ruth and Milton . . ."

"Krompier," Parisi answered. Dellaporta slapped Manny on the back.

"That's right."

Tatorrio asked, "How come Luitu had a different last name?"

"I was wondering the same thing," Ida said. "Turns out he was adopted by the Krompiers, but he was older, so he just kept his name."

"That's great, Tommy, but we've only got half the map. And unfortunately, the Feds have the other half." The mood of the room darkened instantly. For Parisi, the most surprising part of becoming a captain was the emotional volatility of his crew. They were incapable of stepping back from an obstacle and looking for a way around it, preferring to judge the situation by its ability to provide, or prevent, immediate gratification. If denied, an alternative solution was never sought, and a brief lapse into dejection ensued until that, too, required too much effort. Then it was on to the next elusive scheme. The only exception was Tommy Ida. Had it been up to anyone else to research the possibility of the treasure's existence, the entire mini-drama would have likely been forgotten. More than ever, Parisi now understood why someone had to be in charge. For a few seconds, he watched Ida, who was carefully rereading one of the pages he had brought back from the library, making notes in the margin. "Let me take another look at the map, Manny. Gus, do you still have that jeweler's loupe?"

"It's out in the car. I'll get it."

Ida looked up. "Like I was saying, when Schultz and his crew got shot, they were adding up the weekly take from the numbers. After the shooting, the cops got the figures and made them public. Get this—the gross for seven weeks was recorded as $827,253 and the net was $148,369. And that was just on the numbers. So he obviously was making the kind of money that could have accumulated to $7 million."

Parisi had written the figures down. "Man, that's a lot of overhead. If I turned over that low a percentage, the don would have me shot for skimming."

Dellaporta returned and handed the jeweler's loupe to Parisi.

Manny said, "See that X there, Mike, that must be where it is."

Parisi looked at it through the lens. It was drawn right next to the torn edge. "There's a small line that starts on the left side of the X and disappears off the edge. It must be something to help show exactly where the box is buried." Everyone became silent with disappointment.

Finally Dellaporta said what everyone was thinking. "And the FBI has the other half, and they don't have a clue."

"Hey, who knows, we might get lucky. Let's go out there and give it a shot," Manny said. "What do you say, Mike?"

Parisi looked around at the defeated faces. "What the hell, why not? Tommy, how long to drive up there?"

Ida closed his eyes while he calculated. "Two, two and a half hours."

"So, Manny, what do you think? Think this is for real?" Parisi asked.

"You know I ain't the smartest guy in the world, but my father was no dummy. He didn't die of natural causes because he misread people and situations. If he bought Luitu's story, I'd say it's worth checking out."

"Then let's ride."

"Now?" Dellaporta asked. "There won't be much daylight left."

"We'll stay over."

"Where?"

"It's the Catskills, right? Aren't they famous for their hotels? The Dutchman must have had some reason for going up there other than digging a hole."

14

"YOU KNOW I DON'T LIKE TO GO INTO THE OFFICE, especially with the inspectors in town. Have you forgotten the squad battle cry: 'Way out of sight, way out of mind'?" Howard Snow asked. "Can't you go up there by yourself?"

"I need you to stand guard," Jack Straker answered.

"Stand guard . . . stand guard," he said again, changing the accent to the second word, tipping his head in the opposite direction. "You know, Jack, it just doesn't have that keep-your-job ring to it."

With the mock impatience of an adult trying to teach a lesson by repetition, Straker looked up at the Bureau garage ceiling. "Tell me how much money you have left until payday."

"I already told you."

"Tell me again because evidently you weren't listening to your half of the conversation."

"Eighteen dollars."

"Eighteen dollars. Now, do you want to wait to payday to get laid, or do you want to get laid tonight?"

Snow looked away, his left hand tracing the square of his belt buckle. "Tonight."

"Hey, Howard, it's nothing to be ashamed of. We all want to get laid tonight. Did you ever hear a guy say, You know, I think I'll wait until the fifteenth or, if not then, maybe the twenty-eighth? There's only one answer to the question, and it's 'Right now, sweetheart.'"

"This Megan, she's cute?"

"Now the serial virgin is being picky," Straker said. "Have you ever met a Megan who wasn't cute? And by closing time I guarantee she'll be gorgeous. In the meantime, we have to show them we can commit, at least to dinner and drinks, and eighteen dollars won't even get us drive-through privileges. *Now* have we had this conversation for the last time?"

"Sometimes I think you're in love with chaos."

"I'm in love with the possibility of chaos, that things *could* go wrong, but I don't like it any better than you when they actually do."

"How in love are you with this scam?"

"As long as I have a trusted lookout, this can't go wrong."

". . . said Nixon to the Watergate burglars."

"I hope you're this funny with Megan."

As they rode the elevator up to the FBI office, Straker could see that the lure of flesh, which would have overpowered most men's fear, still hadn't captivated Snow. "Do you know why it is absolutely imperative that you get laid tonight?"

"This should be interesting."

"I'm serious. Do you know why that inspector's attempt to flip you is bothering you so much?" Snow looked at him with exaggerated apathy, as if there was only one chance in a million that he would find the evidence Straker was about to offer convincing. "The longer a man goes without getting laid, the more likely he is to be swallowed by his own fear. You probably don't remember this, but when you're freshly laid, you don't give a good goddamn about anything. That's because it's the one thing that truly validates us as men. That's why we think about it constantly. I guarantee you that by tomorrow morning you'll be ready to go in there and kick that inspector's nuts up into his sinus cavities."

"And I was worried about keeping my job."

The elevator doors opened. "Is your radio on?" Straker asked. Snow reached under his jacket and turned on the small radio attached to his belt and twisted the tiny receiver into his ear. Straker stepped out of the elevator and said, "I think the evidence room is this way."

"How did you know this stuff was even here?"

"I know a guy on the squad that seized all of it last month."

"How does someone who gets paid to enforce the law come up with an idea like this?"

"See, Howie, that question proves how badly you need some leg. Trying to divide the world into lawbreakers and law enforcers is, to me, a fairly obvious symptom of being, shall we say, seminally overloaded. You're trying to control the world around you by neatly arranging everyone into categories. To think that by joining the FBI you've surrounded yourself with only good guys is more than naïve, it's grand-theft denial. I hate to break this to you, but there is no moral backpack issued with your credentials. The only thing that separates us from them is a roll of the dice. Don't kid yourself. The whole thing is nothing more than a game of shirts and skins."

Straker stopped at a door and knocked quietly. An attractive dark-haired woman, no more than twenty, opened it and smiled at him. "Jenny, this is Howard." She started to say hello, but he playfully pushed her back inside before she could finish. The door closed behind them, extinguishing her giggles.

Snow leaned against a wall and tried to look inconspicuous in the deserted office. Suddenly, his radio came to life. Straker had switched his on and was evidently leaving the mike open.

Since teaming up with him, Snow had studied all his mannerisms and expressions along with the other iconoclastic quirks that gave Straker his magic, a pursuit that had all the wonder and disappointment of a college class that had promised to change one's approach to life. The first lesson he learned was that no man could copy another man's life, especially when it came to the more desirable of Jack's "talents," like what was going on right now in the evidence room. He was not Jack Straker, but that didn't mean he couldn't become a better Howard Snow by hanging around him.

Decoding Jack's motives was a rambling puzzle he had come to enjoy trying to solve. He considered the open mike, hoping the exercise would shorten the wait. A few possibilities presented themselves. First, it was not an accident that the radio was broadcasting. Despite all the travails Straker had managed to stack in his personnel file like dry firewood, incompetence was never their cause. When something difficult or even dangerous needed to be done, he was the individual who stepped forward or was simply expected to handle it. Like the Dimino chase. Snow couldn't imagine doing the driving. It was all he could do just to hold on. Straker had done it with a casual eagerness. And then, of course, there was the Shot.

Of the millions of rounds that had been fired by agents in the history of the agency, whether in training or actual combat, only one was known as the Shot. Snow first heard about it years before he met Jack Straker and his celebrity had traveled the well-rutted road from legend to infamy to obscurity. Firearm instructors at Quantico invariably cited it as an example not only of exceptional marksmanship, but also of how an agent must be able to adapt to changing situations.

Straker's first year, he was assigned to the Los Angeles office. One day a lone gunman smuggled a small pistol through security at the Minneapolis airport and took over a plane. He demanded half a million dollars, ordered the pilot to fly to Los Angeles, and told them to have the money and a getaway car waiting. The LA office scrambled every available agent and directed them to a hangar at the airport until a course of action could be decided upon. Instead of driving straight to LAX, Straker, seized by some never-explained prescience, went back to the office first and took a sniper's rifle from the gun vault. By the time he got to the airport, the plane was landing, so he worked his way as close to the runway as possible and waited.

And waited. One of the most amazing facets of the Shot, according to the Quantico instructors, was how long Straker had maintained a sight picture through the scope. It was estimated that he kept his eye on the scope for more than twenty minutes. Snow knew from weapons training how quickly the eye becomes exhausted. That Straker maintained his bead that long was a remarkable feat of human willpower. Especially now that Snow knew how completely foreign self-control was to Straker.

When the hijacker finally came down the stairs, he shielded himself with a stewardess. They were more than a hundred yards away from the tip of Straker's muzzle and heading toward a car that was less than thirty. Fortunately it was not between Straker and the gunman. Ten yards from the car, the stewardess's heel caught in the tarmac and she stumbled to one knee. The single shot caught the hijacker under the right armpit. As the stewardess got up, he fell to his knees and reached blindly toward her, but, as she commented later, death had already taken his eyes. He collapsed onto his face.

With predictable bureaucratic high camp, the first-year agent was chewed out for the dozen or so violations of FBI procedure, not the least of which was bypassing the SAC's ego. Then the director of the FBI called. First he congratulated the SAC on such a quick, decisive resolution to an extremely difficult situation. Next he asked to talk to the agent who had killed the hijacker. After Jack hung up, the SAC continued his assault. When Straker stood up to leave, the agent in charge asked where he thought he was going. "To Quantico," he said. "I've just been made a firearms instructor."

But by that time, all new agent classes had women in them, and it wasn't long before the man who had fired the Shot, according to one of his fellow firearms instructors, "became better known for his swordsmanship than his marksmanship." Within a year, he was discreetly transferred to New York.

So whatever Straker's reason was for leaving his mike open, Snow knew it wasn't accidental. Possibly it was to keep Snow alert at his post, but Snow could not sound a warning because a radio cannot receive when it's transmitting. More likely its purpose was to engorge Snow's fantasies, to keep him focused on the evening's eventual prize. He listened more closely, but most of the words were indistinguishable, or maybe he just cared less about them than about the grunting and groaning that seeped into his earpiece. He smiled and shook his head.

Then the most probable reason came to him. Jack Straker, as he had done almost since the moment the two had met, was including Snow in his life. Why, Snow could not imagine. He reached under his jacket and turned off the radio.

Fifteen minutes later, the door to the evidence room opened and Straker squeezed out, carrying something weighty in an oversized brown paper bag. He leaned back inside and Snow could see Jenny's face as Straker kissed her good-bye. Spotting Snow down the hall, she stuck her head out, and he could see that she was naked. She waved coyly and he waved back, not as embarrassed as he would have imagined. He pushed his glasses up on the bridge of his nose to sharpen their focus.

Neither man said anything until they were in the elevator. "See anything interesting?" Straker asked.

"Do you mean before the door opened?"

"She is a doll, huh?"

"She is a doll."

"*Hear* anything interesting?"

Snow said, "I don't suppose she knew the mike was open."

"Hey, it was her idea. She thinks you're cute."

An hour later, the two men walked into Liberty Loan in Queens. The pawnshop's owner, Sam Kasdan, looked up from his newspaper to appraise his latest customers. The short one didn't look particularly bright, and the taller one with an unkempt ponytail hanging out the back of his baseball cap was carrying a glass bowl that had the delicate silhouette and colors of a style that had not been made in almost a hundred years. Dried around the rim was what appeared to be paint, as though someone had used the bowl to clean brushes. Inside sat a couple of handfuls of silver dollars. That these guys were using the bowl to transport the abrasive coins indicated that they had no idea of its value. They had an air that Kasdan recognized—desperation mixed with the stink of low-income impulsiveness.

Kasdan came to the counter. "Hi, how are you?"

Straker pulled the baseball cap down a little farther. "You buy silver dollars, right? The sign says coins, they're coins, right?" He set the bowl on the counter.

"Yes, we do."

"Well, I need to sell these, I mean I'm thinking about selling them. You know, if the price is high enough." He looked around the shop to avoid eye contact.

The pawnbroker smiled professionally. "Fair enough." Had he wanted to waste a little time, he could have gotten him down to a dollar apiece for the coins. He obviously needed money. People did not come to a pawnbroker expecting a fair deal. The trade-off was that the money was immediately available. The pawnbroker had to make a profit somehow, but it was the customer's job to try to minimize it.

Possibly these coins were stolen, and if so, the ponytail would have no other place to sell them unless he wanted to risk going to a bank—with its surveillance cameras.

"Do you mind if I take a look at them?"

"No, go ahead." Straker lit a cigarette. "All right if I smoke?"

"Sure." Kasdan picked up one of the coins. It was in fair condition, with normal wear for a circulated silver dollar. "Mind if I ask you where you got them?"

"Ah, my mother died a ways back. She was a waitress. She collected them for years."

Now the pawnbroker was fairly convinced that the coins were stolen. The two men didn't look like junkies, but he couldn't always tell. "That's too bad, you have my condolences."

"Yeah, thanks." Straker's fingers started tapping the counter. "So what are they worth?"

"How many are here?" Kasdan started digging through the pile but was really examining the bowl, subtly scraping the substance on the rim. It turned to dust under his thumbnail. Watercolor paint. Cleaning it would be only a minor nuisance.

"Thirty-seven is what I counted."

Kasdan stacked them on the counter, verifying the count. "They are pretty worn."

"Meaning?"

"Meaning the market is glutted with them."

"These are pure silver."

"Have you checked the commodities market today? Silver is selling at about the same price as peanut butter. *Mint* silver dollars from this era are worth maybe a buck and a quarter, but these aren't mint."

"How much?" Straker said, his suspicion increasing.

"Forty-five dollars for the lot. And if you think I've got someone waiting out back to make a big profit on this, I don't. I'm going to have to sit on them for a while and hope silver goes up. Or you can take them and wait yourself."

"No, I can't wait. How do I know you're not jerking me around with the price?"

"Go online and check. You'll see there are tons of these things out there that people can't sell. And for the same price I'm offering you."

"Can't you do a little better? I really need the money. It's sort of an emergency."

Kasdan gazed sincerely as if he were considering going against his business sense. "I'll give you sixty bucks for the coins and the bowl. I think my wife might like it. She's into kitsch."

"Kitsch, what's that?"

"It's German for crap."

Straker rubbed his chin. "Can you make it seventy?"

"Sixty-five."

"Wait a minute, Jack," Snow finally spoke up. "How do you know that bowl's not worth something more than twenty bucks?"

Straker turned back to Kasdan. "What about that, is it worth more?"

"Do you see any bowls in here? How am I supposed to know? I told you, it's something my wife might like. Take it, save me twenty bucks. She's not that great a wife."

Snow picked up the bowl and rubbed some of the paint off with a fingertip, as though he were as discerning as Kasdan. As he did the bottom became visible. The pawnbroker could make out "L.C.T." inscribed in freehand in a counterclockwise arc along the outer edge as was the maker's custom. Just as he had suspected. Louis Comfort Tiffany. It had to be worth thousands. It was red, the rarest of Tiffany's colors. The majority of the outer surface was covered with gold leaf, dramatically shaped into a floral pattern.

Snow said, "I say we take it somewhere else, Jack. Get a second opinion." He started putting the silver dollars back into it.

"Hold on a second, let me check something." Kasdan walked into the back room slowly, as if he had no expectations whatsoever. He returned with a pair of glasses that had a magnifier hinged over one of the lenses. He examined the gold portion more closely. "Hmph! That's real gold. Scrap gold is selling less than twenty dollars a gram, but maybe I could sell it to a broker I know."

"Yeah, sure," Snow snorted, "you're just figuring that out now."

"I don't really care for what you're implying," Kasdan replied. "Why don't you take the bowl and the coins and go someplace else."

"Hold it," Straker said. "Howie, go out to the car. I'll handle this."

"Jack, this guy is trying to screw you."

"Just go out to the car, man. I'll take care of this." Snow glared at the owner and left. "Okay, let's quit fucking around. You're obviously interested. How much?"

"Two hundred."

"Three fifty."

"Three hundred."

"Three hundred for the bowl and forty-five for the silver dollars."

"I was only giving you that much because I was interested in the bowl. They're not really worth that much. Three forty."

"Then I'm going back up to three fifty."

For the first time the pawnbroker saw resolve in Straker's eyes. He was beginning to suspect the bowl was worth considerably more. He wasn't going to lose it for five dollars. "Okay, three forty-five."

Straker waited until he had pulled away from the curb before taking off his baseball cap and ponytail. "You played him perfectly," he said to Snow. "I thought his eyes were going to come out of their sockets when he saw the initials on the bottom."

"Great, nothing gives me wood like committing a good felony."

Half a block away Straker pulled over. He lit a cigarette and held it up in a philosophical pose. "You laugh, but this was a good felony. This guy has been fencing stolen property for twenty years, and the pawnshop detail has never been able to catch him at it. You heard him, he thought he was buying stolen property. And he sure as hell thought he was ripping us off on the bowl. I suppose honest people get cheated all the time, but it sure as hell is easier if they're dishonest."

"If I could be granted one wish in this life, Jack, it would be to have your lack of regard for consequences."

Straker reached under the seat and pulled out a black radio

with the initials NYPD stenciled in white on it. "Hey, Nick gave us that list of DeMiglia's associates and told us to see what we could do. So we did."

"He said to target them, not rip them off."

Straker keyed the radio's mike. "Mark, he's got the item. He's all yours." Straker put the radio back under the seat. "Let me offer a few words in my defense: Howie, do you want to get laid tonight?"

The two men watched as two unmarked NYPD cars quickly pulled up in front of the pawnshop and four detectives got out. One of them waved to the agents as they went in. Snow said, "Well, at least he's being arrested. I guess that's the important thing. And I've got to hand it to you, that *was* pretty ingenious dripping those paints over the bowl to make it look like some old discarded piece of crap. But where did you get the coins?"

"My mom did leave them to me. And believe me, she would have gotten a laugh out of what we did with them. Hell, if she was still alive, I wouldn't have needed you."

15

"WE'LL CAMP," PARISI OFFERED.

"Camp!" Tatorrio said and, with a look of burlesqued panic, quickly pulled out his wallet. He extracted a photo ID, pretending to check it. "No, mine says Mafia." He looked to the others who immediately fell in line, holding up a variety of cards and reporting that they too were certified members of organized crime. "Sorry, Mike, no Outward Bounders here."

Parisi's crew was standing in the parking lot of Burbarger's, one of the Catskills' time-weathered hotels. A couple of elderly guests stared at the oddly dressed group of men. "No, it'll be good," Parisi assured them, "it'll make us one with the land. You know, get a feel for where we are. Maybe that's where the others failed."

Dellaporta laughed. "One with the land? No disrespect, Mike, but you've really got to learn what this life is about. When we get back to the city, I'm going to take you out so you can murder someone."

To demonstrate that he was not above being the target of their humor, Parisi laughed. He had yet to tell any of them about DeMiglia's "plan" for the crew. Before, even though ordered not to, he would have needed them to know what a good boss he was, that he had shouldered the burden for them. But instead, he was starting to acquire the vague nobility that came with the loneliness of command. And while it gave him confidence as *capo*, he was still nagged by the feeling that he really didn't belong among these men. Maybe it was their sense of humor, the ultimate marker of membership that comes only from years together in the trenches. But the ribbing was good-natured and, in its own way, a small, inconspicuous medallion of acceptance. That he couldn't return it with an insider's ease made him wonder if he ever would, as Dellaporta put it, "learn what this life is about." The easiest thing would be to pack up and get out right now. Out of Phoenicia and out of the business. And he would have if he hadn't pledged the don his support. But the minute he was back on his feet, free from the latest opportunity of treason, he vowed to find another way to make a living.

And this treasure thing. Now that he was out here, it was hard to believe he had ever taken it seriously. Apparently from their complaining, displaying their usual flashbulb attention span, the others had begun to feel the same way. But something about all of it was calming his mind, arranging all the scattered pieces of a puzzle without his help. What that puzzle was, he had no idea, but its distant promise was demanding that the hunt for Arthur S. Flegen-heimer's metal box be seen through to its conclusion. "Everybody in the cars. We're heading back to that outdoor store we passed on the way up here and get some camping equipment." With unchar-acteristic speed, Dellaporta hurried to his car and got in.

"Where're you going in such a hurry?" Parisi yelled to him.

"To a liquor store. I've got to get my own camping supplies."

With about two hours of daylight left, three Cadillacs and a Lincoln pulled into the Sleeping Bear Campgrounds off Route 28 in Phoenicia. Dellaporta pulled himself from behind the wheel of his new Lincoln and stretched his back from side to side. Manny pushed himself out of the passenger's seat. "Why you blaming me, Gus? I'm supposed to know all the hotels would be booked for a—what was it, Tommy?"

Ida had just exited Parisi's Caddy. "A Washington Irving festival."

"The fuck was Washington Irving?" Dellaporta asked. "That's not that civil rights guy, is it?"

"Christ, Gus," Ida said. "You know, *The Legend of Sleepy Hollow.* Rip Van Winkle."

Turning to Baldovino, Dellaporta said, "I'd like to Rip Van Winkle you, give you the nine-millimeter nap."

Manny went around to the trunk of Dellaporta's car and opened the lid. "I know Mike wants to get an early start in the morning so we can get back to the city by tomorrow night, but this is crazy." Everyone was out of the cars now. "Mike," Baldovino yelled over, "where do you want this stuff set up?"

Parisi looked around briefly and spotted a large clearing with a stone ring for a campfire with wood already stacked in it. "Over there by the fire thing. Must be part of the rental deal. I'm going to go pay this guy and ask him if there's anyone around who might be able to help us find, you know, what we're looking for."

"Make sure you ask him where the men's room is," Jimmy Tatorrio said.

After he was out of earshot, Dellaporta said, "I love a man who's in charge." He reached inside his trunk and took out a long belt, which he wrapped around the elastic waistband of his jogging suit, an outdoor concession from his usual sport coat.

Tatorrio stood watching him, clearly amused. Dellaporta took out a stainless steel automatic and slipped it into the back of his pants under his jacket. "Hey, Gus, we're going to the sleeping bags, not the mattresses."

"The fuck's the name of this place, moron?"

"Ah, Sleeping Bear Campgrounds?"

"That's right. And you know how those old Indians were, they named things by what they saw. And I don't care if they are sleeping, because with that big mouth of yours, I'm sure you'll wake them up. I'm just getting ready."

"*I'm* a moron? There aren't any bears here. The guy who owns this place probably named it."

"Have it your way, Jimmy, but when some pissed-off grizzly has got ahold of you by that bony ass of yours, don't be waking me up."

The group started toward the site, their arms clumsily wrapped around sleeping bags and tents. Coming around a stand of full hemlocks, they found that a half-dozen tents had been set up next to the campfire site. "Hey, Gus, somebody's already here," Manny said.

Dellaporta and Tatorrio walked up. "When they get back, Jimmy and I will see if they don't want to move." Tatorrio opened his arms and let everything fall to the ground. "Manny, the fuck's those sausages? I'm hungry."

Tatorrio, as anyone on the crew could attest, was always hungry, as if his metabolism burned not only fat but the muscle that clung to his skeletal frame. His arms were grotesquely undeveloped, his hands not much more than long, awkward pincers.

"I still think we should of got hot dogs. That's what you eat when you camp, hot dogs," Baldovino said.

"First of all, you eat hot dogs when you go to a ball game or after you beat on some guy what's late with a payment. Second of all, we're not camping. We're . . . just stuck. And third, do you know what they put in hot dogs?"

"Those were one hundred percent beef."

"Everything on a cow is considered one hundred percent beef, even the eyelids and armpits."

"Cows don't have arms," Manny mumbled. "Besides," his voice gained strength as he found logic in the point he was about to make, "you think there's nothing but filet meat in that sausage?"

"Don't start on my sausage, Enzo makes it up special for me."

"Enzo? Enzo the gambler? Enzo who you tuned up once for not covering his bets? Oh, yeah, it's a good thing you didn't get the hot dogs. You never know what's in *them*."

Parisi came walking up. "What's with the other tents?"

"I guess we're claiming squatters' rights," Ida said, pointing at Tatorrio, who was using a switchblade to cut a loaf of French bread into sandwich-length pieces.

Tatorrio said, "Manny, you gonna want some sausage?"

"Sure."

"Now you gonna want it cooked or raw?"

Manny held up his hands to deflect any further orders. "I'll build the fire."

Ida asked Parisi, "Did the owner know anything?"

"I tried to act like I was just curious and told him I heard there was some old gangster's treasure buried around here somewhere and pretended not to be that interested. He kind of smirked like it happened all the time. He showed me how to get to where the creek and railroad tracks were closest together. Like on the map. We'll go over there first thing in the morning."

A half hour later, Manny was still trying to get the fire started. Tatorrio had trimmed a reasonably straight branch into a cooking utensil and a flaccid pink and white link of Italian sausage drooped from the sharpened end, awaiting the miracle of fire. "If I die from hunger tonight, just before my lights go out, I'm borrowing Gus's piece and popping you."

For what seemed like the hundredth time, Manny struck his disposable lighter and lit a small tuft of dry grass. He blew on it gently, trying to get it to ignite. "You know, until this very minute," Gus said, "I could never understand why our crew never got into the arson business."

Manny ignored him. Suddenly they heard the sound of slow, steady movement. Dellaporta drew his handgun as a man in a scout leader's shirt and blue jeans broke through the edge of the clearing. He was followed by a snaking line of boys in dark blue Cub Scout shirts and bright yellow kerchiefs, which had been knotted with as much uniformity as could be expected from nine- and ten-year-olds. The first boy behind the leader was carrying the troop guidon, a pennant of the same predominant yellow. When the scoutmaster saw the men, he held up his hand to halt the boys. As fast as it had been drawn, Dellaporta's gun disappeared. "Hello," the leader said with uncertainty.

Parisi hurried over to him. "I'm sorry, are we in your area here?"

"No, I'm sure there's plenty of room for everyone."

"Hey, Chief," Tatorrio called out, "any of your men there got their badge in starting fires?"

Parisi looked at the fire pit and then the man. "Jesus, I'm sorry, your boys probably put all that wood in there."

"It's okay, one of the things they don't get badges for is sharing. This'll be good for the boys."

Parisi smiled warmly. "That's awfully nice. When you get them settled for the night, we'll buy you a drink."

The scoutmaster looked over his shoulder and in a low voice said, "I'll be needing one. Thanks."

As dusk settled over the Catskills, the air cooled, bringing everyone closer to the fire. As the flames found pockets of resin in the pine logs, they sputtered orange-white and sent up silky helixes of smoke. The scouts, prodded by their leader, started introducing themselves. Not sure of Cosa Nostra–Cub Scout etiquette, or how secret his crew's reconnaissance was, Jimmy Tatorrio gave his fellow campers the alias he had used during his Mohegan Sun junket, Johnny Waylon.

He passed out more sausages to the kids than he had intended and received cracked, blackened hot dogs in exchange. Some of Parisi's crew sneaked off to their ill-slung tents to lace their soft drinks and coffee with whiskey. Dellaporta thinly disguised his bottle in a brown paper bag and, as usual, ate nothing.

When it was good and dark, the natural but uncertain sounds of the woods had a marshaling effect, and Scoutmaster Bob, encouraged by his third cup of "coffee," told the all-too-familiar ghost story that ended with the killer's prosthetic hook hanging from the couple's car door.

One of the scouts, dreading more of the same, said, "How about you, Mr. Waylon, I'll bet you know some great ghost stories."

"I don't know, kid. I think all the ones I know are R-rated."

"Yeah," the other boys chimed in, wanting to hear them more than ever.

The scoutmaster smiled dizzily. "Yeah, Mr. Waylon, come on."

"Well, okay. Let's see . . . Once there was this man who lived in the city, in Brooklyn as a matter of fact. His name was Billy the Weasel, excuse me, William the Weasel." The boys giggled, leaning closer to the fire. "He had made many friends among the poor people by lending them money and charging only seven and a half percent. He was known as a man of great compassion and wisdom because of his understanding when someone was a little late with the vig."

"What's the vig?" the same boy asked.

Tatorrio looked over to the scoutmaster in an appeal for a change of subject, but Bob just stared back drunkenly, apparently as interested as the boys. "See, it's what you owe at the end of the week for what you borrowed. It's like rent, only on the money. It's a good thing. That way the borrower doesn't have to come up with the whole nut, and the lender makes those points every week."

A chubby boy with glasses asked, "Isn't that type of loan considered usury?"

"Ah, sure. You can use it for whatever you want. Just don't be late at the end of the week. Because then you've got to look at some ugly mutt like Gus here. And he won't be bringing hot dogs when he comes, if you know what I mean." The boys laughed harder, delighted at being made part of the story.

Fearing Tatorrio's well-known lack of restraint in front of an audience, Dellaporta, in a strained whisper, which everyone could hear, said, "What the F is wrong with you, telling these kids about me? That one with the glasses probably just decided to become a federal prosecutor."

Tatorrio took a couple more swallows and examined each of the boys' faces. He looked over at Baldovino. "Hey, Manny, I think Gus is right, isn't the redhead one of the Feds that locked you up?" The kids all twittered, and a couple of them slapped the "Fed" on the back.

Baldovino walked over to the boy. "Stand up." Fighting off laughter, the boy stood up, barely coming up to Manny's chest. "He's about the right age, but he's a foot too tall."

Tatorrio said, "Any of you guys wearing a wire? Mr. Dellaporta here is worried." The men's laughter drowned out the boys'.

"And now you give them my name? You are a moron, Mr. *Waylon.*" Dellaporta turned to the kids. "You want to know his real name—"

Mike Parisi interrupted. "Gus, let's keep things in perspective here."

"Yeah, Gus," Tatorrio said. "We're just telling a story here."

"Go ahead, Jimmy," Parisi said. "Finish up so the kids can get some sleep."

"Anyway, boys, don't worry too much about the finer points of banking. You'll learn all that stuff in college. Now back to William the Weasel. While he made many needy people happy, it made rival businessmen very sad because they had always lent money at ten percent. So they decided to do something about it. They got ahold of two, ah, customer service representatives and told them to have a little talk with the Weasel and convince him to either change his rates or, even better, maybe find another line of work. So they drove him over to Staten Island and discussed future business strategies. But William didn't like the tone of the meeting, so he went to those bad people at the FBI and told them about how the other businessmen were charging ten percent and everything else he knew about their operation. When the businessmen heard of this they were very, very upset. So they called in the customer service reps again and told them to make their problems go away permanently—if you know what I mean." A burst of laughter told Tatorrio that no further explanation was necessary. "So they took William up to these very woods, and he was never seen again. The end."

"What kind of ghost story is that? It's supposed to end with something scary," Dellaporta said.

"What, you don't think some guy lending at seven and a half per is scary?"

"You're supposed to scare the kids, not us, moron."

"Okay, okay." He lowered his voice conspiratorially. "When the service reps brought him up to the woods—and I'm sure you've guessed by now, it was to clip the Weasel—they asked him if he had a last wish. Without hesitating, he said he wanted some Italian sausage. The last thing anyone knows is that the three of them were sitting around, on a night just like tonight, cooking sausage. The next day they were all found with their stomachs ripped out. Supposedly something in these woods got all three of them. Something that's attracted to campfires and the smell of freshly cooked Italian sausage. They say it can smell it on your breath while you're sleeping."

Dellaporta looked directly at the boy with the glasses and smiled. "Man, am I glad I didn't have any sausage."

It was after ten a.m. before anyone from Parisi's crew crawled out of the tents. The first one up was Jimmy Tatorrio. He discovered that the scouts had broken camp and were gone. The rest of them rose stiffly, with no espresso or even coffee to comfort them. Parisi told them to pack up and get in their cars. He ran his papery tongue over his dry mouth and watched them stumble around clumsily, complaining, stretching their backs, running their hands over unshaved chins and attempting to reshape their hair without gels or creams or hair dryers. They were obviously incapable of functioning in any setting outside the slender, dark crevice of organized urban crime. Had they wanted to escape, he doubted if they ever could. Their lifestyles imprisoned them. Those Cub Scouts were more self-reliant, more self-assured than his crew, who seemed more like a collection of characters in a failing comedy. Walking over to the clearing where the scouts had pitched their tents, he couldn't detect any evidence that they had been there, while his area was strewn with the debris of a different civilization. He packed up his own gear, taking a little extra time to do it neatly.

Parisi got in his car and had the others follow him to the landmarks indicated on Manny's map. While he, Manny, and Ida spent the next hour trying to figure out how the Rosenkranz map connected to the terrain, Dellaporta and Tatorrio stood around watching them. "Maybe we should give them a hand," Tatorrio said.

"Yeah," Dellaporta said, "let's encourage them. Then we can all become one with the land. Maybe even stay another night or two. I'm sure Manny will be able to start a fire eventually."

When it became apparent that they could not find even the most marginal starting point, Parisi admitted, "We can't figure this out. Anyone have any ideas?"

"Yeah," said Tatorrio, "I was thinking about some nice veal for lunch. Maybe a little wine."

"Anyone else?" Parisi said, dismissing the humor, feeling like an outsider again.

Dellaporta said, "Hey, we had to give it a shot. And we did. It didn't work out, so we go back to the city where we belong, doing what we do."

Parisi knew he was right, but going back meant dealing with DeMiglia. Then an idea came to him. Maybe Dutch Schultz's elusive treasure wasn't a worthless myth after all.

16

THE DOOR TO LIBERTY LOAN SWUNG OPEN AND Jack Straker walked in wearing a suit. Sam Kasdan attempted to flatten his expression, but Straker sensed a small rush of anticipation in the pawnbroker. Kasdan considered everyone who came through that door an impending business transaction. This one, however, had nothing to do with money. He allowed himself a small grin. "Looks like someone got a haircut."

Straker ran his hand through the back of his hair where the fake ponytail had hung the night before. "It didn't go with my official look."

"You mean the suit? I hope my three hundred dollars didn't buy that."

"When I get to know you better, I'll tell you exactly what your money bought."

"As much as I would like to hear the intimate details of your life, with all due respect, I'd prefer to never see you again."

"As luck would have it, I've come to offer you exactly that. And before you say no, you should know it was me who made sure you got out on that PR bond."

"You seem to be skipping over the part that you were the reason I needed bail."

"We've all got a business to run."

"Fair enough. Let's hear the offer."

"Danny DeMiglia."

"Why would I want to trade my little problem for one that

size? My lawyer says I'm looking at probation—if convicted. And because of entrapment, that's a fairly large *if*."

"Let me save you some legal fees. It probably was entrapment, but see, the whole problem is when I get on the stand and the prosecutor asks me why we targeted you, I'll have to tell the jury that we were trying to get at DeMiglia. So then it's in the public record—law enforcement sees you as a link to the Galante family underboss. And I think you know that Danny's a big believer in missing links."

"What is it exactly that you want from me?"

"Judge Ferris." Kasdan started to protest his ignorance, but Straker held up a hand. "We don't think you know anything about it, we're just looking for a starting point with DeMiglia."

"Someplace you can wiretap."

"You know I can't admit something like that."

"How do I know these receiving and concealing charges will be dropped?"

"What, this doesn't look like a trustworthy face?"

"If I was able to judge your face more accurately, we wouldn't be having this conversation."

"Point taken. Just give me something that I can use, and I guarantee that before I leave, your problem will be gone."

"How are you going to do that?"

"Sorry, you'll have to pay to see my hole card."

"And my name?"

"Nowhere to be found."

"Okay," Kasdan said, "I've *heard* that when Danny wants to fence something, or discuss exchange rates, or anything else he doesn't want to hear coming from a courtroom tape recorder, the place he feels most secure is in his car. I know what you're thinking, but that's why he has it checked once a week."

"See, that wasn't so hard."

"That's it?"

"That's it."

"And now I don't have anything to worry about because . . ."

Straker smiled. "That Tiffany bowl, don't give it another thought. We've got sixteen more of them in evidence. And they're all going to be destroyed."

132 • PAUL LINDSAY

"Destroyed?"

"That's what the FBI does with counterfeits."

Lo Kim's was at the end of a narrow curved street, crammed into the clutter of Chinatown. Hanging in its window were half a dozen orange-glazed duck carcasses, but Danny DeMiglia hadn't come for the Peking duck. As part of his personal security program, he maintained a list of places he frequented no more than once a year to discuss business. That way, his attorney assured him, the government couldn't have them bugged. Wiretaps required court orders based on probable cause, something that depended on established patterns. Legally, once a year was not considered a pattern.

Part of Lo Kim's appeal was its small balcony with room for only one table. No one, not even the employees, could get close enough for what the Feds called "an overhear."

Mike Parisi walked in and sat down.

DeMiglia poured him some tea. "You found it okay?"

"If you're asking because I'm late, sorry."

"Only ten minutes." DeMiglia handed him a menu. "You hungry?"

"I had trouble finding parking."

"I like the congestion. Makes it harder to be followed. Especially with Angelo outside keeping an eye on things."

Parisi set the menu down without looking at it. "I had a late breakfast, but you go ahead." He wondered why the volatile underboss was being so accommodating. Ignoring tardiness, pouring tea—these things were not in Danny DeMiglia's nature. Had he found out about the don's improving health and decided to perform some damage control? Parisi doubted it. DeMiglia had never demonstrated any desire or aptitude for long-range diplomacy. He had worked his way up by being impulsive, taking care of problems when and where they happened. He was the noncommissioned officer, the one who got his knuckles skinned so the boss could strike a patriarchal pose. On the rare occasion when an underboss was promoted to don, his tenure usually proved short-lived due to his inability to make the transition from violent enforcer to savvy administrator.

The waiter climbed the stairs and in a thick accent asked, "You ready order?" DeMiglia could smell kitchen odors on him, most prominently peanut oil.

"For now, bring us both an order of egg rolls. With lots of that plum sauce."

Parisi figured he was about to be given *the* order, that the time had come to rob the diamond vault. But DeMiglia's uncharacteristic tact told him that he didn't want that order refused. A charge of disobedience would have to be decided by the commission, and that was always a questionable route. It could backfire and derail his plans. Contrarily, if he could convince Parisi, the don's anointed *capo*, to commit a violent crime and it brought the wolves of notoriety to the mob's door, DeMiglia would be in a position to make a strong case for a change in leadership.

DeMiglia possessed the one weakness that ambitious men of marginal intelligence all seemed to have in common, the need to prove himself smarter than everyone else. He needed to succeed where others failed; in fact, Parisi suspected that their failure was more satisfying to him than his own success. It was how men like him kept score, how they convinced themselves of who they were. He was not a man who lived off dead carcasses, but instead, rapacious, someone who dined on the living. While effective in the short run, his need to succeed while others failed was ultimately a flaw that carried the weight of its own destruction, and Parisi had an idea of how to use it against him. Delaying DeMiglia's plot to take over the family was now Parisi's primary mission. Maybe as much as a month would be needed, even though that now seemed impossible. But he had no choice but to try.

"I hope you're doing something about the Lag," DeMiglia said.

"I told you before, I had a long talk with Manny."

"Why would the Feds go after a lightweight like him?"

"He said they tried to get him to turn."

"No shit, little Manny. Has he got anything that could hurt us?"

Parisi knew DeMiglia was asking him if Manny needed to be eliminated. "Nothing. He couldn't hurt a fly even if he wanted to. But take my word on this, Danny, he'd never go over on us. He'd rather do all day than give any of us a minute of jail time. That's one of his strengths that's easy to overlook."

DeMiglia stared at him for a few seconds, testing the conviction of Parisi's assurances. "Okay, Mikey, but if something goes south with this idiot, it'll be your mess to clean up. As long as you understand that, I'm not going to give him another thought."

"Good." The waiter brought the egg rolls and quickly disappeared.

DeMiglia dipped one into the sweet-sour sauce and bit off the end. "You ready to make some real money?"

Parisi waited before he spoke. "You know, I've been thinking about that, Danny."

DeMiglia stopped chewing, leaned back, and loudly dropped his hands on the table.

Unintimidated, Parisi continued, "This diamond guy, who's into Jackie Two Shoes for two hundred K and obviously trying to stay healthy, says there's ten million in the vault. Which means, because he wants to be in our good graces, there's probably not even five. If we kill more than one person, that means the conversion rate on the stones will be far below the usual. At best, ten percent. Now we're looking at splitting up half a million dollars. After taking care of my uncle, me and my crew are probably looking at something in the neighborhood of fifty grand apiece. To tell you the truth, Danny, I'd rather sell handicap license plates."

DeMiglia leaned forward slowly. "Are you sure you want to refuse to do this?"

"You say this is about money. Is it?"

"What else would it be about?"

"Then I assume you would rather cut up thirty to fifty million dollars."

DeMiglia took another bite of egg roll and then laughed sarcastically. "Thirty to fifty million? Where's someone like you come up with a number like that?"

"Granted, this isn't a sure thing, but there's zero risk."

Ambivalence seized the underboss. He wanted Parisi out of the way, but the numbers he was offering—and, as Parisi had just demonstrated, he knew numbers—were impossible to ignore. He at least had to hear what it was about. "I'm listening, but it better be good."

"Dutch Schultz's treasure."

DeMiglia burst out laughing again. "Dutch Schultz's treasure? You got to be shitting me."

"Then you know about it."

"I've been hearing that tale since I was a little kid."

"What exactly did you hear about it?"

The unsettling sureness in Parisi's voice compelled DeMiglia to answer. "You know, he thought he was going to prison so he buried all this money and jewels in a metal box somewhere upstate. People been looking for it ever since. It's all bullshit."

"Two minutes ago, you were ready to believe in ten million from some degenerate gambler. Did you ever hear anything about a map?"

"Every good buried treasure story has a map—a missing map. I suppose you've found it."

In careful detail, Parisi told him how Manny's father had secreted the map in the New Jersey safe deposit box for twenty years, and how it had just been discovered.

In spite of not wanting to give Parisi a way out, DeMiglia said, almost to himself, "Manny's father wasn't nobody's mark."

"Exactly. So we take a minute or two to find out if there's anything to this."

"Where's the map?"

Parisi took out Joseph Baldovino's notebook and the map. He unfolded it and pushed it in front of DeMiglia.

"Well, it looks old, but who knows. They can make these things look old."

"You use that lawyer Max Stillman, don't you?"

"Yeah. He's the family's lawyer. What about him?"

"He's got to have someone who does document exams. Let him see if this is legit." Parisi had decided on the examination ploy because he knew "experts" usually charged by the hour so they took their time, and time was what he was looking for.

DeMiglia ran his fingertips across his lips three or four times. "I suppose it wouldn't hurt."

"If it's a phony, we haven't lost anything. If it's real, then we can figure out what to do next." Parisi could see the underboss was conflicted. For the moment, the treasure was at least as compelling as his ambition to become head of the family. Parisi just had to make sure the two became inseparable. "Here's what you have to remember, Danny. For three-quarters of a century, the men in our business have been trying to find the Dutchman's treasure. And they've failed. Their explanation is always the same: that the box doesn't exist. But just imagine if we do find it. We'd be as big a legend as Schultz, maybe even bigger. Would anyone be able to say no to the person who found Dutch Schultz's treasure?"

DeMiglia folded the map with unusual care. "Okay, I'll have it checked out, but for now, this doesn't go any farther than you and me. If it's a phony, I don't want to look like some moron."

Parisi handed him the notebook. "You'd better take this, too. It's in Manny's father's handwriting. To my eye, it looks like he's the one who wrote 'Lulu's Map.'" He didn't tell DeMiglia that the other half of the map was buried in some archival catacomb inside the New York FBI office. That would be discovered soon enough because it was spelled out in the senior Baldovino's journal. Also, Parisi hadn't explained how Tommy Ida had traced the genealogies of those mentioned in the book either, even though it would have lent even more authenticity to the map's promise. That trump card could be played later when DeMiglia, confronted by obstacles not yet visible, used the argument that no proof existed that the map was real and ordered the hunt to be abandoned. One problem at a time, Parisi reminded himself. That was the way to keep DeMiglia on the hook: keep the prize large and the hurdles small and distant. The important thing was to distract the underboss of the Galante crime family.

"The minute this comes back as bogus, you're doing that diamond job."

In a tone DeMiglia couldn't fully read, Parisi said, "You're the boss."

DeMiglia reached over and stabbed one of Parisi's egg rolls. "You're not going to eat these?"

* * *

Jack Straker was due for his interview with Lansing in five minutes. The inspector used the time to go through his personnel file again to make sure he had all the ammunition he needed to prove that Straker's performance in the FBI was in an advanced state of disrepair. The file revealed one problem after another, almost without a break. Why he had not been fired was inexplicable. Then he found the letter of commendation for the air piracy case and realized that it was Jack Straker who had fired the Shot. But that was a long time ago. In his second year, without any documented reason, he had been abruptly transferred from the range at Quantico to New York City as a street agent. That winter marked his first full-blown letter of censure and a forty-five-day suspension. Apparently tired of the snow, and without requesting leave, he drove a Bureau car to Florida, charging gas and lodging on an FBI credit card, an act egregious enough to get any other agent fired, but that wasn't the end of it. Once in Miami, he decided that the "clunky"—his word offered in defense—sedan was not suitable for such a well-deserved vacation. He traded it in for a convertible at a less-than-reputable used car dealership, using the Bureau credit card to make up the difference in the down payment.

There were also indications that he had cut a wide swath through the steno pool and other female support employees. No official complaints had been lodged, but the office services manager had filed a written protest that he was constantly distracting her girls. He was called in, and when told about the OSM's concerns, his response was, "Sounds like she needs a little servicing herself."

Without a knock, the door opened and Jack Straker smiled down at Lansing. "Am I late?"

"Yes you are. Have a seat."

Lansing noted that the stitches on Straker's forehead had been removed and the remaining scar seemed to add some ruggedness to his appealing face. He leaned back and pushed his hands into his pockets. "I've got to admit, that is one impressive personnel file you're working on there."

"Thank you."

"That's not meant as a compliment."

"I guess it all depends on your perspective. For me, there's a whole lot of living in those pages. Some *gooood* times."

"Good times? I think it's safe to say that any other agent would have been fired for any one of them. What I can't figure out is why you haven't been."

"I don't know. I guess like anything else, breaking rules can be done with varying amounts of style. I try to make mine as outrageously endearing as possible. Take the time they had a drug wire on some Cubans up here. The Miami office sends up this knockout translator because she was familiar with the dialect. I tried approaching her, but she had been warned not to fraternize with any of the agents. What was I supposed to do, let her slip away? So I got the number that they had the wiretap on, and I called it. The guy answers in Spanish, or Cuban, whatever it was, and I just started talking in English. I tell this gal how sexy I think she is, and if she wanted to see the real New York while she's up here to call me, and then I left my number. Where was the harm? The dope dealer didn't speak English, so he thought it was some wrong number or whatever. But when she was translating the tape and heard it, she called me. A violation of Bureau policy? I'm sure if you looked through enough manuals, you could find a rule or two bent, but the bottom line was that while she was up here she had a much better time. And so did I. Unfortunately, the Department of Justice had to go hat in hand to the judge who authorized the wire and explain what I had done. But after he thought about it for a minute, he laughed. See, that's me. A little bit outrageous, but at the same time begrudgingly admired. Be honest now, wouldn't you like to have that story on your résumé?"

"I'm curious. While you're sitting around dreaming up these excursions into the outrageous, do you ever feel any compulsion to accomplish any part of the Bureau's mission?"

"I've done some pretty fair undercover work."

"Oh yes, I saw the letter from the director's office mandating that you never be allowed to work undercover again. Seems when you were in Los Angeles staying in a four-star hotel, in a one-week period your hotel bill was thirty-eight thousand dollars."

Straker chuckled. "Yeah, and that wasn't easy. I was taking the bad guys out on the town and getting the restaurants and clubs to charge it to the hotel. The bottom line: we recovered three and a half million in laundered cash."

"Twelve of that thirty-eight thousand was for hookers."

"Escorts. Have you ever seen the high-end prostitutes in L.A.? They're beautiful, smart, and they can dance. I mean, you go out on actual dates because you want to be seen in public with them. Hooking those guys up with escorts was what turned the deal."

The interview wasn't going as Lansing had anticipated. "Since you're so willing to discuss your problems, let's talk about the misstep that landed you on this squad. The only thing I see in the file around that time is a very minor infraction of posting the wrong information on your locator card. That hardly seems worthy of a man of your appetites."

Straker smiled. "Do you think I should petition to have it removed?" Lansing just stared back dourly. "Actually, that's all they could put down on paper."

Lansing rolled forward in his chair. "Well, maybe it's time to set the record straight. Save your reputation."

"I'll bet you, right now, that after I tell you this story, you won't want to write any of it down anywhere."

Lansing considered Straker's ability to read the situations he became involved in and set his pen down. "Please proceed."

"As you can see by the date on the memo, it was a few years ago. At the time, we had this assistant director who was a real pain in the ass. I mean he would do anything to stick it to an agent. Fortunately for us, he also had a few weaknesses, two of which were booze and women, something I know about. I was acquainted with this woman who, let's just say, would do just about anything for money. So one night the ADIC was speaking at this corporate dinner, which I managed to get a ticket to. Twelve hours later and with the loan of some FBIHQ night photography equipment, I was able to convince him that a man with such unusual urges needed to treat agents with a little more respect. Which he did until he retired a year later. But I guess he had the last laugh because the last Bureau document he signed was my transfer out here."

Lansing slapped the personnel file shut. "You evidently take great pride in your candor. In fact, I'd say you enjoy shocking people with it. I hope you're going to be equally candid about the night you all were working on the Dimino case. I believe that was the night you were injured."

"Well, I think I've proven during our little chat here that I can be as honest as anyone, but about that night . . . did you know that the cut on my head took fourteen stitches, but the real injury was actually a concussion. Damnedest thing, I can't remember a minute of what happened. I have a note from the doctor at the ER. Should I bring it in?"

Although his mouth was held in a straight, unemotional line, Straker's eyes were smiling. His "candor" during the interview could, if necessary, be later offered as evidence of his not hiding anything, no matter how damning or embarrassing. Lansing felt relatively certain that among an undoubtedly large cache of mitigating documents suitable for every occasion, Straker could produce some sort of medical record verifying a bout of temporary amnesia, or spinal meningitis, or multiple personality. Lansing had been checkmated. Without a word, he bowed his head in defeat and gave a gracious backhand wave toward the door.

17

VANKO'S PHONE RANG. IT WAS AN APOLOGETIC Ralph Hansen. "Nick, I'm sorry I didn't get back to you right away. The chief inspector has been running me ragged. What's up?"

"Sheila Burkhart."

"Who's that?"

"Female agent. Shipped out here. Without a heads-up."

"Oh yeah, yeah. Sorry about that," the SAC said. "Have you talked to her?"

"She said she was working a serial murder too hard."

"Well, it's a little worse than that. According to the supervisor running the task force, she's pretty much lost it. I think his words were 'absolutely obsessed.' He said there was just one homicide, and she was trying to make it into something more."

"You sure he wasn't just trying to get rid of her? She seems pretty outspoken."

"No, it wasn't anything like that. He said she was a phenomenal worker. That was the whole problem. She became obsessed with finding the killer. A couple of the New York detectives read her the same way."

"You mean it's now become possible to work too hard in this outfit?"

"Nick, that's as much as I know about it. Here, I'll give you the number for the task force. Call the supervisor. He can fill you in. She hasn't been causing you any problems, has she?"

"No. In fact she admitted that she had gone a little overboard working the case. She seems a little intense, but, you know, in a good way. I just want to hear what a normal day from her is like."

"Call the supervisor. Bill Henken. He can fill you in. But if you think she's about to start taking hostages, don't hesitate to let me know."

"I'll give him a call."

Vanko was transferred once before getting the supervisor on the line. "I'm calling about Sheila Burkhart. She's been transferred to my squad."

"I'm sorry I had to move her out, Nick; she's a hell of a worker. One of those people with no life outside the job. Unfortunately, it got out of hand. Did she tell you about her *serial killer* case?"

"Just that only one of the victims had been found."

"There *is* only one victim, a twelve-year-old from Spanish Harlem, a year ago. But every time a girl runs away or is missing up there for a few hours, Sheila started looking for a way to link it to the Suzie Castillo case. She runs around interviewing every known sex offender in the tristate area even if they're just flashers, trying to attribute everything to some serial murderer stalking East Harlem. I couldn't get her to go home. I mean I had to threaten her so she'd leave at night, then it got to the point where she'd sneak back after I left."

"So far, she sounds like a supervisor's dream."

"You saw her. She didn't look like that when she got here. I mean—God forgive me—she was no dazzling beauty when she reported in, but she looks considerably worse now. She's lost weight, and I think she forgets to comb her hair half the time."

"She does look a little run-down."

"Some of the guys were having their wives pack an extra lunch for her because either she didn't have an appetite or was too busy and would forget to eat, we don't know. But the final straw was when she moved."

"Moved where?"

"Up to East Harlem. *El barrio.* Didn't give any notice to her landlord in Queens, nothing. Left all her personal stuff behind."

"Do you think the Castillo girl was a serial killing?"

"It was a rape-murder, so it could have been, who knows. But these people get caught for other crimes and spend the rest of their lives in jail and never get matched up. The important thing is no one's killed any more girls since then. There's enough to do in this city without creating monsters, so we've moved on. She couldn't."

"I appreciate the information, Bill."

"Don't get me wrong, she's great. If I had a dozen like her I'd put myself out of business. It's just that she needed to get away from that case."

After he hung up, Vanko buzzed Abby at her desk. "Did Sheila give you her address?"

"Ah, let me see. Yes, here it is."

"Where is it?"

"Can this be right—East Harlem?"

Sheila Burkhart was hunched over her Bureau-issue laptop entering names, dates of birth, and Social Security numbers into it. At it for hours, she was unaware that the sun had set and the only light in her apartment was the optic gray glow from the computer screen. Her workstation was a battered Formica and chrome dinette table that had come with the one-room third-floor walk-up. She had pushed the table against the nearest wall, which she used as a bulletin board. Tacked to it was a detailed map of the neighborhood and five crime-scene photos from the Suzie Castillo case, her twisted body proof of the unmistakable violence that had caused her death, her face blue, swollen, decaying. Above them was a school photo of the pretty twelve-year-old. On the right side of the map, as if buffered from the violence, were photos of eight other young girls, supplied to the police by parents.

A soft knock at the door startled her. For a panicked moment she couldn't recall where her gun was. Then she reached under the table for her briefcase and retrieved her nine-millimeter. Getting up from the table, she suddenly realized it was dark out. Who could this be? She flattened herself against the wall next to the door. As loudly and violently as possible, she drew the slide back to chamber a round. "*¿Quién es?*" she demanded, then lowering her voice into a more menacing range, "*¿Que quiere?*"

"I come in peace, Sheila."

"Nick?"

"Yes ma'am." She undid the locks and opened the door. Vanko stood in the hallway's pale yellow light, a pizza box in one hand and twelve-pack of beer in the other. Seeing the gun dangling from her hand, he suddenly questioned why he had come. He wasn't any more ready for this than she was. "I'm sorry, this isn't the right kind of beer?"

She stepped aside and invited him in. "You know what I love most about New York? Men keep bringing me food. Looks like somebody called my old supervisor."

Switching on the light, she set down the gun and took the pizza box from him, the odor of cheese and sauce displacing the dank, mildewy air. "How crazy did he say I was?"

He looked around the room. "Pretty crazy."

"Pretty crazy by their standards or by yours?"

"They said you moved here."

"Sounds like you're about to agree with them."

"I probably will, but give me a minute to make it look like I'm judging you fairly." He cracked open two cans of beer and handed one to her. The apartment was dismal. The living room, if it could be classified as that, was no more than an extension of the kitchen. Against the far wall was an aged purple velvet couch, its arms threadbare, a folded blanket and pillow at one end. A low table sat in front of it crowded with stacks of folders. She moved them onto the floor and put down the pizza.

He took a sip of beer and walked over to the kitchen table, scanning the stacks of documents and the half-finished page on the laptop screen. Next to it was a small box with young girls' photographs. Each had a pinhole at the top suggesting that at one time they had been tacked to the wall. He looked at the map and photos on the wall. He noticed something curious about Suzie Castillo's school picture. He studied the photos of the eight other girls on the opposite side of the map. Three of them shared the same unusual characteristic, which he decided not to tell Sheila about. The last thing she needed was encouragement.

All four faces in question were distinctly Hispanic, each exceptionally pretty with striking chiaroscuro features. All the reports of Sheila's abnormal behavior made him wonder if she was driven by some sort of delusional fantasy about their beauty. Then, taking another swallow of beer, he decided that if anyone was overwrought, it was him.

He stared at her until she felt his gaze. She had a way of listening to him that made him feel that the only thing more important than what he was about to say was that it was him saying it. He wondered if she was that receptive to everyone, which made him realize that he didn't really know her. It was too soon to be doing this. For two people who were so straightforward, coming here was turning out to be unbelievably awkward.

"Don't get me wrong," he said, "I'm a big fan of obsession. It's made my job a lot more interesting, but in a good year, there are more than a thousand homicides in the city. Why are you letting this one eat you up?"

"One? I guess we know whose side you landed on."

"Do you think I came here because I'm on someone else's side? You were transferred from the task force so you wouldn't work this. You're the one who told me it had ahold of you. And it doesn't look like it's getting any better."

Calmly, she said, "This guy has killed more than one girl."

"Okay, then where are the victims?"

Sheila pointed at the eight photographs on the wall. "Right there."

Vanko went over to the kitchen table and picked up the box of pinholed photos. "Then who are these? Weren't all of them on the wall at one time?" When she didn't answer, he said, "They found their way home, didn't they?"

She collapsed on the couch, trying to decide if this was the same man whose honesty she had found so rare when they met. She knew he was, and that made his judgment about her more reliable than her own. She studied his crooked face for a long time. He didn't seem to mind. This was someone she would always be able to trust. "This is *eating me up* because they are all so beautiful. At that age, they are as perfect as they will ever be, and even if he's only killed Suzie Castillo, that's reason enough." Her tone gave a final surge of protest. "And just maybe I was put here to get a little crazy."

"And who's making sure you don't become a casualty?"

Her eyes softened and she looked down. "I do keep having nightmares. The usual stuff: chasing this shadowy figure, shooting and missing, out of ammunition, being shot at with no place to hide. But they always end the same way: I stumble across another body."

"I've had dreams, too. Mine mostly involve car crashes. Do you know what the worst part is for me? That I'm always alone."

She stared at him for a few moments. "Yes." Then the corners of her mouth curled mischievously. "Well, Nikko, to answer your question about who's making sure I don't become a casualty, I believe that unfortunate torch has been passed to you." She flipped open the pizza box.

He spotted a package of paper napkins in the kitchen. Taking out two, he walked to the couch. With a flourish, he shook one out and covered her lap with it. Her thighs registered the paper's frail pressure, anticipating something more—the weight of his touch. But it never came. Long ago, after declaring loneliness a vice, she had ordered herself to disconnect from those feelings and had pulled a shield between herself and any future expectations. There were other, more "noble" ways to burn each day from the calendar. It hadn't been a perfect diversion, but it worked well enough—until now, when a single moment of anticipation had extinguished a fairly reliable system of denial. But he had given no indication of feeling the same way. She began to wonder if he had come because he was a man, or because he was a good boss.

He sat down across from her, spreading a napkin across his own lap. She watched as his hands settled onto it. Then she realized he was waiting for her to start.

Nick Vanko stepped into his apartment and flipped on the light. The sound had an unusual hollowness to it, as if the one-bedroom loft had been stripped of its furnishings during his absence. It always looked the same, no matter what he was doing. The furniture, most of which had been purchased as floor samples, was arranged like a set for some glossy magazine. He thought of Sheila's apartment and smiled.

The quiet began buzzing in the back of his head like an approaching army of cicadas. Maybe a movie would distract him. He had a collection of more than two hundred black-and-white videos. There was something about the old movies he loved—the lighting, the preposterous sets, the two-dimensionality. But most of all it was the stories' stark moral dilemmas. He pushed *David and Lisa* into the VCR. As the credits rolled, his thoughts raced to the final scene, which he had seen a dozen times. David, a young man in a mental facility who is unable to let anyone touch him, falls in love with another patient, Lisa, and just before the final credits, in another of Hollywood's miracles, lets her touch him. It should have been the perfect distraction, but happy endings sold tickets only because they were so elusive in real life. He turned off the VCR and opened a couple of windows to let in the street noise below his SoHo loft, but tonight it was disappointingly quiet.

He and Sheila had finished the pizza and half the beer. Despite the dreary surroundings, they fell into a relaxed conversation about growing up in places as diverse as Iowa and New Jersey. For someone so obsessed, her sense of humor was uninhibited, and the more they talked, the more incisive it became. Little, it seemed, escaped her notice.

But then an unexplainable silence descended between them. Thinking back, Vanko realized it was simply the point at which a man and a woman, having fulfilled the routine social requirements of an encounter, would have moved on to the physical, would have found a way to touch. Even though both Nick and Sheila suspected the other felt a similar attraction, neither could ask the other to ignore their own unattractiveness. Years of uneasy glances had led them both to fear that only attractive people could feel the warmth of intimacy. To test this hypothesis and fail would leave them without hope.

He had sat parked outside her apartment for a while, thinking about how the evening had ended and wondering if he had missed some cue. Had there been any? Some neighborhood children were playing barefoot around an open hydrant to escape the August heat, their clothing pasted against their chubby brown bodies. Unnoticed by the others, one delighted boy fired his massive squirt rifle at them. Parents sat on cars parked on the sidewalk watching them, placidly smoking cigarettes and drinking beer.

Until tonight, the car accident had been the perfect coupling of crime and punishment for Vanko. At the mirror the first time, instead of pity, he found his mangled image redemptive. A normal progression toward wife and family was over, undeserved, forfeited by a few moments of self-indulgence. But now that desire had been reawakened, his self-imposed exile was in desperate need of revocation. He wanted to touch her. Just grazing her skin would have been enough, even casually, an accident they both would have known was intentional. Unlike visual recollection, aggraded by a million freeze-frames a day, touch was the sense of darkness. He wanted that single, isolated pressure, so distinct, so retrievable, a private channel to reconnect with her on demand. Vanko could still see her profile and, although it remained uncommonly plain, it aroused him. He needed to feel her.

The evening ended all at once. No "It's getting late," not even "I'll see you tomorrow." She walked him to the door, not even shaking his hand, as if she, too, suffered the same fear. They both knew when the evening, along with its invisible borders, had been exhausted. To venture any further might threaten whatever came next.

Vanko hadn't noticed when the four teenage boys came up to his car. One of them knocked on the window to get his attention and threw his palms up angrily. Vanko understood that to mean LEAVE.

He passed a fruit market that was still open, a storefront church, a laundry where the women stood around outside to escape the heat of the dryers. Graffiti was everywhere, some of it exceptionally colorful and well drawn. He stopped at a light. Four or five pairs of old sneakers hung from its crossbar. On a brick wall next to a bodega was a mural of a young brown-skinned man with a black, seagull-shaped mustache. Above the huge head were the words "In memory of Enrique Rabadan." Toward the bottom, now mostly worn away, were the dates his life began and ended—twenty-one years in all. At the next corner was a wrecked NYPD car. A front-end collision with a white airbag hanging limply from the dashboard. The bumper had fallen off and lay immediately underneath. Vanko could see that it had been there for a while. It reminded him of those images in Afghanistan after the Soviets had left, their destroyed tanks along the roadside like some monument to the nation's indomitability.

The humidity felt like it was pouring in the open windows, so he closed them before dialing his sister's number.

"'Lo."

"Nancy, it's Nick."

"Mmmm, hi."

"You were sleeping."

He could hear her turn over. "It is almost one in the morning. Anything wrong?"

"No, nothing. It's nothing. Sorry, I'll call you tomorrow."

"No, it's all right. Just let me slip downstairs so I won't wake the kids."

After a minute, she said, "I don't know which is more surprising, you calling this late or not knowing what time it is. What's up?"

"I've met someone. I think."

"You think?"

"Just recently. I'm not sure how she feels."

"So you're calling in the middle of the night trying to get me to tell you some woman I don't know is interested in you."

"That's what I love about you the most, the way you beat around the bush to spare my feelings."

"As firstborn, that's my job. So, who is she?"

"She's an agent. Sheila Burkhart."

"Interesting that you put her profession before her name."

"Meaning what, Doctor?"

"Like it's something you had to get off your chest. Is there something wrong with a woman having that job? Christ, Phil sells insurance. No, wait a minute. This isn't a test run to see how Mom and Dad are going to react, is it?"

"No . . . well, maybe a little."

"To tell you the truth, I'd be surprised if at this point they'd object to anyone of a childbearing age. Anyway I already like her."

"Why?"

"Because she isn't Greek."

"You do remember that we're Greek."

"Only too well. I'm the good daughter; I married a nice Greek boy."

"What's wrong with that? Phil is a good guy."

"Phil's a great guy. And most of the time I feel very lucky. It's just that sometimes the whole thing gets so Old Country. Every Sunday at the restaurant with the cast of thousands. Weddings are month-long nightmares that seem to occur every two weeks. And funerals, well, you know those are always the Greeks' finest hours."

"Weddings and funerals? Let's slow it down a little, I just met her. I needed to talk to someone. It's all kind of uncharted territory, since . . ."

"The accident. It's all right to say it, Nick."

"Okay, okay. I just don't want to get my expectations up."

"Why not? Life is expectations."

"Even false expectations?"

"You have to look at the possible consequences. Isn't what might happen worth taking a minor ding to your ego if it doesn't work out?"

Vanko laughed. "I'm afraid when it comes to this stuff, there's no room left on my ego for even minor dings."

"Enough, Nikko. Did you call for advice or for someone to listen to you wring your hands?"

"With some reluctance, I'll choose advice."

"Then pick up the phone right now. Calling in the middle of the night will show her you're interested. It sounds like someone needs to take a risk."

"Thanks, Nancy. I'll let you know."

Despite knowing his sister was right, he wasn't ready to completely throw caution to the wind. He could talk to Sheila about what he had seen in the photographs. She answered on the first ring.

"It's me."

"Me who?" she teased.

"The guy who was at your apartment tonight."

"You're going to have to be a little more specific."

"You know, tall, dark, Picasso-esque."

She laughed. "Oh, Supervisor Vanko."

"I need to ask you something, but I don't want to start an argument over it."

"I'll do my best."

"How sure are you that there's a serial killer?"

"Does that mean you don't think I'm crazy?"

"I guess that depends on your answer. The task force says there's only one victim. You said you think there's more."

"Fair enough. I think he's now disposing of the bodies instead of displaying them like he did with the first one."

"Are serial killers able to change their MOs like that? I thought part of their power trip was showing off their handiwork."

"It is. But don't forget what I said. Each one of them is different. After Suzie Castillo was found, we started asking people for DNA samples. The media got wind of it and reported that the killer had left biological evidence at the scene or on the victim. He knew he screwed up. I think he just started disposing of the bodies after that, knowing that a single homicide in East Harlem is much easier to forget about than a serial killer stalking young girls. And if I'm right, it's worked, because everybody has moved on from the Suzie Castillo case."

"Then who are his other victims?"

"You saw the photos on my wall."

"And I saw the ones you took *off* the wall because they had found their way home."

"Most of those eight that are still up there have been missing longer than any of those in the box. Are some of them runaways? Maybe. But I've talked to all these families. Some of these girls are simply not the kind to take off."

"Okay, how many of the eight are possible victims?"

"All of them . . . none of them, I don't know," she said. "If you don't believe there are other victims, why are you asking me these questions?"

He thought again about the way she was living. Even if Suzie Castillo was the killer's only victim, maybe they could get lucky and catch him. "Okay. I saw something in those photos."

He could already hear her moving across her apartment toward the wall.

"Look at the school photo of Suzie. See how there's a faint glow of light around her?" Sheila didn't answer. "You have to look closely. She has a few hairs out of place. They're much lighter in color. It's caused by a technique called rim lighting. It's done by putting a low-intensity light source immediately behind the subject and using a darker background."

"I can see it now."

"I've never heard of a school photographer going to that much trouble."

"Like he enjoys his work a little too much."

"Possibly, but that's not all. Of your eight missing girls, I spotted three of them photographed with the same technique."

"I see it. So out of these nine girls, four of them were photographed by the same person."

"That's what it looks like. It could be just a coincidence."

"Would it be all right if I took a couple of days to check it out?"

"Maybe it wouldn't take that long if some of the squad helped you."

She was quiet for a moment. "You don't know how much I appreciate that, Nick."

"I like the sound of that."

18

MIKE PARISI WAS THE ONLY ONE IN THE KITCHEN when the phone rang. "Hello."

"Who's this?" The voice was a little unsure.

"This is Mike. Who's this?"

"You don't need to know who this is, Mike. I used to live in the neighborhood, and you guys helped me out of a small jam once. I'm just calling to repay the favor."

"Okay."

"I saw that crap in the paper about that Baldovino guy getting arrested and how the fucking FBI made fun of him, but there's something the papers don't know about the FBI."

"Go on."

"I live over in Jersey now, and I got this neighbor, he's with the FBI. He doesn't tell anybody, but his kid told my kid. Couple of days ago I'm watching the news, and they're talking about this broker named Sam Shelby being arrested for insider trading. They show him being brought out in handcuffs. He's holding his hands up trying to hide from the camera, but I see it's this agent. His real name is Garrett Egan. I don't like him. He's one of these people who's always looking down his nose at you. At first I'm thinking this is some kind of undercover deal, but then I figured out it can't be. He wouldn't have been on TV like that where people could blow his cover. And ever since then, we haven't seen him or his family. They don't come out. Our kids play Little League together. They stopped coming to the games. And now their house is up for sale. And it's priced to sell quick. Evidently he needs money. Couldn't happen to a nicer guy. Anyway I just thought you'd like to know. Maybe you could call the reporter who did the story on your friend and tell him about it. I'd love to see that in the paper."

"I'd like to see that myself. I appreciate this, . . ."

"Chris."

"Why don't you give me a number where I can get ahold of you."

"Sorry, I just wanted to help you guys out. Like I said, you helped me out of a jam in the neighborhood a ways back, and I always felt like I owed you one. Maybe this'll even us." He hung up.

Parisi turned around to find DeMiglia's driver, Angelo, standing behind him. It had only been two days since he had given the map to the underboss, and he had hoped it would take a long time to have its authenticity decided.

"Danny would like to see you. Outside. In the car." Had the map proven a forgery—or worse, had DeMiglia found him out? If it was good news, why hadn't the underboss come himself? As he walked out of the club, he silently chanted the don's words: *Panic is an enemy.* Angelo opened the back door to the Cadillac and Parisi got in.

"You think that's cute not telling me it was only half the map? That the Feds have the other half?" DeMiglia said. "What kind of cutesy bullshit is that?"

"I knew you'd find out, it's right in the journal, but you were so skeptical I thought if I told you that, you'd blow the whole thing off without getting it checked. And if it was a fraud, then it wouldn't matter if half was missing."

DeMiglia thought about it for a few seconds. "You're right, I wouldn't have had it checked."

"Is it real?"

Smugly, DeMiglia asked, "Do you know anything about those guys that check documents?"

"Not really."

One corner of DeMiglia's mouth turned up. "All these so-called experts, they're scared to death of being wrong, so they'll never come right out and say, Yes, it's a forgery, or, No, it's legit."

DeMiglia picked up the map from the seat. It and Joseph Baldovino's journal were now encased in a large clear plastic envelope. "The bottom line is, the best these guys will say is"—and now he read—"'no evidence of forgery.' But he did say that the handwriting at the edge of the map with the words 'Lulu's map' was written by the same person who wrote in the journal. Manny's sure that's his old man's handwriting, right?"

"He's positive. You have to admit, it is pretty distinctive."

DeMiglia went on, "Also the paper used for the map was 'consistent in its construction with that used sixty-five to seventy years ago.' The same thing for the paper in the book 'twenty to twenty-five years ago.' And there was 'no feathering of the ink in either document.'"

"What's feathering?"

"The way he explained it to me, when paper gets old, it becomes dry and"—he looked at the second page of the report—"porous. If you try to get old paper and write on it, the ink gets blurry, that's feathering. Not to the naked eye, but he's got one of these super-microscopes and can see all that little bullshit. So what's he's saying is the ledger was written twenty years ago and the map seventy-five years ago. Now the clincher is the 'foxing.' Do you know what that is?"

"Foxing? No."

"Old paper gets these little patches on them. They're different colors. I think he said moisture causes them. Almost like the paper gets moldy. On the map, there was 'evidence of foxing,' while on the journal, there was none at all."

"Why would that be?"

"At first he said he couldn't be sure, but then he asked if I knew where they were stored. When I told him about the bank vault, he said that would prove they were authentic because the controlled temperature and humidity there wouldn't produce foxing."

"But because the map was fifty years old before it was put in the vault, it would have foxing," Parisi said.

"Exactly. Then he said that he had wondered why the foxing on the map wasn't a little more developed, but being in the vault for the last twenty years would explain that."

"So the map is real."

"I finally got him to say that, but only off the record. There's one other thing he found." DeMiglia flipped to the last page. "By the way, I didn't tell him what it was a map to." He went back to the report. "'Next to the X that is presumed to mark the object of the map, there is the beginning of a line drawn leading toward the torn edge of the paper, indicating that a line may have been present before the document was divided. The other detailing on the map indicates that this line may have been consistent with other areas on the map, which contained additional directions.'" Parisi nearly mentioned that he had also noticed the mark, but remembered DeMiglia's disdain for anyone who knew more than he, or as much.

"In other words," DeMiglia continued, "it looks like when they cut up the map, they tried to make sure the treasure couldn't be found without both halves put back together."

"Now that we know it's real, maybe we can find it anyway."

"Hey, it was a fun little pipe dream, but without the other half, it's over. Face it, Mike, it's time to get to work on other plans."

Uncharacteristically, Parisi found himself wondering just how well guarded the FBI office was. Could a good burglar get in there at night or on the weekend? But they had to have thousands of files, how would he find it? Then it hit him.

"Danny, what if I could come up with a way to get the other half?"

"No more bullshitting around. You're doing the diamond job. I'm calling Jackie Two Shoes and buying that hebe's paper."

Parisi gave him the details of the phone call about the FBI agent. Revenge ignited in DeMiglia's eyes. To give the possibilities a few seconds to sink in, Parisi lit a cigarette and blew out a long stream of smoke. "Maybe we can flip this guy. Think about it. We'll offer him money for the file. It's not like he's giving up government secrets, he's just returning our property. He's going to get fired anyway. He needs money to pay back what he stole. It's not that far-fetched."

"How do you know it's even true about this guy? Maybe it's somebody who looked like him."

"Like I told you, the guy who called is his neighbor. The family hasn't gone out since it happened, and they put the house up for sale."

"Can you call this guy back and get some more info?"

"No. He just gave me his first name. Chris." Both men sat thinking until Parisi said, "Wait a minute. The phone in the kitchen's got caller ID."

They hustled out of the car. In the back room, Parisi grabbed the cordless handset and pressed the search button. "Here it is, Christopher's Plumbing Supply. He said the agent lived in his neighborhood in New Jersey."

"Call him."

Parisi hit the redial button.

"Christopher's Plumbing Supply. This is Chris. Can I help you?"

"Chris, Mike Parisi."

There was dead quiet. "Yeah, Mike, how'd you get this number?"

Apparently DeMiglia was right. "We have lots of friends, Chris. And very few enemies. And you called us as a friend, right?"

"Right."

"And we want it to remain that way. I need that agent's phone number and address."

"You're not going to do anything to him, are you?"

"And have the entire FBI after us? No, I'm thinking about your idea of calling the papers. If they had his phone and address we would be taken a lot more seriously. Plus it would be easier for them to make his life miserable."

"Oh, yeah, sure. I'll get it. Hold on." When he came back on the line, he said, "Okay, let me see . . . here it is."

After the plumbing-shop owner gave him the numbers, Parisi said, "Chris, if you ever need anything, you've got our number."

"Thanks." There was some hesitation in his answer. Parisi supposed he was wondering if they were going to call the newspaper with the information or whether more drastic plans were being made. "But I told you why I was doing this."

Parisi hung up. "I've got to say, Mike, that wasn't bad." DeMiglia looked at the piece of paper with the agent's phone number and address and handed it back. "In fact, it was so good I think you can handle Agent Garrett Egan yourself."

Parisi was surprised. DeMiglia had a reputation for believing that revenge was a dish most delicious served hot and from his own hand. As he now did with every order from the underboss, Parisi searched for its false bottom. This one was relatively easy to locate. To turn the agent, a bribe would have to be offered. Ever cautious, DeMiglia did not want to be the one who could be charged with the crime. And at the same time, should Parisi be arrested in the act, it was almost as good as sending him out on the diamond job, which saved DeMiglia the fifty thousand he would have had to pay the New Jersey bookie to assume the diamond merchant's uncollectable gambling debts, an amount he evidently felt worth its potential return. Parisi felt pleased with himself for developing insights into such stratagems. Then another reason for the large payout occurred to him. If the plan backfired and DeMiglia's motives were questioned for sending the inexperienced *capo* to commit such a crime, the large sum of money, out of his own pocket, could be offered as proof of his good intentions.

The important thing right now was that DeMiglia had been sidetracked again. But Parisi had worked himself into the very corner he had tried to avoid: the FBI on one side and Danny DeMiglia on the other. As walnuts went, not very promising.

Garrett Egan let his phone ring a dozen times before he answered.

"Garrett?"

Egan didn't recognize the voice, an occurrence that, since his arrest, had made him extremely cautious. "Who's calling?"

"Someone who wants to help you."

Egan laughed harshly. "This should be good."

"I'm dead serious. You need money; I have money."

"Who is this?"

"Lots of money."

"I'm hanging up unless you tell me who this is."

Parisi sensed Egan's reluctance to do so. Chris had to be right about him being desperate. "You're going to have to meet with me to find out."

"I'd have to be nuts."

Egan sounded like he was trying to convince himself more than Parisi.

"This is all very friendly. I'm talking about a lot of money with a minimum of effort."

"Sounds like a way to get into trouble."

"I was hoping it sounded like a way out of trouble," Parisi said.

"Whoever you are, I'm going to pass. Don't call here anymore."

"I can call you, or I can call the newspapers . . . Sam Shelby."

"Who are you?"

"I'm a person who needs a small favor, nothing illegal. No risk to you."

After a long pause, Egan asked, "How much is a lot of money?"

"It's negotiable, but no less than five figures."

Again Egan didn't answer right away, but Parisi knew the agent didn't have any choice if he wanted to spare his family further disgrace. "Someplace very public. The Green Ridge Mall in an hour. Outside the cigar shop."

"I'll have a newspaper under my arm. And Garrett—or Sam—in an hour and a half, it'll be too late. I'll have called the papers."

With just an hour left until closing, the mall was quickly becoming deserted. Egan sat as far from the cigar shop as he could and still keep an eye on its front door. He watched with dark amusement as the shoppers thinned from around him. *Even here.* Even here, he was becoming more alone by the minute. With the FBI methodically severing all ties to him, it seemed like the entire world was becoming part of the conspiracy. *Great, the first signs of paranoia.* He shifted his weight on the hardwood bench and discreetly tried to read the faces hurrying toward the exits.

The caller was taking advantage of his situation, but right now, as much as anything, Egan needed to believe in something, any pinprick of light ahead, and the promise of money always glowed brightest with the illusion of hope. He closed his eyes and forced himself to forget about the cigar shop. The themeless mall music, which had increased its tempo to allegro, urged shoppers to decide on that last purchase.

Anyone with a shred of sense would have gone to the Bureau

after being approached. He didn't need any more trouble, certainly not any with this potential. But the last thing FBI management wanted to deal with was another problem that had attached itself to the soon-to-be ex-agent. While the red tape of dismissal ground away at its own indifferent pace until it was safe to fire him, he was already being treated like he no longer worked there. The only one who didn't seem intent on stripping him of what little remained of his self-worth was his new supervisor. His offer of time off was an accommodation that, should it come to light, could be interpreted as giving aid and comfort to the enemy. But Egan's situation was well beyond the repair of well-meaning noncombatants. One of the unwritten laws of capitalism was that when money broke something, only money could fix it. With enough of it, he could repay what he had taken. Even if not in full, an earnest down payment could be used by a good lawyer to keep him out of prison. He opened his eyes and started toward the tobacco shop. It was time to meet the caller.

Mike Parisi checked his watch. He bought a newspaper, tucked it up under his arm, and walked out of the shop.

Egan spotted him right away, but waited to make sure he was alone. Finally he walked over to him.

"Garrett?" Egan nodded. "Let's go to the food court, I'll buy you a coffee."

As they walked, Egan examined his face. "Do I know you?"

"No. And like I told you on the phone, I don't want to cause you any heartburn."

"You don't think you've already done that?"

"It was important that I talk to you."

They sat down at a table and Parisi said, "How do you take it?"

"I don't want any coffee. Just get to the point."

"There's something we need for you to get for us. And if you do that, you'll be well paid."

"Who is we?"

"I belong to a certain family."

"Oh, shit."

"Wait a minute. It's nothing like that. There was a piece of property that belonged to one of our previous members and you guys confiscated it twenty years ago. We want it. It's just a book."

"What's in it?"

"Nothing that is going to endanger the safety of the country. It's not even evidence. It's a private matter. Useful to no one but us."

"Just a book."

"A twenty-year-old book."

"How much?"

"I told you, five figures, and that's as specific as I'm going to get right now."

"Well, *right now* I have enough problems. How do I know this isn't going to bring me more?"

"Let's say you get the book and give it to me. I pay you. I'm not sure of the federal law, but I believe that technically puts me in possession of stolen government property. Exactly who do you think I want to tell about that?"

"And if I say no?"

"I think we discussed that on the phone. If you care about your family, you don't have that option."

"You're a cocksucker."

"I know," Parisi said. "And now that that's out of your system, let's move on."

"Can I have tonight to think about it?"

"Not that there's a lot to think about, but sure, I'll call you tomorrow. I know this is out of the blue, but I'm being straight with you. When it wears off, you'll see this as a blessing in disguise."

"Yeah. A really good disguise."

No sooner had Mike Parisi left the mall than his cell phone rang. DeMiglia wanted to know how it had gone. Parisi had some reservations that he had already decided could not be admitted to the underboss, the biggest of which was the possibility that Egan would tell the FBI about the offer to ease his own problems. That didn't seem likely, but then nothing in this increasingly entangled farce did. Divulging even the smallest tremor of pessimism might cause DeMiglia to abandon the hunt for the treasure and refocus on his original, more tangible, target. "He's in," Parisi said. Even if Egan wound up turning him down, the lie might give him another day or two. Right now that was the only out he had. "He needs money, and you know that's the best thing we can ask for."

"When's he going to get it?"

"He said he would need some time to scout it out. I'm supposed to call him tomorrow."

"How soon after that?"

"It depends on what he finds out. I'll let you know as soon as I talk to him."

"You'd better hope you're right about this." The line went dead.

19

PARISI BROUGHT TWO DRAFT BEERS TO THE
darkened booth and pushed one in front of Egan. "So, where we at?"

When Parisi called Garrett Egan at home, the agent had demanded they meet someplace more discreet than the mall. Parisi
took this as a good sign. They agreed on the small neighborhood
bar just outside Newark. Parisi swallowed a mouthful of beer and
wiped the foam from his upper lip. He briefly considered checking Egan for a wire, but decided against it. The truce in their traditionally adversarial roles was tenuous enough.

Parisi hoped he was smart enough to detect any manipulation
of the conversation that would indicate Egan was wearing a body
recorder. The questions would be overly explicit, attempting to
confirm each and every legal element constituting the crime of
bribery. *So you're going to pay me this much if I do that for you.* If he
couldn't detect them, then he probably deserved to go to prison.

"I want some guarantee that I won't wind up in handcuffs
again," Egan began.

"I guarantee it."

"Meaning you can't promise anything."

"That's right. But I think that I can guarantee that if you wind
up in handcuffs, *I'll* wind up in handcuffs, and probably worse."

"For me, worse might be better."

"Jesus Christ, take a breath. This is not a big deal. You go get
the book. You take your money and go home. Even if we got
caught, it's a lousy book, not plans to the A-bomb. It's something

they don't even want. Hell, it's not even theirs really. They don't even know they have it."

"Are you ready now to tell me how much you're willing to pay?"

The way he planned to answer the question would be a test of whether Egan was wired. "I'm still not comfortable talking about money. You do what you got to do, and then you can hold me up for payment."

"Fair enough. Where's this book at?"

It would have been easy enough for Egan to protest, to demand payment up front, but that he hadn't made Parisi more confident that he had the upper hand. "That's what you're going to have to figure out."

"How did we wind up with it?"

"Twenty-some years ago, you guys arrested an old bookie by the name of Gustella Grimaldi. They called him Auggie. It was for some type of illegal gambling operation. In his property was a numbers ledger, I'm guessing something pocket size or maybe a little bigger."

"That's it?"

"I told you this was easy money."

"What's in it?"

"Not that easy."

"You know I'm going to find out when I get it."

"I'm aware of that. But then you'll be involved. Our trust will be a little more *established* at that point."

"That seems reasonable. If this book is not in the bulky evidence room, it'll be in the 1-A section of the case file."

"What's that?"

"It's a large envelope at the back of the file. For things that usually aren't the subject of the testimony. Incidental stuff like personal identification, address books, anything that'll fit in the envelope. Something they wouldn't need for prosecution. Do you know if it was used against him?"

"I think he took a cop, so there wasn't a trial. But when we tried to have a lawyer get it back, he was told the case was under appeal and the book was evidence."

"That doesn't mean anything. They'll tell you everything is evidence just so they don't have to go through the bother."

"What if it isn't in the file, but in that room you said?"

"The bulky room. If it's in there, it'll be more difficult. But let me see. If it's in the 1-A envelope, no one will even know it's gone."

"How soon will you know?"

"What's the hurry? It's been twenty years."

"I think we've discussed this enough for tonight."

Egan shook his head slowly. "You think I'm wearing a wire."

"I'd be an idiot not to think it's a possibility."

"Yeah, you would be." Egan stood up and calmly took off his shirt and undid his trousers, letting them fall to his knees. He turned around and then back again. "Okay?"

Parisi was convinced that testing the agent's sincerity further was probably not a good idea. "Okay."

Egan pulled up his pants and buttoned his shirt. "As long as I'm going to do this, it should be tonight. I could get a call first thing in the morning, telling me I'm suspended. I'll have to go down to the main office in Manhattan, but I'll know something once I do."

Parisi slid a small piece of paper over to him with "M" printed on it with a phone number. "That's my cell, the last four numbers are reversed. Call me as soon as you know."

Charles Lansing sat at his desk out in the bullpen. He had not had one decent overhear since discovering the acoustical aberration between the vault and Vanko's office. He had not managed to elicit any further information about the "Dimino scam" from any member of the squad. Howard Snow was still a possibility, but the young agent appeared to be avoiding him intentionally.

He sat in the vault for a good fifteen minutes hoping someone would speak with Vanko so he could check the sound levels. When he came out, he saw that Sheila Burkhart was at her desk. It was almost nine-thirty. Usually when an office was under inspection, tardiness was nonexistent, which the local management offered as proof of ongoing efficiency. He walked over to her desk. "Hi, I'm Chuck Lansing. I'm on the inspection staff."

"Sheila Burkhart," she answered matter-of-factly.

"I'm sorry I haven't scheduled your interview, but when I was arranging them, you hadn't reported to the squad yet. Would you have time this morning?"

"I have time right now."

There didn't seem to be any reservation in her answer. Most agents would have wanted a little time to realign their perception of the truth, to shut down certain memories and redistribute others behind the impenetrable shield of "to the best of my recollection."

Lansing let her walk into the interview room ahead of him and then closed the door. He flipped open her file. "You're originally from Cedar Rapids."

"Actually we have a farm about fifteen miles south of there."

"You must find this a little overwhelming, I mean New York."

"It takes a little longer to get around, but work's work."

He looked back down at the file. "University of Iowa. Good school, but I don't see much extracurricular activity."

"I had plenty of extracurricular activity. I worked on the farm every day. I was what those who got the *full* university experience called a townie."

"No, no, I admire anyone who worked their way through school. I had a job at the library when I was in college."

"It's like we were separated at birth."

"Well, I know it's not exactly the same, but—"

"I'm just pulling your leg. If I could have sat around a sorority house for four years waiting for Mr. Pretty Boy Trust Fund the Third to show, I'd have been first in line to sign up. But those weren't the cards that came my way. So I did with what I had."

"And did well. A B.S. in chemistry with a three point eight five overall. Are you planning to go to the lab eventually?"

"I'd rather remove both my eyes with a coat hanger."

Lansing gave a short, nervous laugh. "Then what do you want to do with your career?"

"I'm doing it. I'm an FBI agent."

Nodding like he understood, he closed her file and folded his hands on top of it. "I have to admit, I was a little surprised to find a woman on this squad. How did *you* wind up out here?"

"Doesn't it say in there?"

"Actually, I'm finding that none of the personnel files are particularly forthcoming about why people were transferred to this squad."

"I heard that Nick Vanko was a great guy and at the time I was working for one of those supervisors who was just putting his time in until he could get promoted and become a bigger pain in the ass to even more people." Her voice warmed slightly with a trace of sarcasm. "I'm sure you know the type."

He wanted to believe the barb wasn't aimed at him. "I don't know if you've had much chance to interact with the other members of your squad . . ." He let it hang in the air, hoping that she would declare her allegiances without him having to expose the direction he wanted the interview to take. She said nothing. "You know, things like have you had any problems with anyone since you got here."

"You mean like sexual harassment?"

Sexual harassment was perfect. "Yes, anything like that."

"Well, my biggest complaint about sexual harassment is that I have not been the object of any."

When Parisi got back to the club, Manny greeted him as soon as he walked in. "Did he go for it?"

Some of the others at their usual station around the card table looked up. "Yeah, he did," Parisi answered without thinking, but then wondered if he was starting to believe his own lies. "At least he seemed to."

"When will we know?"

"He's going to try for it tonight."

Everyone smiled. "Way to go, Mike," Tatorrio said.

"DeMiglia wants you to call him," Dellaporta reported. "Said he tried to get you on your cell."

"I had it turned off for the meeting." He smiled. "Must have forgot to turn it back on." He went into the back room to make the call. "Danny, it's Mike."

"Well?"

"I just got back. We should know something later tonight."

"You let me know, no matter what time." Parisi had expected him to be a little more upbeat. After all, they were about to turn an FBI agent.

Then it came to him. DeMiglia had not thought far enough ahead. Parisi would be seen as the person who had compromised an agent, a notoriety DeMiglia wanted for himself. Worse, it would give Parisi an unpredictable amount of immunity if he were to be brought up in front of the commission on charges that he refused the orders of the underboss. For the briefest moment Parisi felt relieved. Almost accidentally, he had crawled out from under DeMiglia's authority.

Ironically, the underboss's cautious refusal to expose himself directly was going to paralyze his larger plan to eliminate the don's nephew. But DeMiglia hadn't risen through the ranks because he was incapable of adapting. The last thing Parisi needed right now was for him to devise a new strategy. It was time to put him back in charge. "I got to say, Danny, I didn't think it would work . . ."

"What?"

"I mean, come on, turn one of them? Everybody knows something like that isn't possible. But, goddamnit, you were right. And I played it just like you said, didn't give him room to breathe."

DeMiglia couldn't recall giving Parisi those precise instructions but reasoned they must have been implied in his general approach to the situation. "You got to remember, I've being doing this for a long time."

"And you'll be taking bows for this one for an even longer time. I'll call you as soon as I hear."

"Ah, there's something else I'm curious about, but I need you to call me at that other number first." DeMiglia, ever vigilant of wiretaps, had previously given Parisi the number of the public phone at a restaurant next door to the club where he conducted business.

"Five minutes?"

"One minute," DeMiglia said, the authority back in his voice.

Parisi watched the sixty seconds tick off his watch, then called the number. "What'd you need to know?"

"How much did you tell him you'd pay for it?"

"I haven't given him a number, but I was thinking twenty-five grand."

"That seems like a lot, but since you're not going to pay him, I guess it really doesn't matter."

"Not pay him?"

"Once he delivers that book, you own him. What's he going to do, get a lawyer and sue you? He can't say anything because he stole from the FBI, so anytime you need anything from him you just threaten him with making a call to his bosses. You'll only have to do it once, then he'll understand forever."

DeMiglia's proposal had its usual brutal practicality, but the degree of betrayal didn't seem right to Parisi. Although the agent had previously committed a white-collar crime, his involvement now was strictly to take care of his wife and children. DeMiglia, he suspected, wanted him further humiliated simply because he was FBI. "Yeah, you're right, Danny. I don't have to pay him. But there is one problem that could come up later. Say he does get convicted on that insider trading stuff. What's to prevent him from dealing me for receiving stolen FBI property? He could get himself immunity to do it. But I think if he had to tell them that he put the twenty-five in his pocket, he'll be less likely to do that."

"Hey, it's your money. If you want to throw it away, go ahead. Me, I wouldn't give the prick a dime."

That DeMiglia didn't attempt to argue the point told Parisi that he had considered the possibility of Egan turning on him for nonpayment, another win-win situation for the underboss.

"For me it's just a little insurance," Parisi said. "If he does come up with the other half of that item, what should we do next?"

"Take it to my document guy. Make sure it matches up with what we got."

"That makes sense."

"You really think he's going to come through?"

"I think he's going to try."

"Wouldn't that be something, Dutch Schultz's treasure."

"Not anymore."

"What do you mean?"

Parisi apologized in his head to Manny and Joseph Baldovino. "If it's in your possession, do you think people are going to refer to it as *Dutch Schultz's* treasure?"

It was after one o'clock in the morning when Egan finally called Parisi at the club. "Believe it or not, I got it. It was right where it was supposed to be, right there in the back of the file. I guess in the old days the filing system was much simpler. If you put it in there today, you'd never find it."

"Where are you, I'll come and get it."

"Hey, I'm desperate, not stupid. I believe possession allows me to set some of the rules."

"Within reason," Parisi said coolly. "What's bothering you about me coming and getting it?"

"A few things, like what's to prevent you from just taking the book and not paying me? It's not exactly a case I'd want the circuit court of appeals to hear."

"True. How about I bring you the cash. You can leave, secure it, and then come back with the book."

"That's very trusting of you."

"Do I have any choice?"

"No, you don't. Which brings me to the important part of this. I've looked through the book, and I found a map."

Parisi figured there was a better than even chance that would happen. "Go ahead."

"I want to know what it's to."

"That doesn't concern you."

"I thought you mob guys had a better grasp of the laws of supply and demand."

"And I thought you FBI guys had a better grasp of how appealing vengeance is to us mob guys."

"I think there's strength to both arguments. Apparently, we need to come to some sort of agreement beforehand."

"We can try," Parisi said. "I was thinking twenty-five thousand for a couple of hours' work is more than fair."

Egan didn't say anything right away. "Having a background in business—finance to be specific—I would interpret that to mean that whatever this map leads to has got to be worth at least, oh, four to five million dollars, probably more. Am I close?"

"Close enough."

Egan sounded like he was talking through a smile. "That you would so readily agree means that it's worth two to three times as much. So now we're talking about ten to fifteen million. Isn't that a little closer?"

Parisi couldn't believe he had felt sorry for this greedy bastard. "It was buried over sixty years ago, and no one knows for sure what's inside, but the estimates, in today's dollars, go as high as fifty million."

"Fifty million! Who buried it?"

"Dutch Schultz."

"The old gangster?"

"That's the one."

"How come you're being so straight with me?"

"For one reason, you were pretty much figuring out how much it could be worth on your own. But we've been out to the general area where it was buried, and I think we might need your help with more than just getting the map. Don't get me wrong, the map is important, but a lot has changed out there. And the government has access to things that we don't. We might need more from you. That's why. Now, how much?"

"Help how?"

"Who knows? I'm just trying to think ahead. Maybe some part of the map is in code. You guys got the best code breakers. Or maybe something with satellites. I don't know, something like that."

"Two million."

Parisi didn't want to seem too easy. "One million."

Egan chuckled. "You're forgetting I've got the map."

"Okay, two million, when we find the box."

"No, I can't wait. I want it up front."

Parisi laughed. "Stop and think for a second. I'm going to pay you two million dollars, and we may never recover the treasure? Do you really think I'd do that? Plus, if I did give it to you up front, where's your incentive to continue to help us?"

"Okay, two million when you find it, minus a hundred thousand up front."

"Haven't you been reading the papers? The FBI has put us into Chapter Eleven. We don't have that kind of cash."

Egan was silent for a few seconds. "Then what are you thinking?"

"When this was buried, supposedly it was worth as much as seven million, but who knows. So I propose a percentage. Five percent. So, if it winds up being worth fifty, your end will be two and a half million."

"Ten percent."

Parisi thought about what DeMiglia would do. "There's a reason greed is one of the deadly sins. Right now, I'd say the deadliest."

"Okay, five percent, but I still get the original twenty-five thousand on delivery of the map."

Parisi was pleased. With all the games, he was paying exactly what he had originally offered, twenty-five thousand. He had more than twice that in a floor safe in his basement at home. "I'll need the map tonight."

"Where do you want to meet?"

20

THE AIR IN EAST HARLEM WAS THICK WITH humidity and it was only 7:00 a.m. Vanko's squad sat in the small courtyard between the Church of the Miraculous Medal and the rectory, drinking coffee from a nearby bodega. The shadowed garden with its stunted locust trees and gently overgrown bushes seemed misplaced, anachronistic, a refuge from the very problems it was the church's duty to combat.

Sheila came out of the rectory door with the priest. They shook hands, and she walked over to the group. "Is everyone here?" she asked Vanko.

"Everybody but Brad."

Straker said, "What about that new guy, Mr. Happy Face?"

"Egan? He called me at home last night. Evidently he changed his mind about taking some time off. He's selling his house and needs a few days to do some painting."

"I'm surprised he'd be painting with all that experience hanging paper on Wall Street," Straker added.

"Come on, Jack, you know the rule: we don't insult anyone unless it's to their face. Why don't you get started, Sheila."

She passed out summary sheets. "These are backgrounds and Xeroxed photos of Suzie Castillo and the eight girls who are missing. The first three are the ones we think were photographed by the same person who took Suzie's school photo. Who Father Coyne tells me is," she turned a small piece of paper so she could read it, "Eugene Diaz."

One end of the courtyard opened onto the street, and suddenly the throaty carburetor of a gray Audi roadster drowned out Sheila's voice. It cut hard to the curb and parked in front of a fire hydrant, the only space available. The engine shut down with abrupt precision. As everyone watched, Brad Kenyon got out and retrieved a charcoal blazer from the backseat. The jacket's color was just a shade deeper than the car's and even had the same luxurious sheen. Underneath it he wore a white golf shirt and black dress slacks with razored creases. His soft Italian loafers flashed as he moved through the rising sunlight. He sat down next to T. H. Crowe. "Sorry I'm late."

Crowe said, "Maybe you didn't get the memo, but the dress code is, if you're going to wear a blazer on surveillance, you have to wear an ascot, Mr. Howell."

Everyone laughed, including Kenyon. "Maybe I could borrow one of yours, or did one of your ex-wives get them in the settlement?"

"What do you know about my ex-wives?"

"Enough to agree with them."

Crowe shook his head. "I know you're not gay, but you really are missing a hell of an opportunity."

Kenyon put his hand on Crowe's arm. "Maybe I just haven't met the right man yet."

"Okay," Vanko said, "you two can work on your routine some other time."

Sheila gave Kenyon one of the handouts. "We have the luxury of the killer's DNA profile, so while we're documenting a day in the life of Eugene Diaz, we want to discreetly see if we can't pick up a sample of his. Discarded coffee cups, soft drink cans, cigarettes, gum, anything that a few of his cells might cling to."

Vanko flashed back to Sheila's kitchen wall, the victim's body nude and twisted. He watched her carefully now. Something inside her was gaining momentum.

"Why don't we just go ask him?" Crowe said.

"First, that gives him the chance to say no and disappear before we can get a search warrant. And there's always a possibility that he still has one of these girls. I know it's a long shot, but I don't think that's a chance we want to take."

"How long was the first girl kept alive?" Zalenski asked, his young face suddenly appearing serious.

"The best guess is thirty-six to forty-eight hours."

Crowe said, "So how long have these other girls been missing?"

"The most recent one is about three weeks," Sheila said with noticeably less confidence.

After a few seconds of uncomfortable silence, Howard Snow raised his hand as if in class, causing a faint smile to cross Sheila's lips. "Yes, Howard."

"Have you got any kind of psychological profile on the killer that we might be able to match up with this guy Diaz?"

"NYPD had one done, but it was pretty nonspecific, so I didn't include it. You know the drill, white male thirty to forty years old who may live with a female relative and drive a well-maintained midsize sedan."

"Say, Jack," Snow said, "don't you live with your mother?"

"Anything else?" Sheila asked.

"Nick, how long are we going to run this?" Crowe asked.

"Normally, I say we'd go until we got the DNA sample, but with that inspector watching everything, we're going to have to work around him. Abby's going to tell him we got called out for the next day or two. After that I'll come up with something."

"How are we doing with this inspector?" Straker asked.

"Unless one of you guys has rolled over on me, I guess we're doing all right. But don't kid yourself, this Lansing is on a mission. Just keep it nine-to-five until he gets bored."

Vanko checked the address Sheila had for the photographer. "Okay, for the sake of the new people getting to know you lifers, I want to break up some of the incestuous relationships. T. H. and Sheila take the van. Dick and I'll ride together and Jack and Howard." That Vanko had chosen not to put himself inside the van with Sheila for the next eight hours was assumed to be only a diversionary tactic by the always-observant and ever-prurient men of the squad. "Oh, Brad, I'm sorry," Vanko said, realizing he had forgotten Kenyon. "I made these matches before you got here."

"That's all right, Nick," Crowe said with mock resignation, "Dances with Guccis can come with us."

* * *

When DeMiglia and his driver walked into the Catania Social Club, they found Parisi, Manny, and Tommy Ida huddled over maps of the Phoenicia area and the photocopied halves of Lulu Rosenkranz's map. Ida was studying them with a magnifying glass.

Parisi had met Egan in the parking lot of a strip mall in New Jersey, which, according to the address Chris the plumber had supplied, was within half a mile of the agent's home. As soon as Egan got into the Cadillac, Parisi handed him twenty-five thousand dollars as a demonstration of good faith. "I hope the map isn't too far away. I've got people waiting to see it."

Egan reached inside his jacket and handed over the numbers journal.

Parisi said, "I guess if we were playing poker, I would have lost."

"I think you just identified the problem—we've been going at this like it's some kind of competition. If we want to find this thing, we're going to have to start trusting each other." Then, with some ceremony, Egan offered his hand.

Parisi could see it was a sincere gesture. The agent could have chosen to feel smug about outmaneuvering him, not only on the entire negotiation, but also on the bluff of having the map with him. Instead, he was declaring a truce, offering to work together.

Parisi took the hand. "Fifty million dollars can be a hell of a matchmaker."

Parisi watched DeMiglia as he looked over Ida's shoulder at the map. "Any luck?" the underboss asked.

"Not yet," Parisi said. He noticed that DeMiglia was carrying a folder. "Is that from the document examiner?"

"Could you guys excuse Mike and me?" DeMiglia said. Everyone moved off into the front room.

"Do they match?" Parisi asked.

"They match." A caustic smile pulled DeMiglia's mouth to one side. He took out the report and two plastic envelopes containing the map's original halves and handed them to Parisi. "Now the only question left is, can you find it?"

"We're going up first thing in the morning."

"I'm going with you."

Parisi could see that, despite efforts to keep it in check, DeMiglia's enthusiasm was growing. He hesitated slightly before saying, "Good. The more brains we got working on this, the better."

"What about the Fed?"

"I've got him on retainer, so to speak."

"So you did pay him."

"Yeah, like we discussed, to keep him available until we're done with him. He may be needed for who knows what."

"You know if you do need anything from him, he's going to expect you to pay him again."

"I suppose you're right, Danny, but I can't worry about that now."

"If you did it like I told you, you'd own him right now."

"That doesn't mean he'd help us again."

"So what did you do? You promised him more, didn't you?"

"I told him he could have five percent."

"What?"

"That's what I *told* him, not what I'm going to do. When it comes time to cash out, I'm going to give him the Danny."

"That's more like it." DeMiglia nodded. "Fuck that Cassius guy, I'd better start looking out for you."

It was almost 5:00 p.m. when Vanko called a halt to the surveillance. He told everybody to head back to the cave; he would meet with them there. When they got within a half mile of the off-site, he telephoned Abby. "Is Lansing there?"

"I haven't been in back all afternoon, let me go check." She came on the line. "He's still here and he's got stuff stacked up around him, so it looks like he intends to stay for a while."

"Why don't you take off. I'll talk to you in the morning." He radioed Crowe. "T. H., where are you?"

"Just pulling into the cave."

"The inspector's still there. I don't want to have to meet someplace else in this traffic. Think you could go in and encourage him to leave?"

"Give me ten minutes." Crowe pulled the van into the off-site garage and got out. "Sheila, why don't you stay here with Brad while I get rid of this guy."

Crowe walked into the bullpen area and threw his scarred leather briefcase on a desk.

"Oh, you're back," Lansing said. "Is everyone else coming back here?"

"I don't think so."

"I haven't interviewed you yet, would you have time now?"

"As soon as I download these photos, I've got a meeting to go to."

"A squad meeting?"

"AA," Crowe said with relief, implying that being an alcoholic was preferable to being at Lansing's disposal.

The inspector nodded, trying to give the impression he had simply misunderstood the subtle insult and turned back to the safety of his forms. Crowe took out a cable and linked his camera to the computer and turned it on. He then lit a cigarette and exhaled in the general direction of Lansing, who responded with a small, forced cough. Crowe blew the smoke in a thinner, more aerodynamic stream. Finally, Lansing turned around. "There is no smoking in government facilities."

Crowe walked over to Lansing's desk. With the burning cigarette between his fingers, he leaned forward so the acrid smoke rose up into the inspector's face. In a voice scarred with an inviolable authority of experience beyond the imagination of the man who was now its target, he said, "It's after five. What are you still doing here? Shouldn't you be back at the hotel bar with your inspector buddies playing I Fucked an Agent Harder than You Did Today?" He exhaled another full drag before walking into Vanko's office, closing the door with just enough of a slam to warn Lansing not to be there when he came out unless he wanted more. He could hear the inspector packing up his papers. Crowe called Vanko's cell. "He'll be gone in five minutes."

Once Lansing's vehicle exited the garage, the others pulled in. Everyone went into Vanko's office. Sheila asked, "Did anybody see anything worthwhile out there that I missed?"

Straker said, "We took him from his apartment to his studio and then back. No stops for coffee or a drink. I guess we just need to stay on him until he leaves his DNA on something we can grab."

Sheila made some notes before looking up. "I know there wasn't much going on out there today. Does anyone feel like we're wasting our time?"

Vanko said, "Sheila, this is what we do for a living. Surveillance is ninety-nine percent a waste of time. Actually it's probably closer to a hundred percent. Otherwise the bad guys would be thoughtful enough to show up at the exact moment we did. Then we'd have to call it an appointment."

"I know, it's just when you're planning these things they seem a lot smarter than they do after a day in a metal box."

"Especially if you have to look at someone like T. H. the whole time," Kenyon said.

Crowe said, "I think what bothered her was you humming show tunes and trying to dust."

"I just hate wasting everybody's time. Does anybody have any other ideas?" Sheila asked.

When no one said anything, Vanko said, "Okay then, everyone has the same assignments for tomorrow morning, same time. Any conflicts? No? Then how about we head over to Hattie's for a beer?"

"I'm going to stay and get organized for tomorrow," Sheila said.

"That was an order, not an invitation," Vanko said.

Straker grabbed her hand and kissed it with exaggeration. "You don't want to be in here with these animals. Come with me, we'll fly to Rio, for Carnival."

Vanko watched her hand float back down to her side. He looked away, embarrassed that Straker had done something so matter-of-factly that he couldn't. The visual exchange did not go unnoticed by the others. Sheila quickly regained her composure. "Carnival is just before Lent. You're a few months late. However, since everybody's apparently worked up a thirst on my case, I guess I have no choice but to buy the first round."

"Everyone but T. H.," Zalenski said.

Crowe said, "Yes, I've already had today's allotment of alcohol. In fact, I'm good until 2043."

Sheila jumped to her feet. "Well, as long as Baron von Straker will be there kissing hands, I'm in."

21

ARMED WITH BOTH HALVES OF THE LULU Rosenkranz map and the optimism of having overcome the most recent insurmountable obstacles, Parisi set the departure time to Phoenicia at 6:00 a.m., an hour that he hoped would discourage the notoriously nocturnal underboss from coming along. Initially, DeMiglia did protest the time, but Parisi explained the difficulty they had had getting hotel rooms on their previous trip. "It's what, the Catskills? How can there be no rooms?"

Parisi started to tell him about the Washington Irving festival but considered DeMiglia's disdain for being lectured and said, "I think it was a Jewish holiday."

"Hey, when ain't it a Jew holiday? I guess I'll have to be here at six."

The closer the hour came, the more hopeful Parisi grew that DeMiglia wouldn't show. But at a couple of minutes past six, an unfamiliar white Cadillac pulled up to the curb. The back window lowered with an electronic whir, and the sleep-deprived underboss called Parisi over. "Morning, Danny," Parisi said with as much irritating cheerfulness as possible, "you want some coffee?"

"Fuck coffee, it might keep me awake."

"New car?"

"Loaner. My car's at the dealer. Four months old and already has electrical problems. It's all those goddamn computers they put in these days. How long is it going to take us to get up there?"

"If we watch the speed limit, two, two and a half hours."

"Good. Watch the speed limits, it'll give me more time to sleep. Where's a good place to meet?"

"The old train station. Everyone in town knows where it is."

DeMiglia grunted and fell back onto the seat. Parisi looked around at the others who were glazed by the same fatigue as the underboss. As the last of them pulled away, he got in his car. Leaning back against the leather headrest, he closed his eyes and inhaled the fleeting solitude, holding it in his lungs as long as possible.

Driving by himself would give him time to think, to recheck his increasingly tangled deceptions, their matrix slowly tightening around him. But once he cleared the stop-and-go cadence of the city's traffic, his mind refused to concentrate on anything remotely associated with business. The part of his brain that created and maintained conspiracies was demanding a few hours off.

Streaming along the interstate, he lost himself in the rush of images out the window. Simple stone buildings that would last several more of his lifetimes, constructed for purpose rather than comfort by owners possessing the same character, an earned indestructibility. As he neared the mountains, he began to notice the small tributaries that wound under the overpasses, their course unchanging as they gave life to the triangular evergreens and domed hardwoods that bordered them.

When he pulled into the old train station, he could see the cool green canopy of the Catskills in the distance, a place that had long generated legends and hauntings, one capable of both inspiring Washington Irving and conspiring with Dutch Schultz.

By eight-thirty, everyone had arrived. The night before Tommy Ida had thought to get a metal detector from a cousin who used it to find coins and jewelry on the Coney Island beach. He also brought three shovels and a pick from the club's basement. No one knew how they had gotten there. No one questioned it either.

They tried to visualize the surrounding landmarks' relationship to the rusty, inked lines of the map. It became apparent immediately that the map's X had to be on the other side of Esopus Creek. They found the bridge across and parked along the dirt road. They walked down to the edge of the creek, then followed it east until they came upon a small clearing.

The terrain opened to the west and south, rising gently toward the mountains. The sky was a remarkably pellucid blue, and a dry morning wind was gathering speed. The ground beyond was snared with thick, ropy undergrowth. The men looked for an accessible starting point. A few small clusters of trees were within walking distance, several of their limbs snapped off, as if in the wake of some apocalyptic storm.

Parisi turned the halves of the map in an effort to orient their position. Manny pointed at a scribbled tangle on the paper, then at a stand of half a dozen pines thirty yards away. "Maybe that's supposed to be a bunch of trees. What do you think?"

"Looks right," someone offered more out of impatience than analysis.

"And how we supposed to know when we got the right spot?" DeMiglia asked.

"The most common story," Ida said, "is that when Rosenkranz made the map, he carved an X in the tree that the box was buried under."

"You're going to tell me that people have been looking for this for sixty years and nobody noticed a tree with a X on it?"

A little embarrassed, Ida lowered his eyes. "That's just what I read."

DeMiglia looked at Parisi. "See, it's just like they say, too much knowledge is a dangerous thing."

Jimmy Tatorrio had walked over to the trees while they were talking. "Hey, over here. I think there's an X on this one."

Everyone but DeMiglia hurried over. Sure enough, the vague lines of an X were cut in the bark. "Looks old to me," said Parisi. He stepped aside so DeMiglia could give his opinion.

"Yeah, it could be." He turned to Ida. "Now what?"

"It's supposed to be buried right underneath. We'll go get the metal detector and shovels."

For the next two hours, three of the men followed Ida and his metal detector around, digging at his direction. The only things they unearthed were an occasional beer can or railroad spike. With midday approaching, DeMiglia's mood went from combative anticipation to boredom to embarrassed anger.

Walking around, he suddenly noticed that another tree also

had a shallow X carved into it. He started to tell them, but then something occurred to him. He inspected each of the other trees in the stand, confirming what he had suspected. Clasping his hands behind his back, he walked over to Parisi, who was studying the map yet again. When Parisi saw his contemptuous smile, he knew that DeMiglia had discovered a new problem that he was enjoying much more than Parisi would. "What is it, Danny?"

He pointed to the cluster of the trees. "See those?"

"Yeah."

"Every one of them has an X on it."

"What?" Parisi half-trotted over to the cluster of pines. "I don't understand."

"Think about it. One of these treasure hunters came through here and put Xs on all the trees so he could fuck everybody else up. There's probably not a tree around here without an X on it."

"Even if that's true, we still have the advantage because we've got the map, which we know is good because you had it checked." He knew the argument was weak, but it was all he could think of at the moment.

"Yeah, well, maybe. I'm not sure I know what to believe anymore."

Parisi was glad he had saved a trump card; he hoped it would be enough to keep DeMiglia interested. He turned to Tommy Ida. "Do you still have the genealogy stuff?"

"In the car, but I pretty much remember how it went."

"Then tell Danny." He looked at DeMiglia. "I didn't think this was that important at the time, but Tommy went on the Internet and traced the people in Joe Baldovino's diary."

Ida quickly explained how the map had been passed from Lulu Rosenkranz to Marty Krompier and, when he was shot, to his brother Milton. And that Milton's adopted son was Anthony Luitu, who, according to the journal, gave it to the senior Baldovino in payment for some unspecified debt.

"So not only did your document guy say it was good," Parisi said, "but the Internet confirms the bloodlines. It all fits."

The new, confirming set of facts, while not inarguable, seemed to calm DeMiglia's doubts. "It does makes sense. Let me see that map again."

* * *

At that moment, Nick Vanko was watching Eugene Diaz through a thousand-millimeter camera lens. The photographer was just entering his studio. "Just like yesterday," Sheila said, her voice coming from the speaker under Vanko's dashboard. "And at about the same time." The radio went silent, and, as it had done several times already, Vanko's mind drifted back to the night before.

Hattie's was a neighborhood bar with a small area in the back toward the kitchen where the Opera House crew could discuss business without being overheard.

Sheila had been the last one to arrive. She passed Straker, who was dancing next to the jukebox with one of the bar's regulars, a woman in her fifties who worked in a nearby used-car lot.

As Sheila approached the table, Vanko started to stand up to offer her his chair. She held up a hand. "Thanks, but I've got to use the bathroom."

When she came back a few minutes later, she sat down on the edge of his chair, pushing him over until they each had half a seat. She nodded toward the jukebox. "Looks like my fling with Jack is over."

Vanko closed his eyes, shutting out the blurry images coming through the telephoto lens. It had been a long time since he had felt that tiny arc of electricity that jumps from the touch of a woman . . . obviously too long.

He poured her a glass of beer and she took a hefty swallow. "I didn't get a chance to tell you this morning, but that inspector grabbed me for an interview yesterday."

"How'd that go?"

"He wanted to know exactly how many of you guys were harassing me."

"And you told him . . . ?"

"I explained that I hadn't been there very long, and it would probably take a while for someone to take a shot at me because I'm the kind of woman men generally need to get a good running start at. I told him so far there had been only one problem: someone showed up at my place with beer and pizza." Vanko laughed. "Well, you did come to my apartment—at night, uninvited—with enough alcohol to loosen my moral code."

"I wish I had known your defenses were down," he said, his tone unconvincing. He topped off her glass. "How much beer does it usually take?"

"You're at least a glass and a half past it right now. And speaking of half, could I at least get a quarter of this seat, Slim?" Her hip squirmed lightly against his.

Everyone at the table had turned their attention to Straker, who stood at the bar beside his dance partner, lighting a shot of tequila. He gave a little salute with the flaming liquid and fired it down. The woman did the same and ordered another. Some of her mannerisms reminded Sheila of her mother. She instinctively knew when men were watching her and would arch her back slightly and push her hair behind one ear, her laughter suddenly bubbling more noticeably. Sheila was always relieved when her mother started to take over a room because it allowed her to become even more invisible. She suspected it was one of the reasons her mother did it.

When Sheila first announced her intention of joining the FBI, signaling her more or less permanent departure from Iowa, her mother didn't protest. It seemed a relief for both of them. When allowing herself to think about it, Sheila missed her family, but she returned to Iowa only every other Christmas, and then for no more than three days. If she stayed a minute longer than that, the old feelings began to surface. The thing that she loved most about New York was that it wasn't Iowa. No more of the long, flat winters. No more of the inescapable smallness. Everyone knowing everyone. One of New York's greatest offerings was its ability to distract, enough to convince her that one's appearance was as insignificant as a flickering store window reflection. The faster she went by, the more out of focus she became.

Someone laughed and said something about Straker. "Is he always like this?" Sheila asked.

"He didn't get to the squad on good looks alone."

"Nick?" Zalenski said. "Sheila's trying to get you on the radio."

"Was I sleeping?"

"I don't know. Your eyes were closed."

Vanko picked up the mike. "Go ahead, twenty-three eleven."

"We're wasting time. How about if T. H. and I grab him up for an interview and a cheek swab."

"If you're not worried about him running."

"I'm just not getting much of a vibe off of him."

Vanko knew that no one had a better insight into the person they were looking for than Sheila. "Where do you want to take him?"

"NYPD has a place they use for *special* interviews. Stand by while we get him in tow."

There weren't enough chairs in the small room for everyone to sit down as they watched Crowe on closed circuit television start his interview of Eugene Diaz. The two men were in an adjoining room of a boarded-up grammar school that the NYPD used for discreet "high intensity" interrogations and polygraphs.

Crowe took off his jacket and draped it over the back of his chair, exposing his gun. He started rolling up his sleeves slowly, revealing his thick forearms. "You see, Gene—"

"It's Eugene."

"Is it?" Crowe stared at him menacingly.

"Yeah, it is."

"See, Eugene, I have a problem every time I see a guy with a camera hanging around kids."

"I'm a photographer, so I have a camera. See how that works? And I don't hang around kids."

"That's not what your neighbors say," Crowe lied.

"What, at the festivals? Those are community events that I take pictures of." Sitting closest to the monitor, Kenyon noticed Diaz shift in his chair.

"Ever take any pictures of Suzie Castillo?"

Diaz smirked. "So that's what this is about?"

Crowe leaned to within an inch of Diaz's face. "Did you take any pictures of her?"

"Not that I know of."

"But you know who she is?"

"You can't live in East Harlem and not know when a little girl is killed."

Crowe handed him a photograph. "That's her. Recognize who took it?"

"I've taken school pictures of hundreds, probably thousands, of kids. I don't remember every one of them."

"How much do you know about her death?"

Diaz leaned back and crossed his arms. "I know I didn't kill her."

"You'll forgive me if I don't take your word for it."

"You know what? Whether you're offering or not, I want a lawyer."

"Do you want me to go away?"

"Picked right up on that, didn't you. Who says the FBI has lost its edge?"

Crowe held up a clear plastic package containing long wooden cotton swabs. "Then give me a DNA sample."

"What, so you can frame me? I'll pass."

"You know, that's the number-one answer given by guilty people."

"*Law-yer.*"

Kenyon stood up. "Nick, let me take a shot at him."

Vanko said, "Sheila, any objections?"

"Brad, don't kill yourself. This guy just isn't lighting my fire. If you can get a cheek swab, that'll be enough for now."

Kenyon knocked on the interview room door. "You've got a call." Kenyon closed the door behind Crowe. He sat down and let his blazer fall back so Diaz could see that he wasn't wearing a gun. "That T. H., quite a load, huh?"

"Let me guess—good cop."

"They tell me I'm too pretty to be the bad cop. What do you think?"

"I think you're too well dressed to be any kind of cop."

"Too well dressed as in, This guy looks like a fag?" With a trace of uncertainty, Diaz shook his head. "That's all right, I get it all the time, but you know what, I'm not gay. But short of having public sex with women, I can't prove that to people. You, on the other hand, can prove you had nothing to do with this murder."

"You know, if you had come at me like this first, I'd gladly have given you what you wanted, but your partner shut that door. My people get hassled all the time, and once that happens, I've got to say no, otherwise it's too easy for you guys to disrespect us the next time."

"Like I told you, I have some idea what you're saying. Let me ask you something a little more innocuous. Do you use film or digital?"

"Both."

"At occasions like these festivals—digital?"

"Yes. What difference does that make?"

"How many computers do you have?"

"I don't have any computers."

"Digital photography without computers? You know, Eugene, I believe that is the first lie you told here today."

"Okay, now we're back to the part where I say, 'I want a lawyer.'"

"That's your right. And when you invoke that right, we have to find another way to get your DNA, and that's with a search warrant. See, we've got some friendly judges we go to, and they never mind if we tack on phrases like 'along with all computers in the suspect's possession,' especially in cases where there's suspicion of pedophilia."

"I don't molest kids."

"There's a lot of money in child pornography, even if someone's just the photographer." Diaz started picking at his nails. "Do you know why there are such stiff penalties for just having those images on your computer? Eugene, look at me. Do you know why?"

"No."

"Because it's almost impossible to catch the photographer. But when they do . . ."

"Okay, okay, I'll give you my DNA."

"'If you had come at me like this first, I'd gladly have given you what you wanted'—sound familiar? I'm afraid I'm now going to need something more." Kenyon handed him some photos. "These girls are missing. Three of those are your work. Tell me something that will make me believe that you had nothing to do with their disappearance."

Diaz shuffled through them and put one on top. "I've seen her around."

Kenyon glanced at the name on the back. "Maria Vargas. Around where?"

"Penn Station."

"Doing?"

"There are always kids hanging around hustling the tourists and commuters. I've seen some of the kids from the barrio there."

"And how do you know that? Do you take a lot of train trips?" Diaz looked down. "Now's not the time to stop being honest."

"Sometimes I need, you know, some photography subjects."

"When did you see her there?"

"Maybe two weeks ago."

Kenyon pulled out one of the swabs. "Open wide."

Vanko turned to Sheila. "Think he's telling the truth?"

"Who knows? He might be trying to buy his way out. But it's not going to be that easy." She started scrolling through her cell phone's stored numbers. "I've got some contacts at the Center for Missing and Exploited Children who are going to want to have a little talk with Eugene before he goes anywhere."

22

THE SEARCH FOR DUTCH SCHULTZ'S TREASURE ended with a series of arguments. DeMiglia ordered everybody to meet back at the club, and three hours later they were sitting around the big table eating Thai takeout.

"Before we start on this," DeMiglia said, "did you get this place swept like I told you?"

"The next day," Parisi said.

"Okay then. I think the one thing we can agree on is that the map is worthless as far as leading us to the exact spot where it's buried. Maybe fucking Davy Crockett could find that box with the map, but the last time I checked, he wasn't a made guy. So unless you've got another idea, I think it's time to move on to something more realistic, like that job I've been trying to give you since this all started." Parisi still hadn't told his crew what the job was, but they could see from his reaction that it was not in their best interest.

Tommy Ida said, "Danny, do you mind if I say something?"

"No, Tommy, jump in here." He dug his fork into a carton of spicy noodles.

"While the map probably isn't going to help us find the treasure, it does pretty much prove that it exists. Your document examiner proved that; the genealogies prove that. Through both of those, we can trace it all the way back to Lulu Rosenkranz."

"Okay, so there's a good chance the box is buried out there, but it's a big country. Nobody would like to carve up fifty million dollars more than me, but I don't see how it's going to happen."

"We just have to think of a different way to search."

"Like what?" DeMiglia asked.

Ida hesitated for a second. "Maybe we're thinking too small." He looked over at Parisi. "That kid, John-John, you've got cleaning up, does he throw out the old newspapers?"

Remembering where he hid from DeMiglia the day after his arrest, Baldovino said, "I was down in the basement last week. There were stacks of them down there then."

"I read something last week in the paper. Let me go see if I can find it." Ida headed for the stairs.

As soon as he was out of the room, DeMiglia said, "Again with the fucking reading?" He pushed a forkful of noodles into his mouth.

Not knowing what Ida had in mind but ready to cling to any delay, Parisi shrugged nonchalantly. "Don't sell Tommy short, he's pretty good at thinking on his feet."

Manny watched the underboss carefully. Everyone could see the discomfort he was causing their *capo*. But it wasn't being caused just by the map. Whatever job DeMiglia was talking about, Baldovino suspected it was traceable to his counterfeit license plate arrest. That was the moment everything seemed to change for the crew. The map had changed everyone's mood for a while, but now its "good fortune" appeared to be making things worse. Once again, as careful and judicious as Manny had been, he was failing his friends.

When Ida came back, he was carrying a newspaper. It was folded open, and he handed it to the underboss. DeMiglia glanced at the accompanying photos and handed it back. "Just tell me what it is."

"It's what they call three-D seismic imaging. The oil and gas companies use it to locate deposits under the earth's surface. It's fairly simple. They set out sensors that are connected to computers and then they shoot sound waves down into the earth that make these charts of what's below." Ida turned the page so DeMiglia could see it and pointed to a drawing in the article. A large cutaway section of the earth's crust was divided into grids and color-coded to represent the various substances discovered. "It shows the different densities of what's underground."

"What're you, Mr. Fucking Wizard?"

"I just think this stuff is interesting."

"And you think this little box is going to show up in these hu-mongous chunks of the earth?"

"The article also says they use it to find things as small as util-ity lines or connection boxes. So I guess they can adjust the size of the area they're searching."

"Even if this stuff did work, I don't think any oil company is going to want to help us."

"I just thought it was something we should look at, that's all," Ida said apologetically. "If that box is out there, metal detectors and shovels aren't going to find it. All I'm saying is maybe if we try something never used before, we might get lucky."

Everyone became quiet, and as they picked at their food, Ida took the article back and glanced at the photos. "They're not going to want to help us, but they'd help the FBI."

"The FBI? What, did you *read* somewhere that they were going to start helping us now?" DeMiglia chuckled. "Sure, we'll just give them back the map."

"No, the guy who got us the map, we own him, right? Maybe he can figure something out."

"Like what?" DeMiglia said.

Ida shook his head.

Parisi said, "Hey, Danny, you never know unless you ask, right? The only thing it's going to cost us to find out is a phone call. You never know. What time is it?"

"It's a little after eight," Manny said.

"Let me go try to call him." Parisi went to the back room and closed the door. He dialed the number in New Jersey. A woman answered. "Is Garrett there?"

"Who's calling?"

"Mike."

"Mike who?"

"Just Mike."

He could hear her telling Egan that someone rude was calling for him. He came on the line. "Hold on while I go to another room." He heard a door being shut. "What the fuck is wrong with you calling me here?"

"Do you want your five percent or not?"

"Don't call me here—or anywhere. That's why I gave you my beeper number."

"This is an emergency." Parisi told him about being unable to find the treasure with the entire map, and then about the seismic imaging.

"You know, that sounds crazy, but it just might work. I'd have to make some calls to find out. But even if it's possible, the only people with access to that kind of technology are these international conglomerates. How are you going to get them to help?"

"I thought maybe you'd have some ideas. You know, get the FBI involved."

"You really want to see me go to prison, don't you?"

"If you come up with the right scam, that won't happen."

"Oh, so this is all on me," Egan said. "Well, I'm going to save my own life and pass."

"Ten percent . . . five million dollars."

The silence was so long Parisi thought that Egan might have disconnected the line. "Garrett?"

"Hold on, I'm thinking." After another minute, he said, "The day I reported to my new squad, someone was talking about one of your guys being arrested, Manny something."

"Baldovino."

"They set him up so he would roll over on you. So here's what you do. Have him call the FBI and say he wants to talk, to beat the case."

"But what's he going to talk about?"

"I have to admit this is a stroke of genius—the Mafia burial ground."

"What? There's nothing like that."

"They don't know that. They'll go nuts for it. The only thing they'll be able to see is headlines. *Bureau finds Mafia graveyard!* There won't be a rational thought among them. You'll be able to get anything you want. I guarantee it."

"Are they going to believe a guy like Manny has that kind of knowledge?"

"They did talk about him like he was a lightweight, but look what Joe Valachi did. They teach us in training school that you never know what small-timer is going to break the big one, and Valachi is the example they give to make their point. Besides, they must think Manny knows something. They put a lot of time and money into trying to turn him. Do you think he can pull this off?"

"He isn't the smartest guy in the world, but he does have a pretty good line of bullshit."

"Okay, just make sure you get his mind right first. You'll have to invent some reason he knows about this when he isn't even a made guy. When you think he's ready, we'll meet, and I'll give him a practice interrogation. He knows the area up in Phoenicia, right?"

"He's been up there twice."

"We have to make sure that when he comes in I'm there so I can suggest the seismic imaging. Then I'll be directly involved in the whole thing. While he's getting his story figured out, I'll make some calls to see if that kind of technology can be used for finding buried bodies, then I can be the in-house expert."

"Sounds good."

"And Mike . . ."

"Yeah?"

"If this works, don't try to fuck me."

Parisi hung up. He was about to put himself on a very narrow tightrope between DeMiglia and the FBI again. But this time he was going to attempt a complicated fraud against an agency that, over the decades, had become renowned for its prosecution of swindlers far more accomplished than he. The odds of his not ending up dead or in prison were not worth betting on. Half-heartedly, he cursed the don.

Throwing open the door, he flashed an optimistic grin. He told DeMiglia what Egan had proposed. The other men at the table started leaning back to distance themselves from the anger that invariably accompanied the underboss's cynical responses to innovation. But he surprised everyone. "I like it. I like it a lot. I want to meet this guy." He could see they didn't know how to react, and that pleased him even more.

"Predictability in this business can be life-threatening." He pushed what was left of his food into the center of the table. "You don't get it. If we use this seismic stuff, we might find the Dutch-man's box, but it's probably even money we won't. But even if we don't find it, there's one thing that'll happen no matter what—the fucking FBI is going to make clowns of themselves spending all that time and money to find the Mafia graveyard. Either way, I'm going to leak it to the papers. Right now I think I'd rather have that than the fifty million. Boys, we've been handed a no-lose situation." Then DeMiglia's eyes narrowed. His voice full of warning, he said, "Manny, you do think you can pull this off?"

"Lie to the Feds? How smart you got to be?" The underboss smiled, and everybody laughed.

On the third day, work on the Suzie Castillo case had to be abandoned. Lansing called Vanko at home to tell him he was seriously behind schedule and needed to interview at least T. H. Crowe and Dick Zalenski if he was going to finish on time. Vanko saw the change of plans as a blessing in disguise, because he wasn't sure if there was anything further that they could investigate about the homicide. If Maria Vargas, the girl picked out by the photographer, was a runaway, it lent a little more weight to the idea that Sheila's case was only a single homicide.

While Lansing did want to catch up on his interviewing, a more pressing desire was to have people milling around the off-site, increasing the likelihood of overhearing conversations. He had to admit that when the ASAC warned him not to underestimate the agents' loyalty, he had been right; he had not gotten one bit of derogatory information from any of them. Most frustrating was that he had not been able to find out anything more about the "Dimino scam." He had checked the name in the office indices and found an open organized crime case on a Paul Michael Dimino. After further inquiries, Lansing learned that Dimino had been placed in the Witness Protection Program, and all inquiries would have to be directed to the U.S. Marshals Service, a notoriously close mouthed group when dealing with the FBI. He didn't have the time or the excess of self-esteem necessary to charge through the gauntlet of belittling red tape they would surely lay in front of him.

All he could do now was hope that the vault would eventually give up its potential bounty.

A knock at the door enlarged the already existing lump in his throat. Without a word, T. H. Crowe walked in and shut the door. "Have a seat," Lansing offered evenly, as if he had no memory of their last conversation.

"I see here you're almost fifty. Thinking about retiring?"

"No."

"Hard-core, huh? Going to stay until fifty-seven?"

"Haven't thought about it."

Looking down at the file to escape Crowe's stare, Lansing said, "Looks like your career has had a few bumps along the way."

"Yeah, I spent a lot of years being a drunken asshole."

"And now?"

"I'm just an asshole."

"I'm sure that's not true."

"I think you're very sure that it is true."

Lansing fumbled with some papers. "Your performance appraisals since coming to this squad have been excellent, actually almost completely outstanding. What caused the big turnaround, getting off the booze?"

"Getting sober helped, but I was a dry drunk. Do you know what that is?"

"I think so."

"Then I got shipped out here and Nick explained how ninety percent of the meaningful work in the FBI was done by ten percent of the agents. Up to that point, my time in the Bureau had been spent as part of the other ninety percent. Then he asked me which group did I want to spend the rest of my time in."

Lansing decided this was some sort of motivational speech Vanko had devised. As he had discovered during their initial conversations, the supervisor could be very innovative. "Is that a pep talk he gives everybody reporting here?"

"I don't think so. I guess he knows who needs to hear what."

"And you believe one-tenth of the Bureau does almost all the work?"

"Actually, I think it's more like five to seven percent. But then most people in any organization are in the fat of the curve. I'd rate the majority of agents between a fifty to sixty out of a hundred."

"Interesting. How would you rate yourself?"

"Give or take, an eighty-five."

"But I thought you were in that ninetieth percentile."

"I have some people problems. So I take off five points."

"So you see people as numbers."

"It's just the way my mind works. By training, I'm an accountant."

"What good does it do to turn people into numbers?"

"Isn't that what inspections are about?" Not wanting to acknowledge the statement, Lansing busied himself writing notes. Crowe smiled. "Unless someone is an eighty-seven or above, I don't bother with them. It keeps my blood pressure down."

"I'm curious, how would you rate your supervisor?"

"He's probably the only person I don't think of in terms of numbers."

"I won't put you on the hot seat and ask you to rate me." Lansing gave him a wink, still trying to declare a truce.

"It's no trouble. Invariably, the only people who have winked at me were trying to bullshit me."

23

SHEILA DIDN'T GET BACK TO THE OFF-SITE UNTIL a little after six-thirty. Vanko had sent her on a photographic surveillance requested by one of the counterterrorism supervisors, thinking the distraction might be the best thing for her. He was beginning to regret involving the squad in her case. It gave weight to her questionable theories. The discovery that another of her "victims" appeared to be a runaway should have discouraged her, but through some convoluted psychological process, it had actually strengthened her resolve.

Lansing was still there, dictating the results of his interviews with Crowe and Zalenski. The second interview had been no more productive than the first. In fact, it had been the most boring so far. Even the reason for Zalenski's transfer to the squad had nearly put Lansing to sleep. The young agent had been caught supplementing his income by selling Rolex knockoffs—an inarguable violation of federal copyright and trademark laws—moving in excess of two hundred of them in just three weeks. The biggest disappointment of the interview came when Lansing asked him "off the record" if he had any of the watches left to sell. If such a purchase came to light, he could justify it as an attempt to gain Zalenski's confidence, or, if that proved too unbelievable, as an effort to gather evidence of a continuing felony as part of his larger investigation. And if he never had to explain how he came to possess the counterfeit item, well, he had always coveted the black-dialed Submariner.

But Zalenski swore the last one had been sold. Casually, Lansing asked him if he could remember when, hoping that it might have been after the OPR investigation, thereby generating a fresh criminal count to use against him, a possible crowbar to pry open the sealed, collective psyche of Vanko's squad. Zalenski couldn't remember exactly, but suggested that Lansing call the OPR agent who had interviewed him; he was the one who bought it. As the purchase was finalized, Zalenski explained, the agent slapped him on the back and told him not to worry about the investigation. A week later he found himself reporting to Nick Vanko.

Lansing watched as Sheila walked up to her desk and checked her messages before sitting down. Each day, she seemed to look a little healthier, her face a little fuller, her color not so blanched. Maybe it was just the dim light in the office, or maybe it was her being surrounded by all those hostile males, but Lansing found something unfashionably attractive about her. Her comments about not being sexually harassed enough haunted his idle thoughts, which he dismissed as no more than a temporary distraction. But still there was that confidence about her—that unwillingness to be intimidated by anything. She gave him an almost indistinguishable nod and turned away before he could respond. She packed a few things into her briefcase and signed out.

Now, the only other person left was Garrett Egan, who had inexplicably shown up that morning at the off-site, even though he had asked for time off. Lansing had watched the squad's latest addition most of the day as he tried to acclimate himself to the new surroundings. His movements were disjointed, like those of a visionless creature who navigated by echolocation, trying to orient himself by the memory of a sound given off in the past. Although desperate to make sense of his exile, he could now only feign being an FBI agent.

Egan's beeper sounded. He glanced at Lansing before dialing the phone, turning his back slightly.

Parisi answered, "That you?"

"Now's not a good time. Can I call you back?"

"Where are you at?"

Egan peeked over his shoulder at Lansing. "The office."

"Those have to be the safest phones in the world to call from, so someone must be there."

"I suppose you're right."

"I'm on my way to midtown and my cell's about dead. I really need to talk to you now because I'm going to be asked some questions. If you know what I mean."

Egan turned toward Lansing, who appeared engrossed in paperwork. "Let me call you back."

"Soon, right?"

"Uh-huh." Egan picked up a piece of paper and walked toward Vanko's office, pretending to read it as he went. Once inside, he shut the door. Lansing ran for the vault.

Parisi answered on the first ring. Just above a whisper, Egan said, "Are you and Baldovino ready?"

"As ready as we're going to get."

"Then we need to rehearse his interview." He lowered his voice even further. "There's a motel in Kearny, New Jersey, the Lamplighter. Get a room no later than seven o'clock. What kind of car you driving?"

"Why?"

"Trust, remember?"

"A black Cadillac coupe."

"Do you know the plate number?"

"No."

"That's all right, there won't be many Cadillacs in that place. New York tag, right?"

"Yeah."

"After you get a room, write the room number on a small piece of paper and stick it under the windshield wiper. I'll be there no later than seven-fifteen."

"Okay. There's one other thing, someone wants to meet you."

"Are you nuts, Mike! If there's anyone in that room besides you and Baldovino, it'll be the last time you'll see me." Egan suddenly realized he was shouting. "Don't do this," he whispered.

"You're going to have to meet him sooner or later. He's the one okaying this whole thing."

"My only concern right now is money. I don't care if it is fifty million dollars. The odds that we'll ever find this box are astronomical. If that happens, we'll talk about it then. My priority right now is to make sure this doesn't get fucked up so I wind up in prison. And that means the fewer that can testify against me, the better." Anger raised his voice again. "In fact, you know what, I want another twenty-five thousand to go through with this. I'm risking too much on the if-come. Have it with you tomorrow night when I get there."

"That wasn't our deal."

"That's right. I was supposed to get you that map, and that was it. But *you* came back to me. Right now, I'm the only thing keeping this alive. And we've got a long way to go, so you should be worried about keeping me happy. What's twenty-five thousand to you guys, anyway?"

Parisi didn't like being dictated to. He also didn't like giving up another twenty-five thousand, but the alternative was calling off the deal, which meant finding another way to stall DeMiglia, and he seriously doubted that was possible. "I'll see you tomorrow night."

Egan emerged from the office and glanced at Lansing as he left.

Lansing had heard only bits of the conversation, but had written down "Mike," "Baldovino," "Another 25,000 to go through with this," and "Have it with you tomorrow night."

He waited a few more minutes to make sure Egan was gone, and then walked back through the narrow hallways to check. His own car was the only one still there.

He went back inside to Vanko's desk and hit the redial button. Suddenly something occurred to him: caller ID. If the phone he was calling had it, it might show a call coming from the FBI. Normal Bureau policy was to block that option on all Bureau phones, but with this squad nothing could be assumed. He got his cell phone from his briefcase and dialed the mobile number. As it rang, the display said Out of Range. Good, he thought, the offsite's phones were blocked.

He took a deep breath and hit the redial button on Vanko's phone. The small display window showed the number. He copied it down and hung up before the call could go through.

On the Bureau computer, he typed the phone number into the New York office's indices. After a few seconds, the screen revealed that it came back to Michael Anthony Parisi, a *capo* with the

Galante crime family. The number had been discovered by one of Vanko's agents, who had surreptitiously downloaded the call history from Baldovino's cell phone after his arrest for interstate transportation of forged instruments. The address from the telephone subscriber information had been cross-referenced to the Sons of Catania Social Club in Brooklyn, the known hangout for Parisi's crew. Lansing remembered that during their initial meeting Vanko had offered the Baldovino case as the squad's most recent, and virtually only, statistical accomplishment within the last year.

He retrieved Egan's personnel file from the vault. There was just a short memo, which in the vaguest terms documented his arrest for insider trading. He was looking at jail time or, if he could make restitution, probation and a heavy fine. So plenty of motive existed to sell out. And that's certainly what the little bit of the call he had heard sounded like.

Lansing went to Egan's phone and checked the last call. It was the same number he had called from Vanko's desk. Lansing hit the redial button. When it was answered, the connection was full of static like a failing cell phone. Lansing could hear traffic in the background.

"Mike Parisi, please."

"Speaking."

At a few minutes before nine, Lansing entered his hotel room in midtown Manhattan. He brushed his teeth and recombed his hair. He slipped off his blazer, cleaned it with a lint brush, then put it back on. After adjusting his tie in the mirror, he turned out the light and headed for the chief inspector's room.

Cal Winston double-checked the time before opening the door. Lansing stood there, his face long and tight with attempted sternness, but his boss could see some sort of repressed pleasure in his eyes. "I'm sorry to bother you, sir, but we've got a major problem."

Born and raised in Georgia, Winston had discovered early in his career that unflappability, which as a southerner he had always taken pride in, emitted an aura of command, especially among his skittish peers. He was tall and carried an extra forty pounds evenly across his frame, suggesting that he would instinctively resolve any disorder with a frontal assault. But he had learned that if he just simply nodded at crises knowingly, most problems resolved themselves, leaving him to receive credit for his grace under fire. The simulation of leadership also convinced those around him that a lot more was going on inside his head than he let on. In fact, there wasn't.

"Come on in." Winston's voice indicated that he would rather it wait until morning, but "major problem" was a phrase invariably granted an immediate hearing, a rule Lansing seemed aware of.

When Lansing had finished, he said, "Well, son, you weren't bullshittin', were you? This is my last inspection, too. Before I go out as an SAC. Never fails, if there's one cow pie left in the world, I'm the one meant to step in it. I suppose we should go to the ADIC and let him know."

"With all due respect, they caught this Egan conducting insider trading, and just reassigned him. You know how this office doesn't think it has to answer to anyone. If you go to the assistant director, he might want to pull Egan in and confront him. He's going to accept another bribe tomorrow night, and we can catch him red-handed. This office is honeycombed with leaks and misdirected loyalties. Who knows, a secretary or a clerk could hear something about it, call Egan, and then where are we? I'm not even sure what I heard tonight would be admissible in court, so we'd have nothing."

"You're right about the attitude. They really do think they make the rules. Okay, I'll go along with you and let it play out a little longer. The trick is not to be too hasty. Something like this may be as plain as the nose on your face, but if you grab him tomorrow night and he does have the money, there's a lot of stories he and whoever he's meeting could make up to cloud any guilt. And I suspect these New York juries are just as unpredictable. From what you've said, they're working on some bigger scheme anyway." Winston rubbed his hand along his flat chin as his speech slowed. "I guess that's what we really need to try and uncover. Damn shame there's an agent involved."

Lansing could see some cautionary, bureaucratic switch being thrown. He suspected that hesitation had long been a staple of Winston's "contemplative" leadership, and reconsideration, if given its head, would result in a retreat to the safety of inaction.

"An agent taking multiple bribes from one of the New York families for who knows what," Lansing said. "This could wind up being huge, sir."

"Tell me again what you heard."

Lansing pulled out his notes. "The person called was 'Mike,' who I've identified as Mike Parisi, a Galante family *capo*. 'Baldovino' is believed to be Manny Baldovino, an associate of the family and currently pending federal charges. Also he said, 'I want another twenty-five thousand dollars' and 'Have it with you tomorrow night.'"

"So he's being paid at least fifty thousand dollars. That's an awful lot of money. Do you think it's for information?"

"That's the most likely reason. I noticed he was reading the file on the Galante family today. I browsed through it when I first went out to the off-site. There wasn't much classified information. Mostly generic, the kind of stuff you could have read in the newspaper. Certainly nothing I'd pay fifty thousand dollars for."

After a few seconds, Winston gestured decisively. "Well, that's what we've got to try and figure out. If we can't come up with what he's being paid for, a jury will laugh at us. While we're looking into this, I should let someone back at the Bureau know what's going on, but your argument about leaks is hard to argue with. Just so you understand, this is your baby. You're the one who has to figure out what's going on. We'll call it a preliminary inquiry, so if it comes to light, you're just checking things out to see if there's any substance to it. Nothing more, understand?"

"Yes."

"Good. Think you can handle the bumps that always come with something like this?"

"Yes, sir, I do. I'll have to cut back on the time I spend out at the off-site, but I should still be out there as much as possible in case there's more overhears."

"That's fine. We're going to need some surveillance, and obviously we can't use theirs. I know the SAC in Newark. We were in Cleveland together. I think I can get him to send me a couple of teams on the QT."

"The ideal thing would be Title Threes on Egan's home phone and on that club."

"You've never gotten a wiretap, have you?"

"No."

"It takes a month of Sundays. Plus you have to get the god-damn Department of Justice involved. Hell, the way they like to leak things, you'd be reading about it in the papers before we're up on their phones. No, we'll have to go with surveillance plus whatever intelligence you can pick up out there. It ain't perfect, but the tough ones never are."

What a role model, Lansing thought—aloof, condescending, and clueless. He couldn't wait to become an ASAC.

24

AS THEY SAT WAITING IN ROOM 218 AT THE Lamplighter Motel, Mike Parisi watched Manny Baldovino carefully. In an act of autohypnosis, he was pushing the channel button on the remote, repeatedly working his way through the eight available stations. His eyes were focused at some point short of the screen. "Manny, you all right?"

He hit the power button and threw the remote on the other side of the bed. "Yeah, sure. I mean, I'm a little nervous, but that's okay, right?"

"Being a little nervous is probably good."

"Mike, I'm not *bridge* nervous, if that's what you're worried about." Parisi's head tilted slightly with surprise. "I know you know. When something like that happens, you think nobody notices, but I could tell the way you never sent me anywhere I had to cross over any water. So, yeah, I'm okay."

"It's just that this has got to be a lot of pressure on you."

"This is just a scam. I'm not being asked to kill anybody. It's fine."

"You're sure?"

Baldovino smiled. "The fuck, Mike? We need this, right? Last night, it sounded like Danny was looking to cause you a problem. Which translates into a problem for us. We were talking after you left, and we—you know—thought you might be taking one for the crew."

The sudden endorsement surprised him, and a small rush of

warmth ran up his back. "Take one for you clowns? I'd have to be an idiot. The fuck, Manny."

"Yeah, I guess we think maybe you are."

"I'll assume there's a compliment in there somewhere."

"You're the one always yelling at us for assuming stuff."

"Just for that I'm going to tell you what DeMiglia wants us to do. You think that bridge thing can keep you awake at night?" In full detail, he told Manny about the underboss's proposed diamond vault robbery.

When he had finished, Manny shook his head. "This is my fault. This all began with me getting arrested."

"You didn't bring this on. It has nothing to do with you," Parisi said. He took in a deep breath while he considered what he was about to say. "I don't want this going any farther, do you understand?" Baldovino nodded. "If it got back to DeMiglia that I know about this, I'd be finding the Mafia graveyard the hard way. Do you understand?"

"Absolutely."

Parisi explained everything that DeMiglia was doing, and had done, to become boss, including the murder of Buffalo *capo* Frankie Falcone.

"That would explain why he'd order you to do something as crazy as hitting a place in the diamond district."

"The don just needs a little time, so that's why I've been trying anything I can to delay DeMiglia."

Manny sat quietly for a few seconds. "Does that mean that you've been going along with the treasure thing just to keep him from making his move? Don't you think my father's map is real?"

"Not much is getting by you lately, is it? Actually, I'm fairly certain the map is real, it's been checked. But yes, I have been using it to slow DeMiglia down."

"Fair enough, Mike. And don't worry, I'm not going to let you down."

There was a soft knock at the door. Parisi checked the peephole, then let Garrett Egan in. Not quite convinced of their alliance, the two men shook hands with some uncertainty. "You're right on time. This is Manny," Parisi said, trying to sound at ease.

Baldovino stood up and shook hands. "How are you?"

Egan pulled his hand back and could feel Baldovino's sweat evaporating on it. He wanted to wipe it off, but knew that it would be insulting. The optimism he had talked himself into on the way over was quickly sinking. He had to be crazy to think that they could pull this off. "How do you feel about doing this?" The question was abrupt, suspicious.

"It was my old man's map. Even though it seems like everyone and their brother is getting a piece of it, I know nobody's getting anything unless I do this right."

Egan pursed his lips. "That's good. Keep reminding yourself of that. Just remember, if at any time you feel your knees buckling, you've got to let somebody know so we can pull out. But once we get past a certain point, there is no reverse gear."

"What point is that?" Parisi asked.

"Once the Bureau commits manpower and money, they're not going to look kindly on Manny having a change of heart. Providing false information to the government is five years per count. But as long as you never admit lying to them, they would have a hard time proving it. So once you're in, you've got to stay in."

"I understand."

"I hope so."

"Did Mike tell you that you have become a snitch?"

"You mean pretend to become a snitch."

"You can't pretend. There's going to be too many people staring into your eyes, trying to find the real Manny Baldovino. The problem is you were so standup when you were arrested, and now all of a sudden, you're flipping over. You're going to have a hell of a time convincing these people. There are some you're never going to convince, and those are the ones who you can't let rattle you. But as long as you convince the majority of them, or at least the bosses, this'll work. So you can't pretend. You have to believe you're becoming an informant. Your people know you're not, so you don't have to worry about it. Get yourself into this. Believe me, I worked undercover, and that's the difference between a successful operation and a bust-out. My trouble was I believed a little too much that I was a stockbroker. Anyway, do you understand what I'm saying?"

"Yeah, I got it. I'm a lousy, stinking rat, and, in a way, I kind of like it."

"That's it exactly. And why are you rolling over?"

"I don't want to go to prison. Not for something as embarrassing as selling handicapped plates."

"And what are they going to ask you about?"

"What?"

"Something that you're going to turn down because what you're giving them doesn't require testimony?"

"No, what?"

"The Witness Protection Program."

"Oh yeah, the Witness Protection Program."

Egan looked over at Parisi. "Maybe we should be writing some of this down."

"It'll be all right. Sometimes it takes a while for things to register in Manny's brain, but once they do, they stay there."

"No, no, I got it," Manny insisted. "The Witness Protection Program."

"Okay, I'll give you the benefit of the doubt—for now."

"Don't worry," Parisi said. "I'll keep going over it with him to make sure."

"Just remember, when he walks into that FBI office, he's only going to get one shot, so he has to be completely on. Understood?" Both men nodded. "Okay, let's go over your story. How is it that you know about this burial site?"

"Back when I was on Nino Leone's crew, I drove out with my father and him once to get rid of a body. I was in a second car to cause problems if someone tried to pull them over. When we got to Phoenicia, he had me wait at the old train station while he and Nino took the body across the creek. They were gone about an hour. Nino and I were out drinking later and he told me that he had been there a number of times. On business. He always did talk too much. And he drank too much. That's why he's no longer with us."

"Murdered?"

"Liver cancer."

"And your father's passed, I assume. Otherwise you wouldn't be giving him up."

"Five years ago, a heart attack."

"That's a good story, nice and neat, easy to remember. The

only reason you were trusted was because you were his son. And there's nobody left who can refute it. And you're not being disrespectful to your father's memory because this is a scam, and it'll never see the light of day."

"Actually, from what I've been told about Manny's father, he would be pleased that he's part of this," Parisi said.

Baldovino said, "Screwing the FBI? Who wouldn't be?" Then remembering who Egan was, said, "I mean . . . sorry."

"Goddamnit, Manny, you can't let your concentration drift off like that," Egan said. "But now that you got me aggravated, it's a good time to bring up something else. You do understand that when this information doesn't work out, and you don't give them anything else, they might bust your balls a little harder at sentencing?"

"What the fuck you telling him that for!" Parisi asked.

"Because, if by some miracle all this does work out, I don't want him all of a sudden realizing, Hey, I'm in the joint, and everybody's out there spending what amounts to my inheritance. I'm getting a little lonely, maybe I should get myself some company."

"It sounds like you've thought this through a little farther than we have."

"Well, we'd better all start thinking ahead, otherwise the only discussion we'll be having is who gets the top bunk in the cell."

Manny said, "It's okay, Mike. The lawyer says for a first offense I might catch three years. It's federal, probably minimum security. And I'll have all that bread when I come out. I know you'll take care of it for me. Probably even get me some interest. I think my father would be pleased with me taking the weight on this."

Parisi said, "How sure are you that your people will go to this kind of trouble?"

"I told you before, as soon as they hear 'Mafia graveyard,' there won't be an ounce of common sense left between them. All they'll be thinking about will be headlines and who's going to play them in the movie. This is literally a license for us to steal. Trust me. If you told them it was under Hoover Dam, they'd blow it up for you."

"How about when they take these readings and the box shows up on their charts. Won't they want to dig it up?"

"I spent a lot of time thinking about what could go wrong, and I checked some old cases. They've never tried anything on this scale. Seismic imaging is expensive. I can't even guess how much, probably tens of thousands of dollars a day. So time is money and anything that isn't a body, they won't waste time on. They'll actually be trying to find a way to eliminate any distractions. That's where I come in. I'll suggest they use a cadaver dog. Do you know anything about them?"

"No," Parisi answered for both of them.

"They sniff out buried bodies. I'll simply explain to my bosses that a dog will keep us from doing a lot of unnecessary digging. See, if the FBI finds a grave, they can't just bring in a backhoe and tear it open. Each grave becomes a crime scene and has to be excavated very carefully so evidence isn't destroyed. It takes forever to find out what's buried there. Each grave would take days, if it even is a grave. But these dogs hit on the scent of decaying flesh, even if it's years old. So when they spot the box on the charts, I'll march the dog over to it, and it won't hit because there's nothing dead involved. Then the search will move on. I'll mark the spot and as soon as it's clear, I'll dig it up."

"*We'll* dig it up," Parisi said.

"We'll dig it up." Egan wasn't sure *we* was meant to include him, but since he would be the one to mark it, he would do it in a way that only he could find it.

"What's to prevent them from saying forget the seismic stuff and just use the dog?"

"I looked at a map of the area. Manny's going to tell them they were gone an hour. That would translate into a large area, maybe as much as ten square miles. Don't forget, as the in-house expert on seismic imaging and cadaver dogs, I'll be able to influence the size of the area that needs to be searched. Then even if they have a half dozen dogs, I'll tell them it's too large to search. Plus, dead animals can distract these dogs, and there'll be plenty in that terrain. Once they lock on to one, they're done for the day. I'll also tell them that it could take one dog months to find a body—if it didn't miss it altogether. Then the cost of the imaging will be justifiable because of the savings of having a dozen agents up there working and living in a hotel for months. Besides, they'll love the idea of using cutting-edge technology to solve a crime, especially against the mob. It'll be all over the newspapers, and they'll be doing television shows for years to come about how inventive they are. I've seen this before. They get into a frenzy, which causes extreme tunnel vision. They won't let anything get in their way. It'll be great PR, something the Bureau can't buy these days."

"When you explain it, it sounds reasonable," Parisi said.

"This is just money to you guys; for me, it's my freedom and my family's future. In the meantime I've been learning all I can about seismic imaging, who can do it and how. That way when I suggest it, they'll rely on me for technical advice."

"And that puts you in the middle of the decision making. Pretty smart," Parisi said.

"Hopefully, but, as I'm sure you know, when running a scam, you can't think of everything. That's why you need a good bull-shitter as a front man. Right, Manny?" Baldovino smiled with some pride. "Any questions?" They shook their heads. "Okay, then I believe you have some money for me."

Parisi went over to a dresser drawer. He took out an inexpensive plastic briefcase; its sides bulged slightly. Egan took it from him and peeked inside. "Okay, Manny. Here's how you make sure this is handled by my squad."

After explaining the case-assignment process to him, Egan reemphasized how critical Manny's role was to the success of the plan. Parisi was pleased how focused Manny had become, completely concentrating on each phase of the instruction.

"What is it they'll offer you but you'll turn down, Manny?" Egan asked.

"The Witness Protection Program."

For the next hour and a half, the three men discussed every detail and contingency they could think of. Once he was satisfied, Egan took the briefcase and left. He didn't notice the black Camaro parked across the street in the restaurant lot. As he put the briefcase in the trunk, the agent fired away with his thirty-five-millimeter camera. Nobody on the surveillance team had been told that their target was an agent, only that it was organized crime and very hush-hush.

Egan started his car, and the agent radioed the second team that had been following Parisi for the last four hours. "Our boy's firing up his chopper. Looks like we're about to part company."

"Yeah, ours is coming out, too." The second agent snapped pictures of Parisi and Baldovino emerging from room 218. "Interesting. Our boy carries in the briefcase and yours carries it out. You don't suppose there's anything illegal in it, do you?"

"I'm guessing illegal tender."

As Crowe sat down, Vanko asked, "How'd your interview with the inspector go?"

"It must have gone all right, he's been around here a lot less."

"You do have a knack for cutting through people's BS."

"Speaking of which."

"Okay, I need a favor."

"I guess I owe you one."

"Maria Vargas."

"The runaway?" Vanko nodded. "I was wondering if we were going to get around to that."

"Meaning?"

"It's not like this squad is authorized to conduct homicide investigations. We know you're sticking your neck out to help her, and we don't mind being part of that. But when you didn't pursue the Maria Vargas lead, I thought maybe you were protecting Sheila's feelings. No disrespect, Nick, but it looked like you were trying to keep from proving her wrong."

"I don't want to prove her wrong, at least not in front of everybody."

"Does that mean you don't think there's a serial killer?"

"I really don't know. Sheila's lived with this a lot longer than we have. It *looks* like she's lost her objectivity, but who knows."

"What about your objectivity?"

"It's suspect, that's why I'm asking you to chase this down."

"Then I'll take care of it."

The squad secretary buzzed Vanko. "I've got downtown on hold. They have somebody on the line who says he has important organized crime information and won't talk to anyone but the supervisor of the Manny Baldovino case."

Crowe nodded to Vanko and left. "Okay, have them transfer it over."

Vanko heard the line click in. "Hello, this is Nick Vanko. Can I help you?" He looked at the display on his phone but it read Not Registered.

"Yeah, are you the boss of the guys who arrested Manny Baldovino?"

"That case is on my squad, yes. Could I have your name, please."

There was a slight hesitation. "This *is* Manny Baldovino."

"Well . . . hello, Manny. I'd ask you how you are, but if you're calling me, it sounds like things could be better."

"That's right, they could be."

"They said you had some information."

"That's right, and it's big."

"Big, huh? I guess that means you're looking for some type of accommodation before you tell me what it is." Baldovino's sarcastic laugh was slightly nervous. "How come you're not having your lawyer broker this?"

"Do you know who my lawyer is?"

"No."

"Let's just say he represents a lot of organized crime people. Too many organized crime people, if you know what I mean."

"So you think his interests might be conflicted."

"If you mean me winding up dead, yeah, conflicted."

"So I guess we need to get together and see if there's anything we can do to make each other's lives a little easier."

"I can tell you what I want right now. I want a walk."

"Sounds like you think you've got something substantial to offer."

"This is going to make you a superstar."

Vanko laughed. "No offense, Manny, but I've heard that before."

A little unsure of himself now, Baldovino said, "You'll see."

"Fair enough." Experience had taught Vanko that whatever slight shift in the wind had summoned Baldovino's cooperation could just as easily reverse itself without warning. "Then we need to get together. Tonight."

"It can't be in Brooklyn."

"How about Manhattan?"

"Okay, but no restaurants. These people are always going over there to eat."

"There's a small hotel on East Fifty-first. The Chase. Be at the bar by eight and have a drink. A woman will come and get you. I'll be upstairs." When he didn't say anything, Vanko said, "Is that all right?"

"Yeah, I was just writing it down."

"Good. I don't suppose you care to give me a number where I can reach you?"

"And they say you Feds don't have a sense of humor."

"I'll see you tonight, Manny."

Baldovino hung up and looked at Parisi. "Did I sound *too* nervous?"

"I thought you played it just about right."

"He wants to meet tonight."

"That's a good sign. It means he's hot for it."

"It's just that I thought I'd have a little more time to prepare for it. You know, mentally."

"Manny, you've got good instincts. Just let them take over. You have a tendency to tie yourself up in a knot by overthinking situations."

Baldovino smiled. "The fuck, Mike."

"The fuck, Manny."

Vanko leaned out his door. "Sheila, can I see you a minute?"

She swallowed the last of her coffee and came in. "What's up?" she asked as she sat down in a chair across from him.

"Are you doing anything tonight?" A small flicker of expectation flashed across her face, and he realized that she thought he was asking her out. He looked away embarrassed. The fear of rejection was keeping them apart, and he was about to give her one more reason to think that was not going to change any time soon. "Sorry. I need you to work tonight. If you're available."

A shrewd smile pulled up the corner of her eyes. "Are you sorry because you're asking me to work, or are you sorry about something else?"

Purposely ignoring her gaze, he supplied the details of the call from Baldovino. "We have to be careful how we do this. The hotel isn't the kind that would attract any of his friends, but you never know. If you pick him up in the bar, that would cover him in case someone is around. Any problem with that?"

"Are you kidding? Play a whore? To a mob guy?" she asked in that lilting, agile voice. "You dream about these things in training school, but . . ."

"It's really nice having someone on the squad with your enthusiasm. Never any complaints, never any sarcasm."

"I thought these guys didn't like women around when they're conducting business."

"When I told him a woman would meet him in the bar, he didn't object."

"Maybe he thinks there're more benefits to witness protection than a new identity."

Vanko laughed. "How about I pick you up at seven."

"How about you come by at six and we'll have something to eat. I owe you a dinner."

Vanko pointed at his in box, which teetered with Bureau mail. He felt some relief and wondered if he wasn't using it as another delaying tactic. The two of them seemed to have that effect on each other. "I've got all this to get through, and I still have to make more arrangements for tonight. Some other time—soon."

Soon was good, she supposed. The word seemed declaratory, but it was hardly escape-proof. She wondered if she would ever stop trying to uncover the hidden labyrinth within every syllable. Maybe that's what she really wanted—rest from the endless search for motive. She looked at Vanko's face and, as always, he held it out for examination, as if he were letting it explain his reluctance. His disfigurement provided her with a good deal of safety. Without it, she doubted that she would have remained optimistic. "Okay, but you don't know what you're missing. I order a mean pizza."

25

THE BAR AT THE CHASE HOTEL WAS NOT TO MANNY Baldovino's liking. The decor was Danish Modern. The trail blond furnishings seemed too minimalist, almost surreal, at least compared to the places he hung out. The dozen or so patrons, European he guessed, looked equally misplaced. Thin men with pointed, graying goatees or sharply receding hairlines and women too skinny in the upper body, their hair severely drawn back into knotted puzzles.

He supposed that's why Vanko had picked the place, so there was less chance he'd run into someone he knew. Still, it left him empty, like having only salad with the smell of steak in the air. Maybe he was trying to find something wrong, a reason to turn and run like he had at the bridge. Feeling a little nervous but not quite panicked—not yet anyway—he considered taking one of his pills. He hadn't needed them in a while, but he no longer knew how his nervous system was going to react to stress. While calming, the pills slowed his thinking, a disadvantage someone nicknamed the Lag could not afford. Maybe a little bit of fear was good. At the moment it seemed to be speeding up his brain.

That's when he noticed the man sitting alone at the bar, almost leaning in behind a couple to shield himself from view. His face was tan and his perfectly arched eyebrows were artificially raised in an expression of boredom. His drink was tall and clear with too much ice and too many lime wedges to be alcoholic. He wore an expensively cut white linen jacket over a navy blue turtleneck. His thick brown hair was swept straight back. In the crowd of staid, immobile northern Europeans, he looked like he was in the process of breaking the land speed record. A dazzling Manhattanite.

Manny stepped up to the bar and, as he waited to give his order, tried to catch Linen Jacket's eye to tell him that he knew. Never pass up the opportunity to bust the FBI's balls; it was an unwritten law for mob guys. "Double scotch rocks," he told the bartender.

Bradley Kenyon had seen Manny's mug shot early in the evening. He slipped his cell phone out of his pocket and hit the speed-dial number programmed in a half hour earlier. The phone in the room where the rest of the agents waited rang. Kenyon let it ring for ten seconds and then disconnected the call. He sipped his drink as he cautiously searched the small bar to determine if Baldovino had come alone.

Ten minutes later, Manny was about to order another drink when Sheila walked in and sat down next to him. She was wearing an emerald green silk sheath dress, and while she was as slender as the other women in the bar, her figure was convincingly American. "Hi, Manny," she pecked him on the cheek, "have you been waiting long?"

"Ah, no, not long. How are you . . . ?"

"Sheila."

"Sheila."

"I'm good."

"Can I get you a drink?"

"Red wine would be nice. Why don't I get a booth."

He brought the drinks over and sat down. "Don't you think you should sit next to me?" she asked.

He swung around next to her. Blushing a little, he said, "I thought you Feds couldn't drink on duty."

"Like everything else, it's all right as long as we don't get caught . . . but look who I'm telling that to."

Manny laughed. "So, are you a real lady agent?"

"I've got a badge if that's what you mean. How about you? You a real mob guy?"

"You obviously haven't read my file." He dropped his voice to a whisper. "I'm not made, if that's what you mean."

"We've all got management problems. I've got bosses who think J. Edgar Hoover was a vacuum cleaner salesman. But you're in good hands with Nick. He's someone you can trust."

"You're all right. Too bad we had to meet like this."

"Yes, it is." She patted his hand. "You about ready?"

He fired down what was left of his drink. "Absolutely." She hooked her arm through his and they walked to the elevators.

When they got to the room, she opened the door with a key card. It was a three-room suite with a small bar along the living room wall. Vanko was sitting in a leather chair with his legs crossed. He sat still for a moment before extending his hand. It was a gesture he used when someone was seeing his face for the first time. He smiled warmly. "Manny, I'm Nick Vanko."

Baldovino forced himself to stare straight into Vanko's eyes. He shook hands. "Nice to meet you, Nick."

"Come on into the sitting room. Can we get you anything?"

"Yeah, some scotch would be nice. I'm still a little nervous."

"That's understandable. Water?"

"Just ice, thanks."

They sat down and, when Vanko didn't say anything, Baldovino felt a need to break the silence. "I got to hand it to your guys, they got me good on that license plate beef." He smiled stiffly.

"To steal a line from your outfit's book, it was just business, nothing personal."

Baldovino laughed and seemed to relax a little. Crowe handed him a drink, then disappeared into the other room. He took a healthy swallow. "No offense taken. These things happen."

"So, tell me what you want from us."

"I want this case dropped."

"What about the Witness Protection Program?"

"That would mean I was going to testify. What I'm giving you really won't need any testimony. In fact, part of this deal is that my name never comes up."

"What you're talking about is becoming an informant."

"Just on this one thing. I'm trading it for a walk, straight up."

"I've already talked to the United States Attorney's office, and they pretty much gave me a free hand. So tell me exactly what it is you're offering."

Baldovino bit the inside of his cheek hard. "I can take you to the Mafia graveyard."

Vanko's eyes narrowed slightly. "Mafia graveyard?"

"That's right."

"How come I've never heard about this before?"

"There aren't that many even within the family that know about this place."

"No offense, Manny, but as far as we know, you're not even a made member. How would you know about it?"

"You know who my old man was?"

"We know he was a *capo* until his death."

"He was the most respected man in the family, maybe in any of the families. It was his job to dispose of bodies. One time he took me along. It was only the once, kind of an emergency deal. I was his son, trust was not an issue."

Vanko searched Baldovino for signs of deception. He showed almost none of his initial nervousness. The one advantage to having a disfigured face was that Vanko could use it to gauge people's ability to think on their feet, how fast they could ignore it, how good they were at hiding their true reactions, and how fast they could improvise. Baldovino had adjusted as quickly as any, which did not help Vanko judge the truth of his story. "How many bodies are you talking about?"

"No telling. It wasn't something my father talked about. But think about how many of our people have disappeared over the last ten years. The night I went with him Nino Leone came too. He was my *capo* before Mike Parisi. Every once in a while when we were alone, especially if we were drinking, he'd bring it up. See, when he got drunk, he got religion. He had all this regret that their wives and kids couldn't have a proper burial and mourning. I guess because I was with my dad that night, he felt it was okay to discuss it with me. Sometimes he talked about it too much, you know, like he had to unload."

"He's dead now."

"Yeah, liver cancer."

"And you'll take us there."

"I'll take you as close as I got."

"What do you mean?"

"It's upstate. Near Phoenicia."

"What do you mean as close as you got?"

"Once they got close enough that they didn't need me, they went in by themselves. I may have been his son, but he still followed the rules. It couldn't have been far though, because they were gone less than an hour. Figure in digging time and then covering up, it had to be close by."

"I'm just surprised we've never heard about it before."

"You mean on wiretaps? There's only a couple of guys who knew about it and they're dead. Neither of them ever went to jail because they never said anything on the phone. And tell me this, Nick, what kind of moron would I have to be to come to you and lie when you can put me in prison anytime? I know that if you don't find any bodies, I'm going to prison and maybe for longer for wasting your time."

Baldovino's point was inarguable. As Vanko considered it, he heard the just-audible strains of Sheila's voice from the other room. He thought he caught a hint of her shampoo, that damp, scratchy scent from the car. And that stunning green dress. Surprisingly, she had worn makeup, the first time he had seen her use it. Applied skillfully, it had smoothed the uneven texture of her skin and given it a consistent color. But she had allowed herself to slip into her role only so far. She wore no nylons or nail polish, and when she walked in front of him to the car, he noticed the back of her hair was still wet from the shower. "I hope you don't have any immediate plans, Manny. We'll want to go up there in the morning."

"So I guess that means you believe me."

"It means that I want to believe you."

The squad had assembled in the office by 8:00 the next morning. Vanko had been there since 6:30 making last-minute arrangements for the trip north, an odyssey he hoped would not be filled with the Homeric obstacles it somehow promised. When Charles Lansing walked in and saw all the activity, he headed straight for the vault.

Receiving word that the inspector had shown up, Vanko knew he had little choice but to brief him on the information provided by Manny Baldovino. When Vanko mentioned Baldovino, Lansing realized that his "information" was part of what Egan had been planning on the phone. Aware of Egan's duplicity, plus whatever story Baldovino was telling, Lansing could find out what was really going on. But he would have to be careful not to know too much because Vanko already had two people trying to deceive him; a third might expose everything. "A Mafia graveyard? I've never heard of anything like that, have you?"

"No. But according to Baldovino, it was an extremely well guarded secret. His father was one of only two men who had detailed knowledge of its existence and had involved him only once, peripherally."

"Any problem me tagging along?"

The last thing Vanko wanted was to give Lansing prolonged exposure to his squad. Any one of them might divulge secrets out of boredom or do something stupid simply to get a rise out of the inspector. "It's going to take the entire day."

"That's all right, something like this would probably be worth getting behind schedule a little."

"As long as you don't mind being in the car with me for a couple of hours." He had hoped to make the trip with Sheila, but that small luxury was about to vanish.

"I can ride with someone else if you like."

"No, we can go over some of the inspection deficiencies you've been wanting to discuss."

"I'll get my briefcase."

Vanko instructed T. H. Crowe and Dick Zalenski to make sure Baldovino wore sunglasses and some kind of large hat until they were out of the city on the off chance someone spotted the easily identifiable agents and recognized their backseat passenger. Baldovino expressed some concern for what the hat would do to his hair. Crowe said, "Manny, it's my job to get you to Phoenicia safely. You know, so no one will shoot you. So please don't make *me* want to shoot you."

"The hat's fine."

Crowe looked at his hair. "Guys with your hair usually prefer hats." Zalenski gave a low chuckle.

"What's wrong with my hair?"

"Where it's still growing, I guess it's fine." Zalenski looked over at Crowe and wagged his eyebrows in appreciation.

Manny ran his fingers through the hair at the back of his head where it was longer. "Hey, I've got good hair," he protested, his tone rising. Suppressed laughter shook Zalenski's shoulders. Baldovino looked over at Crowe, who seemed stoically frozen in his seat. The older agent's hair was thick and full, but he was a couple of weeks past needing a haircut. "I spend a lot of money on my hair. I get it cut every week, by a stylist, not some Marine Corps taxidermist. It costs me a half a buck. What do you pay, six dollars at the barber college?"

Crowe turned around slowly. "Okay, let me have a good look. Take the hat off." Baldovino took it off and smoothed down the sides. Crowe tilted his head appraisingly. "I hope that fifty cents included a tip."

After two and a half hours and less than a hundred words later, the three men pulled into the parking lot of the old train station. Vanko and Lansing were already there. Straker, Snow, and Kenyon drove up in one of the squad's surveillance vans, which had been outfitted with as many digging instruments and probing devices as could be rounded up on short notice. Egan and Sheila pulled in behind them. Just prior to leaving Global Fish, Lansing had called the chief inspector from his cell phone, telling him to call off the surveillance on Egan. On that long a trip, and with so many agents, someone might notice they were being followed.

On Vanko's instruction, Crowe and Straker checked around the area before Manny was allowed out of the car and then only with the sunglasses and hat, which he had pulled down as far as possible in protest. But when Sheila got out of her car, he pulled it off and gave her a self-conscious wave.

With Lansing close at hand, Vanko said, "Okay, Manny, is this it?"

"Yeah, this looks right."

"Now that we're physically here, maybe your memory will be a little more detailed. Tell us exactly what you remember."

"Well, like I said, it's got to be close to ten years ago. Like one o'clock in the morning when we got here, maybe later. Pitch black. My old man told me to wait right here while him and Nino took care of the body. They drove out of the lot and over that way." Baldovino pointed in a generally southwestern direction.

"And how long were they gone?" Vanko asked.

"Forty-five minutes, an hour tops. I can't remember for sure."

"When they got back, did they say anything that might narrow it down? You know, like the ground was hard, they had to drive across a stream, any landmarks? Anything like that?"

"I'll have to think about it, but nothing comes to me right at this minute. I'm sorry, Nick, but it isn't easy with everybody standing here expecting me to recall every little detail from a dark night ten years ago."

"I'm sure it isn't. So let's try something else. Do you know the last time they buried a body here?"

"Nino only talked about it in general terms. He wasn't stupid."

"So as far as you know, it was ten years ago."

"That *I* know of, yeah, ten years."

Checking the map, Vanko had everyone follow him down to High Street, where he took a right onto Woodland Valley Road. A bridge crossed over Esopus Creek; on the other side, he drove as far as the terrain would allow. Getting out, he called everyone together and handed out photocopied maps they had downloaded off the Internet that morning. The air was thick with the sour odor of decaying vegetation. He divided them into teams to search sectors designated on the map.

"What are we looking for?" Straker asked.

"Anywhere it looks like a hole has been dug and then filled in. They weren't hauling dirt away, so logically there would be mounds in the spots where the bodies were left, maybe overgrown by now. Aside from that, I don't know."

The small groups, each with a handheld radio, took off along some of the foot trails that generally ran parallel to the creek. A solitary man fly-fishing in rubber waders was startled as the agents streamed past him. It was obvious they weren't there for the trout.

For the next two hours, the squad searched the area, doubling back and crisscrossing paths. After some of them straggled back to his position, Vanko radioed the rest to meet at the van. He asked Baldovino, "Did you remember anything else?"

"Not really."

"And you don't have any idea how many bodies might be here?"

"Just what I already told you."

"Manny?"

"What?"

"Could it be there was just one body?"

"No. Nino said it a couple of times, 'All those poor bastards.' I'm not saying every mob guy that's ever been hit is up here, but I got the impression there's a bunch. I just don't know where."

"Anybody have any ideas?"

Egan said, "When I was in Kansas City, we had a kidnapping that wound up being a search for the victim's body. They brought in this cadaver dog. It was pretty amazing."

"But that was a fresh body, right?" Vanko asked.

"Yes, but there's been cases where they've found them after years."

"Even if they're fully decayed?"

"I guess the soil becomes saturated with decomposition fluid. And they can detect that for years."

"How deep do they have to be buried before the dogs can't smell them?"

Egan hadn't noticed, but Lansing had carefully moved just out of his peripheral vision and was watching his gestures closely to see if he had any "tells" when he lied. "They said there's been instances where they've detected bodies under eight feet of concrete. I don't know how they do it, but they're used all the time to find bodies under water, which is relatively easy because when a body is decomposing it gives off gases, which rise to the surface. It probably works the same way underground."

"How big an area can one of them cover?" Vanko said.

"I'm no expert, but I think it depends on a lot of different things like how long they've been buried, how deep, the terrain, stuff like that. And you have to be careful. They can get overstressed in a hurry, and it makes them hypersensitive. Once that happens, they're pretty much through for the day. A guess—I'd say a square mile, under perfect conditions, would take a dog at least a week."

Vanko looked at his map again. "I'd say we've got at least five or six square miles here, maybe more, and with this undergrowth, we'd probably need a dozen dogs for a month. Can you give us anything else, Manny?"

"I've been trying to remember. It seemed like there was something else, but maybe I'm trying too hard."

"There's too much area to search. Unless you can come up with something that's going to help us narrow it down, you're not going to be able to help yourself."

Manny reminded himself not to look at Egan. "Hey, okay, I get it. I *am* trying."

"I can't think of anything else to do up here. Let's head back. T. H., can you get Manny back?" Crowe nodded.

Egan said, "Nick, can I ride back with you? Maybe we could figure out something with the dogs."

"Sure."

Lansing got in the backseat of Vanko's car and said to Egan, "Why don't you ride up front. I'd like to stretch out my legs."

After they had been driving for a while, Egan said, "As impressive as that dog was, it didn't find the kidnapping victim." Lansing began to wonder if any of his story was true. "A Fish and Game warden's dog more or less stumbled on the body."

"Well, I'm sure there aren't enough of those in the whole state of New York to help us," Vanko said.

Lansing watched as Egan glanced at Vanko, trying to decide the right moment to deliver what he wanted to say next. Then, as if suddenly remembering the passenger in the backseat, he looked at Lansing, who averted his gaze out the window. Finally Egan said, "You know, when I was working on Wall Street, I did a workup on this outfit that the oil exploration companies use. They conduct seismic tests to find oil and gas deposits underground. With the advance in computers and mathematics in the last twenty years they have become very sophisticated. They send these sound waves into the earth and then take a reading when the signal echoes back to sensors. It gives these huge three-dimensional charts showing exactly what's underground. Think something like that could work on this?"

"I don't know. There's a big difference between millions of gallons of oil and a body."

"I remember something about it being used to find utility lines for potential digging problems, so they must be able to scale it down. I could look into it."

"How long will it take you to find out?" Lansing asked carefully.

"I could get on it as soon as we get back."

Vanko turned toward Egan. "Pretty creative for a guy who says he doesn't care."

"That's always been my problem, I let myself get too involved, and then I get carried away."

The only sense Lansing could make out of Egan and Baldovino's ruse was that they were trying to get the FBI to search underground for something. What, he had no idea, but he was sure it wasn't bodies. Whatever it was, when they found it, he would be there.

26

THE AFTER HOURS WAS ONE OF THE HOTTEST CLUBS in Bensonhurst, and just to make sure everyone knew it, the doorman had standing orders to keep a long line of customers outside, even if it reduced profits in the short term. Parisi had been told to bring Baldovino with him and come straight to the side door "to avoid the crowd." These instructions worried him. Why didn't DeMiglia want him to be seen coming into the club? The predictable answer was that he was simply being cautious. As he pulled into the lot, Parisi hoped that was DeMiglia's only reason. Even though the air-conditioning was blasting, the back of his shirt was soaked. As they got out of the car, the hot, sticky night air closed in around him.

After a single knock, the door was opened and Parisi and Baldovino were led upstairs to a private room. DeMiglia sat on the couch with a young woman. He pulled her close and whispered in her ear. She pushed down her skirt and smiled at them as she left. DeMiglia pointed at the two chairs opposite the couch. "Come on, sit." They waited for the underboss to announce the reason they had been summoned.

"So?"

Parisi casually lit a cigarette and said, "From what Manny said, it went well. Like Egan predicted, once they heard 'Mafia' and 'graveyard' in the same sentence their brains disappeared up their asses."

"Did it go that good, Manny?"

"Yeah, they think there's bodies out there." Baldovino laughed. "You should have seen them running around. At times they were actually bumping into each other, afraid someone else was going to find a body first. Egan was right, it's absolutely friggin' catnip."

DeMiglia smiled only briefly. "Are they buying it, or are you two bullshitting me so you won't have to do that diamond score?" Parisi shifted uncomfortably. It was not a question he wanted Manny to try to answer. He started to say something, but DeMiglia held up a hand. "Well, Manny?"

"No, I'm telling you, Danny, they're buying it, completely."

DeMiglia swiveled toward Parisi. "You talk to Egan?"

"Not yet."

"Get him on the phone right now."

"He isn't going to like that."

"My job is getting people to do things they don't like. It's *supposed* to be your job, too. Make the call."

Parisi crushed out his cigarette and dialed. "Garrett, it's Mike. How'd it go today?"

"I'd say it went well," Egan said. "What did Manny think?"

"He said the same thing. What about the seismic stuff?"

"The supervisor's interested, in fact, he's put me in charge of seeing if it can be arranged."

"And you don't think they suspect anything?"

"Nothing."

"Hold on a second." Parisi repeated what the agent had said.

DeMiglia said, "Give me the phone."

Parisi handed it to DeMiglia.

"I know you don't want to talk to somebody you don't know, but just take it easy for a minute."

"I told Parisi I don't need to be dealing with anybody else. One is too many, and now there are three of you."

"Nobody likes a cautious person more than me. It's what's kept me out of jail. And you should take some comfort in that. Because if I ain't going to prison, you ain't going. Understand?"

"I guess."

"Do you understand?"

"Yes."

"Okay, good. Now how sure are you that they're going to go for this with the underground stuff?"

"As I told Mike, they'd do anything to uncover a Mafia grave-yard. They can taste it."

"And they put you in charge of arranging it?"

"The technical stuff, yes."

"Un-fucking-believable. Maybe you guys are overrated."

"You don't know what an understatement that is."

"How soon you think you can pull this off?"

"A matter of days. Don't forget, I don't know how long I've got left, so for me, the quicker the better."

"I'm keeping a close eye on this. Just so you know."

"Please don't waste your time threatening me. My life's a little too fucked up right now for me to care that much."

DeMiglia handed the phone back to Parisi, who said, "Call me when you hear anything." He hung up.

DeMiglia shook his head. "Fifty million dollars. I told you we used to hear about this when we were kids. When I got older, I just figured it was like a ghost story. That there was nothing to it. Do you know what finding a legend makes you?"

"No, what?"

"A legend."

Parisi was pleased that DeMiglia had lost his objectivity so completely and smiled in agreement.

But, after a moment, Parisi's concurrence seemed to sober the underboss. Experience had taught him that no matter what was going on right now, Parisi was ultimately an enemy. "You know something that's bothering me? You have this reputation of being a very practical guy, with the numbers and all. I didn't think someone like you would go for this treasure stuff."

"You're right, usually if I can't touch it, I doubt it exists. But everything checks out. And when you actually go up there and walk around, it feels very real, almost like you can hear it rum-bling under your feet. I think you felt it, too." Although DeMiglia didn't deny it, he gave no indication that he had accepted the ex-planation. But Parisi knew he could always rely on the under-boss's hatred of the FBI. "When I'm having doubts, I think, Hey, what's this costing us? Not a thing. And better than that, it's costing the FBI a ton. And if we get lucky and find the box, they'll never know anything about it. And we can still make idiots of them in the papers."

Parisi could see that DeMiglia was pleased with how "his" plan had evolved into a no-lose situation as he pictured himself walking into the next commission meeting to a round of applause.

Maria Vargas sat on a bench half a block from Penn Station. Next to her was a small, battered suitcase. As she felt the man near, she looked up so he could see her tears. He was older and white, wearing a suit and carrying a briefcase, the kind of individual that had proved to be her crew's best marks. She sobbed just loudly enough. He looked down at her flawless fourteen-year-old face.

"Are you all right, Miss?"

Miss. He was either a very proper person—which invariably translated into a need to rescue the damsel in distress—or, even better, he was laden with white guilt.

"No, I guess I'm okay." Her voice cracked on the last two syllables.

"I'm sorry, but you don't sound like it."

She glanced at the two young Hispanics, leaning against a building across the street watching her work.

He handed her a handkerchief. "Come on, tell me what's wrong."

She pulled a letter out of her jeans pocket and pointed at the return address. "Do you know where this is?"

"Rochester, New York? Yes. Is that where you're trying to get to?"

"I was supposed to take a bus. I had a ticket, but someone stole my purse on the train from Dallas."

"Is there someone in Rochester you can call?"

"They don't have a phone, and I don't know anyone else here."

"How much is a ticket?"

This was the tricky part. If she asked for too much, she might scare off the mark, too little and her boyfriend would beat her. "I think they said forty-eight dollars," she said, adding with childish desperation, "I would pay you back."

"Well, maybe I could lend you twenty."

"Could you make it twenty-five? I haven't eaten since I left Texas."

"I've only got four singles." Her eyes started to well up again. "There's an ATM around the corner." He picked up her bag. "Come on, we'll see what we can do."

She glanced back and one of the young men nodded. "You'll give me your address so I can send it to you?"

"Let's get you something to eat before we worry about all that."

As soon as they turned the corner, she saw a patrol car parked at the curb with two NYPD officers in it. Crowe grabbed her wrist. "What do you think you're doing?" she demanded.

"Sending you home." He opened her suitcase. There were only a few clothes inside.

Just as the car was pulling away, the two young Hispanics came around the corner. When they saw Maria in the backseat, they looked at Crowe. Barely able to contain a smile, he said, "You two, hold it right there, I want to talk to you." They broke into a dead run.

Garrett Egan walked into Vanko's office and sat down. "I found somebody who'll do the seismic imaging."

Vanko set his pen down and slowly folded his hands. "Impressive."

"Something wrong?"

"As much as I'd like to take credit for it, I'm just a little surprised at the change in your attitude."

"My attitude hasn't really changed all that much. I still hate how the Bureau is treating me and my family, but my days are a hell of a lot shorter when I can keep my mind off what's ahead. And who knows, maybe if I do some good around here, it'll be taken into consideration later on."

"Fair enough. I'll get everybody in here so you just have to explain it once."

Vanko called the squad in. Lansing emerged from the vault reading a file. "Chuck, we've got some information on that seismic imaging if you want to sit in."

"Sure."

When everyone had crowded into the office, Egan said, "I got lucky. Downtown had a former agents directory, so I made calls to some ex-agents in the Houston area who got retirement jobs with oil companies. One is a guy named Dave Thornton. He's only been retired three years, so he's still enough of an investigator to appreciate what we're trying to do. He's an engineer and spent a big part of his career in the lab." He looked at Vanko. "Do you want the good news first?"

"Always."

"I told him we were trying to locate some fairly shallow graves. As far as he knows it's never been done, but he'd really like to give it a try. He was telling me a couple of years ago, some scientist used all kinds of land devices to recover a billion dollars of gold from a sunken ship eight thousand feet deep without even getting a toe wet. He thought this had similar possibilities."

"What kind of time frame are we looking at?"

"It's very sophisticated equipment, but it's also highly mobile. Since this project, as he calls it, is government-related, he can make it a priority. Once we give him the okay, he says he can have it here within two days."

"What did he say about targets that are less than six feet deep?" Straker asked.

"He said the Russians have done extensive shallow search experiments, and by changing the frequency of the wave emitted, they could find inconsistencies at lesser depths. I think the chance to break new ground is what's making him so gung-ho."

"So his guess is that it's possible," Vanko said.

"Very possible."

In the vault, Lansing had heard Vanko and Egan's preliminary conversation clearly enough to detect the suspicion in Vanko's voice. The last thing he needed right now was someone else discovering Egan's duplicity. "I'm impressed," he offered, hoping that his optimism might sweep Vanko and the others along, but the only response was a brief, icy quiet.

Vanko said to Egan, "Okay, what's the bad news?"

"It costs seventy-eight thousand a day."

"Did you tell him the size of our area?"

"Yes. He said he couldn't be sure—a lot of it depends on terrain and other variables—but he figured two to three days."

"Didn't take long to get up to a quarter of a million, did it?" Vanko said.

"Some smaller good news—I did find a dog. A state Fish and Game officer who has one said she'd be glad to give us a hand. So that much is free."

"Anyone see any problems?"

Straker turned to Lansing. "Hey, Chuck, isn't a quarter of a million about what they pay two inspectors a year?"

Lansing smiled uncomfortably. "About that."

"Then I vote no, Nick. Why waste money on finding a bunch of dead goombas when we could have two more inspectors to get this office straightened out."

Several "yeah's" chimed in.

"Thank you, Jack. As always, you've helped on so many levels," Vanko said. "Okay, everybody out of here while I try to get authorization. Garrett, stick around in case I need some technical information."

Lansing drifted back into the vault and removed the outlet cover. He listened in amazement as it took Vanko less than fifteen minutes to convince the SAC to risk that much money. Because the SAC didn't know the Mafia burial ground didn't exist, he was throwing away a quarter of a million dollars. Lansing could stop that right now, but if they ended up arresting Egan and any high-ranking organized crime figures, the money would be considered well spent. Besides, whatever the Galante family was looking for might turn out to be invaluable to law enforcement in the bargain. Back at FBI headquarters, Charles Lansing would be seen as responsible for the difficult organized crime arrests and, more important, for preventing yet another disastrous public relations nightmare by interdicting Egan's plans to help the Cosa Nostra. Anyone with either of those achievements in his personnel file might go to the head of the SAC promotion list, but someone with both wouldn't even need a list.

At a few minutes past seven, Vanko was still working. He thought everyone else had gone, but when he looked up, Sheila was leaning against the doorjamb. "Garrett said the SAC pretty much gave you a blank check."

Not used to being watched unnoticed, he involuntarily

touched his face. As her eyes followed his hand, he realized what he was doing and let it drop casually. "A Mafia graveyard is a pretty easy sale."

Sheila sat down. "Can I ask you something?"

"You're asking if you can ask a question? It must be brutal."

"It is."

He forced a smile. "Go ahead."

"No, let's find someplace else to yell at each other, someplace where when we're done, we can leave it. What do you say we go get something to eat? How about Hattie's? I could use a beer."

"You buying?"

"Didn't the SAC just give you a quarter of a million dollars?"

"From that look in your eye, I'm wondering if that's going to be enough."

They sat at the same table near the kitchen. "How about a hamburger?" he offered.

Since leaving Iowa, she had given up eating beef. It was not a political or even health decision, but having eaten probably a good-size herd while growing up on a farm, she had become tired of the taste. Unfortunately a lot of men, especially those who gravitated to law enforcement, seemed to equate bloody meat with strength—not necessarily physical strength, but their own version of fortitude, the kind that allowed them to examine a gory crime scene with dark amusement or to charge recklessly through a door. Things that they sometimes found suspect in women; things she did not want to be questioned about. They sometimes looked at her like they couldn't figure out what a woman was doing in their midst. "Sure," she answered.

He poured beer into their glasses and took a large swallow. He gaveled his glass against the table to announce he was ready. "Okay, fire away."

She gave him an apologetic smile. "Have you ever seen a plastic surgeon?"

He thought he had girded himself against her unpredictability. He felt a sudden pervasive heat under his skin, which he preferred to attribute to the alcohol. "There's no half speed to you, is there? No, I haven't seen anyone," he said with a trace of anger.

His lips pronounced the denial with unfamiliar contractions.

There was also a quickness to his voice that she found suspect. "Whose fault was the accident?" Her words were flat, clinical, suspicious.

Although she seemed to be shifting directions, he was certain she wasn't. "I don't know."

"Whose fault do *you* think it was?"

"I could have been more careful."

"Were any charges brought against you?"

"No."

"So there was no punishment?" Before he could answer, she said, "Except for what you have decided to do to yourself."

His anger started to rise again. "I'm *punishing* myself by not going to a plastic surgeon?"

"Why else would you pass up a chance at a decent face?"

He laughed unconvincingly. "Are you saying there's something wrong with my face?"

"Please listen to me, Nick, because this is something I know about. If that's what you were given, then there's absolutely nothing wrong with it. But it's not the face you were born with. If you want to find a way to blame yourself for everything that goes wrong in life, we can all find something to feel guilty about."

"What do you have to feel guilty about?"

"Not being beautiful. The way people, other than you, don't search my face with any sort of pleasure. Believe it or not, my mother was an extremely good-looking woman. I always thought she loved me unconditionally, but sometimes I would catch her examining my face, trying to figure out what went wrong. You understand what I'm saying. I mean, come on, *the Opera House?* You don't think they call it that because of the architecture, do you? You were out there doing a dangerous job. There's nobility in that. The way I look is more like a birth defect, like a kid in leg braces. My greatest contribution is making people thankful for what they have. I grew up a target. A good day for me, the best I could hope for, was to be ignored. That's a hell of a goal, isn't it? That's what I've had to feel guilty about. And I know what you're going to say—I shouldn't. And that's my point, you shouldn't either."

"It's not like I'm home hiding in the basement. Since the accident, I like to think my life has been more productive. If my face were all right, that might not be the case."

"You Greeks, none of you are missing that martyr gene. Nick, guilt is just another way we feel sorry for ourselves. Life is fucked up—end of mystery. Some people are just luckier than others, or as you Greeks see it, some are just *un*luckier than others. But life comes down to just two choices: either you control it, or it controls you."

"Is that why you moved up to Harlem?"

"That's exactly why. More than my own superficial comfort, I want to solve this case. No compromises. No letting life tell me I can't play because I'm not pretty enough. Every day I get up and look in the mirror and ask myself, Am I larger than what I've been told? Am I better than I've been treated?"

Vanko had failed to confess that he had gone to a plastic surgeon two years earlier. When he was told that the damage could not be corrected, he felt both disappointment and a sense of relief. Until now he had never questioned his response. He had been embarrassed about the vanity that had caused him to go. He studied the crooked index finger on his left hand, the only other injury he had sustained that day. "Actually . . . I have been to the doctor." He presented his face to her, cocking his head to expose its maximum damage. "It's official. Me and the mug? We're inseparable."

She reached up and, with a touch so light he thought it might be his imagination, she traced the scar under his eye. "That's a good thing. I don't need you getting pretty and taking off on me."

27

AFTER SUNDAY DINNER, MIKE PARISI AND ANTHONY Carrera were drinking anisette on Carrera's screened-in porch. Although he still had some paralysis in his left arm and shoulder and needed a cane, the don was beginning to move with an unexpected degree of balance and speed. "It looks like you're mending pretty fast, Uncle Tony."

"Keep that between us. If DeMiglia knew, he might try to speed things up. He's had a taste of being in charge and won't give it up without a fight." Carrera watched Parisi for a moment. "I get the feeling that you're learning a lot of this on your own."

Parisi considered discussing his reservations about continuing in the business, but with the don still recuperating, it would not only be inappropriate, but disloyal. He snorted a single *ha*. "I've learned more than I ever really wanted to."

"Is he still pressuring you about the diamond robbery?"

"I've got him thinking about other things."

"Like?"

"I'm sure you've heard the stories about Dutch Schultz's treasure."

Carrera took a sip of his drink. "Sure. Why?"

Parisi told him about the map and Tommy Ida's seismic imaging idea. He explained how he had recruited an FBI agent and his subsequent Mafia graveyard ruse.

The old don laughed. "You're using the FBI to help? That takes nerve. There must have been more in those walnuts than I knew."

They both laughed now. "That treasure's just an old wives' tale."

"I know it doesn't seem reasonable, but so far everything fits."

"Hey, who knows? Stranger things have happened."

"DeMiglia wants to find that box and at the same time make fools of the FBI."

"Either one would give him a lot of juice with the commission. I've got to hand it to you, Mike, you've done a helluva job playing his weaknesses. Just remember, the higher he's riding now, the more he'll take it out on you when something goes wrong."

"I understand," Parisi said. "How much longer are you going to need?"

"Tomorrow, very quietly, some people are coming to see me. If this goes as I think, a week will be enough. Will your FBI friends and their machines take that long?"

"I'm not sure. We've been lucky to drag it out this long, and as we both know, good luck always runs out."

"You learn quick. I'm sure you will find a way to give me the week. When this is over, we will send the FBI a thank-you note."

"Chuck, the longer this goes, the more I'm inclined to let someone back at headquarters know. For as much as it gets bad-mouthed, covering your ass has stood the test of time," Cal Winston said.

Lansing squeezed his hand into a fist behind his back. "Again, sir, there's no one who can guarantee it's not going to trickle back down here and blow up in our face. If that happens, the headline will be 'FBI Scammed by Organized Crime.' If we make these arrests, it'll read 'FBI Outscams Organized Crime.' To be honest, I think it's going extremely well. Although we don't know exactly what the mob is trying to dig up, we do know who's involved and where they're looking. Parisi and Egan are both under twenty-four-hour surveillance. We've got to keep going because all we have right now is me eavesdropping and the one surveillance of Egan meeting Parisi, which he could easily explain away by saying he was developing him as an informant. It's a reasonable explanation; his squad is assigned to that regime. Parisi could take the Fifth, and no one would blame him because, if he was an informant, he sure wouldn't want the world to know. No, I think this is the only way it'll work. If it does fall apart at the end, then you and I can walk away. No one knows anything except that the New York office wasted a lot of money believing some OC lightweight's tale about a Mafia graveyard. No one's going to notice a couple of Newark surveillance teams working over here for a couple of days. None of this will be our fault."

Winston drummed his fingers on the table. "When is this seismic equipment showing up?"

"We're heading up there tomorrow morning. It's supposed to be in place by the time we arrive."

"I guess the advantages significantly outweigh the risks. But you make sure you keep me posted. If this starts to smell, we're jumping ship."

"I understand."

Vanko went to the Global Fish office early Sunday to make some calls and double-check the arrangements for Phoenicia. Everything looked ready to go. A half hour later, he was driving through East Harlem. He tried to tell himself it had to do with the murder, but he knew it was because Sheila lived there. Did he think he was going to run into her? Probably some hopelessly adolescent part of him did.

The night before had not ended all that well. Burgers were ordered, which he didn't touch and she didn't finish. The conversation turned stilted and they both drank too much beer.

On the drive back to the office, he said, "I would have bet a million dollars we were going to get along."

She smiled with her impenetrable confidence. "We are getting along."

And now it was Sunday, a day designed to consider discontent, to find its cause and pledge its remedy. The traffic was light, and he coasted up to her building. In front of the corner bodega, a man in a suit stood preaching into a microphone. A black woman was dutifully listening while a little girl in a white dress held a tambourine waiting for the next song. He wanted to go up to Sheila's apartment and start over. But ten minutes later, as the minister's group started their song, he turned his Bureau car back toward the cave.

He dialed her number. "Hello," she answered sleepily.

"Did I wake you?"

"A little. I stayed up late working."

"Sorry. I don't know if you heard. The police picked up Maria Vargas yesterday."

"Her parents called me last night," Sheila said. "How'd you know?"

"T. H. sort of rounded her up."

"On his own?"

"No."

"And you couldn't tell me you were going to do that?"

"I was just trying to avoid the argument I'm pretty sure we're about to have."

"Sounds like you still haven't figured out whether I'm crazy or not."

"If there are other victims, we need to know exactly who they are."

"*If?* So you do think I'm delusional?"

"I'm on your side, remember?"

"Oh yeah, that's right. I don't know why I keep forgetting."

"Sheila, you know we had to find out."

"This doesn't change a thing. Seven girls are still missing."

"That's right, now you have seven to concentrate on instead of eight."

She wondered if she wasn't deluding herself. Maybe all the girls were runaways. But all the families had said the girls would never run away, even Maria Vargas. God, she was tired. "Okay, you've made your point. Just let me know up front if there's a next time."

"I'll see you tomorrow."

By six o'clock the next morning, the squad had assembled. Given the unpredictability of the day ahead, the group was relatively quiet, except for Jack Straker, who couldn't stand the thought of an audience being allowed to go fallow.

"Did I ever tell you guys about the time I was dating a mother and daughter?" Howard Snow looked over the lip of his coffee cup and rolled his eyes. "I'm sorry, Sheila," Straker said, "it isn't too early for a little sex story, is it?"

"Where's that inspector? I want to change my plea to insanity."

Straker laughed. "Okay then. This was six or seven years ago on Saint Paddy's Day. A bunch of people from the office used to turn out for the festivities after work. We're up at this Irish place in Queens and as the night wore on, there was this mother and daughter who both worked in the office. The daughter was just out of high school, working in indices, and the mother, a divorcée, who was extremely well-preserved—"

"Not that it would have mattered," Snow interjected.

"Again with the sniper fire, Howie? Are you trying to break up with me?"

"Jack, it wouldn't have mattered if they were Cinderella's stepsisters. The reason you wanted to—and I'm *guessing* this is what happened—double team them was to add the evening to your fantasy résumé." Snow started tearing the lip of his cup into a thin cardboard spiral.

"Isn't that why we all get up every day, to add to our résumés?" When no one answered, he said, "Anyway, in the shank of the evening, I find myself out in the parking lot with the daughter in my Honda while the mother's waiting for me in her van." Straker beamed, Cheshire-like. "Can anyone guess what happened next?"

Sheila said, "You started cursing the Japanese for making your car too small?"

Everyone laughed. "You've never gotten over me kissing your hand that night, have you?"

"Neither me nor my mother."

"You're dying to hear the end of this story, aren't you?"

"I'm guessing this episode fades to black as some body-shop employee tries to reconcile the excessive damage to your Honda with the story you gave the insurance company."

Lansing walked in and everyone nonchalantly scattered to their desks. A few minutes later Vanko came out of his office carrying a large canvas utility bag. "T. H., you and Dick are picking up Baldovino, right?"

"In about twenty minutes."

"Everybody here? Then let's get going."

Despite the early hour, the heat and humidity were heavy

again, and as they drove out of the city, the promise of the Catskills' cooler air seemed a good omen.

Two hours later, when the squad reached the search area, the equipment was in place. Egan hurried over to three men standing alongside the seismic recording truck reading some computer-generated charts. One of them identified himself as Dave Thornton, the retired agent who had set up the search. His voice was full of friendly Texas confidence.

"This is a helluva deal you've brought us in on. We're pretty sure this is going to work." He introduced Egan to the other two, who were geophysicists. They shook hands with academic aloofness and went back to their charts.

Parked next to the large recording vehicle was an even larger truck carrying the sensors and cables. A third vehicle, off-loaded from a flatbed, had enormous wheels and a large piston suspended from the middle of the truck body. The piston would be raised to its highest position and released, sending a shock wave into the ground, which would then be picked up by the geophones and transmitted along the cables back to the recording vehicle.

Parked off by itself was a New York State Fish and Game SUV. Inside a dog cage in the back, a large black German shepherd prowled restlessly.

Vanko spread maps across the hood of his car and sent Jack Straker over to the officer, a stocky blond woman with a pleasant face.

Thornton said, "We've already fired some test shots and run some charts. We're up and ready to make some thunder. Just tell us where."

"We'd like you to start about a quarter mile west of here and generally walk your charts in a west-northwest direction for about another two miles," Vanko said.

He walked over to Crowe and Baldovino in the van. "Manny, have you thought any more about this?"

"All day yesterday. I'm afraid this is as close as I can get you."

"All right, just sit tight while we see if this is going to work."

Assuming he had finally accumulated enough camaraderie with Crowe, Baldovino asked, "What happened to his face anyway?" Crowe just stared at him with his heavy, penetrating eyes.

Baldovino watched all the activity with increasing apprehension. The oversized seismic equipment seemed like a tormenting dream, the point of no return Egan had warned against. No longer was this a game of busting FBI balls. Money and man-hours were being spent—retreat was no longer possible. He closed his eyes and summoned his father's image. Manny walked him through the story that had been given to the Feds. The thud of a body hitting the bottom of a hole. He could see his father slapping him on the back after the body was buried and telling him to be careful driving home. Now he could see sound waves snagging on body after body and charts filling up with human-shaped irregularities. He opened his eyes. Now he would be as surprised as anyone when no bodies were found.

Vanko checked to see if anything needed his attention. Sheila was talking to the Fish and Game officer and leaned down to pet her dog. Lansing had ridden up in one of the other cars. Normally managers wanted to be with whoever was in charge, to insulate themselves from the rank and file, their potential targets. He found him standing in a small group of agents, but he clearly wasn't paying attention to their conversation. He appeared to be watching Egan, who was twenty feet away. At one point Egan moved from the recording truck to the dog handler, and Lansing moved, too, to keep within earshot. Finally Vanko walked over to him. "Is something wrong?"

"No, why?"

"Why all the interest in Garrett?"

"Ah, I think it's interesting. Here's a guy who could wind up in prison, and he's out here more or less running this three-ringer. I'm just trying to figure out what makes him tick."

"And that's it? I'm surprised that you would burn up energy on someone like him. I got the impression that you thought his kind didn't belong in the Bureau."

Without effort, Lansing summoned some condescension to add conviction to what he was about to say. "I do. That's why I find it interesting, because if you watch him not knowing his circumstances, it seems like this is the most important thing in his life."

"Maybe he's not guilty of insider trading. Maybe he's just a good agent wrongfully accused."

Lansing couldn't help but smile. "Maybe."

Egan walked up. "Nick, they think they may be able to cover the area in two days."

"If they can save us a day, that'd be great."

"They're ready. The way I think it'll work best is when they get a chart for the area, I'll take the handler and her dog to any points that look like a possibility. If the dog hits on anything, we can start digging."

"I'll have a couple of agents standing by with shovels and the evidence kit."

Two technicians had inserted a series of the geophones about ten feet apart along the perimeter of the first area to be searched. They were mounted on thin, frail-looking rods that had been driven into the ground and linked by white cables that ran into the recording truck. One of the technicians radioed the truck and said they were ready. The piston on the truck had been raised. They said they were ready, too. The geophysicists gave the go-ahead.

The piston dropped and everyone felt the resonating thud. It fell again. The process was repeated for the better part of an hour before Egan and Dave Thornton came out of the recording truck reading a chart. They walked over to Vanko. "There's a couple of possible spots we can have the dog check while they're moving the geophones."

"So you feel you got a good reading?" Vanko asked the retired agent.

"As good as we're going to get with this shallow search."

"What do you mean?"

"This equipment is designed to explore what's hundreds of feet below the surface. You're looking much shallower."

"Garrett said something the other day about changing the frequency."

"We did. We tried a lot of frequencies. This terrain is an unusual mixture of rock and soil, hard to get a shallow reading on because the sound waves have to pass through so many different and repeating densities. But we'll give it our best shot."

Vanko called Sheila over. "I'm not completely sold on Manny's selective memory."

"You think he could be making this up to get off the hook?"

"He wouldn't be the first. The little he has told us seems awfully well rehearsed. But being responsible for all this probably doesn't make me the best judge. That night at the hotel it seemed like you two got along pretty well."

"I guess so."

"How about getting him away from T. H. for a while and see what you think."

She walked over to the van. "Manny, I'm going to get some coffee. Want to take a ride?"

Glancing at Crowe, he said, "I could use a change of scenery. Sure."

As he got in the car, there were a half dozen photographs on the seat. "What are these?"

"That's a case I'm working on. Twelve-year-old girl from up in East Harlem."

He was unable to take his eyes off the image of Suzie Castillo, her naked body rigid with death. "Raped?"

"Yes."

"Fucking animal . . . sorry."

"Actually, I haven't been able to find a better description myself."

"Who are these other girls?"

"They're missing, too."

"The same guy?"

"We're looking into it. This whole thing is a lot of pressure on you, isn't it, Manny? All this time and money being spent on your being able to remember something from ten years ago."

"Yeah, it is. I'm doing my best."

"Any chance you're blocking something unintentionally because your father's name might eventually surface?"

"I don't know. I guess that could be. The mind's a funny thing, especially mine." He smiled weakly and considered telling her about his bridge phobia to help convince her that her theory might be valid, but decided that he liked her too much to expose such a deep weakness.

Sheila pulled up to a convenience store. "What do you want in your coffee?"

"Two creams, two sugars."

When she got back, he tapped the photos with his finger. "What do you know about the guy who did this?"

"Other than his DNA profile, not much."

"Want to know what I think?"

She handed him his coffee. "Sure."

"I think this guy was trying to send a message."

"How do you figure that?"

"When it comes to leaving a body as a message, the Cosa Nostra invented it. See the way she's positioned, naked with her knees up and her legs spread. She didn't die like that. This guy is saying 'Screw you' to somebody."

"To who?"

He looked closer at the photo. "I thought you said this was in Harlem. It looks like Bensonhurst."

"It is. She was taken in East Harlem, but the body was dumped in Brooklyn."

"Sure, I remember this. About a year ago."

"That's right."

"I mean we heard it was a kid, but we didn't know it was anything like this."

"What about the message?"

"I can't believe this piece of garbage did this in our neighborhood."

"Manny, please focus. What message?"

"I think whoever he's sending the message to lives in the area."

"What makes you think that?"

"I'm pretty insensitive, but this makes even me cringe. That's what he wants, to shove it in whoever's face. You know, like some girlfriend who dumped him, something like that. Don't the cops talk to everybody in the neighborhood?"

"They interviewed some of the residents and checked them for criminal records."

"I don't think this guy lives around there. He has no respect for the neighborhood. You got to look for who he had the beef with."

"There's an awful lot of people living around there, and besides, what would we look for? It'd be tough finding the connection. But I'll give it some thought." When he didn't say anything, she looked at him. "What is it, Manny?"

"Say I could get you all the names that live around there, would you have to know where it came from?"

The radio broke the silence. It was Vanko. "When you get back, I need to see you."

She knew he was just making sure everything was okay. "On my way." She turned back to Baldovino. "Manny, I appreciate the offer, but the way you asked makes me think I'd better pass. Besides, with all this going on, I don't know when I'd get to them."

"Got a pen?" She handed him one, and he wrote his cell number on the folder that had been sitting under the photos. "Just in case you change your mind."

28

VANKO SAW SHEILA COMING TOWARD HIM, TALKING on her cell phone, her lips a thin, flat line of anger.

"I've got to get back to the city," she said.

"What's the matter?"

"That call was the task force supervisor. Another girl's missing." When he didn't say anything, she knew what he was thinking. "This time it's real, Nick. The media's all over it. She vanished on the way home from school. They found her messenger bag with her wallet and money in it. They want all my files, and my help."

"Where did it happen?"

"Saint Michael's. Another Catholic school in East Harlem, and like Suzie Castillo, she was wearing a school uniform. I've got to get down there."

"I understand, but . . ."

"But what?"

"You know what this case was doing to you when you weren't sure there was more than one victim. Now that it's a full-blown serial killer investigation . . . well, I'm a little worried."

She stepped closer. "There are some things you don't know about this case—like the autopsy—because I thought Suzie had the right to some dignity. Unless you're getting too much sleep, I don't think you want to know what's in it. But the important thing is he kept her alive for thirty-six to forty-eight hours. They need everybody they can get. So even if I have to hitchhike, I'm going."

"Give me five minutes."

"For what?"

"I'm going with you."

"Okay . . . good," she said, but her expression was still suspicious.

He told Egan and Straker to take over, then motioned to Bradley Kenyon and Howard Snow. "Brad and Howard are coming, too."

"Why?"

"You said they need everybody they can get."

"All right."

The trip of a hundred and twenty miles took under an hour and a half. Vanko had Kenyon and Snow drive one of the vans in case surveillance was necessary. He and Sheila went in his car.

She spent most of her time on the phone, calling her contacts at the task force and Homicide, figuring out how the agents could best be deployed once they got there. As she was about to dial again, Vanko interrupted her. "Mind if I ask you something?"

"What?" she said distractedly.

"Put the phone down and talk to me for a minute." She turned it off and locked her hands between her knees. "What do you think the odds are that we're going to find this girl alive?"

The word "alive" seemed to slap her across the face. "If you start playing the odds right now, you'd might as well drive straight to the church and start making funeral arrangements. This isn't about probability, it's about never *ever* giving up."

"Nobody's giving up. I'm just concerned about you."

She pivoted away from him and lapsed into a ruminative silence. The thousand-yard stare that had been so startling the first day had returned. "I'll be fine."

"You're not fine now. Just because you were right about there being a serial killer doesn't mean that you're going to find him. What if you don't? This could swallow you whole."

"And if I don't slow down, you're going to run and tell the SAC."

His voice flat, he said, "I'll assume that you didn't mean that."

"Don't assume anything. If I say it, it's what I mean."

Vanko didn't say anything until he was sure he could maintain his calm. "I'll tell you what, we'll help with this, but when this girl is found, even if the killer isn't, you've got to promise me you're out for good. You'll move out of the neighborhood and let it all go blank."

"I can't promise anything right now. But whatever way it goes, I will sit down with you and try to be rational."

A small smile lifted the undamaged side of his face. "Considering who I'm dealing with, I'll accept that as a major concession."

In the city now, Vanko stopped at a light. "What about that photographer Diaz? Anybody looking at him?"

"That was the first thing I asked. They just cleared him on DNA."

"So much for the obvious."

"You know, Manny said something interesting."

"About the graveyard?"

"No. But I think, for whatever reason, there's something about that he's not telling us. No, he looked at the crime scene photos and said he thought the killer was sending a message."

"A message? To who?"

"Someone living around there. Let's go over to where the body was found."

With the van close behind, Vanko headed out to south-central Brooklyn. A half hour later Sheila had him pull over. "This is it."

"This small playground?"

"She was found over by the swings." They all got out of the vehicles.

"What are we doing here?" Snow asked.

Sheila explained Manny's theory.

Kenyon said, "And you think we're going to find whoever he was sending a message to? Bensonhurst has to have, what, a hundred fifty, two hundred thousand residents?"

"Homicide talked to the neighbors around the playground, but . . . Give me a couple of minutes, would you?" While the men stayed on the sidewalk talking, she walked over and sat down on one of the swings. She checked the crime scene photos, trying to determine if the positioning of the body could reveal anything further. Then she watched the people passing by for a while before rejoining the others. "There's a lot of foot traffic along this street."

"Eighth Avenue is two blocks up. Stores, banks, bus stops," Vanko said.

"Did you notice the church we passed? It's only a block away."

"What's that got to do with this?" Snow asked.

"It's Catholic, both victims went to Catholic schools. Maybe there's a tie-in."

Vanko said, "She could have been displayed for anyone passing by."

"But there's got to be hundreds of people who live within walking distance," Kenyon offered.

"And right now I'd like to have a list of their names." She turned over the folder with Baldovino's cell number on it and then retrieved her phone from the van. "Manny, how's it going up there?"

"Okay, I guess. They haven't found anything yet if that's what you're asking."

"No. If it's not too late, I'd like to take you up on your offer to get those names of people in Bensonhurst. I need everybody who lives within walking distance of Saint Teresa's church."

"Where you at?"

She explained about the latest abduction and that the victim might still be alive.

"Let me see what I can do."

"We need at least a half mile in every direction."

"I'll call you in a couple of minutes."

Baldovino was sitting alone in the van. Crowe had gotten out to smoke and was watching the seismic crew work. Manny called the club and Parisi answered. "Mike, those names Tommy's been collecting for that bank scam, do you know if any of them are around Saint Teresa's?"

"I'm not sure, some maybe. Why?"

"The Feds need the list."

"The fuck, Manny! You telling the Feds about that?"

"No, no, nothing like that, I swear. I just told them I could get a list of names as long as they didn't ask where it came from. Mike, I thought before I offered. I could've told them how to do it themselves, but I didn't want them to know we had any connection to that stuff, you know, in case we decided to do the bank scam later on. I figured if I did, we'd be the first one they would have looked at when the bank started screaming."

"I don't know, Manny. This has trouble written all over it."

"I know you watch the news. That little girl that's missing up in Harlem, it's for that. It ain't going to come back on us, honest."

"You're sure about this?"

"Remember a year ago that little girl that was found dead over by Saint Teresa's? It's supposed to be the same guy, only they think this one might still be alive."

"Let me put Tommy on."

Baldovino told Ida what he needed. "How long you think, Tommy?"

"Hold on." Ida turned to Parisi. "It'll be a lot quicker if you, Gus, and Jimmy can help me."

"What do we have to do?"

"They got four computers at the library. Everything's in the tax records. It's easy. It'll take two minutes to show you."

"What if somebody's using the computers?"

"Gus can explain how Christian it is to share."

Parisi took the phone from him. "Manny, with you up there, how we supposed to get them to the Feds? If they figure out it's us, they might put two and two together about the graveyard thing."

"That kid who cleans up, John-John, he can deliver it. He knows how to keep his mouth shut." Baldovino found Sheila's cell number on his incoming calls. "Write this number down. It's a lady agent—Sheila—have John-John call her when everything's ready."

"Sheila, huh? Not Agent So-and-so, just Sheila. You're not getting a thing for this broad, are you?"

Baldovino could feel himself blushing. "Come on, Mike. Don't bust my balls."

"You'd better be sure about what you're doing. I want to help with this, but let's remember why you're up there," Parisi said. "Anything happening?"

"I've been watching the dog. They haven't gotten him off his ass yet, so I don't think there's anything worth digging up."

"We're going to head out and take care of this then."

Baldovino called Sheila back. "It's being worked on. As soon as it's done, you'll get a call to arrange delivery."

"How are you going to—"

"Remember what I said, no questions?"

"Thanks, Manny."

"I hope it helps. I really do."

The parking lot of Saint Michael's school was crammed with cars, a large number of which belonged to the NYPD. Vanko drove up to the door and Sheila got out. "I'll be right back."

Ten minutes later, she got in the van and handed him a stack of fliers with the missing girl's photo on them. "They're getting ready for a news conference, so I've got a few minutes."

"Good, because we're going to get something to eat. None of us have eaten today, including you."

"I can't leave."

"Am I ever going to get my way?"

"Probably not very often. Sure you want to waste one on a sandwich?"

"It's not just a sandwich. I'm getting fries, too."

Vanko found a coffee shop two blocks away. The four of them found a booth and ordered sandwiches. The news was on, and the abduction was the lead story. The reporter was standing in the parking lot of Saint Michael's. "As I speak, the New York City police are meeting inside to discuss what should be done next in the case of missing twelve-year-old Adelina Lopez. She was last seen on her way to school this morning. The police have stated that the latest abduction may be related to the year-old murder of Suzie Castillo, a student at the Miraculous Medal Catholic school, who was also on her way to school when she was reported missing. The police refused to speculate whether there could be other victims. Forensics and the autopsy in the Castillo case indicate that she was kept alive for as long as forty-eight hours after the abduction. The police have spent the day searching the East Harlem neighborhood and talking to residents in hope of finding the girl. Sources report authorities are considering their next move very carefully."

Vanko asked, "Did it look like they had anything going on?"

"Nothing. They're rounding up known sex offenders, more out of frustration than hope. They need as many of us with experience on the case as possible to conduct interviews. Looks like we'll be at it all night. Most of these guys have been interviewed, alibied, and DNA'd. Like I said, it's pretty much out of desperation." She took a bite of her club sandwich.

"We'll head back to Bensonhurst."

"Thank you. I'll call if we get anything."

Vanko threw some bills on the table. "If we don't hear from you, let's all meet here at eight tomorrow morning for breakfast."

Half turning her back to the other two, she tugged at Vanko's sleeve. "You're bound and determined to keep feeding me, aren't you?"

Parisi stared at the screen as he queried lot numbers in the Kings County tax assessor's website. The library's computer room seemed too small for the four men who were pecking away with unusual diligence. Dellaporta was wedged into one of the desks and punched the keys with the merciless piston strokes of his index fingers. Tatorrio, unable to exist without some degree of human communication, hummed the music from a series of TV commercials as he tapped the keyboard with the flair of a concert pianist. Ida was the only one who knew how to type and was working at a rate three or four times faster than the others.

Parisi's cell phone rang. It was DeMiglia. "Mike, have you heard anything from the Lag? Is that typing I hear?"

"My wife's typing a letter. Let me go in a different room." Parisi jumped up and signaled the others to stop by pulling his hand across his throat. "Manny's called me a couple of times. They got some ape watching him. He has to ask to go take a whiz in the woods so he can call. Says they got all this equipment up there. He laughed, said it must be costing the Feds a ton."

"What about our guy?"

"He's managed to get himself put in charge. Pretty much running the whole show. Their boss had to leave and come back to the city on some emergency, so I guess he'll be able to keep running things, pushing them in the direction we want."

"Anything about the box?"

"Well, I can't be sure, because if it comes up on one of those charts, Egan can't just dig it up and call us."

"If he finds anything, he's not digging up without us, right?"

"That's what he said."

"I don't give a fuck how much he says no, when he comes back, I want to meet with him. I've got to find out face to face if he's jerking us around."

"What could he gain by doing that?"

"You know, sometimes it's like you're trying to prove that you're a moron. You know what I'd do if I was him and found out where the box was?" Parisi didn't answer. "What, did I hurt your feelings?"

"What would you do if you were him?"

"That's better," DeMiglia said sarcastically. "First, I'd tell the FBI, Okay, no bodies, let's go home. Then I'd call you up, because probably he got the impression—I don't know from where—that you're easy, and tell you, Sorry, didn't find the box. This treasure must all be some kind of bullshit. Then in a couple of days, I'd take a nice drive up to the Catskills with a shovel and keep all fifty million dollars for myself. Call me paranoid, but that's got to be going through his mind. Or did you forget that the reason we were able to flip him is because he's a fucking thief."

"I never thought of it that way."

"That's because you're not really one of us."

It was almost two hours past the library's closing time when Parisi and his men finished. Ida was organizing the printouts alphabetically into two large stacks. "Tommy, get those over to John-John right away and tell him what to say when he calls that woman agent. Then drive him to wherever she wants to meet. Just don't let anyone see you."

As the men filed out, the librarian busied herself trying not to look frightened. Parisi went up to her. "Thanks for your understanding." He took out four one-hundred-dollar bills and pushed them across the counter. "You know, for the late charges."

The three agents drove back to Bensonhurst, and, using the playground as a starting point, went off in different directions. They started knocking on doors, showing Adelina Lopez's photo and asking if anyone had seen her. They continued until almost midnight, when knocking on doors no longer brought cooperative responses, especially when it was Nick Vanko's face at the door. A monster had taken another child, and then this man knocked on their door, wanting them to open up. Sure he had a badge, but maybe the killer did too; he was getting the girls to go with him somehow. This man looked the way monsters looked. That's why they became monsters?

Finally Vanko radioed the others. "Let's call it a night. We'll meet at that coffee shop in the morning."

Vanko sat in the darkness of his apartment unable to sleep. He was still thinking about the people he had tried to interview but had failed to enlist their help. Snow and Kenyon, on the other hand, had received almost unanimous support.

He imagined looking at himself through their peepholes and tried to understand what they saw. He dialed Sheila's cell phone. The anonymity of the telephone was always a welcome alternative.

"Hello."

"It's me," he said, his voice unintentionally low. "Can you talk?"

"Hold on one minute." He heard a chair scrape across the floor and a door open. "I'm in an interview, but I need a break anyway. Did you do any good?"

"As far as we went, nothing. Anything going on there?"

"Oh yeah, we're partying. Wall-to-wall pedophiles and rapists. Just talking to these guys makes you feel like you've been sexually assaulted."

"I certainly don't want to keep you from that. I just wanted to call and let you know how miserably we failed. I'll see you in the morning?"

"I'll be there. And, Nick, thanks again."

"For?"

"Hanging in. I know at times I don't make it easy."

"No one ever promised me being a martyr would be easy."

The next morning, the three men sat drinking coffee, waiting for Sheila to show up. Snow asked, "Did you call Phoenicia last night, Nick?"

"Yes, they should be getting started right about now."

"So nothing yesterday?"

"Not so far."

"When are you going to have to get back up there?"

"I figure I've got the rest of the day before I have to worry about it."

"Does that mean we're through here after today?" Kenyon said.

"I hope so."

The news came on and everyone in the restaurant stopped eating to listen. "Today the police are calling for volunteers to search abandoned buildings and go door to door with photos of Adelina Lopez, who has been missing since yesterday morning. They have asked that anyone wishing to volunteer come to the gymnasium at the Saint Michael's school by nine a.m."

Sheila came in. "Sorry I'm late." She ordered coffee to go.

"You have to get back that soon?" Vanko asked.

"Actually, I've gone AWOL. They wanted me to sit on the phones all day, taking tips. I think it's the task force supervisor's doing. Some bull about having a female the callers can relate to. But at two o'clock this morning, I got a call from this kid. He says, 'I've got something for you from Manny.' We meet in the school parking lot, and he gives me printouts with the names of all the families within a half mile of the Castillo crime scene."

"I'm impressed," Vanko said.

"Me, too. And it gave me a better idea than answering the phone all day. If you guys are game."

Vanko said, "You say that like we've got a choice."

29

HOWARD SNOW PULLED THE FBI VAN TO THE CURB outside Saint Michael's school. In the back, Sheila was working her way through the Bensonhurst printouts. When she flipped over the last page, she said, "No one I recognize." She handed the stack to Vanko. "Okay, here's what I've got in mind. Some serial killers, given the opportunity, will involve themselves in the investigation if they can do it without being too obvious. For one thing, they get a firsthand report of what's going on. They can find out if the investigation is getting closer to them, or if they need to do anything different to avoid detection. Also it can give them an insight into what to avoid the next time they grab someone. It's also a power thing. Here he is, sitting right among us, and we can't catch him. And who knows, maybe he's even scouting his next victim. A lot of young people come out to help when something like this happens. He could introduce himself to one of them without being that noticeable, and when he wants to get the next one into his car, she'll recognize him and since he was helping, he's got to be one of the good guys."

Kenyon shook his head. "It's a little frightening that you understand this kind of individual so well."

"It helps to be equally disturbed, something I've worked at very hard."

"So we're here because you think this guy's going to show up as a volunteer," Snow said.

"It's a possibility. How likely, I don't know. But I'd rather be doing this than looking for a body. The downside is, if he does show up here, the girl may already be dead."

"How do you figure that?" Kenyon asked.

"If she's not dead, she needs watching, unless he's got a sound-proof, escapeproof hiding place."

"Just tell us what you need," Vanko said.

"While the volunteers are checking in, we're going to mingle and look for anyone who doesn't quite fit in. We know he's a male, not too old or too young. He's intelligent, probably neat in his appearance. He'll come alone and probably won't know any-one else. And of course, if you can observe him during the search, he won't be working very hard at it because he already knows where she is. He'll be more occupied watching the searchers, maybe pumping them for information. If he does show up, it's because he's getting a little bored and wants to ramp up the thrill factor. That could be in our favor, because what would be more thrilling than being out with the police looking for the girl he has alive back at his home. He's the only one in the world who knows where she is and can decide whether she lives or dies. And when."

"If we spot someone who doesn't look right, what then?" Snow asked.

"I'll leave my laptop here. It has everybody's name that has come up in this investigation. I have a feeling this guy could be in there. If not there, maybe it'll be in the Bensonhurst names. So the first thing we have to do if we see someone suspicious is get his name and call it back to the van. Someone will have to stay here and radio in indices and criminal checks and coordinate the whole thing."

Vanko said, "Sounds like the perfect place for me."

Her stare hung on him a moment longer than necessary, and he knew she had read something in his response that he had not intended to reveal. But the truth was he was relieved not to have to go out among strangers again.

"And what if we do find someone that's listed?" Kenyon said.

"Then we'll have to take a look at his residence," Vanko said.

"Since this is all based on assumptions, I'm guessing we're not going to slow ourselves down with anything as cumbersome as a search warrant?" Kenyon asked.

"We can always claim exigent circumstances afterward," Vanko confirmed. "But participation is strictly voluntary."

Kenyon smiled. "No, it's fine. If we can get the girl, I don't imagine anyone's going to be worrying too much about the letter of the law."

Taking handheld radios, Sheila, Kenyon, and Snow got out and walked toward the school entrance.

At the Phoenicia search site, T. H. Crowe got out of the van and went over to Garrett Egan. "The office is on the radio. They want to talk to whoever's in charge."

Egan picked up the mike. "Garrett Egan."

"This is Assistant Director Beck Logan. Where's Vanko?"

"He's not here right now."

"I didn't ask where he *wasn't*."

"He had to go back to the city."

"Where in the city?"

"I'm not sure. There was some type of emergency."

"And he left you in charge?"

"Yes, sir."

"Aren't you under investigation by OPR right now?"

"Yes, I am."

"And you've been put in charge of spending seventy-eight thousand dollars a day. Perfect," Logan said. "I want everything stopped up there until I get some answers."

"Sir, this was cleared with the SAC."

"The SAC is standing right in front of me and says he had no idea of the cost."

"With all due respect, if we're successful, sir, this will be a landmark case."

"Save the marketing for the tourists, Egan. Shut it down. *Now*."

The phone rang and Tommy Ida put down his newspaper. "Hello."

"Tommy, it's Manny. Is Mike around?"

"Yeah, hold on, he's out front. Where you at?"

"We're headed back to the city. There's a problem."

After a minute, Parisi picked up the phone. "What's the matter, Manny?"

"We got shut down."

"What do you mean, shut down?"

"Hold on."

Egan came on the line. "Parisi?"

"Yeah."

"The assistant director shut us down. I guess the SAC, who my supervisor cleared this whole operation with, never told the ADIC about it. Somehow he found out, and when they told him how much it was costing, he went nuts. He called in the SAC, who denied knowing the cost. So now everybody wants to talk to my supervisor. The assistant director called *me* on the radio. I tried to tell him about the graveyard and all the bull that went with it, but he said he wasn't authorizing anything until he talked to Vanko."

"So why doesn't he talk to him?"

"He's disappeared, and no one knows where he is."

"What, he just disappeared?"

"He went back to the city with three agents. Some emergency that no one seems to know anything about."

"Did he go with that female agent?"

"Yeah, how'd you know?"

"Never mind."

"Anyway, they've tried to get ahold of him, but evidently he's got his phone turned off and nobody knows what scrambling code his radio's set on. But even if they find him, it doesn't mean the ADIC is going to okay this."

All of a sudden Parisi felt the disappointment that he had previously dismissed in his men. He hadn't realized how close they were to finding the Dutchman's treasure and how important it had become to him. Millions. Money without responsibility and effort. Best of all, it was his ticket out of the life. "Who's with you and Manny?"

"Nobody. When we were ordered out of there, I volunteered to drive him back."

"What about all that seismic stuff?"

"They just shut it down. They're not leaving until their boss tells them, and he isn't going to do anything until my supervisor gets this squared away with the ADIC."

Parisi, recalling DeMiglia's suspicions of Egan, spoke with a forced casualness. "Before you shut down, were you making any progress?"

"Not that I know of, but to be on the safe side, I took all the charts with me. The geeks running the equipment didn't particularly like it, but I told them they would help convince the ADIC. I haven't had a chance to take a good look at them yet."

"I'd like to see them." Good, Parisi thought, this was an opportunity for Egan to meet with DeMiglia and sort everything out. Knowing the agent would not agree to meet the underboss, he would just have to surprise him

"Sure. That would be good because I'd like to get a look at that map of yours. I've been out there tromping around enough, maybe I can make some sense out of it now."

"Eight o'clock tonight?"

"Yeah."

"Have Manny give you directions to the After Hours in Bensonhurst. Use the side entrance and come upstairs to the office."

"Don't forget the map."

"I've got the map. Just make sure you bring those charts."

"Sounds like we're back to not trusting each other."

"Let me give you my take on that—*fifty million dollars.*"

Dusk was settling over the city. Word had circulated through the small groups that they were to finish their searches and make note of whatever abandoned building they were in so they could start there the next day. Sheila had been shadowing a man for almost an hour. A couple hundred volunteers had shown up, and she had wandered among them, eliminating possible suspects as quickly as she could. This guy was the first one all day who had met the profile she had provided to the others. He was compulsively neat and slender, even a little on the emaciated side. His clothing, while inexpensive, was a bit too formal. And there was a stiffness, a sterility to him that did not fit the personality of a volunteer. He wore hiking boots, and when Sheila saw that they'd been spit-shined, she decided to concentrate on him.

Their group was working with one of the three NYPD tracking dogs assigned to the search. The handler had been given an article of Adelina Lopez's clothing. Sheila's suspect was staying close to the officer, asking questions. The rest of the time, he tried not to be noticed as he listened to their conversations. She wondered if she was trying too hard to convince herself that she had found a candidate. Maybe this was just someone who was genuinely trying to help. They were about to finish for the day, so she decided it was time to resolve it one way or the other. She moved close to him. "Long day, huh?"

He looked her up and down. "Yes" was his single-syllable answer.

She held out her hand. "Sheila Burkhart."

The man looked at her impolitely, but then surrendered. "Alex Tolenka." It was pronounced with an eastern European formality, no more removed than one generation.

To give the impression she had taken the hint, Sheila wandered away and turned as if heading back toward the school. When out of earshot, and with no detectable urgency, she dug out her cell phone.

Vanko had already taken three calls from Howard Snow, each offering what he thought was a good suspect, each "really" fitting the profile. None of them was in the laptop's file. Kenyon had called once, and the name he provided wasn't listed either. When Vanko heard Sheila's voice, he sensed some urgency. "Have you got something?"

"I've got a possible. Al-ex To-len-ka." She pronounced each of the syllables distinctly. "Right now, we're heading back."

While he searched the name, she told him what she had seen. "Sounds good . . . but he's not in the file."

"How about the names from Manny?"

"Hold on." After a minute, he said, "Jesus, Sheila, there's a Tolenka family. The property owner is listed as Anya Tolenka."

She started to tremble. For the first time she understood just how much she had given up. She had forgone sleep, food, and the reassurance of social convention until only the case existed. They said she had let the case consume her, but it was all about to pay off. She glanced back to make certain Tolenka was still in sight. "That has to be a relative. We're just starting back. Manny predicted that he wouldn't live where he left the body. Can you run him through DMV and see if he has a different address?"

"Sure. Do you need some help keeping an eye on him?"

"I don't think so. It looks like he's staying with the group."

"Good. The people at the church are having a potluck dinner

for the volunteers. He wouldn't miss an opportunity like that."

"I'll be there as fast as I can."

"As soon as you get close, call. You can hand him off to Brad, and he can watch him inside the school."

Vanko radioed Snow and Kenyon to get back to the van. By the time they got there, he had obtained an address for Alex Tolenka in Queens. Vanko filled them in. "Brad, you've got to stay on him. Sheila, Howard, and I will head over to his residence. Let us know if it looks like he's heading home. I don't know how much time we'll need, but with any luck he won't leave before we're done."

"And if he does?"

"You'll have to find a way to slow him down."

Vanko pulled the van up in front of Tolenka's house. Sheila said, "I guess the laugh's on me."

"Why?" Vanko asked.

"I moved so I could be closer to the case, but my old apartment is less than a mile from here."

"Okay, Howard, man the radio," Vanko said. "You've got to let me know right away if any cars show up that look like they might belong here."

Vanko unlocked a hidden cargo well and took out an over-sized pilot's map case. After checking the street for anyone who might be watching them, they walked up to the front door of the small bungalow. He rang the bell and looked around while discreetly trying the door. It was made of steel and locked tightly. He scanned the neighborhood again. He and Sheila went around back and he knocked on the door. It had a glass window, and he placed both hands and an ear against it and closed his eyes, trying to sense any movement inside. He opened the briefcase and took out a lock-pick gun, inserting its shaft into the keyhole. He clicked the trigger carefully while slowly turning the grip. The lock rotated open.

He locked the door behind them, and, using a pocket flashlight, they moved through the house quickly. There were two bedrooms and no basement. Once they got through the kitchen, living room, and the first bedroom, Sheila stopped. "Hold it a second," she whispered. He turned off the light. They stood motion-less, listening . . . nothing. With the light back on, he examined the room more closely. He walked back to the kitchen, and then to the second bedroom, which appeared to be Tolenka's. Sheila checked the closet and the dresser. Hanging items were all faced the same way, the hangers perfectly spaced. All the shoes were still in their original boxes, stacked on the floor with architectural precision. Socks, underwear, and shirts sat in the drawers with the same pathological alignment. She took Vanko's flashlight and went back into the living room. A vacuum cleaner leaned against the wall next to the front door. The carpet was marked with the symmetrical patterns of a recent vacuuming. The only other impressions on it were the agents' footprints. "He vacuums his way out of the house so he won't leave footprints," she said almost to herself. She yelled, "Adelina! Where are you? It's all right, it's the FBI." She waited a few seconds. "Adelina! It's the FBI." She called out a third time, but there was still no response.

"If this is the right guy," Vanko said, "where can she be?"

"He has to have her somewhere else. That means we'll have to follow him when he leaves the school. The forty-eight hours are almost up."

As they headed out the back door, Vanko said, "Do you want to do anything about those footprints?"

"No, let's leave them. If nothing else, they'll make him paranoid."

They relocked the door with the pick. In the backyard was a one-car garage, unusually tall and of noticeably newer construction. Checking the next-door neighbor's house for signs of anyone watching him, Vanko started toward it. As he did, a motion sensor set off a pair of floodlights. Hurrying into the shadow of the house, he handed Sheila the map case. "Wait here, I'll be right back."

Vanko rushed to the van. Snow asked, "Find anything?"

"Not yet, let me have the BB gun." Vanko had equipped each of the surveillance vans with a CO_2 pistol for long-range night surveillance. It was not unusual for their targets to be erratic drivers, which made following closely difficult to conceal. At an opportune time, they would discreetly shoot out a taillight, rendering the vehicle more distinguishable at night, the single light easier to track at a distance.

"Brad just radioed. He followed Tolenka back to the school. First thing he did was go to his car and change his shirt. Brad's going to set up on the car."

"If he starts to leave give me three blasts on the horn. Any other problems out here, give me two."

Vanko approached the garage, keeping his distance from the motion detector. He checked the adjacent houses again. Then he quickly fired a quietly hissing shot into each of the floodlights. He tried the overhead door, but it was locked. He told Sheila, "Wait here a minute." He walked completely around the structure. Even though it was a good six feet longer than a standard garage, there were no windows or walk-in doors.

He opened the map case and took out a nondescript black metal box about the size of a cordless phone. He flipped a switch on the top, and it emitted a low, steady hum. As he turned a small, ratcheted dial, its pitch rose slightly. After a dozen or so clicks, the motor in the garage kicked on, and the door rose smoothly. They walked in under it and Vanko closed the door behind them.

The garage was as meticulously ordered as the house. Even the floor had been painted. Then Sheila saw the shelves.

The entire back wall was filled with floor-to-ceiling shelving. On small wire stands stood dozens of two-foot-high female dolls, each with elaborately painted porcelain faces and hands. The colors were natural and perfectly applied, except for the eyelids, which were completely covered in Wedgwood blue, and the lips, which were coated with a thick Gothic cordovan, giving the faces a vandalized look. A few of them were clad, not in elaborate old-fashioned doll dresses, but modern children's clothes: jeans, tank tops, short cotton summer skirts, and kneesocks.

Sheila swept her hand along the floor but couldn't find any dirt or debris. "He doesn't park his car in here."

Vanko stared at the shelves. The wall behind them was finished with painted plywood where the other walls were bare studs. He went to the corner and paced off the length of the wall. Eight and a half strides, somewhere around nineteen feet to the shelves. He turned toward the door to pace it off outside, but suddenly felt the pull of tacky paint on his right shoe. "This spot has been painted recently."

Sheila touched the floor with her fingertips and tested a widening pattern with her toe until she could visualize the shape of the still-wet area. It was a ninety-degree arc about two feet long. "It's fan shaped. It looks like the wall in front of it swings open and scraps the old paint. So he repaints it. Just like the carpeting inside, he likes to cover his tracks."

Vanko examined a seam in the wall at the pivot point of the freshly painted arc. "If this is a hidden door, its hinges are on the inside so it can't be detected." Grabbing the shelves at the end that would have opened, Vanko pulled, at first carefully and then with force. It felt as solid as if it were embedded in concrete. He inspected under the shelving for some type of lock or release.

The van's horn sounded three long blasts. Tolenka was moving. Vanko jerked at the wall with his entire weight. Sheila grabbed hold of it next to him. "Adelina!" she started yelling again. "It's the FBI, are you in here? Adelina!" she screamed. She stopped pulling. "Maybe he has her someplace else." Vanko opened the garage door, and they ran to the van.

Snow said, "Brad said he's coming out to his car."

"This is our guy," Sheila said, "but we're not sure where the girl is. Get us back over there, we can't lose him now." Vanko picked up the mike. "Brad, I don't care if you have to shoot him, don't let him get away. We'll be there in two minutes."

"Well, don't rush." Kenyon's voice came back with its patrician calm. "It seems someone has let the air out of one of his tires."

30

GARRETT EGAN DIDN'T LIKE THE SIZE OF THE MAN standing in front of the second-floor door at the After Hours, but he no longer had the luxury of options. "I'm here to see Mike," he said. Without the slightest change of expression, Angelo swept the agent's upper body with a small electronic security wand. "I'm not carrying a gun."

"I'm not looking for a gun." Angelo ran the detector along Egan's legs.

"Then what do you think I—" Egan realized he was being searched for a transmitter.

As soon as the door opened, he was surprised to see a third man with Parisi and Baldovino. "Who is this?"

DeMiglia extended his hand. "We talked on the phone. I'm Danny." Egan glared at Parisi, who busied himself with a cigarette. "Don't be upset with Mike, he didn't have any choice. This little get-together was my idea."

Egan shook hands.

"Things don't happen in my territory unless I say so. Remember, we brought you in on this."

"And don't forget, without me, you guys would be sitting around the old gangsters' home playing gin and talking about how nice it would have been to find fifty million dollars."

"That's right, so like it or not, we're a team. Quit being so pissed off about it. If we're going to have a shot at finding the Dutchman's box, we've got to work together."

Egan took a moment. "Okay, since this can't be undone, let's move on."

"Good. You want a drink or something?"

"You got any Drambuie?"

"I've got whatever you need. Manny . . ." Baldovino went to the bar and poured him a small glass. "So tell me how the search was going before they stopped you."

Egan recognized that his credibility was being questioned. "Pretty much according to plan. They ran several charts."

"But no sign of the box?"

"To tell you the truth, I haven't really looked at them."

"How do I know that's true? How can I be sure you haven't found the box on the chart and are telling us there's nothing so you can go back and dig it up?"

"This is why I'm here?"

"You have to admit, if you were in my shoes, you'd be asking these questions."

"What have I done to make you distrust me?"

"Let's not forget why we came to you in the first place: you were arrested for insider trading."

"Well, yes—"

"That's not petty theft we're talking about. How much was it?"

"The indictment said over a quarter of a million."

"Which means you're not only capable of—let's be nice and say *diverting* large sums of money, but you need large sums to make problems go away."

"Okay, I get it."

"I'm curious, how does someone with your education—and background—wind up doing that?"

"Well, let me see if I can put this in terms you can understand. You're out in Vegas, and you're given a job in a casino counting room with so much cash in it that money loses its significance. It's just green paper or worse, some other form like credit card receipts. Although they tell you what your job is, they don't really tell you all the rules. You start to notice all the people around you gambling, and some of them are actually winning. So you place a bet, but you lose. But it's not really losing because you can take some of that money in the counting room, or shift around some numbers, to cover your bet. It's not stealing because it's all going back in the system anyway. You're just moving it around, which is kind of your job anyway. You start gambling more because you like it and because you really can't lose. Then one day they walk in and put handcuffs on you. And that's when they explain *all* the rules. I suppose I did step across some imaginary line, but you tell me, Danny, where was it?"

"And you lost it all in the market?"

"That and a couple of hundred thousand more in accounts in my undercover name." Egan took a healthy swallow of his drink.

"So we're back to my original problem. How do you convince me that you don't know where the box is?"

"How do you convince someone you don't know something?"

"Let's just say it would be in your best interest if you could think of a way rather than *me* thinking of a way." DeMiglia smiled.

"The charts. I've got all the charts they ran. They're in my car. I'll go get them."

DeMiglia held up a hand. "Angelo'll go."

He handed over the keys. "It's a brown Chevrolet four-door. They're in the trunk. There's also a briefcase with some equipment I 'borrowed' from the seismic geeks." His confession of an additional theft made DeMiglia smile. Egan said, "Since I'm showing you mine, how about you showing me yours? I'd like to see this famous map. I've only seen the half I got for Mike, and that was very briefly."

"Mike, did you bring it?"

Parisi picked up a large envelope from the desk. "Here."

The two halves were still in the clear plastic envelopes from the document examiner. Egan laid them side by side, matching the edges as closely as the plastic would allow. He tried to visualize the terrain he had tromped across the last two days. "This X, this is where you figure it is?"

"What else could it be?" Parisi answered.

"This line drawn across the tear, that starts by the X, the symbol at the end of it, do you know what it is?"

DeMiglia said, "Yeah, that's right. The document guy said something about that."

Egan pulled out the report from the envelope and read the first two pages. "Here it is. He says that since it's right where the map was divided, it might be significant."

"I remember that, but we could never make anything out of it," Parisi said.

"If this is what I think it is . . ." He opened and closed his eyes several more times trying to link something in his memory to the map. Finally he said matter-of-factly, "I'm fairly certain this marking represents a small but distinctive rock outcropping that's north of the creek. If I'm right, we've been using the equipment in the wrong area." DeMiglia and Baldovino crowded up to the table.

"We thought those squiggles was supposed to be trees," Manny said.

"Yeah," DeMiglia said. "How do you figure they're rocks?"

"First, remember that sixty years ago, the roads probably weren't paved, and even if they were, they might have been in slightly different locations, but the creek hasn't moved. If you look at this map in relation to the creek, and take into consideration where that outcropping is, the X is on the other side of the Woodland Valley Road. See how the creek is drawn here, the way it bows. The actual course of the creek isn't that pronounced. Now look at the X in relationship to how he drew the creek. See how the outcropping symbol kind of points to it. That's how you were supposed to locate the X, from its position relative to the creek and the outcropping. He exaggerated it for that purpose and in doing so threw off the rest of the map's proportions. If you know where that point in the stream is, you're much closer to where the box is buried. I think all the seismic tests that have been conducted the last day and a half are just off to the east of it." Angelo brought in the charts and briefcase. "Let me have those."

Egan unfolded the charts. He took a moment to orient himself. "See, here's where the creek cuts through. And this shading here? That indicates a different density—the rock outcropping, or actually the underground base of it. If I'm right," he consulted the map again, "the X would be over here." He pointed at an imaginary spot past where the chart ended. "We've been testing in the wrong area." He collapsed into the desk chair. "Goddamnit, I should have seen this map before we started. I should have thought of it. This is my fault."

"So you'll have them look in the right area now. What's the big deal?" DeMiglia asked.

Egan laughed sarcastically. "Did you miss part of this conversation? We're shut down. And it isn't looking real good to start up again. Maybe we should just cut our losses and forget it."

"Cut our losses?" Parisi said. "What losses do you have? You took fifty grand from me. That's my loss." He stubbed out his cigarette in the ashtray, breaking it in half.

"Jesus Christ, Mike, we don't even know if this treasure exists. You want your money back? I'll give it back. I'm out."

"Yeah, I want it back."

DeMiglia had heard enough. "You two, shut the fuck up! Nobody's getting *in* or *out* unless I say so. We've come this far. The FBI is paying for this, and if nothing else, when that fact comes out, they're going to be as embarrassed as we were when Manny the Moron here made headlines. Nobody's giving up, so just shut up. You two sound like my fucking kids. And especially you there, FBI, you'd better figure a way to pull this off or that ledger you stole with the map in it—which I'm sure has your fingerprints all over it—is going to show up at the federal prosecutor's office with a note explaining where it came from."

To hide his anger, Egan started fidgeting with the map and charts. Then something seemed to catch. "Wait a minute." He grabbed the smaller pile of charts that had been put off to the side.

"What are those?" DeMiglia demanded.

"These are the test charts taken when they were checking and calibrating their equipment, before we told them where to look. Before we even got there. There was no reason to look at them before." He started aligning and overlapping the edges of several charts while moving the treasure map on top of them. Opening his briefcase, he took out a large rectangular magnifying glass. "Yeah, see this test chart is right at the edge of the area I think we're interested in." At the corner of one of the seismic charts, he brushed at something with the flat of his hand. When it wouldn't move, he bent over and looked at it more closely with the glass. Then he stood up and smiled.

"What?" DeMiglia demanded.

"Take a look."

DeMiglia took the lens and moved it until the item came into focus. "You mean that square thing? You're telling me that's it?"

"Actually, if you look closer, it's rectangular. See how everything else on all these charts is irregularly shaped? This is something man-made. How big is this box, do we know?"

DeMiglia looked at Parisi and Baldovino. Parisi said, "If anybody does, it's Tommy. Call him, Manny."

While Baldovino called Tommy Ida, Egan went to the bar and poured himself another drink.

Baldovino hung up. "Did he know, Manny?" Parisi asked.

"Yeah—"

"Hold it, Manny. Before you tell us, let me see if I can figure it out."

Egan took his drink and went back to the table. He got out a small, clear plastic ruler. "This is calibrated to read the charts." Placing it on the rectangular mark, he measured its width and length. He took out a small calculator. After taking a minute to double-check the figures, he said, "This isn't real accurate, but I'd say this rectangle is approximately two feet by two and three-quarters feet."

Everyone looked at Manny and he asked, "Now?"

"Yeah, moron," DeMiglia said, "now."

"Tommy said it was supposed to be eighteen inches thick, two feet wide, and three feet long."

"I'll be damned," DeMiglia said. "That's it."

With a small flourish, Egan dropped the pen on the charts and held up his glass in a silent toast to no one in particular.

DeMiglia said, "So we're done with all this imaging stuff. And the FBI. We can just go get it."

"It's not quite that easy. This chart will get us . . . I'd guess, within two hundred yards. See, it isn't like the other full-blown charts, it doesn't have these grids on it. With them, you can pinpoint everything within a few feet. We're going to need one more day of testing. I know exactly where they have to place their equipment now."

"So how do we get your bosses to go for that?" DeMiglia asked.

"To tell you the truth, I don't know. The assistant director was pretty hot about not being told about the cost. The only thing he can see come out of this is that we spent a quarter of a million dollars and have nothing to show for it. Compounding that, the inspection team from Washington is in town this month second-guessing everything, so it's twice as hard to get anyone out on a limb. See, if you look at this from management's standpoint, they're spending all this money and man-hours on Manny's word, and there's no way to know if he's telling the truth. I mean, we've been out there twice now, this time for the better part of two days at seventy-eight thousand per, even with a body-sniffing dog, and nothing. It's starting to look like we got beat." Egan took another sip of his drink. "Unless we can think of some way to corroborate Manny's information."

Everyone sat quietly until DeMiglia said, "When I was in prison, there was this grifter I knew. He was big in stock swindles, oil wells, gold mines, all that sort of stuff. Do you know how he sold shares in gold mines? He'd take the mark out to an old abandoned shaft. Then he'd take one of those hand picks and break off a chunk of rock and give it to the guy and tell him to get it analyzed. It always came back with a high gold content. What the mark didn't know was that Billy went in there the day before with shotgun shells that had been hand-loaded with gold dust. He'd fire them into the wall and that's where he cut the chunk from."

"That's clever, but I don't see how it applies to our problem."

"Salting the mine. We'll salt the mine." Egan still didn't seem to understand. "You college boys, all that training and you can't see the nose on your face. We'll plant a body."

Egan set down his drink. "Yeah, that's perfect. If they find a body, they'll authorize whatever we want."

No one wanted to ask the obvious. Finally, Parisi lit another cigarette and said, "Where we going to get a body?" He blew a protective cloud of smoke as if to suggest that he had identified the problem so its solution was not his responsibility.

Egan said, "I think this is a matter better discussed without me." He stood up to leave.

"Sit down," DeMiglia ordered. "Mikey, that's your job. You come up with one. I said sit down."

As Egan lowered himself into his chair, Parisi asked, "Where am I going to get a body?"

"I don't know, whack a wino, break into the morgue, dig one up at the cemetery. There are millions of dead people on this planet, we just need one."

"It's not that easy, Danny."

"I suppose I could make one locally." His eyes drifted toward Baldovino.

"Okay, okay. We'll come up with something."

"Good. Now, Mr. FBI, when are they going to pull out up there?"

"They gave us a three-day commitment. Which means they'll have to leave the day after tomorrow."

DeMiglia looked at Parisi. "That means you've got to find a body tonight and put him in the ground before morning so Egan can find him first thing tomorrow."

"That leaves one problem," Egan said.

"Now what?"

"I have to come up with a reason to be up there looking for a body after the operation has been shut down."

Everyone was quiet. Baldovino said, "Maybe you could get that woman with the dog to stumble across it. From what I saw, she liked you."

"Manny, that wasn't me. She was all over Jack Straker. But that's not a bad idea. If I give her the impression he'll be there, maybe I can get her to come back once the body is planted."

"Your bosses won't have a problem with you going up there on your own?" DeMiglia asked.

"You're forgetting they can't find my boss, so I'll take the initiative, so to speak. And when I find the body, nothing will be able to stop this."

"Think you can steer that dog to the body?"

"As long as I know where it is."

"Then you'll have to meet them up there while they bury the body."

"I'd really rather not."

"If you can't find that body, this is over. So far your people haven't been able to find their ass with both hands. You will be up there when they plant the body tonight. Do you understand?"

Reluctantly, Garrett Egan nodded and started packing up the charts.

"Leave those here."

"I'm going to need them so I'll know exactly where to put the body."

"I want to look at them some more. Mike can swing by and get them on the way up there."

"You're keeping them so I couldn't go up and find the box by myself."

DeMiglia smiled. "The thought never crossed my mind."

Egan's mind raced into the dark corners of the plan. It had become far too complicated. Buried treasure was supposed to require only a map and a shovel. Now they were going to have to come up with a body; who knew how? And they would have to make a grave look old; the Bureau would see through it. Lifting a worthless notebook from a decaying file had evolved into possible involvement in murder. He had rationalized doing everything for his family's sake, but he had actually put them at much greater risk. DeMiglia was still staring at him, rudely now. Egan understood just how expendable he would be should anything go wrong.

31

HOWARD SNOW ACCELERATED THROUGH THE clogged streets of East Harlem and slid the boxy, top-heavy surveillance van precariously around corners. As soon as they were in sight of the school, Vanko picked up the mike. "Brad, have you still got him?"

"Yeah, he's just getting the flat off. He's going to be at least another ten minutes."

"We're pulling in the lot. Give us a minute to get organized." Vanko turned to Sheila. "How do you want to work this?" She hadn't spoken the entire way back and seemed lost in thought. He waited.

"If the girl is still alive, her time is just about up. So chances are when Tolenka leaves here, he's going to kill her. If we follow him and he loses us, she's dead. So I say let's grab him now. I know it's taking a chance. If she's not in that garage, I'm fairly sure he's already killed her."

"And if you're wrong?"

"I would give anything to have some divine ability to know the right thing to do, but that's not how it works. We have to take chances. I've been trying to get in the killer's head for a year. Now that I've met Tolenka and been in his house and that garage, the blanks are filling in. You saw where he lives. He's so controlling, he needs to have her close at hand. That garage wasn't built like that for his car. Either the girl's dead, or she's in that garage."

"You're the one who got us this far, so we'll grab him." The van pulled into the lot and Sheila opened the door. "Where are you going?" Vanko asked.

"This is an NYPD case. They're the ones who have to prosecute it. I'm going to run inside the school and find someone I can trust with our probable cause."

Again Vanko was amazed at her calm. Maybe the case didn't have the hold on her everyone had thought. "We'll sit on him with Brad until you get there."

He closed the door and they drove through the lot slowly until they spotted Kenyon's car. "Brad, do you want us to take the eye?"

"No, I've got a clear shot at him, and he has no idea I'm here. You probably can't see him right now, he's putting the new tire on. It's the black four-door Ford Taurus two rows east of me." Kenyon tapped his brake lights twice.

"Okay, we've got him. Keep us posted. We're going to get into position to cut him off if he tries to leave." Kenyon acknowledged the order with two pushes on the mike key.

Sheila came out at a brisk pace with a man who looked like a detective. Vanko slid open the side panel and they got in. "Nick, this is Stan Lasky. When I was on the task force, he was my partner on the Castillo case." They shook hands and Vanko pointed out the black Taurus. As soon as he did, a man stood up next to it.

Kenyon's voice came on the air. "Nick, he's got the tire changed and is putting everything in the trunk."

"We're ready, Brad. Stay loose, Sheila's going to grab him." Vanko's cell phone rang. It was the assistant director. After listening for a while, he said, "Yes sir, I'm on my way."

"You're leaving?" Sheila asked.

"He's been trying to get me. Something's come up."

"Bigger than this?"

"I'm sorry, but I've got to go."

She followed him out and in a whisper said, "I'm kind of hanging everything out here, Nick. It'd be easier with you backing me up."

"I have no choice. And it's not like you need me."

"You're sure about that?"

"You are going to solve this case." There was a weariness to Vanko's voice that somehow qualified his omniscience.

She nodded like she understood. "Come on, Stan, let's go see if we can give Mr. Tolenka a hand with his tire."

They got in Lasky's unmarked NYPD car and, almost at an idle, pulled up next to Alex Tolenka. "Need some help?" Sheila asked.

Tolenka looked up at the sound of a female voice, but when he saw that she was not alone, and in an unmarked police car, he went back to the task of placing the flat tire in the trunk. "No thanks, I'm finished."

She got out of the car and imperceptibly hit the thumb release on her holster. "You're Alex Tolenka, right? We met today during the search."

He seemed caught off guard. "Ah, yes, that's right." Lasky quietly came around behind him.

"I'm with the FBI, Mr. Tolenka. Somebody called us with your name," she lied.

"Isn't that what the police always say when they're fishing?" Glancing behind him, he noticed Lasky.

"If we were fishing, would we know about Anya Tolenka?"

"My mother? What did they say?"

"That you may know something about Adelina."

"Me? I'm a volunteer. How could I be involved in this?"

"I know. I'm a little embarrassed by this, too, but I'm sure you understand why we have to check these things out. The quicker you can help us resolve this, the quicker we can concentrate on finding the person who is actually responsible for taking her."

"What do I need to do?"

"That's the spirit. Do you mind if we take a quick look through your car?"

"Go right ahead."

"You got this?" Lasky asked her.

She smiled. "Mr. Tolenka's on our side, Stan. Go ahead." The detective gave the trunk, glove compartment, and floor of the vehicle a quick search. "See, that wasn't too bad. Now, what do you say we finish this up by taking a quick look in your house? Where do you live, Alex?"

"You want to search my house?"

"I'm sorry, it won't take long. Unless you have a garage or something."

His eyes dropped and he shifted his weight from one foot to the other. "Maybe I should get a lawyer."

"I was a lawyer before I came to work for the Bureau," she lied again, "so let me give you the same advise I used to give my clients. If you're guilty, don't say another word except 'I want a lawyer.' If you're innocent, give the police what they want and save yourself three hundred dollars an hour."

He shoved his hands in his pockets and slumped his shoulders forward. "Okay, I guess so."

"Good, we'll take our car."

As they were getting in, Sheila waved at the van to let them know everything was under control. Snow pulled out. She could see Vanko on his cell phone. He gave her a single wave good-bye. Lasky radioed for additional cars and a tracking dog to meet them at Tolenka's residence.

By the time they reached the house, half a dozen other units were already there. As they got out, Sheila recognized the glaze that had numbed Tolenka's features; it was a sociopath's lack of emotion. "The keys," she demanded. With a smug grin, he handed them to her.

"How about the garage?" Lasky asked. "I don't see a door. How do we get in there?"

"The opener is in my car back at the school." He gave the detective the same arrogant smile.

"Alex, I'd be real surprised if we don't find a second opener just inside the door. You know, so you can get it open when the car's already in the garage. They usually come in twos, don't they?" Tolenka's face reverted to its amorphous mask.

Lasky led a team of uniformed officers into the house. A few seconds later he came back out alone and handed Sheila the garage door opener. He looked straight at Tolenka and returned his earlier sneer.

Sheila pointed the opener back over her shoulder and pressed the button. "Shall we?"

The cops rushed in and were stopped by the sight of the doll racks. Sheila led Tolenka by the arm. "Your hobby?"

"Yes." His voice was unreadable.

The K-9 car rolled up. The officer let out the German shepherd and it moved quickly back and forth, sniffing the ground.

The cop took an article of clothing out of a plastic bag and held it close to the dog's snout. "Find her, boy," he commanded.

"Can you have him work at the back of the garage," Sheila said. Tolenka's head snapped toward her. Her eyebrows lifted and she smiled at him as if in appreciation for his reaction.

The dog pulled its handler along as it ran to the base of the shelving and sniffed to the left for a couple of feet and then accelerated in the opposite direction. Reaching the corner, it pushed its nose hard against the crevice between the floor and the wooden base of the racks and started scratching at the junction. "Good boy," the officer said, pulling the animal back, patting him on his powerful shoulder. "Good boy."

Sheila turned Tolenka toward her. "Well?"

The handler noticed some paint on the German shepherd's nose and claws. He tested the floor with his fingertips. "This has recently been painted." He walked around. "But just in this corner."

She walked over to the spot and looked at the pattern of tacky paint. "Looks like that part of the wall swings open, Alex. What's behind there?"

"I wouldn't know."

"Are you going to make us tear this wall down?"

"If you think you can handle the lawsuit, go right ahead."

As the uniformed officers pulled and prodded unsuccessfully, a trace of confidence crept into Tolenka's demeanor. She began to wonder if he had already disposed of the body. Lasky came out of the house and, not wanting to give Tolenka any sense of hope, discreetly signaled Sheila with a thumbs-down that a search had failed to find any evidence of the victim. She decided to call Tolenka's bluff. If it was a bluff. She said to Lasky, "Call for a wrecker."

When the tow truck arrived, it backed up close to the garage. The driver let out the steel cable and found a place to anchor the hook into the wall. Everyone cleared out and watched as the slack in the cable was slowly taken up. When it was taut, the driver looked at Sheila for the final go-ahead. "Okay, let's see what's behind door number one."

The winch strained and the edge of the shelving pulled away, then with a sudden crack the whole section ripped free, twisting in the air before it hit the garage floor. Behind the shelving was a room twelve feet wide and six feet deep—completely empty.

Manny and the rest of the Catania Club crew sat in the back room trying to figure out where to get a corpse. Preferably, they decided, one that had been shot. "Could always go over to the Bronx and wait for one to fall," Dellaporta said.

"Yeah, that's good, Gus, a *tutsone* in the Mafia graveyard."

"Hey, what're you trying to say, we're prejudice? We kill blacks, too," Jimmy Tatorrio offered.

"It's got to be tonight," Parisi said.

"Mike, how about the morgue? There's got to be someone we can buy down there," Baldovino said.

"Jesus Christ, will you guys give me a break. It's got to be a white man, shot, and dead for a while. You know, rotting."

"Sounds like he's going to stink," Dellaporta said.

"Now you're getting it."

"There's only one place that has moldy dead people—the boneyard," Tatorrio said. "And I ain't robbing no graves. At least not for a body."

Tommy Ida said, "We can always shoot an old body. We only need it to look good initially. They're not going to do an autopsy for days. Hopefully by then, we'll be long gone with the box."

"You're right, Tommy," Parisi said. "So now we just need a real dead white guy."

"I don't like all that digging," Dellaporta said.

"Then we'll break into one of those mausoleums," Parisi said. "It's better anyway. If we're careful, they won't discover it for a while. In the ground you've got to fill the hole back in. Tommy, you and Jimmy go scout a cemetery for us, huh?"

Tatorrio said, "Here's a scene you won't be seeing in *Godfather Four.*"

All the cops turned to Sheila. They waited for her instructions, not because they thought she was the only one who knew what to do next, but because they wanted to be able to say unequivocally that it was all her idea. The smirk had returned to Tolenka's pasty gray lips. Seeming to draw strength from the impossibility of the situation, she said, "Get the dog in here."

The German shepherd went to the far corner and, as it had outside the room, started clawing at the point where the wall met the tiled floor.

She looked at Tolenka. "That dog's a real pain in the ass, isn't he, Alex?" His grin retreated. To the dog handler, she said, "Can you give us a little privacy?" She stood in front of Tolenka. Her nose was almost touching his, but his eyes wouldn't focus on her. "You see all those cops out there? Most of them have been working this case since you started killing these girls. I'm about to make an enemy of all of them by offering you a way to prolong your life. Look at me, goddamnit . . . look at me!" Finally Tolenka focused on her. "Right now, you've got a very good chance of getting the needle. No, let me correct that. We've got your DNA on the first victim, so you *are* going to get the needle. And believe me, that's one of the last things on this earth I want to prevent. The only thing I want less is for Adelina Lopez to die. Now, we're getting under that floor if I have to dynamite it myself. If there's an accident, and something happens to her while we're trying to get her out, it's all on you. So tell me, Alex, are you in the mood to save your own life?"

She could see the suspicion in his eyes. He was trying to hold on to any thread of hope, telling himself that nothing could be proven. "Alex, why do you hate your mother?"

He glared at her. "I love my mother."

"Is that why you put Suzie Castillo's body in that disgusting pose so close to your mother's home? 'Disgusting'—is that what she called the things you did growing up? Tell me, Alex, did it work? Did she actually see the body? I guess it doesn't really matter. You raped and killed Suzie, that's really how you got even with all of us women, isn't it?"

His eyes slowly traced the details of her face. His cold, salacious grin caused her hand to slip to her weapon involuntarily. "Ironic, isn't it?" he said. "Driven by jealousy, I would assume."

"What is?"

"That someone as unattractive as you would solve the killings of such beautiful creatures."

Sheila felt her heart pump three hard strokes. He had said "killings." Did that mean Adelina Lopez was already dead? "Open it."

He forced a final arrogant snort through his nose and then said, "The release is on the wall outside. I'll have to show you."

"You wouldn't be thinking about running?"

"I'm doing this to prolong my life, not to end it."

"Good read on your part."

"It's spring-loaded. Someone will have to stand in the corner where the dog was to take the tension off the release."

Sheila started to ask him how he had done it when he was alone, but then realized he must have used the weight of his victim. She directed one of the uniformed officers to stand next to the wall.

At the back of the garage, Tolenka pulled up the lowest strip of siding, which was connected by two hidden hinges. A long metal rod was held between two eyebolts. He slid it clear.

A small section of the floor lifted. One of the officers grabbed the edge and pulled it up, shining his light into the chamber below. Sheila looked down into the squinting eyes of Adelina Lopez. She was still in her school uniform and her mouth, arms, and legs were heavily taped. Sheila jumped down the five feet. Stan Lasky followed. The two of them lifted her up so she could be pulled out. Lasky shined his light around the underground room. There was a single folding chair and a large cardboard box. Reluctantly Sheila looked inside and recognized the two items sealed in clear plastic bags—Catholic school uniforms, one from Miraculous Medal, Suzie Castillo's school, and the other, the same as Adelina Lopez's, from Saint Michael's where some of the other missing girls had been students. Another girl was dead. Sheila collapsed onto the chair. She would be the one who would have to figure out who it was—and then tell the parents.

32

IDA AND TATORRIO ARRIVED AT THE CLUB TO report that they had located a cemetery that would suit their needs. It was an hour north of the city on the way to Phoenicia and fairly isolated. But as soon as they walked in, someone flung open the door and more than a dozen cops streamed in behind them, guns out, telling everyone to freeze. They were from the state police organized crime unit. Their lieutenant announced that a search warrant for the premises had been issued, and they had arrest warrants for everyone present.

"On what charges?" Parisi demanded.

"Violation of state gambling and loansharking statutes." The detective then started droning their Miranda rights, as a pair of cops frisked each man and put flex-cuffs on him.

"Can we post bail?"

"Not tonight, it's too late."

"I don't suppose you waited until now just so we'd spend the night in jail."

The cop smiled. "I'd like to think I'm that clever, but actually we've been waiting for the last two of your little ensemble to show up. We wanted everyone at once."

"But I've got something I have to do tonight."

The detective laughed. "Oh, in that case you can all go."

DeMiglia had fallen asleep on the couch in his office, and his cell phone rang three times before he answered it. "Yeah."

It was Garrett Egan. "We've got a problem."

It took him a moment to recognize Egan's voice. "Why're you calling me?"

"Parisi and his entire crew have been arrested. And they're not being arraigned until tomorrow."

"Where are you calling me from?"

"Don't worry about the phone, I'm in my supervisor's office."

"What are you doing there now?"

"I had a late meeting with my lawyer when I got the call on my cell. I decided to drive over here; I know these lines are secure."

"What were they arrested for?" DeMiglia said.

"Gambling and loansharking. Parisi had some guy from the lockup call me. He didn't want any calls directly from him to you or me. He told this guy to tell me that he wouldn't be able to make that funeral arrangement, and I should call you. Gave me your number."

"Motherfucker! I should have never relied on that amateur to do anything. That *motherfucker.*"

"Stop and think about it," Egan said. "Which is better—splitting whatever's in that box with Parisi and all of his crew or just between you and me? I think we're at a point now that you and I could find it without anybody's help. You supply the body, and I'll locate the box."

"What do you mean by *split?*"

"I could be greedy at this point, but I have to respect your, ah, position in the community. I was thinking twenty-five percent."

"That's a lot of money."

"Exactly one-third of what you'd be getting. We're talking about millions of dollars. Does it really matter if I'm getting someone's share who's in jail?"

"What if someone decides to cut a deal and tell the Feds about the treasure?"

"First of all, none of them know for sure that it exists. Hell, we're not even sure. We saw a rectangle on a computer printout, nothing more. So if you and I don't ever say anything about finding it, how are they going to prove it? Parisi can't say anything because he'd have to tell them that he set up the whole Mafia graveyard scam. They're just going to have to sit and take it. Even if the Bureau find out that it exists, we'll have the assets hidden by then. There's nothing they can do. Believe me, I know, I've been on the other side."

"What about Parisi, is he going to prison?"

"That sounds almost like you want him to."

"Never mind what I want, is he going to prison?"

"I don't know anything about the case. Traditionally, gambling and loansharking cases are not prison makers. Gambling is usually a slap on the wrist, and loansharking—well, I don't have to tell you—the victim has severe memory loss just before the trial. So I'd have to say no. If for some reason you do want him out of the way, that's something you're going to have to take care of yourself. But I sure as hell don't need to know about it."

DeMiglia looked over at the ashtray on the table. One of Parisi's filtered cigarette butts was standing up in it. "I'll meet you at four a.m. in Phoenicia in the train station parking lot."

"Four a.m., in Phoenicia. Don't forget my briefcase and charts," Egan said. "And I am assuming you're bringing that extra person?"

"Yeah, I guess I'll have to. You know what they say, if you want something done right, you have to do him yourself."

Egan hung up Vanko's phone and listened for a few seconds. Had someone come in while he was on the phone? He peeked out into the bullpen. No one was there. He listened for a few more seconds and left.

Charles Lansing came out of the vault. When the Newark surveillance units put Egan, Parisi, and DeMiglia at the After Hours together, they had called him. He met up with them and waited for Egan outside his lawyer's office. When Egan came out, he was talking on his cell phone. He hung up and headed for the off-site.

Lansing called the surveillance units. "He's on his way out. Whatever you do, don't lose him. It's going down."

He then called the chief inspector. "Cal, it's me. Looks like tonight is the night. He's meeting with the underboss up in Phoenicia. Surveillance is on both of them. He was talking about bringing another person. And he used the phrase 'millions of dollars.'"

"Think it's the head of the family?"

"Well, it was cryptic enough that I think it's a good possibility."

"When are they meeting?"

"Four a.m. Up in Phoenicia."

"Pick me up at the hotel at midnight."

Danny DeMiglia and Angelo sat in the silver Cadillac at the Phoenicia train station. It was four-fifteen. "Where is this guy?" DeMiglia said. "You got those cigarette butts, right?"

Angelo patted his jacket pocket. "This FBI Mok, you really giving him twenty-five percent?"

DeMiglia gave him a sideways glance. "Of course." Both men laughed. "As soon as he shows us where the box is, he's going to become a *fugitive*. Couldn't take the idea of prison for that insider-trading rap. Maybe we'll bury him in the same hole that the Dutchman dug to hide his treasure. It gives the whole thing a nice, what do you call it, symmetricalness. Yeah, the Dutchman would have liked that, taking the treasure out and putting a Fed in."

Lansing and Cal Winston were parked a hundred yards away. They watched the silver Cadillac, its exhaust rising through the red glow of the car's taillights. On the Bureau radio, they listened to the slow, rhythmic cant of the New Jersey agents following Egan. "It sounds like they're almost here," Winston said. "When do you think we should move in?"

"You're the boss, Cal, but I'd say if we see any kind of exchange, that'd be the time. We certainly missed that chance at the New Jersey motel."

"That 'millions of dollars,' you don't think that's a payoff, do you?"

"I really don't know. We know they're trying to find something buried in the ground. Whether it's a payoff or some kind of hidden cache of money, it'll play well either way with the media."

One of the surveillance units called in. "We're coming up on the railroad turnoff. How close do you want us?"

Lansing picked up the mike. "We've got an eye on the target, so you can lean back a little. We'll give you the word when we're going to take them down."

Less than a minute later, a second set of headlights wheeled into the parking lot. Egan pulled up next to the Cadillac.

"Nice night for a burial," Egan said.

"Where do you want him?" asked DeMiglia.

"I want to take one last look at those charts to make sure."

Through the binoculars, Lansing watched DeMiglia pass the briefcase through the window. He immediately radioed, "All units move in."

By the time the two inspectors got there, the Newark agents had the three men spread-eagled against their cars. Lansing retrieved the briefcase. "Well, well, well. I wonder what's in here." He pulled open the case and was stunned to find nothing but charts in it.

Suddenly two powerful searchlights snapped on. At the same time, Beck Logan, the assistant director in charge of the New York division, walked out of the station with Nick Vanko. Logan glared at the inspectors. "What are you two doing here?"

A dozen New York agents stepped out from their hiding places, mostly in the heavy woods around the parking lot.

Lansing said, "We developed information that this agent was involved in supplying information to members of the Galante crime family. We had reason to believe he was about to meet with the head of the family and be paid a bribe."

"Since this is my division, and my agent, did it occur to you that you should have come to me?" Logan said.

Winston said, "No disrespect, sir, but we were afraid of leaks."

"No disrespect! This breaches every protocol within the Bureau. Who are these agents?"

"They're from the Newark office."

Logan shook his head and turned around. "The agents from Newark, I'm Assistant Director Logan. There's been a misunderstanding here. Thank you for your efforts, but you can go home now. You will be contacted for statements by someone from this division in a few days." The New York agents took custody of DeMiglia and his driver. Logan looked at Winston and Lansing. "Tomorrow morning in my office, nine a.m. You've embarrassed me not only within the division, but evidently Bureau-wide. Better make it ten o'clock. I need to make some calls about your futures before we speak. Let's get this over with, Nick."

DeMiglia had been handcuffed. Vanko unbuttoned the underboss's shirt and stuck a folded document inside. "Daniel DeMiglia, this is a search warrant for your car." He leaned in the window and took the keys out of the ignition.

"Hey, I want a lawyer. You've got no right to search my car."

Vanko opened the trunk and was hit by the stench of a decomposing body. He looked at DeMiglia. "Judge William Ferris, I presume." Egan walked over and looked at the body. DeMiglia suddenly realized that the agent wasn't under arrest, and a mixture of confusion and anger knotted his face. Vanko smiled. "It's really not that hard to figure out. When you started talking about getting a body any way you could, Garrett knew he was in over his head. So he had his lawyer call the assistant director. I had the state police arrest Parisi and his crew so you'd have to come up with a body. We kept our fingers crossed it would be the judge."

"I want my lawyer."

"As soon as we get back to the office, you can give him a call. You can also tell him that we installed a GPS unit on your car a week ago. Remember when you had to leave it at the shop because it wasn't running right? Nice thing about the device is it just receives, so when you had your car swept for a transmitter, it couldn't be detected. As soon as the techs pull the device off, it'll tell us where you dug up the body. I'm sure a thorough crime scene investigation will tie up all the loose ends nicely. The jury is going to love this—no thinking required."

Lansing spent a restless night trying to deny the insistent image of his career plummeting to earth, leaving only a tiny, silent puff of dust to mark its impact. But somewhere in his subconscious his mind forged a maxim: Mistakes don't end careers, regret does. He awoke and went to the window, a porthole of light, of safety. Below was New York's great wheel of humanity—eternally resilient, proudly defiant, its discontent suddenly reassuring. He resolved never to allow himself the luxury of remorse. Even though Logan was about to throw an oversized monkey wrench into his career, Lansing could see past it. Logan was powerful but would retire soon. Lansing had to append himself to someone who would have rank in the future. Cal Winston was in position to be a perfect host.

First, the damage Lansing had inflicted upon himself had to be minimized. All the cases of misconduct he had investigated had taught him that however counterintuitive it was, the best thing was to take full responsibility for his actions. Besides, trying to blame the entire incident on Vanko's lack of leadership, or any other vaguely conspiratorial act, would not sell to a pragmatist like Logan. Instead, this tactic would not only deflate Logan's bloodlust, but, more important, seal Winston's gratitude. Then, in the not too distant future, after the assistant director's retirement, Winston would be made an SAC somewhere—because of this setback, probably some urban, third-world office. But that was good because the overwhelming majority of aspiring ASACs had a historical aversion to such dismal assignments, which would make it easier for Lansing to gain the promotion.

At breakfast, Winston gratefully accepted Lansing's offer to take the lion's share of blame and noticed that a new indifference settled over Lansing as he offered to "fall on this grenade." Winston found himself admiring such a senseless act of bravura and chalked it up to the shortsightedness of youthful heroics.

At exactly 10:00 a.m. Lansing and Winston entered the office of the assistant director in charge of New York.

Beck Logan ran his hand through his already disheveled hair, a warning that what little patience he had left was highly flammable. "Without the headquarters bullshit, I want to know how this happened."

Lansing described how the whole situation had been predicated on an overheard conversation between Egan and Mike Parisi. Although Winston had arranged for the Newark surveillance teams, Lansing said the rest of it was his idea. And then he explained how everything had come to a head the night before when he had heard Egan conspiring with the Galante family underboss, Danny DeMiglia, on the telephone.

Logan burst out laughing. Lansing's first impulse was to ask what was so funny, but he had to act penitent, as if he deserved each hammer blow of the ADIC's wrath.

Logan said, "After being told they didn't trust him, Egan left that club last night and saw that he was being followed by men he assumed were DeMiglia's. He was already worried that somebody was going to be murdered to provide a body. But it wasn't the mob following him, it was you. That was enough to convince him to go to his lawyer, and the attorney had enough sense to see that Egan would never survive his involvement with the mob. When we set our plan in motion, we also figured it was DeMiglia's men and decided to use it to our advantage. We told Egan to act exactly as if DeMiglia were calling the shots. We even had him make the call to DeMiglia from Vanko's office because he had called from there in the past and they knew the lines were secure. He had to go to the off-site because we thought the bad guys were following him and would report to DeMiglia where he was, making him that much more credible. If he hadn't made the call from there, you wouldn't have been able to overhear the call setting up DeMiglia and wouldn't have blundered into the arrest. Your surveillance caused him to go to the only place you could overhear him. You've done this to yourself."

Lansing lowered his eyes. "I can't argue with anything you've said, sir."

"The one thing you haven't told me is why you didn't come to me when you first discovered all this. Did you feel you couldn't trust me?"

"To be completely honest, we were afraid of leaks. New York can be very contrary."

"You're damn right it is. That's the first thing you've said that's been worth hearing. You could have blown the entire case. We weren't ready to spring the arrest until we knew for sure that there was a body in the trunk. You are extremely lucky there was."

"I understand that now."

Logan sensed Lansing was being a little too contrite and leaned back in his chair as though trying a new angle of perception. "I'm curious. Now that you know the facts, do you feel you made the right decision?"

294 • PAUL LINDSAY

"If you're asking me if I'd do it again . . . yes, I believe I would."

"Your shamelessness is frightening. The reason I find it so disturbing is that I know just how far someone with your disregard for propriety will go in this organization."

It was all Charles Lansing could do not to smile.

33

WHEN MIKE PARISI CAME THROUGH THE LOCKUP door, T. H. Crowe and Dick Zalenski were waiting for him. He offered them his wrists. Crowe said, "That won't be necessary."

"I appreciate that."

"Personally, I'd like to see you try to run."

In the car, Parisi asked, "Which jail are you taking me to?"

When neither of the agents answered, Parisi understood he wasn't supposed to ask any more questions.

Forty-five minutes later, Crowe pulled up to an anonymous single-story brick building.

Parisi asked, "Where are we?"

"At a restaurant. There's somebody inside you need to talk to."

Zalenski steered him toward the heavy oak door. Inside, an attractive woman in her fifties approached them. Her hair was honey blond, expensively highlighted and wound into a meticulous French twist. She smiled with an elegant patience. "Right this way, gentlemen."

Parisi couldn't help but notice the restaurant's unusual layout. The tables were grouped in clusters, isolated by curved walls. Those groupings formed an even larger circle, at the center of which was a jazz combo with a woman at the piano. She was dark, her race unidentifiably mixed. Her voice rose like liquid smoke, dusky, narcotic.

They were led to a semiprivate section with its own bar. The bartender placed two paper napkins in front of them. "Gentlemen?"

"What'll you have, Mike?" Zalenski asked.

Parisi surprised himself by ordering scotch and took out his recently returned money clip. "Everything's taken care of," the agent said. Parisi held his glass up in appreciation and tossed a ten-dollar bill on the bar for a tip. He surveyed the room. Off to the side was a large table he hadn't noticed when they walked up to the bar. Half a dozen men sat around it; one of them had something wrong with his face. The others seemed to defer to him. The man gave Parisi a single nod of acknowledgment. Manny had told him about the supervisor that night at the hotel and how his face was disfigured. So this was the man he had been brought to meet. The question was why. The possibilities were not promising.

He ordered another scotch. He took a small sip and made his way over to the table. "Have a seat," Vanko offered.

Parisi slid into the chair next to him. "I've got to hand it to you, I was up most of the night trying to figure out which part of this thing was real and which wasn't."

"If I were smart, I'd let you keep wondering."

"It's not really that hard picking out the smart people in the room."

"Actually not all that smart. I didn't have a clue until Egan left the After Hours last night. Not that it matters when we found out what. By the time Washington gets through spinning it, everyone will think we planned the whole thing."

"It wouldn't take much to convince me, and I was there," Parisi said. "But one of the things I can't figure out was the map. Was it real?"

"That was a question I had too, so I had it flown back to the lab this morning. It's a forgery, a very good one."

"What about the expert? He's been used by the family for years."

"Experts make their living by telling lawyers what they need to hear."

"So there's no treasure."

"Not that you'll find with that map."

"Then what about that little rectangle we saw on the charts?"

"It could be anything. If the map were real, it might be worth pursuing, but it's fairly unlikely that a forged map is going to lead to mythical treasure."

"So Manny's father got beat?"

"We all got beat."

"And just to be clear, the state police arresting us last night, that was your doing?"

"If it had been the FBI, DeMiglia might have become suspicious. And we needed to get you out of the way so he'd have to come up with a body."

Parisi shook his head appreciatively. "You were pretty quick on your feet."

"When you find out one of your agents has turned, you'd better be," Vanko said. "We were already looking at DeMiglia hard for the judge's disappearance and had installed the GPS in his car, so the rest of it didn't take that much work."

"How'd you know he'd bring the judge's body?"

"We didn't. But we knew he wanted you out of the way. So when Egan called about you being arrested, we had him tell DeMiglia that you weren't going to prison, and if he really did want to get rid of you, he'd have to figure out something himself. Like I said, we couldn't be sure he'd use the judge's body to frame you, but we thought we'd plant the seed anyway."

"How'd you know he wanted to get rid of me?"

"I'm going to leave that unanswered. A little paranoia can be useful when trying to get someone to see my side of things."

"So DeMiglia really was trying to frame me. Or is that part of your paranoia tactic?"

Vanko leaned over and took something out of his briefcase. It was a plastic bag with four cigarette butts in it. "Recognize these?"

Parisi examined the bag. "That's my brand."

"Not only your brand, they're covered with your DNA. From the After Hours. DeMiglia's driver had them on him. They were going into the ground with the judge. Then all it would have taken was an anonymous tip, a court order for your DNA, and so long, Mike. You'd be out of the way permanently, and he'd be off the hook for the Ferris murder."

"I'm getting the impression you think I'm in the wrong business."

Vanko smiled. "Hey, it's organized crime—somebody's got to do it. I'd rather it be you than someone who makes public officials disappear. I don't need to go through this again."

"Maybe I'm hearing what I want to hear, but it sounds like I'm not going to prison."

"The probable cause for last night's arrest wouldn't stand up at trial. And as far as the whole thing with Egan, it's not something we'd like to have aired in open court. Besides, if you and he hadn't come up with that Mafia graveyard idea, we wouldn't have gotten DeMiglia. Think of it as reluctant appreciation on our part."

Parisi drained his glass and rattled the ice cubes as if trying to shake out the uncertainty of the argument he was about to make. "Does this mean you think I owe you?"

Vanko shrugged. "What I think is that you're basically an honorable guy."

"I'm not going to be your snitch."

"I know. But I also know if I really need something in the future—something as important as finding out who murdered a judge—you'll do the right thing."

"Don't bet on it."

"I believe I already have."

"So you're going to take care of Manny's case?"

"Manny helped solve a serial murder." Vanko tapped a finger on his lip. "But I have a feeling you already know something about that. Besides, what's not to like about Manny?"

Parisi stood up and offered his hand. "Thanks."

"My pleasure."

As Parisi was leaving, several more members of the squad came in. A couple of waiters set down trays of hors d'oeuvres that no one seemed to have ordered. Straker started telling one of his stories, more off-color than usual. Snow noticed that because of the celebratory air of the evening, certain details were growing with the size of the audience.

Abby, the squad secretary, walked in and signaled Nick that she needed to talk to him alone. He drained his beer and wandered toward the bar. "Nick—," she said.

He held up his hand. "Let's get a drink before you start telling whatever it is that's making your face so long." Vanko handed her a glass of wine and said, "Fire away."

"I think you're about to get some bad news. The SAC called

as I was leaving. When I told him you weren't there, he asked if Snow was around. I told him no. He said you should give him a call."

"Okay."

"I do have some good news. There was a certain somebody who called looking for you."

"Sheila?"

"How many friends do you think you've got?"

"Did you tell her we were coming here?"

"You did instruct me to let everybody on the squad know."

"Well, with her case breaking all over the TV, I thought she might be hard to run down."

"Yeah, maybe now you two can get on with things."

"What things?"

"You and her. You know, *thangs.*"

"What do you know about that?"

"I know something when I see it. You *were* working on her case? And I hear stuff, like sharing a chair at Hattie's."

Vanko laughed. "You black women think you know all about men."

"If I knew anything about men, I'd never go near one. But I'd have to be blind not to see it in you."

"Do you see it in her?"

"Now *you* must be blind."

"Can you stick around for a while?"

"I'm finishing this glass of wine and going home to the relative safety of my kids. Besides, I've seen this act before. You putting this bunch in a room with free liquor; you're going to need someone sober enough in the morning to post bail."

"I'd better go call the SAC."

When Vanko came back ten minutes later, he told Snow he needed to talk to him.

"I take it this isn't about a promotion."

Vanko smiled unhappily. "You've come a long way being able to read people, Howard."

"So it *is* bad news."

"I just talked to the SAC. The Bureau called. You're to be offered a chance to resign."

"Or be fired."

"Or be fired."

Vanko waited for him to say something. Finally he did. "When?"

"Tomorrow."

"I'd like to be the one to tell everybody. And since we're rarely all in the same place, would you mind if I put a little dent in the festivities?"

"I think they'd like to hear it first from you."

They walked back to the table. Vanko said, "Everybody, Howard has something to tell you."

Everyone could see how serious Snow looked. The color went out of Straker's face. "Let me give you the bottom line first. Tomorrow I will be resigning. The Bureau has given me that option. It's not what I want but when it comes from Washington, when is it ever what we want. Please do not feel sorry for me. I've been an FBI agent for four years. No matter what I accomplish after this, it will be the standard by which I judge the rest of my life. To know all of you, to work with you . . . in a way, I'm glad that I screwed up that search warrant and was sent to this squad and made part of that amazing resolve you have when the chips are really down. And I'd like to thank Jack Straker, a guy who is much too cool to be hanging around with the likes of me. There's one other person I have to thank, Nick Vanko. No one knows better than you, Nick, that I'm not perfect. But I am better than I would ever have been without working for you. We all are indebted to you for that."

Everyone held up their drinks and took solemn, contemplative sips. It was a sequence of events that was not unexpected, or unprecedented. One by one, they came up and shook Snow's hand.

Vanko sat down next to Brad Kenyon. "I made a call back to someone I know at headquarters this afternoon. Your old supervisor will be getting orders back to Washington within a couple of weeks. Our stock is pretty high with the front office right now, so if you want to go back to working art thefts, it'll just take one quick phone call."

"If you don't mind, I'd like to stay here for a while. After all this, art theft seems a little too civilized."

"Well, this hasn't been exactly a typical week, so it might get boring. But I think I can guarantee it'll never get civilized."

"What's going to happen to Garrett?"

"Fortunately for him, when he figured out he was in over his head with DeMiglia, his lawyer negotiated a no-charge deal in return for his cooperation on the whole graveyard scam."

"I'm surprised the Bureau went for that."

"They have a tendency to listen only to the loudest headline. Today that turned out to be the solution to the Judge Ferris murder. Besides, he still has the insider trading charges to deal with."

"Are you going to get any heat over the money spent on the seismic imaging?"

"When the oil people found out what happened, they were nice enough to give us a discount rate, I guess because they had been scammed too. The fifty thousand Egan got from Parisi and turned over to us will pay the majority of it. And the rest—well, we would have spent a lot more trying to get DeMiglia."

"And we're all a little bit wiser."

"Hopefully."

Kenyon offered his hand. "Nick, what Howard said . . . me, too."

As the two men shook hands, Vanko looked up and saw Sheila talking to Abby, but watching him. She was wearing the green silk dress she had on the night at the hotel. He went over to her.

"Hi."

Abby said, "This is where I wander away nonchalantly." She walked over and sat down next to Jack Straker, who put his arm around her, and while he laughed at something Snow was saying, pulled her closer.

Without a word, Sheila took Vanko's hand. Hers was trembling slightly and she squeezed his to try to stop. "Why didn't you tell me why you had to leave last night?"

"You had enough going on. Which, rumor has it, turned out well."

"Not that good. It hasn't been on the news yet, but there was a third victim. I spent most of the night with her parents. It's so sad."

He squeezed her hand now. "How's the Lopez girl?"

"You can never be sure what's buried underneath, but all the signs were positive. She was unbelievably calm and focused, extremely strong-willed. He hadn't done anything to her."

"*Yet* . . . thanks to you. And how are you doing now?"

She thought back to Tolenka's cruel remark similar to those she had endured many times before. Maybe that's why she had zeroed in on him during the volunteer search. Maybe that's what she had recognized—his need to terrorize. "Better."

"I'm sorry."

"For what?"

"For thinking I knew what was best for you." He stepped closer to her, his lips barely touching the side of her face. "I was just worried about you."

She pulled her head back to look at him. Some mischief had returned to her eyes. "If that's a sincere apology, really sincere, you'll dance with me."

"It's not that sincere."

"Please."

"It's been a long, *long* time."

"For both of us. You're not going to try and tell me you've forgotten how?"

"Well, I am Greek. We do have two extra genes, one for tragedy and the other for dancing. Hopefully my feet won't get them confused."

He led the way to the small dance floor. "Before you hear it from the front office," she said, "I wanted to let you know I'm going back to the task force."

He carefully put his arm around her. "A media star like you, I'm not surprised."

"It is tough keeping a good obsessive-compulsive down."

"Are you going back to your old apartment?"

"Yes I am, and you're going to help me move. How else can I be certain you'll know exactly where I live?"

"I know what you're trying to do, but it's Bureau policy that once someone is reevaluated as sane, I have to stop delivering pizzas."

She put her cheek against his. "That's all right, I think I've found something else to be crazy about."

He dug his fingers into her waist and gently pulled her closer.

Mike Parisi stared lazily through the thick shafts of afternoon sunlight slanting across Anthony Carrera's den, trying to avoid any immediate decision about the future. The easy money and respect of organized crime would be difficult for him to give up, but its bounty would always be complicated by men like Danny DeMiglia. Then there was the FBI to consider. Once they locked on to a target, their ingenuity seemed especially ominous to him. That they had eliminated someone like DeMiglia—a man far better built for the scheming demands of that life than he—presented a strong argument for Parisi's retirement. But in all likelihood, the worst of it was over, and everyone, with reassuring indifference, would now be able to get back to profiting from the venial sins of mankind.

The old don came in, and Parisi couldn't help but marvel at his resilience. The cane hardly seemed necessary, his veined hand balanced lightly on its ebony crook. He had put some weight back on, eliminating the spectral profile that just a week earlier had seemed so tentative. "You look terrific, Uncle Tony."

"I feel good. You should feel good, too, no? You could have had a much worse week." Even his speech was quicker and more enunciated.

"You're right, I have to consider my blessings. I could be in a cell with DeMiglia."

"That particular cell is reserved for murderers."

"I know, but still, I can't help thinking my luck with these other things of ours might be running out."

"Of course you feel that way, you were in jail. It'll pass."

"I don't know. The FBI ran circles around us. I can't help but feel that as soon as I come up on their list, I'll be gone."

"You may be overestimating them. They tried to get to you through Manny, and it didn't happen. What they did with DeMiglia was impressive, but they would never have been able to do it without your involvement. Their success was possible only because you made DeMiglia vulnerable while protecting this family from him."

"I was just trying to do what I could to help."

"You did what had to be done, even though it was against your nature. That's who you are. That's the kind of person I need as an underboss."

"Me? I appreciate your confidence, but if I've learned one thing from all of this, it's that there's too much of this business I don't understand."

"That may have been true when this started, but you have learned a great deal. I am not a sentimental old man, I would not offer you this position strictly out of gratitude."

"I am honored, but I came here to ask your blessing to leave the family. And now you offer me this."

"Do you know why your regime is successful, even though you have men who are not the most talented? You maintain. DeMiglia murdered and look where that got us. But somehow through all the turmoil, you maintained. If you can bring that to the rest of our people, I think the FBI will find better ways to spend their time." There was something playful in Carrera's tone that hinted he knew more about the motivations of the government agency than he was revealing. As Parisi tried to figure out what it was, Carrera said, "This is a lot. Go home, kiss my niece, and think about it. I don't need an answer today. You come Sunday for dinner, we'll talk some more then. In the meantime, I have a small gift for you to remember this little training exercise." Carrera handed him a wrapped present.

"Training exercise" seemed an odd choice of words, but it brought a glint of amusement to Carrera's eyes. Once before he had referred to the problems with DeMiglia as instructional. Parisi opened the flat package with careful curiosity. It was a picture frame. Inside was the Dutch Schultz map.

"How? This was sent to the FBI lab just this morning."

The don's only response was a sly smile.

Parisi tilted the frame against the strong sunlight. "There's no seam. This is a whole map. Where did you—" Carrera's smile remained patiently in place. "You planted it in the safe deposit box?"

"Sometimes tests have to be untraditional."

"This was all a test?"

"Maybe not all."

"Wait a minute. Half of the map we used was found by that agent in the FBI files."

The old don shrugged modestly. "This is a funny business. Sometimes you have to make friends with the most unlikely people."

About the Author

Paul Lindsay was born in Chicago. After graduating from MacMurray College in 1968, he served a tour of duty in Vietnam as a Marine Corps infantry officer. He later joined the FBI and worked in the Detroit office for twenty years. He is the author of five other novels—*Freedom to Kill, Code Name: Gentkill, Witness to the Truth, The Führer's Reserve,* and *Traps.* He lives in Rye, New Hampshire.